PRAIRIE
PERPENDICULAR

MARSTON MOORE

Beaver's Pond Press, Inc.
Edina, Minnesota

PRAIRIE PERPENDICULAR © Copyright 2006 by Marston Moore. All rights reserved. No part of this book may be reproduced in any form whatsoever, by photography or xerography or by any other means, by broadcast or transmission, by translation into any kind of language, nor by recording electronically or otherwise, without permission in writing from the author, except by a reviewer, who may quote brief passages in critical articles or reviews.

Artwork by Gerry Thompson

ISBN-13: 978-1-59298-148-9
ISBN-10: 1-59298-148-8

Library of Congress Catalog Number: 2006925046
Printed in the United States of America
First Printing: May 2006

10 09 08 07 06   5 4 3 2 1

Beaver's Pond Press, Inc.

7104 Ohms Lane, Suite 216
Edina, MN 55439
(952) 829-8818
www.BeaversPondPress.com

To order, visit www.BookHouseFulfillment.com
or call 1-800-901-3480. Reseller discounts available.

Dedication

To all who populate

The empty space

With memory

Doug,
Here's a story of small town life in 1970's North Dakota.
Bill Ouseley
(aka) Marston Moore

Dakota Wind

Wind is a constant companion to all prairie dwellers. For animals, it signals change, threat and renewal of life. For men, wind is a theme of conversation and a marker of special events that signal the passage of time. Wind begins outside the bounds of the prairie and slides down the eastern slopes of the Rockies, accelerating as it follows the gradually lowering elevation toward the Mississippi valley. In summer, the wind forces its way northward through the plains bringing heat and moisture, its flow extending into Canada. In winter, Canada sends the wind back—this time a carrier of cold and blizzard.

These continent-sized movements of air are the bearers of cyclonic high and low pressure areas. As they follow one after the other—highs rotating clockwise, lows counterclockwise—winds shift to blow from every point of the compass, erratic pressures against all that stands above the level of the prairie.

Prairie dwellers who attempt to make their mark with trees and structures are continually engaged in a struggle with wind. If wind has a mind, its sole purpose is to return perpendicular to horizontal. Trees in windbreaks are twisted into grotesque forms and broken stubs. Buildings are stripped of any loosely attached features and are, when abandoned, tilted, flattened and covered by wind-blown dust. Even people are effectively shoved out of the prairie by the wind—dry land agriculture is ruled by a wind that capriciously holds out promise—only to evaporate opportunity. In all these ways, wind is expressive of the intolerance of the prairie for all that is unnatural.

The events and persons who inhabit this story are moved about by winds of weather and economics, unconscious of their exposure to elemental forces. Lives that cry out for order are transformed by a prairie that refuses to recognize humankind or to be in any way shaped to the designs of men.

BOOK 1

FARMERS ELEVATOR

CHAPTER ONE

Eight Cents under Minneapolis

Tom Cooper could not remember when the Elevator started sharing their bed. Upon becoming the manager of Sheffield Farmers Elevator two years ago, confidence had given him uninterrupted sleep. Shortly thereafter, the Elevator came to bed. At first, it was an inert idea that gently pushed him closer to Janet where their love protected him from this newcomer. But it wasn't long until the Elevator came between them—shoving them further apart day by day.

By this November morning, the Elevator had full control of Tom's thoughts—it shook him awake. "My God! Five already!" he mumbled as he reached for yesterday's clothes on a nearby chair. The frigid floor called for socks and he threw his cold-stiffened shoes down the bedroom stairs to the warm kitchen. Then he and the Elevator followed.

Whenever the Elevator presented an especially difficult problem, Tom experienced a vivid recall of some event in his past where he had failed—or where family emotions took control. These flashbacks came more frequently now, disturbing sleep and family life.

In the kitchen, Tom brewed the only cup of fresh coffee he would have this day, and sipping it, looked out a window at the snow-covered yard—lit by a full moon. A hint of wind animated this scene with darting waves of snow. As he stared, the picture gradually changed to the farmyard of his childhood. There snow banked itself around the debris of farm life: an abandoned mower; an old sleigh used for hauling wood; the stump of an elm tree downed by wind. He saw figures moving through the snow, his father leading the family toward their barn—images so vivid that they called for action. Then the wind died and there was peaceful moonlight on the prairie.

He turned away from the window. "Must be below zero," he said aloud. "That'll play hell with corn dryin' today." He drained his cup, rinsed it under the faucet and set it on the kitchen drainboard. At the door, he pulled on a heavy parka and leather gloves. Switching off the kitchen light, he left what remained of family life and entered the prairie with his constant companion—the Elevator.

The first breath of frigid air set him coughing—and intensified the headache left over from last night's party. "Gotta go easier on the sauce," he gasped as he opened the door of the old Plymouth Fury. "Jesus! It's even colder in here! Should have put the damn thing in the shed. Hope to hell it'll start."

He fumbled his key into the Fury's lock and cranked the engine. "C'mon! C'mon! You sonofabitch!" The Fury stammered and gagged into life. Tom relaxed and waited for the engine to run evenly before moving out of his farmyard.

When he left his drive and turned onto the township road, prairie replaced the Elevator as his companion. Like every other human creation, the Elevator was impotent in the face of elemental prairie forces. In winter, wind told of the prairie's power—today, it buffeted the Fury so that Tom was conscious of an empty darkness around him. He steered carefully, centered on the path of light that held the prairie at bay. Three miles to Highway 13 and a right turn to the east placed wind behind him and he moved smoothly toward Sheffield.

In summer, this was usually a journey of promise. Summer prairie surrendered to the ever-increasing appetite of world markets. Tractors and combines mechanized agriculture and forced the land into regular patterns of planting and harvest. Strips of grass modulated wind, isolated farmsteads thrust their defiance against the sky, and the land was bounded by a neat geometry of roadways, plots one mile square—the garden of Sheffield.

Sheffield was grain, a living organism of agribusiness whose purpose was to husband the prairie, to manage it, and to receive its harvest. As the community exercised its control, it gave form to the lives of those whose vocation was grain.

All the activities of Sheffield's residents defied the fundamental forces that shaped the prairie and its environment. Their lives were built on an illusion; wind, rain, snow or drought could erase any trace of human dominion. Thus, the garden of Sheffield existed because the prairie allowed it, and the impression of settled community was transient.

For Tom Cooper, driving the last miles of Highway 13 before starting down into Sheffield defined the mood of the day. On optimistic days, when Janet had given him a joyful send-off, he was like a skier—taking a giddy plunge into anticipated thrills of commerce. On bad days, he drove the Fury more slowly and eased up to the valley edge, afraid of Sheffield and the problems that waited there.

The Elevator also took on an appearance that depended upon his mood. When he was in an optimistic mood, he was reminded of how his ten-year old daughter Christine had seen it on her first trip to Sheffield. To Chrissy the Elevator looked like Camelot, a magical place where adventure would lead to wonderful outcomes. During Tom's darker moods, it was a bleak castle where judgment on his decisions would be handed down; or worse, a prison where the results were already in and a sentence was waiting to be served. Today was an average day, fifty miles an hour, determination, and one hell of a hangover.

Then the hill with its sign—TRUCKS USE LOWER GEAR—and the swaying sweeps of Highway 13 leading down into Sheffield. In years long past, pathfinders stopping here were weary of exposure and looked for a burrow of their own—like other prairie dwellers, man and beast, before them. Sheffield was a refuge from the limitless scope and power of the land, a place where men could define their world as they wished; built against the skyline of river hills.

The half-dark of this November morning hid the town from Tom's determined stare. Only the Elevator was defined against its background of early snow blotches on the surrounding bluffs. Lights of its central structure, housing the main elevating leg and distributors, gave shape to its outline, and plumes of vapor from grain dryers added a mantle over extended bins and silos.

Tom made the final turns off Highway 13 onto Main Street. In fall and winter Main Street didn't belong to Sheffield. It belonged to the Elevator. Piles of corn and wheat—a spilling of the Elevator's guts—were marks of plenty and measures of the year's crop. When children romped through the piles of grain, everyone knew debts would be paid and a few dollars left over. Then Tom could forgive the spreading of priceless grain and the kernels that dribbled down nearby streets from shoes and cuffs.

When dry years came, play in the grain piles was forbidden and every kernel cherished to keep farms and town economically alive for the next spring when planters would roll again. This year was marginally adequate, not enough, but…

"If I manage this right, I can keep the annual report in the black and get a new line of credit for next year," he mused. "Better take a look at the Elm Street pile."

As usual, Tom murmured continuously about decisions he must make as he drove from one mound of grain to the next. Turning sharply at the Citizen's Bank corner, he pulled up in front of its gilt-lettered door to wave to Ben Waters, the community's financial gyroscope and the Elevator's main creditor, early to work as he had been for all of his twenty years as bank president.

"Hey, Tom." Ben's breath was expelled in little clouds, like a miniature grain dryer. "How's things this morning?"

Tom responded out his car window. "Not too bad, Ben."

Waters laughed. "Shouldn't drink so much at parties–should have gone home like me. And, don't worry about your grain. You'll get through it in time to cross off your note."

"Sure hope so," Tom replied. "You seen anything of my crew?"

"Yep. They're workin' on the south dryer. Seems to be shut down."

"Dammit." Tom frowned. "That one's been givin' us problems all fall. I'd better get over there and see what's wrong. See you, Ben."

"So long, Tom. Drop in soon."

As he drove away, he reflected on the problem that had been with him every day this past month. Grain wasn't coming in, and it wasn't just the short crop. Something would have to be done to promote the Elevator to new customers and to those who had left to trade at neighboring towns.

Turning onto Elm Street, he remembered how he had to struggle to convince the Elevator Board and Ben to approve a budget last spring. In addition to a line of credit that grew by several hundred thousand dollars each year, Tom had seen a need for additional storage space and the potential profit it could turn. Board members were, as always, conscious of the farmers who owned the cooperative. Expenditures of any size led to questions and opposition. Last spring, Tom's argument had prevailed, at least in part, and six new concrete silos were nearly finished–maybe even this week–but far too late to make a smooth flow of harvest possible.

"Tom's losin' his touch." The word was out among farmers. "Expanded too fast over to Sheffield." "Better take your crop somewhere else if you don't want it to rot in the street."

Little spurts of steam from the Elm Street pile confirmed farmers' suspicions; this corn was rapidly going out of condition and would soon be worthless if not dried immediately. Any visible vapor indicated that the grain was rotting—even in below-zero weather.

Fat chance of saving this stuff, he thought. South dryer's down, night crew can't fix anything, and probably can't even get organized to get outside the office in this weather. These thoughts crowded one on another, the same voices he heard on the hundreds of days he had come to work to face problems. There were always unending lists of troubles he had to master immediately upon arrival at the Elevator. Each problem suggested a remedy in his mind: put Andy on the corn pile, let Pete get that dryer goin', have Helen call Sioux Falls for those Bobcat parts.

Then, as soon as he entered his office door, all solutions proved worthless. He was invariably besieged by new problems of even greater urgency that involved legions of critical jobs so that the original problems multiplied and pressed on him another day.

Tom stopped the Fury, got out, and thrust his hand into the pile of wet corn. Down at arm's length, the grain was hot. A few moldy kernels stuck to his hand as he pulled it out. He could see that this corn had to be taken care of today. At least they could move the pile and give it some air. Maybe that would buy two or three days of time. He straightened, holding his left hand to his temple. Too much booze last night.

The Elevator's Bobcat loader clattered down Elm Street to load another truck for a short haul to the dryers.

"Hey, Andy," he shouted, "how we comin' on this pile?"

"Jesus, Tom, the dryer's been out since 2:00 a.m. and we can't find the trouble."

Two o'clock! God! Tom calculated. More than three thousand bushels hadn't been processed. They were nearly a carload behind on filling the train parked on the Elevator siding. And Northern Pacific would come by for the cars today.

"What's she do, Andy?" Tom asked.

"Nothing. Fan runs, but we can't get her lit. The old bitch is on the wagon."

"Pilot okay? Remember, we had trouble with the sail switch, too. It always freezes on these cold nights."

He ran through the major causes of dryer shutdown in his mind. Usually there was a fault in the electronic controls that monitored temperature and airflow. The result was a closed gas valve and no heat. Sometimes chaff and dust clogged the tiny orifices of the inaccessible pilot light, or the heater that vaporized LP gas failed.

"Yep," Andy replied. "And we got gas at the valves."

"Okay," Tom said, "I'll take a look. Maybe we'll have to call the dryer man. Say, Andy, let's tear into this pile. Stir it up, even if you can't get it to the dryers. Maybe it'll cool down some in this weather."

"You're damn right!" Andy grinned. "It's colder than the hind tit on a polar bear out here."

Donkey! Tom turned away, reflecting on his employees. They were all donkeys. Couldn't think for themselves. Couldn't finish any job without having something to complain about. Some days the Elevator was a whole stable of donkeys, each braying a list of complaints and questions in his ears.

He pulled the Fury into the Elevator lot, next to Bob Clauson's four-wheel drive GMC pickup. The fertilizer salesman always had cash to travel in comfort. "Must be a better man with the pennies than I am," he mumbled as he climbed out of his car. Well, at least Bob was always on the job and put in countless hours on the phone to make the Elevator's fertilizer operation its most profitable division.

Bob's ready smile and wave brought many customers to the Elevator. Cold mornings were no match for his good humor. "Hi, Boss. How's she hangin'?" Bob called as he opened the door of his pickup.

"'Bout knee high," Tom responded with a sickly grin, holding his head with both hands.

Bob chuckled. "Ain't everybody can hold his likker. Say, where did you and Jan go after the 66 Club?" He swung out of his pickup to join Tom.

"Oh, she wanted to go home," Tom replied, "but I decided to head down to the VFW to have one for the road."

"More like one for the ditch." Bob peered owlishly at Tom. "Bet it was more than one, your eyes look like two pee holes in the snow."

"Well," Tom admitted, "the big farmer, Barney Jacobs, was there and one wouldn't do."

"Say, ain't that right? Ain't he just one hell of a guy?"

"Yeah," Tom said. Barney was one hell of a guy, he thought. But one who wouldn't be put off. Barney wasn't fooling last night when he said that he wanted his grain check this week or else. They'd better get the dryer running today and send the unit train on its way. Only six cars to go.

Tom looked to the side of the main elevator building, an old tin-covered pile, the main Sheffield landmark since 1920. To the right of the building stood two dryer towers, the north one spouting its customary clouds of vapor with the accompanying wail of high-speed fans, the south a silent monolith.

Damn those Chicago salesmen. And damn the Elevator Board for placing the order for a Chicago dryer instead of the American he had recommended. That Chicago was a fire trap. No way anyone could prevent a build-up of chaff in one of its columns. Then, a puff of gas—ignition—and the smell of burning corn. And, if the crew was on the ball, the stink of fire extinguishers and another three hundred bushels of ruined grain. Well, no such problem today. Just cold fingers and worrying through the operator's manual to find a solution.

As Tom and Bob climbed the office steps, the outdoor telephone horn bleated its message, the first of a hundred calls reaching out to welcome them. Inside, Tom stamped a mixture of stale corn and snow from his boots and gave his hands a brisk rubbing.

"Morning," he called to his secretary, Helen Fredericks. "How you takin' the weather?"

"Just fine, Tom. Say, there's a call for you on line one. I think it's someone from the railroad about the train we're loading."

Oh, shit, he thought, now he would be hung for demurrage on the whole damn train, with only three cars left to load. This was another of the problems associated with grain movement. Railroads parked cars on the Elevator siding and arranged to pick them up on a specific date. If they were not filled and ready to move, the Elevator would be billed for demurrage—an unplanned expense.

"Ummm, hello. Tom speakin'."

"Tom? Dick Ferguson. How you comin' with that unit train?"

"Just about done, Dick. Should wind her up today."

"Great! Boy, have I got a deal for you!"

"Oh, that so? The last time you had a deal for me, we ended up loadin' ten old boxcars by hand." Tom smiled, remembering a week of backbreaking work occasioned by Ferguson's 'deal'.

"Got another fifteen-car train," Ferguson said. "Elevator up to Grandview couldn't take her now."

"Christ! Fifteen cars? All hoppers?"

"Yep. Three thousand bushel apiece. Can you fill her up?"

Tom considered a moment. That was one hell of a lot of corn.

"Well, I don't know, Dick. What's the freight break?" He held his breath, waiting for the answer. A few cents freight might make this deal worthwhile.

"How's five cents per hundred?"

"Not bad, Dick. Make that six and you got a deal."

"Done. She'll be in tomorrow night and the locos will take the one you got on track now. Thanks, Tom. You always seem to be able to get me out of a jam. I ordered that train on the chance that the Grandview Co-op would take it. When they turned me down, I thought I'd wind up workin' the switches at Wolf Point."

"That'd be too bad, Dick. Who'd sweep out the toilets in Sheffield?"

Ferguson swore and laughed. "So long, you son of a bitch. Don't forget the train's comin'."

Tom put the phone back on its cradle carefully. Boy! That sure increased the pressure. Fifteen cars meant forty-five thousand bushels. Nearly all the grain in one of the concrete silos, a big share of the corn farmers had in storage. But the freight rate was right and they should be able to dry corn fast enough to shape up the books in a week or two, especially if late year-end sales came through on schedule. Now all he had to do is to sell those forty-five thousand bushels at a good price.

Selling corn farmers had stored was a risk every manager took. Frequently, managers marked some of this grain as 'sold' or 'priced' in their Daily Position Books and hoped to buy it back from farmers at an anticipated lower price. This 'pricing' and 'replacement' was a delusion. In fact, elevator managers who manipulated their books were speculating with crops that belonged to farmers.

What made the practice risky was the fact that the Elevator was legally required to produce grain at the request of farmers who had stored it. The Daily Position Book showed how much grain the Elevator owned and how much it held for farmers and for federal loans. If Book entries failed to balance with warehouse receipts held by farmers, the Elevator was guilty of stealing grain. The widespread nature of the practice didn't ease Tom's mind when he took advantage of an attractive price spread by selling farmer-owned grain.

Conflict between the rules of the grain trade and the practices of elevator managers resulted from a fundamental change in the business of farming. Rules made when trade was largely a matter of storage throughout winter months in expectation of higher spring prices no longer worked. Grain wasn't the 'stock' of storage. Instead, it was a 'flow', constantly in motion. Where once price had been determined by the costs of storage for a regional market, farmers and elevator managers now faced a global market and prices that changed day by day. These were the facts of a new agribusiness. However, the rules were still in place, and they were enforced.

"Hello, Tom speakin'." He picked up the second line in response to the flickering of a lighted button on his phone.

"Tom, this is Hank Sawyer from Continental Grain in Minneapolis. How you doin' out there?"

"Not bad, Hank. How's the market?"

"That's why I called. Corn looks awfully chancy in the next several weeks. It just isn't being used up by cattle feeders and the market the way we hoped. In fact, I look for a hell of a price slide come the first of the year."

"Just about the way I see it," Tom agreed. No wonder Hank could be so matter of fact in that paneled office with those sexy chicks around. He didn't have several thousand bushels of corn rotting in the streets.

"Tom, do you have anything on track that could arrive here in the next couple of weeks?"

"You bet I do." He sat back in his chair. Here was a chance to price Ferguson's 'deal'.

"Well, if you can get us corn, I'll give you spot rail price ten cents under the market."

Tom calculated, jotting figures on his desk blotter. Let's see…ten cents under. Allowing for the six cent break on freight from the railroad, which would be a premium of seven to nine cents over the normal market–not too bad a deal.

"Hank, how far would you go for a fifteen-car unit train?"

"A fifteen-car train? You got something like that loading? Just what you got out there, the Chicago Terminal?"

"Nope," Tom laughed, "just helping out a freight agent. But what do you say? Shoot me a price."

There was prolonged silence and Tom could imagine Hank working ever closer to Continental's margin to make what was obviously a good-sized purchase.

"Okay, Tom, we can give you another penny on that much corn."

"That's not quite enough." Tom shot back, hoping his voice sounded confident. "Give me another two cents and you got a deal."

"Tell you what," Hank said, "let's split the difference. I'll take the fifteen cars at eight cents under Minneapolis cash market. How's that sound?"

"Fine, Hank, you got a deal. Send me the papers and I'll call you for a firm delivery date when the railroad spots the train for me."

He hung up his phone and walked into the glass-enclosed office where Stub Thompson kept the Daily Position Book and Grain Assembly Sheets. It bothered Tom that he couldn't handle these critical records himself. They were the only way the Elevator could track its dealings. Weight tickets on farmers' trucks were accumulated on Assembly Sheets and entered in the Daily Position Book as 'open' grain, for which no storage receipts had been issued. When a farmer filled a contract, or delivered all he planned to store, the total amount was transferred to 'Elevator owned' or 'stored' in the Position Book. Warehouse receipts were then issued to the farmer confirming grain that was 'stored'. The fact that few farmers asked for receipts did not change the obligation of the Elevator to honor these commitments.

In addition, the Elevator served as a warehouse for commodities that farmers pledged as collateral for federal loans. These stocks were under the supervision of the Commodity Credit Corporation and were to be held intact and apart from Elevator stock. Keeping all these records in balance with daily transactions and inventory was a major feat, to say nothing of the manipulations that Tom made to keep the Elevator in the black.

If you looked at the glass inner office in just the right light, Stub's full, spectacled face resembled that of a giant fish in a surrealistic aquarium. Some of the farmers who waded through his complex accounting system felt that Stub kept most of the facts about their grain under his scaly hide rather than in the Elevator account books.

"Say, Stub," Tom said, leaning through the office door, "we're gettin' a unit train in the next couple of days. I want to load out about forty-five thousand of number-two yellow corn for Continental at eight cents under Minneapolis spot rail."

"Jeez, Tom, that'll really cut into our stored corn. If the federal inspectors hit us with that much of the farmers' stored grain gone, they'll hand us our asses."

"Yeah, but what if we buy replacement corn with another dime in our favor? Then the Board will have us eatin' steak at the annual meeting."

"Okay, Tom, you're the boss; I just lick the pencil."

That could be, Tom thought, but if Stub didn't lick it right–the fishy bastard–everybody would be on Tom's neck. Federal inspectors, the Board, and the farmers whose grain he had just sold. He shoved a wooden pencil up under his cap band and turned to go.

Stub drew in a deep breath, halting Tom in the doorway. "Say, Tom, a few of the farmers have been takin' out those official lookin' warehouse receipts from us. I think they're takin' them to the bank to get a loan."

"Why the hell didn't you tell me, Stub?" Tom turned back, anger showing in the stiffness of his body.

"Well, I didn't think it would really make any difference. The grain belongs to the farmers anyway."

"Dammit, Stub, how much do you have out on warehouse receipts?"

"Geez, Tom, I don't know for sure—probably something like two hundred thousand bushels." Stub looked down at his boots, afraid to meet Tom's eyes.

"Well, keep me posted. I guess we can price enough to fill that train without cutting into receipted grain."

He pivoted to leave, but once again Stub took that deep breath that was always a prelude to some kind of bombshell.

"Just for the record, Tom," Stub said in an even voice, "I don't think we should price that much grain without some insurance, like a position in the futures market."

"Stub, you just said that I call the shots. We've got to do it to fill this train and to get a little breathin' room in our cash accounts. Now, make the entries."

"Okay, okay, Tom. You don't have to read me the riot act. I'll get her done." Stub hunched his shoulders over the Daily Position Book, his arms like flippers scooping papers right and left.

Tom edged behind the narrow counter, shoving several little seed promotion leaflets into a neat pile. He took the pencil from under his hat band and clamped it between his teeth, gnawing at the uncertainty raised by Stub's rebellion. Just what the hell was wrong with pricing grain, selling it, and replacing it? Everybody did that, and made a pile of money when the market was falling like it was now. He paced the length of the counter and considered the alternative. But what about an up market? Nope, that just couldn't happen. He, and everyone else in the trade, was convinced of a continued downward trend. Even though the Dakotas had experienced a dry summer, the Corn Belt was coming out of a bumper crop–circumstances increasingly reflected in declining prices. Anyway, he would be short of grain for only a few weeks at most before he would be able to buy back the amount sold to Continental.

This internal argument was broken by the arrival of one of the scale operators who shoved his wind-reddened face through the door leading to the main elevator building.

"Tom, we got a problem with the auger over the north row of silos."

"Now, what the hell!" Tom exploded. "We put new bearings in the whole line last month."

"I know, Boss, but the bitch is poundin' something fierce. I think you should give it a look."

"All right, all right!" He grimaced, picking up the dusty coveralls he wore when he worked in the Elevator. He struggled with his sleeves. That extra weight he had picked up this fall didn't make it easier to wiggle into this straitjacket. He'd better take off a few pounds—good New Year's resolution.

"Okay, Ronny, take the manlift and I'll be right behind you."

"Boss, I got to hit the can. Why don't you go ahead and I'll be up in a jiffy. The trouble seems to be between the old and new silos where the auger is jointed."

Tom's sudden fear of the lift and height stopped his answer for a moment. Then he replied, "Okay, Ronny. See you up top."

He stepped through the door into a cold blast of dusty air in the scale house driveway, across the empty scale platform and into the towering manlift shaft. The lift was a holdover from the earliest elevator construction in Sheffield. It was an endless vertical belt running in an open shaft from the base of the elevator to the top of the structure. Spaced on the belt were small wooden platforms on which riders stood, and tiny hand grips that enabled them to maintain balance. The lift motor located at the top of the elevator was operated by a rope knotted so that a person might stop the belt at a particular floor. Riders could also step on and off the slow-moving belt, swinging across the dark emptiness of the shaft to the safety of a floor level.

Tom never made these daring steps. He stood firmly on a platform and pulled the control rope. The ancient machine ground to life, and he was swept slowly up the hundred fifty foot shaft. As he rose, vertigo seized him. Shadows on each side were hands trying to tear him from the moving belt. He clutched the handhold. Sweat formed on his forehead. He gritted his teeth; the urge to cry out was overpowering.

God! He must be crazy. How had his fear of heights got this delirium started? Boy, did he ever need a drink, something to calm him down.

As he reached the top of the lift, his hand slid over the worn control rope, feeling for the knot that would cut his umbilical tie with earth. He stopped the lift and stepped carefully backward over the lift shaft opening to the distributing floor of the head house. There the vertical elevator leg discharged grain into a waiting hopper on an auger that moved it out to the storage silos. For a moment he waited, letting his sweat cool in the icy breeze coming toward him from the auger tunnel. Then he began to walk beside the thumping screw on a narrow catwalk over a hundred feet of emptiness.

Eyes straight ahead. He had to pay attention to the job, and not think of the space underfoot.

Yeah, Ronny was right. Something was wrong over silo three.

Walk along; careful now, here was a joint in the catwalk. Slide feet, hang onto the flimsy railing. Don't let the sleeves of the coverall get caught in the open auger.

Dim corridor, dusty with the smell of countless harvests, ghostly with the pathway of all the elevator men who had worked there in the past. Vertigo. Hands reaching, voices pulling him from one side, then the other. Misty dust.

Now snow banks, the walkway a path from the country road to his childhood house. Home from school…walk carefully…slide one foot then the other. There, ahead…an open door…Mom waiting…

"Tom, Tom." Her call, half-heard…

"I'm coming,"—whispered.

"Hey, Tom!" Ron shouted from the headhouse. "Watch it! There ain't no railing on the end!"

"What? Huh? Uhhh, Ron, glad you yelled at me! Must have been thinkin' about the auger–sure glad."

Tom's voice trailed off, his whole body was now covered with icy sweat. He put his hands in the pockets of his coveralls to hide their shaking.

"Yeah," Ron replied, "silo six is empty and you would have taken the deep six." He laughed and swung his arms wildly as if falling.

Tom turned abruptly away to break this horrible vision.

"Looks to me as if the bearings between silos five and six will have to be changed again. What do you think, Ron?"

"That's the way I see it. Who do you have to give me a hand?"

"Take Timmy off the dryers. Only one running anyway, and let's get this thing fixed. We can't hold too much more dry corn in the surge bins. Have to get it into the silos."

"For sure!" was the grinning reply. "I'll get at it right now."

A good man. Not enough like him to go around. Everyone was needed to make the Elevator run smoothly with a big train load-out coming up and an increased pressure for dry corn to balance the books.

Tom moved carefully along the catwalk following Ron. Back over the full silos. Three…two…one. Now, more confidence, a grown man again, not afraid, no sounds, no voices.

He waited for Ron to get some way down the manlift before choosing one of the platforms for himself. As he stepped easily on, he heard the lift gearing protest as it adjusted to his weight.

"Hey, Tom, you better get some of that lard off, or this lift will be going forty miles an hour."

Tom glanced down into the depths of the lift shaft. "Forget it! If you were as skinny as me, we wouldn't be able to make this thing go down at all."

A burst of laughter floated up to him and Ron gave the belt a tug that was amplified by Tom's weight.

"Hey! Cut it out! You wanna kill us?" Tom hugged his handhold, hoping that this joke would end.

Then the lift ground to a halt as he pulled the knotted control rope and stepped back onto the ground floor. Relief!

"Well, Ron, you hit the bearings and I'll see if we can get the dryer back into operation."

Inside the office, several farmers greeted Tom, each expecting private minutes with him to discuss markets, their harvest, and whatever local gossip they had in mind. God, how he hated those sessions. Forcing a smile, hearing the same comments about the market—"Man, she's sure up–or down–today."

Weather–"Ain't this a bitch? Never seen it so hot–or cold."

And the never-changing jokes—all of them uniformly foul.

Helen waved to him. "Tom, Barney Jacobs is on line two. Said he wants to talk to you. He's been waiting for the last five minutes."

Now what? He picked up the phone. "Ummm—Tom speakin'."

"Tom. Barney Jacobs. Just calling to be sure you understood me last night at the VFW. I'll be down there today and you better have my grain check ready."

"Sure, sure, Barney. No problem. I'll have Helen make it up this afternoon and I'll buy you one tomorrow just to show you I understood."

"Fine," Barney responded. "Just making sure that friendship doesn't get in the way of business. See you later." And there was only the buzz of the open line.

As he put down the phone, Tom recalled how other farmers felt about Barney. "He sure don't let friendship get in the way of makin' a dollar."

Well, as far as he was concerned, that could be Barney's motto, and he could have it painted on that black Cadillac, and nobody in town would give it a second look.

"Barney Jacobs–Business First, Friendship Last."

Well, getting enough cash together to cover Barney's grain check would be tough, but it had to be done. If he received a check, Barney might have more corn on his farm that could be moved into the Elevator to help cover the Continental sale.

"Helen, figure up Barney's grain account and make out a check. I'll sign it this afternoon."

"Okay Tom, but that will take most of our cash balance and we just got done covering the overdraft we had last week."

Tom thought back to that embarrassing talk he'd had with Ben Waters lecturing him like a schoolboy on the need to keep a positive balance in the bank. If only that goddamn Ben weren't so stingy with the Elevator's line of credit, Tom wouldn't be painted into these corners. He no sooner got several hundred thousand ahead than some farmer or supplier would show up with a hand out for the whole amount. Then, back to the endless moving of grain to corral enough cash to make ends meet.

"Don't worry, Helen," Tom said, "we'll be fine as soon as the checks for this trainload and the Continental sale come back." He would have to talk to the Board again about a bigger operating loan from the Central Bank for Co-ops and maybe another couple of hundred thousand from Ben's bank, too. He couldn't run a business this size on a shoestring.

At last year's regional co-op meeting, he had talked with several managers about this problem. The rapid movements of grain now possible with unit trains coupled with wildly fluctuating prices, and high costs of supplies all came together to make million-dollar businesses out of those that had run on a cash basis in the late 1960s.

Sure was rough to be caught with a loan made when grain and fertilizer prices were low. All of his line of credit had been soaked up by harvest time purchases that now had to be held for spring price run-ups. Neither cash nor credit remained for collecting anything like an adequate inventory of fertilizer, seed, and chemicals.

The phone interrupted Tom again, as it would countless times that day.

"Hello, Farmers Elevator. Tom speakin'."

"Tom, this is Ernie Larsen. What's corn doin' today?"

"It's steady now, Ernie, but I just got word from Continental that prices are going to slide for the next couple of weeks at least–if not for longer than that."

"Hmmmm…" There was a pause as Ernie digested this report. "What'll you give me today for delivery by the end of the month?"

"Well, Ernie, I just made some good sales and can do about $2.50 a bushel for you."

"That ain't too bad, but I got about twenty thousand here and would like a little price break on volume."

Tom considered…twenty thousand…almost half of what he needed to replace the corn sold to Continental. Better do this right. Knowing Ernie, the corn would be in on time and it would be top quality.

"Ernie, for that amount, I'll go to $2.55. Is it first class?"

"You bet! You just made a buy. I'll come in first of the week and sign the contract. We'll start hauling by the middle of the week. You got room?"

Man, have I got room, two trains pullin' out with nearly one-third of the silos empty. Room!

"Sure thing, Ernie, we'll take it as fast as you can haul. Want any help trucking?"

Larsen hesitated. Tom smiled at Ernie's caution. Obviously didn't want anybody cutting up his driveway.

Tom pictured the Larsen place in summer–irrigated lawns and almost obscene prosperity. The land, and probably God, had been in partnership with Ernie and his two sons to make his farm the envy of the community.

"Tom, if you can get Ted Schultz to come down with his semi, we'd be happy for his help. I'd like to get some money in here by the end of the year."

"No problem, Ernie. I'll talk to Ted and we'll set it all up. So long."

"See you, Tom."

He let out a long breath. Larsen's deal would go a long way to picking up the slack in his stored grain. A couple more purchases like that and he'd be out of the woods. Especially with a down market.

A cold draft across his feet announced the opening of the door leading to the dryer yard. The hulk of his dryer operator, Pete Sondal, loomed like a large, dusty cloud against the background of the snowy yard. Pete was a key man in the Elevator operations. His judgment in setting the big dryers could spell the difference between barely making expenses and realizing substantial profits for processing wet grain. All elevators dried grain to fifteen percent moisture, the Minneapolis Terminal standard. However, farmers were docked for moisture above thirteen and a half percent, which meant that they had to absorb the resulting shrinkage in weight and were paid for fewer bushels. This difference in moisture not only paid the cost of drying, but was a windfall of 'extra' bushels that all operators counted on.

This year, corn was somewhat wetter and the potential margin for the Elevator was very significant, but only if the dryers were going around the clock, and if they were set properly.

"What's it look like to you, Pete?"

"I've been through the damn thing from top to bottom and the only thing it can be is the safety relay that opens the main gas valve."

"Haven't we got a couple of those on hand?" Tom asked.

"Not any more. That crazy machine eats them up like a Norwegian at a corn feed."

"Goddamn. That means that we have to call Sioux Falls and maybe send somebody down there for it. Nobody else in the area has one of those Chicago junk piles, right?"

"Nope, Boss, nobody else is that dumb."

"All right, Pete. You call Sioux Falls. Take Andy off the Bobcat, and get him on the road. It'll take him two days—one down and one back."

"Will do." Pete moved into the bookkeeping office with that offhand salute he always used to acknowledge Tom's orders.

"Hey, Stub," Pete jostled the bookkeeper. "Get your coat on and do a little work."

Their thinly veiled enmity was always ready to break through the surface of customary Elevator byplay, like one of the submerged snags coming down the Thoms River in spring. Like those snags, these breakouts could be dangerous to the normal interactions necessary for a smoothly running business.

"Go to hell! If I didn't keep track of your mistakes, we'd all be shoveling like crazy to keep this place running." Stub glared, red-faced.

"Well, we all gotta put our hands on the shovels if we don't want to be buried in problems!" Pete avoided confrontation and turned away to pour a cup of coffee from the office urn, holding both red hands close around the cup to draw warmth from the hot liquid. Cup in hand, he strolled over to Helen's desk and carefully perched on its edge, using the clean cup to shift papers away from his dusty clothes.

"Hi!"

"Pete, look at you! You're a sight!"

"Yeah, but underneath I'm still your honey, right?"

"Now, Pete, one date doesn't make a romance." Her blush made her pert face even more attractive.

Their voices lowered. Their relationship was a good thing since both Pete and Helen were lonely people with no family in Sheffield and no interests outside their work.

Looking at the two inexperienced lovers gave Tom a pause that pushed his problems into the background. As long as he and Janet were together, there wouldn't be problems they couldn't deal with. Maybe it would be the same for Pete and Helen.

Pete came out of the inner office now, with the empty cup a paper ball in his hand.

"Tom, this dryer breakdown means I can't keep up the schedule we planned."

"I know, Pete. I told Andy to stir up the Elm Street pile this morning. Some air drying might take up the slack."

"Boss, you and I know that there ain't no air dryin' that's gonna keep that pile from heavy spoiling."

"Yeah, you're probably right," Tom admitted. "How much do you think we got left in the street?"

"Ohhh...," Pete considered for a moment, "I'd say about thirty thousand."

"Ummm, thirty thousand," Tom jotted the figure on the blotter in front of him, and then he twirled the pencil. "That's the corn I bought cheap on a wet basis so we could lose as much as twenty-three thousand bushels if the whole pile goes."

"What about preservative?" Pete suggested.

"That's taking a hell of a chance." Tom frowned. "If we put acid to it, we got to move the stuff to cattle feeders by spring and you know how weak the feed market has been."

"Well, it's either feed or shit. In my book, we got about two days to treat that corn or write it off. Less than that, if the weather warms up."

"Okay, Pete, let me think about it, and we'll decide this afternoon."

Propionic Acid. The corn preservative could be applied by running the pile through a portable auger into one of the smaller storage bins while metering acid into the corn. However, once acid was on the corn, it couldn't be marketed to terminals in Minneapolis, but had to be fed to local cattle and, if it wasn't sold by the beginning of warm weather in spring, he would have a bin full of badly spoiled corn and complaints from townspeople about its smell.

These thoughts were brought to an end by the roar of a diesel truck on the scale outside the office window, accompanied by a blast of dual chrome-plated air horns on the big Kenworth mountain rig that came to a stop abreast the scale operator's station.

TED SCHULTZ TRUCKING was the name on this imposing truck, along with stars and comets that decorated a sleeper cab behind the driver's compartment. The visual impact of the truck announced that Ted Schultz wasn't the type to lay back in traffic while his fellow truckers led the way past the Smokies. Like the blast on the horn, Ted surged into Tom's office.

"Hey, you Elevator turkeys, Schultz is here! Schultz wants corn! Now!"

"Hi, Superstar," said Tom. "What's the latest from your rollin' whorehouse?"

"Hey, Boy!" Star responded. "Two new waitresses in Fargo country and about three wives of elevator men who were too busy watchin' their scales to keep an eye on the Star."

"Well, us elevator types don't have to worry too much. Like most stars, you fade when a little sunshine hits your stories."

"Say, old Thomas, think you can get your thumb off them scales long enough to load me with number two yella for Montana?"

"Sure, Star. Let's have the boys load you, and I'll plunk for lunch downtown."

"Fine as silk! But tell those cats to go light on the chaffy shit, cause it's the old Star who has to sweet talk them cowpunchers into buyin' the crap you load here."

"Okay, okay," Tom chuckled. "Have the boys load him, Pete, with about forty-six thousand out of bin seven. I'll be back after lunch."

"And, be sure it's forty-six right on the money, and don't add the Boss Man's two hundred pounds to my ticket," Star laughed and clapped Tom on the shoulder.

Forty-six thousand pounds of corn was automatically translated into the eight hundred fifty bushels that could be billed to Ted Schultz Trucking, an ongoing record of transactions that dominated all his waking—and most of his sleeping—hours.

They crowded out the door together and raced each other to the Fury. Tom immediately lagged behind as Star's lanky frame rocketed ahead.

"The Star wins!" shouted Star, and they both piled into the car and set off for downtown Sheffield.

CHAPTER TWO
VFW

There were three major social groups in Sheffield. Each provided an opportunity for people to meet with others who thought alike. Special rules for behavior, though unwritten, limited what one might be expected to say and do in most situations. These customs made for relatively comfortable exchange in all that was done in town. However, under the smooth, predictable surface of town life lay divisions of opinion and action that occasionally resulted in open disagreement between these groups and among their members.

Tom and Janet, as newcomers, were acquainted with the community through several of these groups. Janet numbered her friends among those who attended Our Savior's Lutheran Church, where many farmers of an older generation belonged. The youth activities of the Church offered a setting where Chrissy made her friends. And, as time passed, the Church became a substitute for a family weakened by the Elevator.

In contrast, Tom was drawn into the business life of Sheffield. He was welcomed by younger residents, including the most financially successful and socially powerful who came together through the Commercial Club and casual meetings in Sheffield's business district.

Even though Tom was one of the leading businessmen in town, he was never comfortable with their association.

Instead Tom was an enthusiastic member of another category of citizens that cut across age, religion, and social status to bring people together in drinking, talking, and card playing at several Sheffield taverns. He was always able to find a large contingent of this group at the VFW Club at one time or another during the day–except on Sunday, when all Sheffield gave in to the wishes of the churches and refrained from drinking, at least in public.

Whenever Tom reflected on the nature of social Sheffield, he could see that many young people looked for life and work in larger towns in the Dakotas or in other urban areas. Those who stayed behind were not necessarily less ambitious, but were readily pleased by the diversions offered by the VFW Club and able to limit the scope of their ambition to allow time for pleasures of sociability. As the older generation of church goers declined in number, more money became available for the interests of the business community, culminating two years ago in a new parish hall for St. Stephen's Catholic Church and the bar-restaurant of the VFW Club.

Every noon, the VFW offered a simple sandwich lunch that drew businessmen as well as Commercial Club members who had their weekly meeting at the VFW. These individuals lent a veneer of respectability to the Club and prevented complete stagnation of business that might have occurred on those days when too many productive hours were spent in casual drinking and talking after lunch.

Evenings at the Club were no different. Last year Tom took Janet to dinner at the Club's Rodeo Room. Her enthusiasm for a private dinner was dampened by the need to cross the barroom with its tables of partygoers. Décor in the Rodeo Room did little to restore her delight. Wall-sized murals of bronc riders alternated with pictures of the Dallas Cowgirls and football greats. 'All you can eat for $4.50' was a fitting anticlimax. That was the last time they tried an evening out in Sheffield.

On a winter day like this, with a half-hidden sun giving faint glare, entering the Club was like coming into a cave where a holiday was in full celebration. Tom's eyes adjusted slowly to the relative dark of the

Club. Gradually, he could see other forms, then faces in the light of bar signs and candles burning in their red containers of corrugated glass.

"Hey, it's Tom and Superstar!" Bob announced. "C'mon, I'll buy one!" Bob had beat them to the Club and was already drinking his second Walker's and charged water with Jim Leach, a small, paunchy man who was the area fertilizer representative for Farmhand Cooperatives. Leach supplied most of the fertilizer and chemicals purchased by elevators in this part of the Midwest and was a fixture at any meeting of elevator managers.

"Hi, Bob, Jim. Didn't see you guys up at the Elevator." Tom hung his Farmers Elevator jacket across the back of a chair and joined the two at their table.

"Nah," Bob answered, "we took off for lunch as soon as Jim drove in. Better to talk business down here without that damn phone."

"You think the phone's bad now, Bob, just wait 'til the first of the year, when farmers find out that fertilizer's goin' to be short as Superstar's pecker." Leach chuckled at this rare opportunity to beat Star to any obscenity—no matter how mild.

"Hey, you, Leach! Watch how you poke fun at the Star! I might decide to muscle into your territory with that Betty over to Minot," Star replied, turning his chair backward and leering across the table as he joined the party.

"Jim," Tom interrupted, "is it possible that we might not get as much fertilizer as we did last year?"

Leach looked at something in the middle distance through the top of his bifocals. Tom recognized this as the Leach 'deal look' which invariably resulted in a profit for Farmhand. That profit was guaranteed by the bottom of Leach's bifocals where the details of a transaction were hidden from the outsider. In all his dealings with Leach, Tom had never penetrated the bifocals to discover a real person behind the glasses.

Before Leach could reply, Kate Christensen, the Club waitress, made her way to their table.

"What'll it be for you boys? Drinkin' or eatin' today?"

"Drinkin'," Tom replied. "Double Manhattan on the rocks for me and a double rye for Star."

Kate took their orders and left—leaving a special smile for Star.

Tom looked at Leach and repeated his question. "What about spring supplies, Jim?"

"Well," Leach said, "I don't know for sure yet. But seems to me that we could easily have a situation where we can only come up with about half of your normal supply."

"Christ!" Tom exploded, "that's all we need. We've had a booking day at the Elevator and sold about twenty percent more already than we sold all last year."

Each considered this problem in momentary silence as Kate brought their drink orders.

"You boys want a sandwich?" she asked.

"Kate Baby," Star grinned, "I'll take that sandwich and be back for you later."

"C'mon, Star," Kate laughed, "you ain't growed up enough to hang around a mature woman."

"Well, I don't know…," Star pretended to think about the problem of aging. "Kate, you're sure enough mature but I'll bet the old Star's hung enough for hanging around."

Bob laughed, "Kate, you know you can't beat Superstar at those word games. Better bring our lunch so the poor child don't get all overheated."

Blushing, Kate moved smoothly off to the kitchen. All four men watched her closely, Star staring over the rim of his glass. "Man, I'd sure like to take that for a ride in my truck."

"She'd be too much for you, Star," Bob grinned. "You'd have to put training wheels back on your Kenworth." He reached over and carefully turned Superstar's head back to the table.

"Bob, did you know this fertilizer squeeze was comin' on?" Tom's forehead showed wrinkles of concern as he carefully drained his glass and signaled the bartender for a refill.

"I kind of suspected it. The world market has been tight this fall and seems as if foreign buyers are stocking up for a big plantin' season next spring." Bob showed the insight that made him one of the top speculative authorities in the trade.

"That's the way I read it too," said Leach. "We're even getting calls from foreign traders at our headquarters in St. Louis, and that means that New Orleans and East Coast supplies are getting low."

Tom considered this for a moment. "Well, we had better book more product, Bob. We can't let our farmers down, 'specially on the heels of the low crop we had last summer." He left the table and walked slowly and steadily to the bar to pick up his Manhattan. He scooped two sickly cherries from the drink and tossed them into a nearby ashtray. Then he looked around the dark room—noticing Barney Jacobs at a distant table.

"Jack," he called to the bartender, "give the boys back with Barney a drink on me and let's have a refill at our table."

"Will do, Tom. You guys going to have a party?"

"Sure could use it, but we probably ought to tend to business. Takin' off on Friday's too much of a temptation and the work's pilin' up back at the Elevator."

He took the four drinks, including his now half-empty Manhattan, and went back to the table where Star was talking.

"Isn't there some way we can get access to the Canadian market for 0-0-60?"

"Oh, sure," said Bob, "but you gotta have friends in Canada at the allocation department–right at the potash mines."

"But, Bob," Star said, "I thought you met some of those boys when you were on your fishin' trip up that way last year."

"Sure, I got lots of friends in the trade, but you need cash to play in that league."

"The same's true in the phosphate market," said Leach. "There's always some surplus material on track somewhere that can't be unloaded in time. You got cash and a place for that stuff, and you got yourself a load of 18-46-0."

Tom listened to the exchange. These were the two most popular analyses of fertilizer: 0-0-60, sixty percent potash; and 18-46-0, eighteen percent nitrogen and forty-six percent phosphate. They were also the fertilizers used by Sheffield farmers for spring planting. If Leach was right, the Elevator would probably be caught short, especially given this year's level of demand.

He leaned forward, tapping his pencil on the table. "I'm sure the Elevator Board would increase our loan to get a sure supply of fertilizer for this spring."

"That may be, Boss," said Bob, "but until the contacts and the cars are in the bag, there ain't no use in getting your hopes up."

"It's also hard for a co-op elevator like yours to come into a speculative market," added Leach. "My people get all pissed off when one of our customers tries to muscle into our wholesale trade."

"Yeah, I suppose so," Tom reflected. "Last year when I sold that Lasso to Grandview Elevator I sure got hell from your credit department."

"That's just it!" exclaimed Leach. "Those boys get in the way of sales. We can't move product around to where it'll do the most good without some bullshit about allocation and customer relations from our St. Louis desk boys."

"If you had more truckers in this, you wouldn't have any problems," said Star.

"What do you mean?" asked Bob.

"Like, well, you could take guys who have made a run to, say, Louisiana. We could pick up phosphate on the back-haul and the desk jockeys would never be wiser. We could do just the same on hauls to Canada, except that the back-haul would be potash."

"Maybe you got a point, Star," mused Leach. "Direct trucking would bypass the bottleneck in our rail department. Without the car invoice, the St. Louis office can't get on our case about diverting fertilizer from one customer to another."

"Jim," Tom interrupted, "I don't like the idea of diverting fertilizer. Sounds like you would be taking from one elevator and moving to another just to get a better price."

"Nope," Bob cut in, "you are just takin' material that's left over and above the normal allocation that any elevator will pay a premium to get." Half-moons of sweat on Bob's brown work shirt became visible as he hoisted his glass in a sweeping gesture that enclosed their conversation.

"We're all still fartin' in the wind," said Leach. "This is only talk. We might not see a shortage. Trade could loosen up by spring."

"I'll bet one of the top nights on the town in Minot that it don't," said Bob, wiping a hand over his bald head.

"Hell! All there is to do in that town is watch the snow pile up!" Star snorted. "Or, see how long it takes one of them drunks to come in out of the cold!"

They all laughed at the low value of this wager as Kate brought their sandwiches. Talk of fertilizer dwindled, but not before Leach and Bob exchanged glances that spoke of a 'deal' in the making.

"Thanks Kate," Tom said, "bring us coffee all around and get me a refill on this Manhattan—hold the cherries this time. How about you, Bob? Jim? Another one?"

"No." Bob shook his head. "Me and Jim'll pass. We got to get back to the Elevator and look over our customer orders for next spring."

"Me, I'll take one," Star said. "We truckers can't let you fat old elevator boys pass us by."

The two fertilizer salesmen finished the last of their sandwiches and put on their coats. As they were about to leave, Barney Jacobs called to them from the rear of the Club. "Hey, Bob, c'mere a minute."

Bob wound his way through the maze of now-empty tables with Leach following

"Yeah, Barney. What's on your mind?"

"Just checkin' up on you. What's the scoop on my fertilizer for next spring?"

"Hell, Barney, you know we'll take care of you. We got your check and you're on the books for $80,000 of the stuff. In fact, I was just talking with Jim here, from Farmhand, about our supply and it looks good."

"It sure as hell better look good. You've got my cash and I don't plan to get caught short next spring. I can read the papers, and one hell of a shortage is comin' up." He turned his massive body back to the other farmers at his table, dismissing Bob.

"Sure, sure, Barney," Bob flushed at this rebuff. "You're probably right on the shortage thing, but we noticed that in early fall and got our orders on top of the Farmhand list. Ain't that right, Jim?" Bob looked to Leach for support.

Leach moved into Barney's line of sight. "That's right, Bob. You are one of the few elevators who were looking ahead." Jim extended his hand so Barney could not ignore him. "How do you do? I'm Jim Leach."

"Barney Jacobs is the name," he growled, his huge hand engulfing that of the smaller salesman. "You better keep old Bob in line, Leach. Just ask around town and you'll know that Barney Jacobs makes his deals stick."

"That's the only way," mumbled Leach.

Bob straightened. "Well, Barney, we got to get back to the Elevator. See you later."

"Damn right you will. So long, Bob. Nice to meet you, Leach." They were sent off with a wave of a giant arm.

As the two passed Tom's table, Bob stopped. "Boss, Barney is sure on the warpath. Did you do anything to set him off?"

"Christ, no. He's got a check coming on his grain, but that's in the bag with our new train shipment comin' up."

"Seems to me you better keep your eye on him. He don't act like he trusts us."

No trust from Barney Jacobs could be something that might keep the Elevator from expanding. Not one to hold his opinions to himself, Jacobs could spread the word that the Elevator wasn't to be completely trusted. Then farmers would start to demand their cash on delivery of grain. The resulting outflow of money would make it impossible to build up a stock of Elevator-owned grain to compensate for unavoidable delays between the purchase of grain from farmers and the final receipt of a check from the Minneapolis commission firms. Because he was a regular fixture in the Sheffield downtown area, Jacobs had the contacts with Elevator customers to make him a real threat.

"Guess I'd better talk to him and try to find out what's buggin' him." Tom sighed and finished the last of his drink. "Star, you going back to the Elevator?"

"No, think I'll hang round here a while," he grinned, looking over to where Kate was waiting on Jacobs' table.

"I see your point," said Tom, following Star's gaze. "Since you're going to stay, let's go over and join Barney–his friends are leavin'."

They took their coats from the backs of chairs and walked to the rear of the club, Star casually brushing past Kate on the way.

"Hi, Barney. Got time for one before we go back to work?" Tom smiled down at Jacobs, waiting for a summons to the throne.

"Sure, hell, why not? Hi, Superstar."

"Hello, Barney, how's it goin'?"

"Could be better—if this here elevator man could stay on the ball."

"Say, Barney, what's eatin' you about the Elevator, anyway?" Tom lowered himself onto the chair across from Jacobs and waved his drink order to Kate.

"I think you're losin' your touch," Barney growled. "I see that hot corn on the ground and I know that you've been stallin' me on my check. Well, I don't like that, but I'll go along with you for a while 'cause you used to be a top grain man and we need that sort of person at the Elevator."

Tom sat silent for a moment. This was the sort of blunt talk that nobody else in town would give him and it hit very close to home. Maybe he was losing his touch. Who wouldn't with the poor season and upside-down markets, and those donkeys at the Elevator. Sometimes he took too much time for lunches like this and drank a little too much. But these escapes were the only way he could fend off the terrible visions that came with every problem. Jacobs couldn't know the real story or he'd see that the Elevator Board fired him immediately.

"Okay, Barney," he said evenly, "I deserved that. I do have trouble with some corn and I've been taking a lickin' on the markets, but I have a hell of a deal on a big shipment that will make farmers and the Elevator a lot of money in the next month. If the weather changes, and our dryers keep running, I'll have this thing turned around."

Tom paused to watch Kate's hand set a brimful glass in front of him—liquor-rich syrup straining against a glowing meniscus on the rim of the glass, a true witch's brew—erasing memories and present strain. His hand, now steady, replaced Kate's and he lifted the glass and carefully sipped–forgetting.

"And," snorted Jacobs, "you drink too damn much!"

The liquor spilled—now only wet and cold, down the front of his shirt—across the script letters 'Tom.' Barney's comment was a source of guilt. Each drink taken today was a betrayal of the Elevator. With effort, he tore himself from this thought and faced Barney. "I guess that's right, too, Barney. Sometimes I do, but I think that it's under control and I'm cuttin' down every day."

"Bullshit!" Jacobs exploded as he stood, wriggling into his three-hundred-dollar sheepskin coat. "I'm tellin' you, Cooper, you keep swillin' that stuff and you'll leave this town in that beat-up car of yours damn quick!"

Jacobs wheeled out the door, leaving only guilt and shame in his wake.

Superstar averted his eyes and motioned to the bartender for another drink. "Might as well have a party. There ain't nothin' goin' on today."

"Might as well—nothing much could help me today. Anyway, I gotta get on my way home. It's Chrissy's birthday and I still have to stop for her present."

Star ignored these comments and focused the conversation. "What kinds of loads you got for me this month?"

Tom responded to Star's attempt to change the mood. "Corn, for sure, for Havre Feedlot. Should be a good run for you."

"Maybe. Depends on the back-haul. Should take a good day and a half if they can find me a load in Havre." Star made a few mental calculations. "Could take me a rider along and have a bang-up time."

"Heavy on the bang, I bet," Tom replied with the lift of spirits Superstar always gave him. "How's that Kenworth running?"

"That was the best buy the old Star ever made. I clear a pretty good living after paying for truck and fuel, and I'll have enough equity come next fall to add a truck and maybe a driver for this one. Then the Superstar will take to the desk and let somebody else work his balls off loading at midnight and rub the nails off his fingers trying to keep awake on forty-eight-hour round trips."

"I'll drink to that!" Tom looked at Star, now a little blurred in outline, over a fresh glass.

Star responded with a toast and suggestion. "Hey! Let's bug out of this joint and go over to River House. Usually there's a party there on Friday afternoon."

"Good idea. Have Kate bring our check. I'm going to shake hands with the man who stood up at my wedding." He headed for the men's room. When he returned, Star was waiting, holding their coats with a wide grin. Reaching the Fury, Tom saw the reason for the grin. Kate was waiting for them, bundled in her old coat in the front seat.

"Well, look here," Star said. "We got us a passenger for Fun City."

"Oh, come on, Star, get this car going. It's cold in here!" Kate shivered and moved to the center of the seat. Star slid behind the wheel, taking Tom's keys from under the driver's seat.

"Lemme show you how to handle this rig." He struck the classic pose of a semi-truck driver. Back erect, arms straight on the wheel and an over-the-road look in his eyes. Both Kate and Tom laughed. Star started the Fury and pretended to shift a Road Ranger transmission using Kate's knee as a shift lever. With her squeals of protest and the jerky missing of the Fury's engine, they moved out of the parking lot, headed for Fun City.

River House, Friday's Fun City, was across town from the VFW Club. To go from one to the other, it was necessary to travel the length of Main Street, past most of the stores and services of Sheffield. At the end of Main, Highway 13 curved gently up a small incline to a bridge over the Thoms River. About a mile from the bridge, Highway 13 moved reluctantly from the river and ascended a small knoll. This knoll, covered with cottonwood trees and sprinkled with rough cedars at its top, was the site of River House. Anyone climbing the knoll from Sheffield in winter was led through bare trees toward a thin wall of cedars. At once, through a gap, the plastic sign of River House Motel and Bar could be seen.

WELCOME BACK COOPERSTAR–TGIF!

"Jesus!" groaned Tom, "Look at that!"

"Hey! Great!" Star shouted, "How's that for top billing?"

"I knew that party we had last Friday was a little too loud." Tom slid down in his seat, pulling his Farmers Elevator cap to one side. Although he saw and enjoyed the humor, he couldn't help but think of the impact the sign would have on some of the farmers who traveled Highway 13 on their way to and from Sheffield. Chris Odegaard, Chairman of the Elevator Board, was sure to be offended by the sign—if he could place the reference correctly. Odegaard wasn't one to take a drink, nor did he approve of others who indulged. For him, Church and Elevator were one and the same, each to be given complete loyalty and each to receive its tithes in profit while maintaining a proper image.

"If Odegaard sees this, I'm going to get a lecture on Monday!" said Tom.

"Oh, don't worry," giggled Kate, "that old bastard ain't smart enough to figure it out."

"Let's see if we can get KISS ME KATE up there next week," said Star as he wheeled the Fury up to a parking lot snowbank and killed its engine with the impact. They rolled out of the car and made their way to the River House door, like sailors who have had a particularly rough crossing, their steps made unsteady by the stability of land. Tom held the door for Kate and Star, who stumbled past, arm in arm.

"Here's CooperStar!" yelled Star, as he burst into the bar. The dozen or so patrons waved and greeted them with varying degrees of obscenity and levity.

"Welcome, honored guests. May this humble hostel be worthy of your knightly presence." Al Austin, the bartender, raised a bottle in each hand and, with a practiced flourish, brought them down neatly, their metal spouts touching the rims of two highball glasses.

"Let there be a toast to the Knight of Road and the King of Grain!" He pushed the full glasses across the bar to Tom and Star. Each hoisted the offering and, with solemn glances over the customers, drank deeply.

Star held up his free hand as if giving a benediction to some mass of followers. "May this kindly gift warm this knight, all night, and, especially tonight." He curved his arm around Kate and let her drink from the now half-empty glass—to the accompaniment of loud laughter from the assembled.

Tom stepped up onto the bar rail and the rung of a barstool and, precariously balanced, delivered a blessing. "Hear ye! Hear ye!" he coughed. "Ye King of Grain tells ye peasants that today is proclaimed for feasting and drinking and anyone not following ye orders will be put in ye jail!"

Amid the laughter following this announcement, the King toppled with a distinctly unroyal lurch onto the floor.

Star leaned over and helped Tom to his feet, signaling Al to replace the spilled liquor. The royal party then made their way to a table near the bar and prepared to hold court.

"Tom, we got to have peanuts or this ain't no party," Star pronounced with an owlish gaze.

"Correct, Sir Star. Barkeep! A bowl of peanuts for my people!"

While this request was being carried out, Star's attention was drawn to a middle-aged woman who was making a purchase at the off-sale counter.

"Say, Ma'am, that there is sure a big box for you to carry. Let me help you."

"Oh, thank you," the woman replied with a grateful smile. "I'm not sure I can carry these to my car. It's much too slippery outside."

"A box of bottles?" queried Tom. "And what might be in them, Ma'am?"

"Just some wine that I'm taking home for my bridge club tonight," she said. "I do wonder, though, do you think that a red wine is okay with snacks?"

"Hmmm…," Star considered, "I don't know. Sometimes red wines are a little off. Ain't that so, Tom?"

"Oh, yes, definitely. The reds are often off in taste. Especially if the year is a poor one," affirmed Tom.

"My!" said the woman. "Do you suppose that I might have a poor year here?"

"Only one way to tell." Star made a great effort to control his glee. "Why don't we open a bottle and sample it?"

"Oh, would you?" the bridge club woman said, with evident relief.

Star escorted her to the royal table and, in passing, picked up four wine glasses which had appeared almost magically on the bar. As they joined Kate and Tom, the woman introduced herself.

"I'm Helga Olson," she said with a smile.

During the introduction, Star deposited the case of bottles beside his chair. With a flourish, he produced an opened bottle of wine wrapped in Tom's Elevator jacket.

"Ladies and gentlemen! Here is a specialty of the house! Old Elevator, 1976. Do you wish to sample the wine, sir?" he said, looking at Tom with a wink.

"Oh, no, that will be fine. I know the brand and it's always excellent."

The four held their full glasses carefully and Helga raised hers tentatively and said, "I hope that this will be good enough for my club."

With that toast, the glasses were emptied and quickly refilled by Star.

"Well, what do you think?" Helga asked worriedly. "Will this do?"

"Hmmm, I can't really tell." Tom pretended to savor the bouquet of the cheap wine. "Often these red wines are hard to taste properly. I thought there was a hint of a problem here, didn't you, Star?"

"Definitely. We had better check again," Star agreed quickly.

Again the glasses were filled, and the empty bottle placed in the box.

"I regret to say, Helga, that this bottle is quite inferior and in no way fit for your bridge club," stated Tom.

"Oh, no!" she replied, "I had better return the others and get my money back." She began to rise.

"No, don't be too hasty. These other bottles look fine. Why don't we take another sample and we'll probably find that you did the right thing." Star held her in her chair with a fatherly hand on her shoulder.

"Okay, but I do have to be going. It's only a couple of hours until the girls will be arriving and I have to get everything ready."

Another bottle was enveloped in Tom's Farmers Elevator jacket and all glasses filled.

"Kate, what do you think of this one?" Star peered over his nose at her.

She giggled. "I'm no judge of wine. This one tastes fine. Just like the last one."

"There you are!" exclaimed Tom. "This is a better bottle. Looks like you have a winner, Helga. Can't you taste the difference?"

"Yes, yes, now that you mention it. This is much silkier—is that the way to describe it?" she looked at Star questioningly.

"Why, Helga, you got a natural taste for wine. I couldn't have said it better. Silkier—ain't that so, Tom? Here, taste it and see." He poured refills again and slipped the second empty bottle into the box.

"Yessiree, Mr. Star. It definitely is silkier, but I hate to say this, the bouquet is off."

"There ain't no flowers on the bottle, Tom," said Kate in drunken seriousness.

"Not flowers on the bottle, my dear woman," pontificated Star, "but delicate flavors of flowers in the bottle."

Helga looked puzzled. "What do you mean? Is this a good wine or isn't it?"

"I guess we don't know," Star paused and studied the label on the bottle. "This doesn't seem like 1976 vintage to me. We had better try another bottle to make sure there hasn't been some tinkering with the label."

"Oh, please do," Helga placed an imploring hand on Star's arm, knocking her half-empty glass over in the process.

"I think you're right, Helga," said Tom, as he mopped up the spilled wine with his napkin. "There's no reason why we shouldn't be one hundred percent sure."

Once again, Star served and the guests sampled. This time there was almost uniform approval, somewhat unintelligible and slurred in the case of Helga, who clearly lacked the robust constitution needed by an experienced wine taster. Despite this limitation, she was warming to her work and considering her new vocation with an inner pleasure, never before experienced.

"Just to be sure, we better take a little out of each bottle," she said. "I must know that I'm doin' the right ting…I mean…thing," she added, with a determined glance at Star.

"Who else could be so careful," Tom added with pride. "I knew you were fooling when you said you didn't know anything about wine."

"You betcha!" Star decided. "Helga, your choice of wine is right on and the ladies at your party will be very happy."

"Oh, my!" she replied, "I haven't been watching the time. I'll just have to go pretty soon or I won't have things ready."

"Right. But first let's check the rest of these bottles." Star drew the corks from the remaining three bottles and poured a little of each into the four glasses, spilling quite a bit in the process.

"Oh, Star!" Kate said, with a hand pressed to her forehead. "I don't think I can drink any more. I'm getting a little sick."

"Don't worry, Kate, Tom and I can take over for you. We can't let Helga down, can we, Tom?"

"No way!" Tom exclaimed, tossing off a full glass and pouring the balance of Kate's into his own.

As the tasting progressed, the group became silent, each coming to terms with an oversupply of alcohol in his or her own private way. For Tom and Star, experience made possible a gradual transition from gaiety to a condition where large quantities of alcohol could be consumed without appreciable impact on behavior. In fact, the wine could be viewed as an interlude in the day's party, where each man took stock of his condition and formed some vague plan that would guide him in his choice of drinks and predetermine the total amount to be consumed. If either were to take the trouble, he would admit to some such subconscious calculation, often intermingled with questions about other demands such as driving, lovemaking, or even business decisions to be made.

Helga was in that early stage of drunkenness when it seemed that mind could control body. Her pleasant feelings and heightened perceptions helped her to appreciate her newfound friends and enhanced her understanding of fine wines. How pleasant it would be to share this experience with the girls at her club party. How proud she would be to describe her reasons for choosing each wine…silky…fine bouquet…a good vintage year. This silence and the varied thoughts, and turmoil it concealed, was broken by the arrival in the barroom of Mary Austin, the wife of the bartender.

"Helga Olson! Whatever are you doing here? Isn't this the night for your bridge club?"

"Why, Mary! Yes, it is. And I'm teen—unh—testin' some these wine for the gals."

"Helga, you're drunk. And the party is starting in an hour. What will we do?"

"Let the old party start!" she said defiantly. "It won't go anywhere without us and the wine."

Mary turned to the men. "Ted Schultz! Tom Cooper! You should be ashamed of yourselves! You knew that Helga was taking this wine home. Now look at what you've done! What will her friends say? Her husband?"

"Aw, Mary," Star mumbled, "we didn't mean nothing."

"That's a lie!" Mary stormed. "Both of you know exactly what you're doing when you drink. And you knew that Helga couldn't stay with you."

"Oh, Mary," Helga pleaded, "these guys both know wine and we were comparin' notes. Ain't that so, boys?" She winked carefully, leaving her eye closed.

"Yeah, Mary," Tom added, "we were just tryin' to help Helga."

"Is that so! Well, you can just help her into her car so I can drive her home. You, Ted, take her other arm and we'll be going. Tom, you bring her purse and the box of wine bottles and make it snappy!"

Both men hastened to their feet and to their appointed tasks, motivated by a vague feeling of guilt and the real threat of Mary Austin's anger, which was a local legend in Sheffield.

As Tom watched Mary and Star half-carry Helga from the bar, he could see how their innocent fun might produce a real crisis for her. Taking the box of wine bottles, he stumbled to the bar.

"Al, I guess I'd better replace Helga's wine. Give me six more bottles." He pulled out his wallet and gave the bartender two twenties, money that had been earmarked for Chrissy's birthday present. No matter now; this was a fine that had to be paid.

"You're right, Tom," Austin said, as he placed the fresh bottles in the box. "This party's pretty important for Helga and she'd be disappointed as hell not to have wine when she gets home."

This analysis did nothing to relieve Tom of his growing guilt. He quickly picked up the box of bottles and stepped out into the cold evening air of the parking lot. Mary and Star were trying to persuade a giggling Helga to enter the passenger side of her Mercury.

"Oh," she protested, "I never let anybody else drive. My husband gets real mad if I don't take good care of our car."

"Helga," Mary said firmly, "this time I'm driving, so in you go."

Tom put the wine in the back seat and closed the door while Helga continued to wave through a rapidly fogging window. Mary glowered at Tom and Star as she drove the Mercury out of the River House parking lot.

"Cold out here," Star said, attempting to make conversation as they watched the car turn down the hill from River House toward Sheffield.

"Damn right! Let's go back inside and get some chow. It's gettin' close to supper time."

They welcomed the overheated air of the bar and moved, almost sober, to their table.

"Boy, we sure have poor luck with our drinkin' partners today," Star said, pointing to Kate, who had lost her battle with alcohol and sat slumped in her chair, face down on the table.

"Passed out," observed Tom. "Well, let's order some food and some black coffee and see if we can bring her around."

"Hey! Al!" Star called. "Bring us a couple of burgers and fries and a pitcher of coffee, okay?"

"Comin' right up—the works?"

"You bet. Tom and me'll share an order of onion rings, too."

"Say, Kate, you okay?" Star asked. There was no reply, merely heavy breathing with an occasional sigh. "You know, Tom, I think she's really sick," Star said in a kindly voice. "Here, give me a hand. Let's see if we can find a place where she can lie down."

They carefully helped her to a standing position and, sharing her weight, took her to a bench near the shuffleboard table in the rear of the barroom. Star folded his coat for a pillow and gently covered Kate with her own coat and Tom's jacket.

"She'll get a little sleep and be plenty fit by the time we're ready to go, don't you think?"

"Yeah, she'll be all right." Tom looked down at Kate, lying sick and helpless, her condition in marked contrast to the idea of wellness. Again grief swelled up to fix itself as a lump in his throat. Kate's dependency on him seemed like that of those who looked to him for support. Janet…Chrissy…people who came to him for advice at the Elevator.

"Let's hurry and eat, Star, and then you can take Kate home and we'll all feel better." He turned quickly back to their table so that Star could not see his clenched hands and the working of his throat as he fought to regain control over his emotions. Once seated again, food and coffee helped to restore a sense of rationality to the day's experience and he was able to look with more confidence, if not approval, at the evening.

"Star, I got to be gettin' along. Can't have another night on the town. It's Chrissy's birthday today and I promised to be at her party. Better finish up here and check the Elevator before I move out for home."

"Let's do that. I'll ride back with you and take Kate home in the Kenworth." He held a paper napkin to his face to hide the foolish grin that came at this prospect.

"My God, Star, you don't ever stop thinkin' of women, do you?"

"Nope. I don't. And that's a fact. But you're right. She is sick and I got to put that right with her." Star stopped chuckling and looked thoughtful, as if he was connecting his behavior to the consequences of the afternoon. "I guess the party didn't work out so good. Better luck next time."

Tom silently agreed. He couldn't help thinking, as he paid their bill, that next week River House would have a cooler welcome for CooperStar.

The two men easily carried Kate out to the Fury. Once outdoors, the cold air revived her and her sickness was more apparent. Only a few steps from the door, she tore herself from their support and was immediately sick. While Tom turned politely aside, Star held Kate as she retched her way back to unpleasant consciousness.

"Poor gal," Star tenderly wiped her face, "here, c'mon, we'll get into the car out of this wind."

Tom slid behind the wheel and started the tomb-cold Fury while Star enveloped Kate in her coat and a blanket from the back seat.

"Get this thing goin', and let's get warm." He hugged Kate and she leaned on his shoulder, sharing her sickness with him. Nobody said anything on the drive back to Sheffield, in contrast to the holiday mood of the afternoon.

The guilt Tom felt as he followed the snow swirls down Highway 13, around the sharp turn onto the bridge, was a complex emotion. The most immediate was the responsibility for the effect of the party on two women. Of these, Helga weighed more heavily in his thoughts. She was an innocent bystander who had been drawn into barroom life by the chance of her purchase. The results of her afternoon provided Tom with many scenarios as he drove, each of great embarrassment to Helga, and each, it was clear to him, the direct result of his actions. For Kate, it was not so much that they had drawn her into their party, but that they had pushed her to her limits and made her sick. Kate had no reason to expect anything but heavy drinking and had gone along with them, knowing that a party was in the making. However, the very cleverness of their wine tasting gambit had not only fooled Helga Olson, it had disarmed Kate's natural, and experienced, vigilance over her drinking with a very unpleasant end to an afternoon's fun.

These feelings crystallized as they approached the Elevator. Here was tangible evidence of his responsibility. He had not returned to work after lunch. He had not made the decisions expected of him. He had not laid plans for tomorrow's work and for the purchases and sales necessary to keep the Elevator actively in business.

The darkened stores on Sheffield's Main Street reminded him that he had promised to find a birthday present for Chrissy—her tenth birthday was to be celebrated this evening. With stores closed, there would be no present. Another failure added to the weight he was carrying.

As he pulled the Fury into the Elevator parking lot beside Star's Kenworth, Tom was almost in despair over the demands on him and his inadequate responses.

"What you goin' to do?" he asked Star as he halted the car.

"Goin' to get this gal into that truck so she can sleep this off." Star gestured to the sleeper cab on the Kenworth and wound down the Fury window to listen to the reassuring rumble of the big diesel. It had been set idling by one of the Elevator employees before they left for the day. "She'll be nice and warm and them blankets will sure feel good. Guess I'll drive along to Minot or some such place before I hit the hay."

"You goin' to take Kate with you?"

"Yep, she don't have to be at work 'til Tuesday morning and I should be back in town by then." Star grinned, his customary self emerging from the veneer of tenderness that had covered it on the drive from River House.

"Here, I'll give you a hand with Kate." Tom stepped out into the cold wind and walked around to Star's side of the car. Together they opened the door of the Kenworth and lifted the sick girl into the sleeper behind Star's driving seat. As Star climbed in, he grinned at Tom.

"Wasn't that a hell of a party? Wonder what they'll have on the sign for next Friday?"

"Probably 'Hello Dummies,' or something like that. We sure didn't act too sharp this afternoon."

"Guess that's right," Star considered the party. "Anyway, we'll have more fun when I get back and everybody'll be happy, too."

The gleaming exhaust stacks of the diesel gurgled as Star eased the full truck out of the Elevator lot. When he turned onto Main Street, a gentle blast on his air horns told Tom that Star understood and that, in his own way, he felt the afternoon could have turned out better.

Tom shuffled his way through bees' wings of corn that had drifted into miniature dunes between the parking lot and the Elevator office. He climbed the steps to the office door, taking care not to stumble, and fumbled his key into the lock. Inside, the smell of parched corn was stronger and the dusty surfaces of the desk were broken only by whispers of the last transactions of the day. On his desk was a note from Pete.

"Sorry I didn't catch you this afternoon. Decided to go ahead and add acid to the Elm Street pile. Should be done in a couple of days. Both dryers down—so I sent the boys home. Chicago dryer man will be here on Monday—so I didn't send Andy for parts. See you in the morning. Pete."

They were now committed to treatment of the corn for feeders—no way could it be added to dry storage to replace what would be shipped out in the next weeks—30,000 more bushels to find. No drying this weekend either—another 10,000 bushels short in dry corn. That was what he got for his afternoon at Fun City.

On the other corner of his blotter was a note from Helen. "3 pm. Janet called. Be sure to find a present for Chrissy." Tom sank in his chair and held his head in both hands. After a moment, he reached out for the phone. "Better call her," he mumbled. When the receiver was in his hand, his resolve collapsed and he left it lying on the desk.

He sat for some minutes, then rummaged in the back of a lower drawer of the desk. The bottle of Jim Beam was still more than half full. He splashed whiskey into a paper cup and added water from the office cooler. Drink in hand, he sat at his desk again.

"Sorry I didn't catch you." Pete's way of letting him know that he should have been on the job. Tom Cooper should have made those decisions. He was the only one who knew the overall picture of grain flow through the Elevator, and the monstrous commitments made this very morning. "… find a present for Chrissy." Janet trying to hold him within their family circle.

He refilled his cup, this time with raw liquor, and drank it off quickly. A little of the liquid ran from the corner of his mouth and dripped on the bills of lading Helen had placed on his blotter. One train loaded and ready to go. Another coming. Where in the hell was he going to get corn to meet all those commitments?

He replaced the Beam bottle and closed the desk drawer with unnecessary violence. Now, as he rose from his chair, alcohol was making itself felt. He wavered and placed both hands on his desk to avoid falling. His normally limitless capacity had been severely taxed and Tom Cooper was nearly falling-down-drunk.

He felt his way along a wall to the outside door. Not until he was groping for the iron stair railing leading down into the parking lot did he realize that he had left the lights on and the door unlocked.

Deliberately, he lurched back to the door. His hand groped around the door jamb for the light switch—then he pushed the lock button on the door and felt it engage after three tries. Finally, he stumbled hand-over-hand down the steps.

Once on solid ground, he fell heavily, drifts of bees' wings puffing up. For almost a minute he lay on the ground until cold penetrated his consciousness, or more accurately, his unconsciousness. Then, on all fours, he crawled to the Fury and into its still-warm interior, closing out winter for the moment.

Drunkenness was eventually penetrated by the 'whirr-click' of the dashboard clock as it rewound itself every seven minutes. This disturbance gradually became perceptible. God! Was it cold! The plastic seat covers were stiff with it against his cheek and his hands were numb where they lay against the floor of the car. Slowly he raised himself, hands clawing at the icy wheel. He fumbled for his key and cranked the engine—no luck. Carefully now, he pumped the accelerator once, then held the pedal to the floor and tried the starter again. Luck. The engine caught–coughed as it protested against the cold air being drawn in, then ran roughly, but steadily.

Tom pushed his frozen hands inside his coat and leaned his head and shoulders against the side window, running the engine at fast idle in a haze of waiting for warmth. Finally, a breath of heat came from defroster vents, and a small, dark delta appeared in the clear white of the frosted windshield. Frost receded slowly, reluctantly guarding the fine tracery of its design as if each line constituted a dike over which heat must spill. He held his fingers to the vents, drawing warm air into his tingling hands, all the while shivering, his body fighting burning liquor within and expending the little energy it contained in useless shaking for warmth.

Now the engine was running smoothly and his hands had warmed enough that he could switch the heater to the floor position and begin to work on his feet. The Fury might be junk, but Jesus, did it have a heater—a lifesaver. The temperature must be well below zero, and it was late as hell. Better try to get home. God! The temperature had dropped twenty degrees since noon. The tires crunched, wrenched from their beds of ice and forced to roll over the frozen parking lot.

He drove slowly across the lot and came to a full stop at the entrance to Main Street. Trying to collect himself, he wiped his hand across the chill sweat of sickness on his forehead. Hadn't had this much to drink in years. God! Was he sick! Better get home. Better drive slow—the thoughts tumbled one on another—each fighting liquor for attention.

The pull of home and comfort won out. He turned onto Main Street and headed toward the hill leading west out of town. Few cars were out and he was able to strike some semblance of sobriety by aiming the Fury's hood ornament between the rows of buildings and lamp posts.

As he left the bright illumination of town, he couldn't recognize objects as they sprang into being in the wash of headlights. The STEEP GRADE sign came on him and he braked roughly, thinking he was on his way downhill, rather than climbing to the prairie above Sheffield. CURVE signs and their arrows leading upward were negotiated in a series of abrupt right- and left-hand turns, jerking the car dangerously close to hillside cuts or guardrails.

Once on the prairie, the road ran straight for many miles. Now it was covered with patches of drift, and little wisps of snow were blown around his car. These movements increased Tom's sickness. He began to feel as if he were a passenger on a ship, a feeling heightened by the bobbing and dodging of the Fury on its worn shock absorbers.

He could go no farther. He stopped the car in the center of the road and lurched out to expel the liquor and his supper in violent heaves. Retching drove him to his knees, and he ground his hands into the icy pavement with each spasm. He shook with cold as he wiped his mouth on his handkerchief. It fell from his hand to be whirled away by the wind.

Crawling back to the car, he lowered himself into the seat and pulled the door shut, huddling over the steering wheel while the car gradually warmed again. Now when he drove, he was less drunk—only weak and sick. As perception gradually cleared, he was able to guide the car more smoothly with less surprise from the revelations of headlights.

The five miles to his side road were negotiated successfully and he turned smoothly onto the township road and adapted to its narrowness. This road set off at right angles to Highway 13 as if taking an abrupt tack into the wind and made a straight path for Tom to the driveway of his home. At his drive, the gravel road came to a 'T'; anyone not visiting the Coopers had to choose one of the right-angled options. His driveway was to the right of the 'T'—and memory guided his turns—right, then left.

Tom slowed and drove into the familiar space of his farmyard. The Fury's lights pointed the way to an open shed where the car was kept, and now he could see their house. A light burned over the kitchen sink–a light Janet always left on when she had gone to bed and was no longer waiting for him.

A white plume of vapor rose from the chimney, bright against dark pine trees behind the house. The headlights shifted, picking up an old well house and a long-disused concrete stock tank at its side, then the shoveled mounds of snow at either side of the shed door.

Tom took deliberate aim and slipped the Fury between these guideposts into the shed. Home at last! He sat minutes with his head resting on arms folded on the steering wheel. The Fury idled quietly and the interior of the car became pleasantly warm. Drowsiness became sleep.

He awoke with a start. It was cold and the engine was no longer running. Must be out of gas. Shit! There were only a couple of gallons left in a can from last summer's mowing. Enough to get to town!

Outdoors, he was even colder as a sharp breeze propelled him toward the house. Once inside, he leaned back against the kitchen door and gazed around the room. On the table was their glass-covered cake holder. Inside, a birthday cake with ten candles—all that remained of the party that was to have been.

Tom stumbled to the kitchen sink and ran cold water in his hands, scooping the flow against his face. He had to sober up. Jan would be hurt—and angry—if he came to bed drunk. Sitting at the kitchen table, he stared at the cake. Next to it was a note from Chrissy. "Dad. Sorry you couldn't make the party. Let's have it tomorrow. I can wait." A smiling face served only to increase his misery.

A half-hour later, Tom was able to make his way upstairs to their bedroom. In the faint light from the hallway, he saw that Chrissy had joined Janet in her bed. They were asleep, with Janet holding the child.

The image was too much for Tom. He turned and stepped carefully back down to the kitchen where he once again sat at the table. He was excluded from his family—alone with the cake and Chrissy's note. He stared at the note. And, after a long time, slept.

CHAPTER THREE

With Gusts to 70 MPH

Hints of movement filtered through the haze of sleep and drunkenness. Finally, the smell of coffee and sounds of Janet, busy at the kitchen counter, wakened Tom. He raised his head from the kitchen table and straightened against the pain of cramped muscles.

"…umm…Hi honey," he mumbled. "Got home late and didn't want to wake you two, I…"

Janet swiveled to face him. "Tom! You were drunk! And you missed Chrissy's party!"

He was startled by her anger. Other drunken nights had been ignored or glossed over in the hope that they would not occur again.

"…well…Star and me…"

"I don't want to hear about your party! Just tell me how you think we feel when you are off with your friends on another bender!" She picked Chrissy's cake from the table and set it roughly on the counter. "Look at this! Chrissy sat at the table for hours waiting for you. I can't tell you how many times she went to the window to look for your lights!"

"…we got to visiting…and…"

"Don't give me that line! I know how it goes with you and Star! How many afternoons have the two of you taken off?"

There could be no response to these accusations. Her anger sank him into a silent depression.

Finally Janet said, "Now, that's enough! There are fresh clothes in the basement. Get cleaned up and we'll see what needs to be done."

Like a meek adolescent, he stood up and went down the basement stair. Shower and shave made him into a human being on the surface, but failed to restore his confidence. How could he make things right with Jan? What would reconnect him with Chrissy? These questions held him in suspension—standing and staring at a basement wall.

"Tom!" Janet called. "Please come up. We need to talk before Chrissy gets up."

There was less anger in her comments and questions. However, he was not comforted, nor did he supply comfort. For the first time in their marriage, Tom could see that drink was creating a wall between them—a wall that only he could tear down.

The magnitude of the discord in their relationship was too much for him. "Honey. Please listen. I won't let this happen again! I…"

"Tom," she interrupted, "you have to change your behavior. You can't live two lives—choose between your family and your buddies."

The choice overwhelmed him. He stood with arms hanging, looking at her. Janet waited, watching his face. Neither spoke nor moved.

Then she came toward him and they hugged, like two strangers greeting one another in an unaccustomed social embrace.

"Well," he said, "I better get to work. I'll come home as soon as I can…"

She cut in. "I need the car today. The old Ford won't start. It's Saturday and I promised to take Chrissy and a couple of her friends into town. You had better call Bob or Pete and have one of them pick you up."

Tom went to the phone obediently and dialed the Elevator.

Pete was, as usual, on the job. "Hello. Farmers Elevator. Pete speakin'."

"Pete. This is Tom. Can you run out and pick me up? And bring a can of gas—I ran out last night."

"Sure. No problem. I'll be out in a jiff."

They waited for Pete in silence. Tom looked out the kitchen window into the growing prairie dawn, hoping to see Pete's headlights. Janet busied herself with unnecessary tasks, wanting to be free of this problem for now.

When Pete arrived, Tom donned his coat and hat and waved a perfunctory goodbye. "Well, Pete's here. I'll start the Fury and warm it up. Don't let it run too long. There's just enough gas for you to get to town."

Janet followed him to the door. "When will we see you? Do you want me to pick you up?"

The offer was there, he only had to accept. "Sure. That would be fine. Come by the Elevator anytime after five o'clock. Maybe we could catch a sandwich downtown." He was out the door without noticing Janet's grimace.

Gasoline, jumper cables and cursing prodded the Fury to life. When it finally ran steadily, Tom and Pete left it for Janet and took off to Sheffield.

"Pretty cold," Pete observed. "Nothin' will start at the Elevator. That'll put us further behind on loadin' them cars."

Tom accepted these comments in silence, realizing that they contained unspoken criticism of his absence yesterday.

Pete drove on for a time, then said, "What's on the program for today, Boss?" With that question, Pete put Tom back in charge—with implied forgiveness.

"Let's get things moving first," Tom said. "Then we can decide what's next. By the way, thanks for dealing with the Elm Street pile. Putting the acid to that corn probably avoided a total loss."

"Thought so," Pete grunted. "We got enough problems without a pile of rotten corn."

The morning went surprisingly well. By noon, all equipment was running. Drying and car loading were proceeding at a good pace. Tom's hangover was nearly gone. He reflected on his 'bender'—*gotta stop drinkin'—wreckin' my family—killin' myself.*

This reverie was interrupted by the violent opening of the office door. Marvin Olson stormed in and planted his massive hands on the counter. "What the hell's the idea of makin' my missus drunk? She's the laffin' stock of her bridge club and it's all your fault!"

"Marv…," Tom began.

"Don't you give me any crap. I'm about ready to mop the floor with you and Star! I want you out at my place pretty damn quick with an apology for Helga!"

"Sure…glad to do it…I'll come by…"

"And, you can total up my grain and write me a check right now!"

"But, Marv, are you sure? Maybe you should hold on for a better price, and…"

"Nope. I'm through with this place! Now, hop to it!"

Tom moved briskly to the cubby where Stub had been listening to this exchange with open mouth. "Stub. Total up Marv's grain account with today's prices and write him a check."

"But, Tom. We don't have…"

"Stub. The check! Now!"

Moments later, Tom had copies of Olson's Assembly Sheets and Warehouse Record along with a check. "Here, Marv. Please think this over. I'm sorry for what I did. Don't take it out on the Elevator."

There was no answer as Olson marched out of the office.

"Sonofabitch!" Tom growled. Now a little bit of fun had wrecked a relationship and lost the Elevator a good customer!

"That cleans us out of cash," Stub said. "Until we get the Continental check, we're broke."

"Don't I know it!" Tom said. "You try to put off any other sales 'til the money comes in. I'll see if I can speed up the loadin'."

He worked through the afternoon under a weight of shame, often stopping and staring at what could have been a better day. When Janet pulled the Fury into the Elevator parking lot, he almost ran to her for support.

"Jan! Honey! Where's Chrissy?"

"Get in, Tom! We have a lot to talk about!" She waited until he was seated, then continued. "I've never been so embarrassed! The story of what you and Star did to Helga Olson is all over town! How could you be so stupid?"

"But…we were just havin' a little fun…and…," he said lamely.

"Fun is right!" she blurted. "Everybody is laughing at you and Star—a couple of grown men acting like teenagers!"

He shrank in his seat. "I know, I know. Marv Olson was in and read me the riot act. He pulled out of the Elevator and wants me to apologize to Helga…"

Janet was silent, then she said, "Think about what you've done. Look at the consequences. Disappointing Chrissy. Spoiling Helga's party. And, losing a good customer. Doesn't this tell you something?"

Tom put his hands over his face. "God! How can I put this right?" These familiar lamentations received an immediate answer.

"I'll tell you what you can do." Janet said. "You can start by apologizing to Helga. Then you can make up with Chrissy. And, you can cut out drinking!" She turned the Fury onto Main Street and headed the car out of town toward the Olson farm.

When they pulled into Olson's yard, Tom broke the silence. "I gotta do this myself. You wait in the car." He moved reluctantly out of the car and crossed to the Olson house.

Helga answered the door. "Tom! I'm glad you came. Come on in."

This unexpected invitation was too much for his overloaded emotions. "Helga, I…" He came into her kitchen, cap in hand.

"Tom. Before you start, I want you to know that we are both responsible for what happened yesterday. You should have known better and so should I. Now let's try to forget what happened."

He couldn't speak. Choked with guilt, he could only nod and mumble. Finally he said, "Helga, I'm so sorry. It was my fault and I should have known better."

They stood looking at one another. Then, Marv Olson came into the room. Tom looked at him, afraid of the wrath of the afternoon.

"Tom. I didn't think you had the guts to come out here. I gotta hand it to you." He reached out and gripped Tom's hand. "I popped off at the Elevator and I'm sorry for that. Let's see if we can't start back where we were. I'd like to return my check and keep tradin' with you. That OK?"

"Sure…great…," Tom stammered. How could these people share in his guilt and make him feel welcome at the same time?

They talked about nothing for a few minutes. Then Tom said, "I'd better be goin'. Hope to see you at the Elevator soon."

"I'll be there, you can bet on it!" said Marv.

"And thanks for coming out. It means a lot to me," added Helga.

When Tom reported this interaction to Janet, she was both amazed and relieved. "I can't believe it!" she said. "They reached out to you. See how doing the right thing helps everyone."

As they turned back toward Sheffield, Janet reached over and took his hand. "This is a good first step. Now, let's pick up Chrissy and make things right with her."

He was still overcome with emotion and he gulped his agreement. "Yeah…I gotta…" He hung his head and clasped his hands between his legs.

Janet stopped the car and held him until he was able to speak.

He sat up and wiped his eyes with the backs of his hands. "I guess I'm ready to go now. I hope Chrissy can forgive me. Think she will?"

"Don't worry, she loves you! All you need to do is show her that you love her."

In the two weeks that followed, Tom and Chrissy reverted to a happy relationship. Janet was supportive, but reserved—watching Tom for signs of his resolution. Life at the Elevator was a mixture of familiar routines. Daily trading and grain processing, giving Tom freedom from the press of agribusiness.

At the end of the second week, the weather turned unseasonably warm for the Dakotas. So much so that Elevator conversation invariably started with some reference to climate change, comparison with some vaguely remembered year past, or joke about a 'banana belt'. Tom tolerated these comments and used the days to speed the fifteen hopper cars on their way. Luckily, the new loading equipment installed last summer worked to perfection and he was able to blend a considerable amount of off-grade corn into the shipment, thereby improving the quality of stock remaining in storage.

His days were full. This was the first real opportunity to test the new machinery, and he took great pleasure in making fine adjustments to feed augers from various bins to make up a uniform grade of grain flowing down the curved, flexible spouts into the open hatches of the hopper cars. Each hour he climbed the steel ladder of the car being loaded to run a pointed grain probe into the mounting pile of kernels. Clutching samples, he hurried back into his office and tested the grain for moisture and weight. He lavished love on the grain, on its golden color, like the hair of a lover, and on its earthy, dusty smell–the sum of all the energy and sensuality of growing things. His sifted the corn with a gentle, nervous caress, and chewed a few kernels to gratify his romance with grain.

Looking at the little slips of paper where he noted test results, his pleasure at meeting goals of 15.5% moisture and 54 pounds per bushel test weight was like the joy he felt when Chrissy attained a prize: a sense of mutual achievement, a sharing of victory over criteria set by others.

Occasionally, it was necessary to make adjustments in the flow of grain so that these standards could be met to the letter—no more, no less. Then, Tom might introduce a fine water spray into the loading spout to add a trace of moisture. This was especially necessary this year, for grain that had come into storage this fall had been set aside by farmers for long-term federal storage loans and had been reduced to 13.5% moisture, a figure far too low for maximum payoff in the Minneapolis market. When he turned the valve on the water hose, he was conscious of his decision to use farmer-owned grain to make up this train load. How else could he realize the bonanza of a top price in a falling market? In much the same manner, he rationalized the use of the water valve. He wasn't adulterating grain, merely using the arbitrary standards set by grain companies so he could maximize Elevator profit.

Days rolled one into another. As they grew shorter, he increased the time he spent on the loading project, feeling the pressure defined by the sun's shortened course. These were good days, full of work with no time for drinking. He felt only the exhaustion of effort, something he experienced rarely these days. He actually felt better now that he could act like an elevator hand and not a manager.

Tom realized that the telephone didn't ring as often; rarely was he called from his supervision of loading. At first this didn't seem to be a problem. He welcomed release from the clamor of two phone lines constantly in action. Then, as days passed, his concern grew. Farmers weren't coming to market rapidly enough to restore the corn he had 'borrowed'. Evidently good weather gave farmers time to renew field work and left them with little opportunity for leisurely discussions with elevator managers and no time to move grain to market. For Dakota farmers, grain marketing wasn't a science, but something set by undefined, yet very definite moods. Some days, long lines of trucks would show up at the Elevator, top full and bulging with grain when the market was down or in a prolonged depression. As if resigned to being victimized, farmers brought in their offerings. On other days, good prices and a chance to make substantial profits called in only a few stragglers, despite Tom's efforts to spread the word by phone. This was one of the latter times. When he did take time to phone, farmers invariably voiced unconcern or spoke about plans for other kinds of work not related to selling grain.

"Market up? Eh? Good! Let the bastards bid for it. We can sure use a boost out here."

"Yeah, but Nick," Tom would argue, "this is only a temporary run-up and we're bound to get a slide into the New Year. In fact, I got the word that foreign sales will be way down and you know what cattle feeders say—no profit in feeding high-priced corn to them cows."

"Sure, Tom, but I don't believe that bullshit. How many times we been euchred by them reports? I ain't buyin' it now. I'll just wait and see. When she turns around, I'll be in for sure and you better have room for me."

"We'll have room, Nick, but I think you should move now. I can even give you a two-cent premium for corn this week."

"That's great! Just you hang onto them cents and lay 'em on me when I come in first part of the year."

Tom would hang up his phone with the sinking feeling he had whenever he calculated the amount of grain to be replaced. Where the hell would it come from?

"Hello, Mrs. Rasmussen? Jack in? Good! This is Tom Cooper—let me talk to him."

Faint shuffling sounds from the Rasmussen kitchen, explanations—"It's the Elevator man"—and grunts of acknowledgement.

"Hello, Tom. How's it goin'?"

"Not too bad, Jack. Just thought I'd call to see how you were doing now that you're retired for the winter."

"Retired, hell! I'm just sittin' here for a last cup of coffee before I fire up that Steiger again."

"You back in the field?"

"You bet. This here weather is too good to pass up. I got 3,000 acres to make black before spring and this is an opportunity. I can't sit on my ass like you elevator boys."

"Ha!" Tom snorted. "While I'm sittin' here, I figured out that there ain't no time like now for you to move some of that grain you got comin' out your ears."

"Why? What's so good about now?"

"Jack, I think that we're seeing the last of some good prices and I'm looking for a hell of a sinking market toward the end of this month." Just the right note of urgency in his voice, he thought. Confidence guardedly given, bait dangled–now to set the hook.

"I got some open space in the silos now, and can give you a bonus over the usual Minneapolis basis for corn this week or first part of next. How about it?"

"Say, that sounds good! Can you guarantee that this weather will hold for the next two weeks?"

"Huh? Uh no, I guess that's a little out of my department."

"Well, you get it under control. I'll have to hit the ball while the dirt's ready. See you later. Don't you worry; I'll be bringin' you my corn. Wouldn't do business nowhere else."

The hum of a dead line as Jack hung up was a poor promise of no real use to meet his immediate needs. These conversations were repeated many times in the next days, with only small variations on the theme. "Let 'em come beggin' for our grain," and "We're too damn busy now to worry about haulin' corn. Wait 'til next year."

That was all very well, but moving in this amount of grain didn't happen overnight and there was more than a remote possibility that

Department of Agriculture grain warehouse inspectors would show up late this month or, at least, in the early part of January. If they found him short, there wouldn't be a simple warning notice. The Elevator would be put on probation. That would be a hell of a note. Without a Federal Warehouse License, he was no more than a country store. Thank God for the Ernie Larsen sale. Even though it didn't cover the shortage, it was a good step in that direction. Just the other day he had talked with Ernie who confirmed the sale with another promise to come in to sign a contract and begin hauling as soon as he wound up the last of his field work. This delay could be tolerated; that grain was as good as in the bin. Ernie was known never to go back on his word.

The delays that were tough to handle were the indefinite ones of other Co-op members. Sure they would sell, but would it be soon enough to put his house in order? This question haunted Tom as he loaded the train. Whenever he had the opportunity, he mentally calculated his weekly needs for grain and the cash flow necessary to pay for it. He couldn't buy too much too soon, for he needed the money from the sales of two trainloads, money that wouldn't be back in the Citizens Bank for at least two weeks. This was a delicate balancing act. Buy farmers' grain, even sell it, but put off payment until there was sufficient money in Elevator bank accounts. Without physical work, this problem would be too much to bear and he would have needed alcohol to cope.

The frustrations of Tom's talks with farmers were enhanced by the evident correctness of his reading of the market. Each day, small declines were posted in all grains–oats, corn, wheat and barley–with corn leading the pack in a downward tumble of price. Tom had no question in his mind but that he had done the right thing in selling the second trainload of corn. In fact, he stood to make substantial profits for all farmer members when he replaced high-priced corn with lower-priced purchases from those who held grain on the farm.

The daily call from Continental Grain marketing service was getting repetitive.

"Hello, this is Sally at Continental. Are you ready to copy?"

"Sure, Sally, shoot!"

"All grains down slightly today with January bids two to three cents lower and March down four to six cents on corn…"

As she read on, Tom mentally calculated storage costs for each month and noted a diminishing premium being paid for holding grain into spring. Normally, grain markets paid higher prices for commodities in future months. These prices reflected costs of storage and interest, so that farmers could expect to recover their investment in storage bins over time. This year was clearly building up to be an exception to the rule. Even if farmers weren't selling now, he was sitting on a situation that could do nothing but good for the Elevator. The pattern became monotonous. Not until the day before Christmas did any break show up in the price toboggan. That day, markets were to close early so that business would be down for the holiday. He planned to close the Elevator at three in the afternoon, after a short Christmas coffee party for employees.

When Sally called, there was a holiday mood in her voice.

"Hello, this is Sally at Continental. Merry Christmas—good news today!"

"Hi, Sally, same to you from Farmers Elevator. What's the good news besides tomorrow off?"

"Well, markets are slightly stronger today. No reason for it, but there is speculation in the trade that some deals may be in the making with foreign buyers."

"That so?" Tom frowned. Foreign rumors abounded in the market, but they could play havoc with prices as doctors, housewives, and other speculators fed on rumor to swing futures prices in dizzying gyrations. "What's corn doing?"

"Oh, not much," she said. "It's up three on the nearby and up four on the March. Wheat and barley are both up a nickel and oats is steady."

"Hmmm," he reflected, "say, Sally, keep an eye on that corn for me and give me a call first thing after Christmas. I may want to take some protection by going long."

"I'll do that, Tom. Tell all of your people Merry Christmas from us at Continental."

"Sure thing, Sally, and you go straight home from that office party."

She laughed and hung up.

As Tom sat back in his chair, he reflected on her news. Up a couple of cents—no particular cause for worry, but generally the market was very static on pre-holiday closings. It was unusual for a change of this type to occur on such a day. The long price slide had broken. Not by tailing off, but by reversing and turning upward. This could give some support to Sally's reference to foreign sales. If the Russians were to come back into the market, corn could go wild. Tom had seen it happen before. The momentary panic this thought caused him was squashed by his good sense and the frequent confirmations he had received earlier concerning diminishing foreign trade this coming year. Better keep an eye on the markets right after Christmas. If they opened strong, he might have to buy nearby futures to protect the price he had received for the trainload of grain. Then, if prices rose, money he would lose in paying higher prices to farmers would be offset by a rise in price of futures he would buy. Gain on one would compensate for loss on the other.

No particular reason to worry, but damn good reason to stay the hell out of the yard and watch price fluctuations from his desk. He sighed, feeling as if he had received a second sentence after completing one prison term. He had enjoyed and thrived physically on hard work. This was a reminder that he was the manager of the Elevator and not just an employee.

His depression carried through lunch at the VFW with Star.

"What's eatin' you, T?" Star asked. "No spirit of Christmas?"

"Yeah, I'm looking forward to tomorrow and a couple of days off. Guess this last two weeks of car loading is finally getting to me."

"Maybe, but let's have another for the road and I'm splittin' for Minot. Kate's goin' with me for the holiday with my brother up there."

"Huh? You getting serious about her?"

"Nooo—don't hardly think so—but she sure is a comfort to have along. Good talker and better listener."

"That all?" Tom leered over his drink.

"You bastard! Here, drink up and let's get going."

Tom downed his Manhattan, the second of the day, and walked out with Star.

Outdoors, the sun was glassy and a strong, warm wind blew at them from the southeast.

"Jesus, Star, this here's like March, not like Christmas."

Star agreed. "Yeah, but the word is that we'll be gettin' some snow tonight and tomorrow. A low's comin' in from Canada."

"That so? Well, it'll have to get one hell of a lot colder or else another rainstorm will hit us, like the one we had last week."

"We sure don't need another like that. Must have had two inches of rain," Star recalled. "Drivin' through that is okay in the spring, but not in December."

"You leaving for Minot now?" Tom asked.

"Yeah, just goin' by Kate's place for her suitcase. Should be in Minot by midnight."

"Well, good sledding," Tom grinned. He held out his hand. "Merry Christmas, Superstar."

"Hey, Big T, same to you. See you in a couple of days." He bounded into his Kenworth and sped off down the street. A Star going into orbit.

Tom turned into the wind for the six-block walk back to the Elevator. The wind was strong, and he had to lean forward, just as in March, conscious of air pressure forcing him back. Like a salmon going upstream, he thought, as he entered the Elevator parking lot. He looked up. The long pipes leading down from the outdoor grain leg were swaying in the wind.

"Hmmmm…that damn wind would like to rip the place apart. Better check upstairs before I head home." He mouthed these words and forced his way into the office, closing the door gratefully.

"Some wind, huh, Tom?" Helen looked up from her desk.

"Yep. Sure will be tough going for Santa coming down from the Pole against this breeze."

"Oh. Janet called. She said to tell you that school closed early and Chrissy's bus just dropped her off. Something about a possible blizzard."

"That so? Maybe we should start the Christmas party now. No use keeping everybody here. Nothing to load out and nobody will be coming in this afternoon."

"Oh, fine, Tom. They'll love you for that."

She left her chair and went into the coffee room and carried out two pans of rolls from the Sheffield Bakery and placed them on one table, then added a coffee urn and cups on another. Sprigs of holly and some pale evergreens made centerpieces, with a model of Superstar's Kenworth, 'Farmers Elevator' written crudely on it.

Not much of a spread, Tom thought. About what the boys would expect.

This celebration was merely a preliminary to after-work parties at the VFW or River House before family gatherings in the evening. In the inner office, Stub was listening to Bob talk about his last trip to Canada.

"Them mines is somethin' else, Stub. Big shovels and trucks like you never seen. They load out one hell of a lot of potash in a day."

Tom interrupted the travelogue. "How come we don't get it down here, then, if they produce so much?"

"Well, they're behind on orders, you know. Nothin' like big demand to run up price," Bob explained. "C'mon, Stub, let's knock off and have a little Christmas party before we go home." Bob waved his arm and the three moved toward the coffee table.

"Yeah, not much corn movin' these days," Stub said, as he stretched his fat body. He then carried the Daily Position Book to the safe and spun its dial, locking away business, much as Scrooge had done years ago.

Stub and Bob fell into line and helped themselves to rolls and coffee. One by one, Elevator hands came in and discussions drifted from work to holiday plans. A general feeling of good will grew, even though each would have liked a more active party—and some liquor.

Before joining the group, Tom made a few last calls confirming some small corn purchases and some futile attempts to sell the acid-treated corn to cattle feeders. That was shaping up to be one hell of a mistake. Well, couldn't blame Pete for that one; he should have been on the job himself. As he was sitting at his desk listening to the shocks of wind against office walls, he noticed that party laughter and talk grew with each additional gust, as if speakers were modulating their talk to the wind's sound. Tom lifted his phone again and dialed the familiar number of Ernie Larsen.

"Hello, Ernie, Merry Christmas. This is Tom Cooper."

"Hi, Tom. Good to hear from you, and the same to you. You still on the job? Thought you'd be knocking off early for the holiday."

"Yeah, Ernie, just thought I'd tie up a few loose ends. When are you planning to come in and sign that contract on your corn?"

"Golly, Tom, I forgot to do that this week. Tell you what. I got a few things to do here at home, then I'm coming in to do some last minute shopping. I'll drop by, if you're still open."

"Great, Ernie. If I don't catch you today, I'll run the contract out right after Christmas."

"Okay. Say hello to your family and have a good holiday."

"Thanks, Ernie. Take it easy."

He hung up. Some load off his mind. At least that one was still in the bag. Now he could feel a little more in tune with the party. He stood and turned off his desk lamp. As he left his office, he looked out of the window. The sun was now behind some clouds off in the southwest and condensation had formed on the upper half of the window.

"Looks like it's cooling off," he muttered as he switched out the overhead light and, almost as if in response, the wind shook the building, like a dog with a rag.

Everyone at the party talked of wind. "Really picking up out there. Probably just the hot breath from Santa's reindeer." "Naw, that's just the backwash from his sled." "That'd really blow me home." "Yep, right into the VFW…" Nervous laughter came to him. They all sensed the wind and expressed their doubt as to its meaning. As he picked up a coffee cup, Andy came in from the scale house.

"Jesus, Tom, you better come upstairs. It's blowin' like hell and, man, is it gettin' cold! Off to the west there's one big cloud bank. Bet it's goin' to storm."

"Aw, Andy, you got a bottle hid up there," Tom joked. The man's white face was his bond; there was no doubt, Andy was frightened. Tom had better follow up on this one.

"Andy, you get yourself some coffee and rolls and I'll give her the once over." He pulled on his light jacket and leather gloves and opened the door to the scale house. At once, he was aware of a change in temperature. A blast of wind probed the old building, sending a chill through him, even though he was fresh from a warm office. Reluctantly, he stepped onto a manlift platform and pulled the starting rope. As he rose up the Elevator's height, he felt a clammy breath on his back through each lift shaft window. By turning his neck awkwardly, he could glimpse the west side of the valley. Andy was right; it was dark and no doubt about the cold.

When he stopped the lift at the top of the structure, he could feel the forces that had frightened Andy. The elevator was rocking in the wind. Each cable cried out its own note in a raucous symphony of terror. The building talked with itself, as if to gain courage to combat savage attacks from the elements. From the west windows of the head house, Tom could look across prairie uplands. One massive bank of fog squatted at ground level with mighty piles of black clouds pressing it toward the valley. All around the western sky, this curtain of danger was being drawn. One hell of a storm was coming, and damn quick. Tom knew at once the urgency of getting back down and sending his help home to safety.

He stepped onto the lift, his own personal fears of height forgotten in the urgency of the moment. On his way down, he remembered another time he had seen a sky like this. Back in Minnesota in the forties, a November day had turned from sun and breeze to a roaring blizzard in less than two hours–a temperature drop of sixty degrees, driving wind, heavy snow, and death. These prairie storms were serious business.

Tom stepped off the manlift and quickly pulled the main power switches. Then he halted for a minute to listen to the wind. God, how quickly the temperature had fallen! Better give it to the boys straight. They all had time to make storm arrangements before leaving. He walked into the party. Everyone turned to him quietly; they knew he had news for them.

"How's it look?" Bob questioned.

"Bad. We'd better close up right now and hit the road. Everybody who has more than ten miles to drive or anybody who is heading west better find someplace to hole up in town. We won't have more than fifteen or twenty minutes before we're drivin' blind."

"God! Really!"

"I'm cuttin' out right now!"

Each adjusted to the news, and within five minutes, Tom was the only one left with remains of the Christmas party. He left everything as it was, hurriedly turning out lights and emerging into the beginning storm. He took another minute or two to start the Fury and force it out of the parking lot exit against a wind that shook everything, even in the shelter of the valley. As he pressed down Main Street, he turned into Quality Market to stock up on extras that a storm might require, additional gallons of milk, dried and prepared meat, and cereal. At the off-sale counter where he collected three quarts of Jim Beam, he confirmed the clerk's anxious questions.

"Sure. Gonna storm, probably in the next fifteen minutes."

"Well then, you're the last customer. I'm not spending the night in this place." She rang up the sale and was turning out lights as Tom carried packages to his car.

With one gloved hand, he opened the car's front door and slid himself and his packages in through the opening with one motion, pulling the door closed behind him. Wind rocked the car, sending wisps of dust through edges of windows and rattles of gravel against them. He moved the heater control to 'full on' as he pulled away from the store and headed out of town. The heater made little headway against cold and wind. Already little circles of frost were forming on the corners of side windows that faced into the wind. The climb out of Sheffield was made easier by the shelter of the bluff. Tom switched the radio on as he negotiated the first switchback.

"Warning to all residents of central and eastern Dakotas and southern Manitoba. There will be blizzard conditions for the next twenty-four hours, with gale force winds and subzero temperatures. Travel is expressly prohibited and police will turn back cars at the edges of all towns within the half hour. West central North Dakota reports winds gusting to seventy miles per hour and minus-five degree temperatures with heavy snow. Here in Grandview it is now ten above with winds out of the north-northwest gusting to sixty miles per hour. Residents of Sheffield and Grandview should be in their homes. Do not attempt to travel or, at any time, leave your house."

Tom snapped the radio off with the uncertainty of one who has committed himself to a foolhardy course of action. Halfway up the hill, he abruptly plunged into thick fog. Moisture condensed on all windows making visibility even worse. Inside the fog it was quiet. There was no noise of wind and the Fury purred smoothly upward. Tom could hear the irregular whirr of the heater fan as it carried out a losing campaign against the frost. The quiet of fog was more threatening when contrasted to the violence of wind.

Tom guided the car almost by feel around steep turns. Only occasionally could he glimpse guard rails or roadsides. The many times this trip had been taken in drunkenness were now a help. Limitations of his senses imposed by fog could be mastered by experience.

When the Fury crested the bluff, fog ceased and the blizzard roared in full force. The suddenness of this onslaught drove the Fury nearly into the south road ditch. The pressure of wind was so great that he had to steer into it to prevent overturn. With wind came snow, not gradually, but all at once. A blinding curtain of white was cast over the car, shutting out all sense of landscape. Immediately, north windows were plastered with snow, frozen to moisture left by fog. Snow also forced its way past chinks in weather-stripping around doors and windows so that the inside of the car was dusted with fine snow that hung in the air.

Now lights and past experience were of little use in determining Tom's location or direction. Only by putting one set of wheels off the road could he sense ruts of the past week's rain and know that he was pointed in the proper direction. This delicate balancing act continued, except for spots where groves of trees had already deposited drifts that masked the features of ground. At these obstacles, he set a tack, like a sailboater leaning against the wind, to keep on course. The powerful blast that hit the Fury when he passed these landmarks was a signal to resume his navigation by feel. Tom's mind was intensely alert to changes in the wind's velocity suggested by the landscape: the grove of cottonwoods by Ben Telford's driveway…the old schoolhouse on County Road 20…that abandoned barn before Barney's driveway.

On Tom went, hands sweaty on the wheel, and anxiety honing his perception. Nevertheless he nearly missed the top of Hendrickson's Coulee…three miles to go.

The heater made little headway with frost. Only a small half-circle was clear in a lower corner of the driver's side windshield. Not of much use, as headlights only intensified the storm's cloying whiteness. Tom tried not to remember tales of old-timers, of those who were dumb enough to venture out in a Canadian Norther. Most of these stories concerned people who were trying to make it to their homes; all died short of their goal. People in stalled cars sooner or later were faced with a choice. If they elected to continue on foot they usually died just yards away from their vehicles. If they stayed in their cars, they risked freezing to death or an endless sleep of monoxide poisoning as exhausts plugged with snow.

Tom suppressed these thoughts, concentrating on his only hope for survival–recall of bumps and ruts bounding his path toward home. His main worry was identifying the turning onto the township road to his farm. This was unmarked and would have to be hit dead-on, or he would wind up in a ditch and become one of the characters in a blizzard story. He continually checked the car's odometer.

Two miles to go–coming up to that row of grain bins on Olson's farm. The windbreak of the bins–the short relief from constant steering into the wind–then, the renewed fury of the blizzard.

Time passed slowly. Even though he has expended a great deal of effort, he had only been out in the storm for about fifteen minutes.

Still making a mile in five minutes-should be home in fifteen more at this rate.

Now, the first real trouble began. Snow was growing deeper the farther west he went, rapidly covering ruts he had been using for guidance. He could feel only heavy thumps as the car plowed through drifts cast by clumps of grass, fence posts, and clods of mud. He looked again and again at the odometer and continued to calculate his progress, allowing for some wheel-slip.

He tried to open his door in an attempt to see the road below. He could see nothing. Wind carried a thick stream of snow underneath the car, and the open door was an invitation for back drafts of snow and exchange of heat for cold. Tom closed the door and let the car force its way along without him for a moment. Now his only hope was knowledge of obstacles remaining between him and his side road.

The last mile was a nightmare of narrow escapes from wheels caught in ditch edges, first on one side, then the other. He accelerated in erratic bursts of speed to cross foot high drifts, then he frantically braked in fear of sliding off the road. Finally, the odometer showed figures indicating that he should be at his crossroad. He let the Fury drift with wind to the south side of the highway, searching for the stop sign that marked his road.

Providentially, two ruts emerged in his path. Someone had crossed Highway 13 within the last few minutes, leaving a track in frozen snow. Tom stopped the Fury and backed past the bumps of this track. Slowly, he turned, feeling each front wheel into these faint ruts, keeping wind at his back. The track was fairly well-defined, a guide toward home. *God! I hope that whoever made these tracks isn't in front of me… or off somewhere in the ditch!*

Headlights bored into falling snow leading him into a gleaming darkness with traceries of white. The car's interior warmed perceptibly now that wind could not work directly on chinks in its armor. Less effort was needed to guide the Fury, and its engine purred as it followed the path left by the previous auto. In his relief at finding the ruts, Tom had forgotten to check his mileage, and now could not recall exactly what the reading had been when he turned off Hwy 13. *Was it 302 or 303?* He tried to remember, thinking always of the dead end "T" in the road coming up and the way his driveway laid a bit to the right of the "T". No use. He couldn't recall the figures. Better just to go slowly and hope that he could find some sign of the road's end.

As he went along, driving grew more difficult. The track he was following filled in rapidly and the Fury could barely forge through drifts.

Wind was blowing snow into the engine compartment; now and then, the engine stuttered until the motor's heat dried the ignition wiring.

His concern for the engine diverted his attention and he ran directly off the "T" into the ditch, burying the car to the top of its hood in a firm snowdrift. He restarted the engine and tried to rock free of this prison. He only spun the rear wheels and made slippery chocks that held the Fury more firmly in place. He shifted out of gear and let the engine idle while he considered his problem. He was only about three hundred yards from his house, straight down the driveway on his right. He had less than a quarter of a tank of gas left, not enough to ration his way through the storm, no matter how careful he was. Either he had to take the chance of finding his house in this impossible night, or dying slowly in the tomb of car.

He leaned over to look in the rear seat for anything that might help him on his trip. There was a dirty blanket and several gunny sacks. He took two sacks and, putting a foot in each, wrapped them around his ankles. Another sack he used to hold the groceries, meat on the bottom, milk and whiskey on top. He took one pull on a fresh bottle to arm himself for the ordeal ahead, and then another. The dying of the Fury's engine came to him, a warning that death had no respect or pity for drunks. He had to act now.

With the engine stopped, the car quickly became very cold, rocking in its bed of snow with each gust of wind. Tom tried to restart the motor, but it was evident that there was no longer enough gas to feed the engine—or else the gas line had frozen. Time to leave. He pulled the blanket over his head to make a hood against the storm. With several twine strings from the back seat floor he tied the blanket securely around his shoulders and suspended the sack of groceries in the middle of his back, that way keeping his hands free and providing additional protection from the following wind.

He considered his route. He would have to walk off a little to the right of the Fury to reach his driveway. The entrance to his farm was marked by Chrissy's small school bus shelter—now invisible. Along the left side of his drive was an old fence that should still be above snow level. He could find his way by feeling along the fence. Since his back would be toward the wind, he should have no trouble breathing and would only have to be careful to maintain contact with the fence in order to bring himself into his farmyard. He pulled his jacket closed at his neck and tightened the thongs on the back of his leather gloves; they weren't very warm, but would have to do. The trip shouldn't take more than ten minutes.

The beginning of his journey involved getting out of the car on the passenger side since snow blocked the driver's door. He crawled across the seat and opened the passenger door. At once the wind tore it from his hand, and the blast almost pulled him out of the car. Icy force took his breath away and sent freezing fires into his lungs. He struggled out of the car into snow that was now halfway to his waist. With difficulty, he forced the car door shut and half-turned his head and shoulders from the wind to set a direction for a point where he supposed his driveway to be. He carefully counted his lurching steps, conscious now, as he had been on the highway, of the need to be absolutely certain of distance.

When he had gone thirty paces, he turned his back to the wind and, like a bit of paper or dry leaf, allowed it to carry him forward as he searched for the fence. Almost at once, he was wallowing in snow up to his waist. He had plunged into the ditch along the "T" road and could be on either side of the drive to his farm.

Slowly, he beat a path through the snow and up the far side of the ditch, feeling in front of him like a blind man for some landmark, and for the fence. It took great effort to go slowly now. The wind pushed him along, giving wings to his feet in a ghastly parody of play.

"Come, run with me—run 'til you drop—then I will bring snow to cover you while you sleep."

He mustn't give in to the urge to run with the storm. *God!*

The wind was like a knife, cutting through the blanket into his shoulders. Already his hands were numb and he could hardly hold the blanket from the wind's whipping force. He took careful steps, lifting first one foot out of the drift—then the other. Then his foot caught in a tangle of fence wire that marked the corner of his driveway. The relief he felt at this luck gave him encouragement and he quickly moved, hand over hand, to the fence corner and to the line of wire that led down the driveway.

Overhead, electric and telephone wires screamed in the wind. The deep bass howl of larger wires was a counterpoint to the whine of smaller ones, a gigantic organ on which blizzard played a wild jumble of notes, terrible in their intensity and in the absence of pattern. The storm was disorder, a compelling force that sought to penetrate, level, and destroy any perpendicular object.

Tom shivered violently, knowing that he would not be able to continue much longer. His breath came in short, painful gasps. His hands were almost too numb to feel the fence-path he was following. Only the push of wind kept him going now—plant one foot in deep snow, reach a hand forward for another grasp on wire, then lift the other foot, set it in snow and reach forward again. Step…reach…grasp…lift…repeated over and over, following the storm's perverse melody.

Then, one reach–and no wire to be found! He lost his balance and fell. Icy crystals grated his exposed wrists and face. Exhaustion forced him to rest. He did not attempt to get up. The instant he hit the snow, wind began to pile it over him. His body was covered and the blanket around his head formed a small drift downwind of where he lay. Gradually, but steadily, the drift moved to fill the gap between the top of his head and snow, as if to enfold him in storm.

When the drift grew to a mound, it diminished the wind's noise and he became aware of a growing quiet, along with a misleading sense of warmth. Only with the cutting of his air supply, did he realize that he was being buried alive. Already, snow around his legs was wind-packed and hard. He had to roll over in order to free himself. Rotating his body to bring his back to the wind, he raised himself to his feet. Now he dared not hunt for the fence. If he moved too far to one side or another, he would miss his farmyard altogether.

He tried to remember the sensation of wind on his back when he was following the fence. Carefully, he stood still and turned one way, then the other, until the pressure of wind seemed right. Slowly, he allowed himself to be moved along, praying silently for a tree or building or another object that would be a signal of the farmyard. Nothing was met. He knew, however, that the direction was generally correct; he could still hear screams of storm in overhead wires, but he could not tell exactly where he was in relation to them. Their numbing cries dulled his senses and lulled him to submit to his environment.

He was a fool. He should have stayed in town, or at least tried to survive in his car. His ten minutes were gone, and his last reserves of strength with them. Soon he would fall again and not be able to get up. He would become another of those whose judgment of their own power was proved frightfully wrong by the storm's immense energy. His stumbling steps were paradoxically quicker now, as wind met less resistance in his muscles and hurried his walk along. He was beginning that endless journey across the prairie. In its press, wind was bringing him a sort of peace. No longer need he fight to make his own way. Wind and storm would care for him. He would find a place where he could rest and snow would provide him cover against cold.

As Tom went on, he encountered less resistance. He felt bare ground under his feet. This unreasonable sensation came at the same instant that he caught a glimmer of light at the corner of his eye. With effort, he stopped and tried to recapture this perception. Bare ground meant that wind was accelerating in this spot. Some obstacle nearby caused the wind to speed up and scrape the ground free of snow. The glimmer of light had been just above eye level on his right. He stared out of frost-rimmed eyes, using his right hand to shield his face from the driving snow.

Again, the glimmer came, now directly in front of him. For a moment he was looking into a room. Then the storm blotted the scene from him. He lurched forward toward the image and came up short against the wall of his house. His searching fingers found the sill of a small kitchen window, just at eye level. He had almost walked with the blizzard right past his house.

He caressed the wall, as he felt his way back into the teeth of storm to reach the kitchen door. He stumbled onto the porch, his icy hands fumbled at the door, and he was inside, out of the wind. Finally. In front of him, the kitchen door was flung open and Janet stood there, lamp in hand–the glimmer of light he had seen.

"Merry Christmas! Here's Santa," he mumbled as he propped himself against the doorway.

"Tom! Tom! Oh, God!" She drew him in and the door closed against the blizzard.

CHAPTER FOUR
Limit Up

Janet held Tom, too filled with emotion to speak. Then she helped him to his chair at the kitchen table and began to work at the frozen zipper of his coat. All he could feel was relief at escaping the storm. He worked at his gloves but when his numb hands proved ineffective, he gnawed at the straps that held the gloves to his wrists. The straps were frozen into rigid bands that cut off circulation. Gradually the heat of his breath loosened them and Janet was able to pull the leather from his fingers.

"Tom, your hands! They're all white!"

He looked down at them; in the light of the lamp his hands appeared lifeless with only a trace of redness where he had chafed his wrists in removing his gloves.

Janet moved to the sink and ran warm water into a bowl. "Oh, I hope it's hot enough. Power has been off for about an hour." She brought the bowl to him and he gingerly put his hands into lukewarm water. At first there was no feeling, then fingertips began to tingle, as circulation slowly returned and finally excruciating pain shot through his hands. When he withdrew his hands, he could see that there were one or two places where traces of frostbite appeared. He rubbed each spot and began to work at the strings holding the gunny sacks to his feet. These were still snow-covered and the touch of cold made him shiver violently.

"Here," she said, "let me do that." Janet crouched at his feet.

Though few words had been spoken, they both knew the narrowness of his escape, and their closeness at that moment was a mixture of relief and thanksgiving. While they were working at his clothing, Chrissy came into the room, dressed in her flannel nightgown.

"Dad! I was sleeping and I was dreaming that I heard you talking." Her eyes enfolded him.

"Hi, honey. I'm sure glad you weren't dreaming. I'm really here and plenty happy to be home."

"Oh, this is the best Christmas present ever!" She came running into his arms, hugging him, her body still warm from sleep.

"We all feel that way," Janet added.

He gazed at the two of them, glowing in the soft light of an old kerosene lamp. "Where did you find that lamp?" he asked.

"It was up in the attic, and we had some kerosene left over from the camp stove this summer. I was just lighting it when you came home."

He did not answer. The knowledge that he would have bypassed the house if she hadn't chosen that precise moment to turn up the lampwick sent a new wave of cold through him. He wrapped his arms around himself.

"Let me get you some coffee," Janet said. "I think it's still warm." She went to the stove and poured two cups full from an old white coffee pot. He held his cup tightly in both hands, trying to draw its warmth through the pottery. The blizzard was a present thing; shutting it outside had only muted its howling. The house shook as a particularly violent gust wrenched at it. Faint wisps of snow, blown in around the edges of windows where loose weatherstripping allowed wind to penetrate, touched Tom's face. Lamplight was a feeble indication of how close they were to the storm's power. Without electricity, they had no furnace and no water could be pumped from the well. When the pressure tank emptied, there would be no more water. And, when the reserves of warmth in the house were used up, they would be no better off than he had been in his car. Both Chrissy and Janet were already wearing heavy sweaters, and the kitchen had grown colder, even in the short time he had been home.

"We've been busy all day getting ready for the blizzard," Janet spoke, as if in response to his worry.

"Yes, Dad," Chrissy added, "we've been hauling firewood into the basement for the little stove. We've got stacks and stacks of it."

Janet smiled. "Chrissy has been a real help. She hauled load after load of wood from the barn with the wheelbarrow, and I carried it downstairs. Come, see what we've done." She held out her hand with a welcoming smile.

Together, they filed down the basement stairs, Tom carrying his sack of groceries, Janet in the lead with her lamp. Downstairs, the basement was lit with prancing flames from the tiny Franklin stove he had added to their game room last summer. The air was pleasantly warm and the noises of storm were distant overhead. In this burrow, there was security and a wholly different mood. Each person seemed to change in this refuge.

For Chrissy, descent into the basement was a return to anticipation of Christmas. Earlier that day, she had trimmed cellar beams with evergreen boughs from their pine windbreak. She and Janet had moved the Christmas tree Tom had brought home three days ago from the upstairs living room to a basement corner.

The faint odor of wood smoke and fragrance of pine gave Tom a vague recollection of other Christmases spent at his grandparents' home, where lamplights and candles defined the environment. Here, the only candles were two burning on a table beside the old sofa.

Janet placed her lamp on a similar table across the room and turned to Tom. "Well, how do you like our new home?"

He smiled, "How did you get all this done? What made you think of everything?"

"We heard on the radio at school that the storm was coming," Chrissy said. "We started to work as soon as I got off the bus. Jean Jacobs was here this afternoon. She talked to her uncle on the phone from Minot, and he told her a blizzard was coming."

"When did she leave?" Tom asked, thinking of tracks he had found at the Highway 13 crossing.

"Oh, a long time ago…before the fog came. Why?"

"There were some tracks on the main road before I turned off. Just wondering who had made them."

"Nobody was here other than Jean," Janet replied. "How was the storm? How could you see where you were going?"

"Just lucky, I guess. This is the kind of weather you get lost in. I ran the car into a ditch…couldn't see the front of the hood. If I hadn't followed the fence down the driveway, I wouldn't be here now."

They were all quiet, each thinking of what 'not being here' meant. They knew that the storm would claim many lives and that it had come very near to taking Tom as its first forfeit.

He sensed the intensity of their mood and reached into the sack for his purchases. "Look, see what old Santa has in his pack." He lifted items out one by one.

"Here's some milk for good little girls. Isn't that just what you ordered for Christmas, young lady?" he teased Chrissy.

"Dad!" she protested. "That's for all of us!"

"Here's the food you asked for, ma'am." He handed several items to Janet. Three bottles of whiskey went along the cellar wall. "Thought we might be having company," he explained.

They all knew the lie and were quiet again. Then a holiday mood grew. They were drawn to the fire and its play of light and shadow outlined their faces as they looked into the Franklin's open doors.

"We filled the old cistern, too," Janet said. "When I heard that power failures were likely, I took a garden hose and pumped water into it." The cistern was a concrete room in a basement corner, holding about a thousand gallons of water. When the house was new in the 1920s, this reservoir was the sole source of water—now a protection against the threat of storm.

"Great!" Tom hugged her. "We should be able to ride out the weather without any problems."

"Did the radio say how long it would last?" he asked Chrissy.

"They say that it will snow for about two days and blow for another couple of days," she replied.

"Then we had better plan our Christmas…since we're stuck here anyway."

They laughed and found places to sit around the stove. Janet brought the old white coffee pot from the kitchen and set it on top of the Franklin, where it soon added its fragrance to the smell of evergreen. Tom now began to feel warm for the first time since he had come home. He sat back on the sofa, relaxed, safe from storm and secure in knowing there would be no work for several days. No responsibilities and no demands.

"What did Jean have to say?" he asked.

"Oh, she talked and gossiped, as usual," Janet hesitated. "I think she feels that there's some problem between you and Barney."

"Yeah, I wondered about that. Barney's been acting real different lately."

"Why?"

"I don't know," he frowned. "We haven't seen much of them in the past few months. I suppose they might be sticking closer to their other friends."

"I don't think that's it," Janet said. "Seems like it's something to do with the Elevator."

"Hey, this is Christmas," Tom interrupted, "let's don't talk about business now." Nevertheless, he reflected on her words. Yes, that would be about right. Somehow Barney had the feeling that he was doing a poor job as manager and that he couldn't focus on his job. That would be a definite reason for limiting their friendship. With Jacobs, you were a friend only if you could be counted on in business. If you couldn't, or weren't making it on some sort of balance sheet, there would be a cooling of manner, if not an outright break in association. They had been close over the past three years. At least once a week the two couples had gathered for a few drinks or a game of cards, lingering well into the morning and their gatherings were anticipated by everyone. Now it had been at least two months since they had visited.

It was a good thing, he thought, that his other friends weren't so demanding. Superstar would stick with him for sure. He recalled Star's plan to take Kate to Minot in his truck and Jean Jacobs's report of the intensity of the blizzard in that area. He hoped that Star would make it to town or to a farmhouse before roads were blocked.

Paradoxically, knowledge of the storm warmed him. He became intensely aware of the fire and the security of their basement shelter. Wind could not tear at this space. Here was warmth and companionship that was not measured by business or jealousies of ordinary sociability. He smiled at being safe at home with his family.

Christmas for the Coopers was always a private affair. Family ties for Tom and Janet were tenuous at best and were growing weaker because Sheffield was so far from places where relatives lived. Only Janet's mother in Minneapolis still kept in close touch with them, visiting each summer and fall.

Their little family always celebrated the holiday with dinner in the evening and some quiet moments around a Christmas tree. Gifts were an important part of the event, especially for Chrissy, who had spent most of the month decorating the house and their tree.

The blizzard did little to change this evening. In fact it was powerless to disrupt the family's closeness. Instead, the storm made them more aware of their interdependence and sensitive to the security of their commitment to one another. Janet had made Tom's favorite dinner earlier in the day and kept it ready on the Franklin. After they had eaten, Tom and Chrissy sat together on the old sofa while Janet washed dishes in their improvised kitchen at the bar sink. Sitting there, looking into the fire, Tom was drawn into recollections of other fires and other Christmases.

At his boyhood home, all days of the year were ordered by a need to care for animals. From early morning to late evening, dairy cows had to be served and each member of the family took part. At Christmas time, there was a special satisfaction in knowing that chores were to be done before the holiday could be celebrated.

On Christmas Eve, Tom would find a way to be last to leave the barn, waiting to savor the environment that had been created. He would stand just inside the barn door in the dark, smelling the winy odor of corn silage freshly piled for the animals' morning feast. Mixed with this smell was a dusty vapor of hay that diffused through the barn as cows shook loose mouthfuls, their reward for milking. Security of the dark barn was enhanced by quiet noises of cows gnawing at hay and the subdued jingle of stanchion chains as one animal reached for spears of hay hoarded by another. Overlaying this was the strong smell of the animals themselves, an odor that never varied in winter—something that was carried with each member of the family in hair and clothes.

Perhaps his desire for security and isolation had its roots in that farmyard. There one's life could be defined and managed with only the interruptions of weather. Once he had stepped out of that surrounding, he had opened himself to the uncertainty of commerce and to demands of roles that were defined by others. When pressure of these uncontrolled expectations increased, he could find no release except in mental images of the past or in the numbing refuge of alcohol.

Tonight there were no expectations, no demands—and no Elevator. Occasionally, as they sat together looking into the fire, the storm would force a gust of air down the chimney and stir sparks. Then, the triumph of heat would set the flow right again and fire would burn more fiercely. Renewed gusts were a source of comfort to Tom, evidence that this evening belonged to them and that forces outside were, for the time being, unable to penetrate their Christmas.

Chrissy's question, "Can we open our presents now?" interrupted his reverie and gave him an increasingly rare experience of being completely a part of events moving toward a positive outcome.

"Sure, let's get going," he said. "Maybe I'll get the presents I've been asking Santa for the last five years."

"Oh, Dad," Chrissy gave an exasperated shake of her head, "you always get the most presents." She ran to the couch and hugged him. Then, there being more hugs available, she held Janet close before falling to her knees in front of the family Christmas tree.

He reached to accept a small package from Chrissy, who was making a game out of passing out presents. "Finally!" he sighed. "I've been waiting for this tie clasp." He shook the package.

Chrissy laughed. "You're so wrong! You'll never guess what's in it. C'mon, open it."

He carefully removed the little pinecone elf she had made to decorate the package…something to put in his drawer of memories of her…and opened the box. Inside, there was a photograph of Chrissy in a pile of golden straw. The photo had been encased in a block of plastic, a paperweight. A wave of emotion ran through him. How beautiful she was—her flax-colored hair melding with the brilliant yellow of straw. She was like grain, a child of the prairie, vibrant, colorful, alive.

"Honey, thanks. I remember that pile of straw. You sure had a good time jumping in it. I'm going to take this to work and put it on my desk. Every day I'll look at it and think about you."

She came to him and hugged him, her grasp drawing a lump to his throat.

"Where did you get that idea?" he asked Janet.

"Oh, I remembered how you talked about that threshing bee and how much you liked the picture, so I had it made up one day when I was in Grandview."

Threshing bee—that had been the day Odegaard had asked him if he wanted the manager's job at Sheffield. How happy they had been to get out of the apartment at Grand Forks and out of the traveling job with the Peavey Elevator Company. That had been a day! The problems came later.

Each gift of the evening had some personal meaning. Sometimes it was only through knowing the giver, more often it was a gift that meshed with desires the recipient thought had been hidden. The joy at being found out was a pleasure of being cared for and understood.

Tom hadn't spent much time on Christmas this year, or for that matter, for the past several years. As a result, his gifts tended to be on the expensive side, and less meaning was wrapped with them now than in past holidays. It was only with Janet that his emotions had completely melded in one gift this year. During a trip to Minneapolis last fall, he had come upon a rare book store and found there a collection of first editions of Laura Ingalls Wilder's books. When Janet opened the oblong box and found the musty, faded volumes, and her face lit, he knew that he had understood her. Janet's house on the prairie was real and complete when the three were together as now.

Chrissy's final gift from Tom was a small transistor radio in the shape of a ball, to be hung in her room along with other trophies of girlhood.

"Dad, what is it?" she asked, holding the radio in two hands like a softball.

"It's a radio. See. Here's the switch and this knob's for tuning." He held the ball and manipulated its controls to bring in GVC, the Grandview station.

"... weather is likely to remain with us for the next two days. No travel is possible in the Dakotas or western Minnesota. Power is out in the following counties ..."

He switched the radio off. No need to let it remind them of the storm; their mood had been changed by the announcement. Janet rose and went to the Franklin stove and poured coffee for herself and Tom and carefully heated milk for Chrissy's cocoa.

"Say, you're pretty good with that wood stove," Tom joked. "Maybe we should disconnect our electricity for good."

She waved a spoon at him. "You had better not, or you'll be hauling wood and ashes every day."

They laughed at the idea of cooking at the wood stove as a means of survival. Over coffee, they occasionally fell silent, again conscious of wind outdoors.

"I suppose I'd better drain the upstairs pipes in the morning," he said. "I can do that and we can still use the upstairs bathroom, just carry water from the cistern to flush with."

"Good!" cried Chrissy. "I was afraid I'd have to go outside." She held herself and gave a mock shiver.

"Don't worry, honey," Tom said. "We'll see to it that you're comfortable these next few days."

"How glad I am," Janet said, "that we're trapped here. We'll be together for a while. It will be just like when we were first married and nobody called us or expected us to do things on Christmas."

They cleaned their cups in the bar sink and made ready for bed, using the furnace room for dressing. When Tom came out in his pajamas, Chrissy raced down the stairs.

"It's so cold up there!" She had been up to the bathroom, and this time there was no mockery in her shiver.

"That so? Maybe I'd better go see for myself." He wrapped himself in a blanket and pretended to lean against a wind coming down the stairwell.

Chrissy giggled. "You look like the headless horseman."

"Arrgh!" he growled, and turned toward her, chasing her to the safety of the couch with a galloping rush. This game went on until Janet intervened.

"Enough, you two! Get into bed so I can turn out this lamp!" She gave the kerosene can a shake. "Not too much left. We better go easy on the light from now on."

They finally complied, Chrissy on the couch and Tom beside Janet in sleeping bags on the carpet in front of the stove.

Throughout the night the blizzard beat against the house. For a long time, Tom laid awake listening to the storm and watching the stove's red glow expand and contract in sequence with pulses of wind. When the glow grew dim, he rose and added fuel, closing the Franklin's doors to control draft. Each return to his sleeping bag made him more awake and thoughts tumbled through his mind. Relaxed feelings of the evening were gone. He was alternately fighting the blizzard for his life, and the press of business for his job. Finally, toward morning, he rolled up the bag and dressed.

He went quietly upstairs into the chill of the first floor. Wind had piled a drift of snow from the back door halfway across the kitchen. Each gust added to the pile that was now almost two feet deep at the door. The room was cold. The difference between indoors and out couldn't be more than twenty degrees, enough to ensure that each window was covered thickly with frost so that nothing of the outdoors could be seen. Tom went to a kitchen window, scraped a hole in the frost and peered outside. Snow had drifted higher than the windows on that side of the house.

He walked into the living room where a picture window faced to the lee of wind. There, frost had not completely blindfolded the house and he could see into predawn gloom. For twenty feet around the house on that side there was bare ground, surrounded by a wall of snow piled to a height of five feet or more, smoothed by wind into a white dune.

He noticed no letup in the storm. New snow fell at a constant rate and the wind was as strong as it had been the previous evening, but today it was colder. Chill penetrated his clothes and he could feel sensations of cold with each breath. He made quick work of his personal chores in the first-floor bath and returned to the basement and warmth.

The other two were awake now.

"Good morning, Dad. Merry Christmas!" Chrissy called from a pile of blankets on the sofa.

"Merry Christmas, darling." Janet smiled at him from the stove, where she was making fresh coffee. "How is the storm today?"

"Merry Christmas, you two." He sat in a chair near the stove. "Looks just as bad as last night, and a lot colder."

"Goody!" Chrissy snuggled in her blankets. "We're snowbound!"

"That's for sure," Tom agreed. "There's no way we'll be getting out of the house for the next couple of days. Guess I'll call over to Pete's and see how it is on his side of town."

"Oh!" Janet exclaimed, "I forgot to tell you, the phone's been out of order since yesterday afternoon. A line must have broken in the wind."

"Fine!" he scowled, then smiled. "That means that nobody can get at us and we can really relax for a couple of days."

"Great, Dad!" Chrissy cried. "Then we can play games and you can read to me. You never have time otherwise."

"Agreed," he said. "After breakfast, we'll get started with one of your new games."

Janet brought coffee and their hands touched as she passed the cup to him. "Merry Christmas, T," she whispered.

He looked steadily into her eyes. "Merry Christmas, hon." He lifted his cup, as if in a toast. That moment brought with it the peace and contentment he hoped for in this holiday and, in its passage, held him safe from the pull of the past and threats of the present.

They gathered around the small card table for dry cereal and canned fruit. Tom made a wall of cereal boxes and peered around it suddenly at Chrissy, catching her daydreaming with a spoon in her hand.

"I see you, Dad," she announced.

"No, you don't…you see…you see…the world's greatest athlete!" He peered around the Wheaties box. Then the other way. "The world's greatest tiger tamer!" He peered past Tony the Tiger on the Sugar Frosted Flakes box.

Fascinated by this play, Chrissy eagerly munched her way through breakfast.

Janet was amazed. "She never eats anything when we're alone. She is so relaxed with you here. I can't believe the difference."

"We're a family now," Chrissy concluded.

They laughed, together. After breakfast, Tom and Chrissy sat on the couch with new games and some old standbys around them.

"Okay," he said, "what do you want to get beat at?"

"We won't know who will win until the game is over. Let's try Aggravation." She uncovered her favorite old standby, tipping the colored playing counters into her lap.

"Good!" Tom said, "that one's easy for me to win."

"You'll see, Dad. I'm getting pretty good at this. I beat Mom three times last week."

They set the game in motion. Each roll of the dice sent their counter in a circular path around the board. Each time one overtook the other and returned the opponent's counter to 'home', cries of victory accompanied moans of defeat. Tom watched his daughter's intense concentration in the game more as an observer than a player. When she leaned to make a move, her hair fell forward, making her peer out from a frame of wheat, just as she was in the photograph, where plastic held her image for him. His love for her, always concealed by the tensions of life, or by the confusion of drink, was unexpressed, but evident in the way he followed her emotions in the game and in the compliant patience with which he played his part.

Throughout the morning they played at this or other games, while Janet read or knitted a scarf she was making for Tom. The only interruptions were those for feeding the fire and for commentary on the storm that accompanied that task. After lunch, Tom lay on the sofa and listened for a time to the Christmas Day football game on Chrissy's new radio. For the first time in several years, he allowed himself to sleep during the day. It was not until Janet urged Chrissy to wake him, late in the day, that he got up.

"Who's been feeding the stove?" he asked, stretching, his hands reaching the ceiling joists.

"We've been taking turns," Chrissy said proudly. "I even went out on the porch to get more wood. Did you know the porch is full of snow and the kitchen has a drift halfway across, up to here." She marked a point between her shoulders and her waist.

"Really!" he yawned. "Is the storm still going?"

"Yes," Janet answered. "The radio says it won't let up until tomorrow morning. Lots of people have been stranded. Gas stations along the freeway are jammed with people and all schools in town are full. They are pretty worried about those who haven't turned up."

"Guess I was lucky to get home and not have to spend the holiday stranded in town." He sat up. "What's for supper?"

"I've been cooking a stew on the stove all afternoon. We'll see how good a frontier cook I am."

"Sure smells okay." Tom lifted the cover on the simmering pot. "If this works, we can save a lot of money."

Chrissy busied herself setting the card table with Christmas napkins, paper plates, and candles.

"Hey!" Tom exclaimed. "Dinner by candlelight. That's pretty fancy for the Coopers."

"Dad!" She tossed her hair in frustration. "This is my dinner party and I want it to be nice."

"How can I help, honey?" Janet asked.

"Mom, if you would bring the stew and dish it up, we will be ready to eat." Her busy reply, a copy of her mother's, made both Janet and Tom laugh.

As they sat together, they talked of the storm and people they knew to be traveling or away from home when it had begun.

"I hope that Jean made it home okay," Tom said. "Did she leave here in time?"

"I think so. But that was when I found the phone was out. I tried to call her shortly after she left…" Her voice trailed off.

"I know how you feel," Tom said, reaching over to take her hand. "Superstar and Kate were going to Minot and I know they didn't have time to make it all the way. They are probably holed up in some truck stop along the way."

"Say," he paused, "I remember that Ernie Larsen was coming in to see me at the Elevator yesterday afternoon. He never did show up. Probably decided that the weather was too bad and stayed home."

"I bet he did," Janet agreed. "His place is three miles farther from town than we are and he would have had trouble making it home."

They stopped to consider the implications of what they were saying. "Trouble" meant that those out in the storm might be dead or hopelessly marooned in dying cars. It meant that many people had a personal stake in the storm, had even stronger reasons than the Coopers for hoping that someone had reached a sanctuary.

"Let's get the weather report." Tom broke the silence by picking up Chrissy's radio and tuning it to GVC. Every few minutes the programming was broken by announcements concerning the storm and reports of persons who had successfully made their way to safety; many of these stories were fully as incredible as Tom's.

"The storm could blow itself out tomorrow," the announcer said. "Cold weather will continue, with readings from ten to twenty degrees below zero for the next two days. The cold will hamper efforts of highway crews to clear snow from the roads. Highway Department personnel told GVC today that most county roads and township roads would remain impassable for the balance of the week."

"That means that you'll be home for the rest of my vacation, Dad! And we can play games every day."

"That would be nice," Janet agreed. "How long do you think it will be before they get to our road?"

"I don't know, sounds like a couple of days. I have to pull the car out of the ditch—probably three days before we can get out."

"What about the Elevator?" Janet raised the subject reluctantly.

"It'll be okay. Pete lives on the main highway and the plow garage is over on that side of town so he'll be in before I will. He can do the job. Anyway, there's nothing pressing on the agenda."

Let's hope he can. Tom reflected on his words. No grain would be moving for at least a week, and they would just have to sit on the shortage until farmers could begin hauling again. The storm could act in his favor, too. If prices continued to slide, he would be covering his trainload sale at an even lower price and would have a larger profit to show.

These thoughts relaxed him and made the evening special. Janet joined in the games and the lamp-lit intimacy of the basement drew them together in a bond of feeling. When they finally went to their beds, Tom had lost his apprehension about work and was content to let tomorrow come, hoping for another day like that just past.

That night, he slept soundly. The untended fire went out. The chill in the basement woke Tom. Guilt came on slowly as he gradually realized there was something he was supposed to do and he had failed. The cold grew more intense, until finally he sat up. He was fully alert at once.

He got up hastily and dressed. He opened the stove's door; no sparks or heat there. He crumpled some Christmas wrappings into a pile in the stove and added kindling. He lit the pile and arranged sticks so that they remained in the midst of the flame as the paper burned and the sticks caught fire. He added first one, then another, larger piece of wood until the fire was fully involved, then adjusted the damper for maximum draft. Soon the fire was roaring and the stove radiated heat in a comfortable circle.

When Janet poked her head out of the sleeping bag he said, "Better stay in there. The fire went out. It will be a while before the basement heats up again."

"How is Chrissy?" she asked. "Is she covered?"

Tom bent over his daughter on the couch. She was curled into a small ball with covers pulled tightly around her chin. He stooped and added his sleeping bag to the nest and tucked it tightly on all sides.

"She looks so darned warm," he grinned. "Look. Just like a kitten." He smiled and pointed to her head, now barely visible above the covers.

"She's so cute!" Janet laughed and drew herself into a ball, in mimic of Chrissy.

"So are you." Tom kneeled beside her and mussed her hair.

She turned her face toward him. "I love you."

He reached down, lifted her shoulders and held her close, conscious of the warmth of sleep in her body. "I love you, too," he murmured.

She kissed his cheek. "I've got to get up. It's getting warm enough and Chrissy will be wanting breakfast soon."

He released her and watched her movements as she swung out of the bag. Her nightgown outlined her body as she walked to the furnace room. A beautiful woman, he thought.

"Hi, Dad. What's the storm doing?" Chrissy looked out from her cocoon at him.

"Say! Are you awake?" he asked. "I don't know about the weather, but I guess we'd better find out." He moved the curtain on a basement window high on the wall. He could feel the flood of cold as air trapped between curtain and window flowed down like an icy waterfall. Through the layer of frost on the window there was a brilliance of light. Sun, magnified by millions of crystals of snow, showed that the blizzard was over and that high pressure dominated the environment.

"Honey, look! The storm's over. The sun's out."

"Good!" she cried, "now I'll be able to make snow houses in the drifts like we used to. Will you help me?"

"Sure, why not? We'll go out after breakfast and see what we can do."

Throughout the meal, they planned the mansion they would build. When they had finished their breakfast and each had dressed in their warmest clothes, Tom and Chrissy climbed through the drift of snow in the kitchen and forced the back door open. On the enclosed porch, the blizzard had declared its tenancy. The porch was filled with snow, level and sculpted at the sides to a depth of four feet.

"Oh!" Chrissy exclaimed. "Look! We live in a snow fort!"

They romped through the drift together and plowed to the outside door and opened it to a world possessed by snow. None of the familiar surroundings could be identified. On the north side of the house, the ground was swept clean; even the leaves and twigs of autumn had been carried away by wind. The west and south sides were drifted to a height of six feet. Chrissy's swing on the cottonwood tree now terminated in a snow bank, two ropes reaching into snow that held the anchor of the seat. The several pine trees at the north side of the yard wore enormous mantles of snow and ice, and their tops bent low to the ground, forming a tunnel. The entire outdoors sparkled and blazed in sun. Only by carefully shielding their eyes could they look any distance from the house. All around were great piles of snow; cold penetrated their clothes with the steady breeze blowing out of the northwest.

"It's so beautiful!" Chrissy stood amazed at the changes in her yard.

"That's for sure!" He squinted at the unaccustomed light. "But, man, is it cold!" He turned to the side of the porch where the thermometer proclaimed the fairness of Farmers Elevator along with temperature. "Look, honey, it's twenty below zero."

"Is that cold?" she asked.

"You bet! We'd better get busy if we're going to do any building. We can't stay out in this very long." He rummaged in the snow on the porch and found a snow shovel where the wind had dropped it. "Okay, where you want this castle?"

Chrissy ran around the corner of the house to the south side, where the building held back the wind. "Here. Dig here." She danced and pointed to the side of a huge drift.

"Stand back!" he shouted, and attacked the drift. The hard crust resisted, so he chopped with the shovel to break through to less compact snow below. Once he had created a small opening, he hollowed out a cave large enough for Chrissy to crawl into. When he stood back, she entered the cave on all fours and turned, a snow queen surveying her subjects from a palace window. He smiled at her joyfulness. The cave had brought her pleasure, just as many such caves had done for him years ago. They worked for some time, enlarging their tunnels and adding openings and rooms. Finally, he sank back into the mouth of the cave, exhausted from cold and unaccustomed work. Chrissy scrambled in and out of the cave, stopping only to lick snow from her mittens.

As Tom sat, he grew cold. The sweat of his exercise turned to ice and a chilly breeze enveloped him.

"C'mon, Chrissy, we better go in. It's too cold to stay out any longer."

"Aww, let's make some more caves."

"Maybe later." He got up and walked stiffly to the house. She followed, still pleading for more of the game, but finally giving in and leading him to the porch with a rush. They tumbled into the kitchen and down to the basement.

"You're back!" Janet came to them and untied Chrissy's scarf from her face. "Honey, you're frozen!" She held Chrissy's face in her hands, allowing warmth to penetrate the rough cold. "And Tom, you look like you've got frostbite on your cheek again."

He involuntarily raised his hand and felt the numbness that signaled frozen skin.

"You had better get some warm water on your face." She undressed Chrissy, bundled her into the sleeping bags on the sofa and took Tom to the laundry tubs where a teapot of warm water steamed. Slowly he worked circulation back into his cheek.

"I can't believe it. Can't be that cold." He shook his head in amazement at the tingling of restored circulation. "We were only out there for half an hour."

"They say that it will be much colder this afternoon, maybe forty-below tonight." Janet held a warm washcloth against his cheek. "They're also talking about people lost in the storm."

"Anybody we know?" he asked, drying his face with a dishtowel.

"Yes. Jean Jacobs waited out the storm in her car." She turned her face to him, anxiety in her eyes.

"Was she okay?"

"Yes, she had several bags of old clothes in the car and was able to keep warm enough. Lucky for her, she was able to start the car several times to take away the worst cold. And, weren't we talking about Ernie Larsen?"

"Yeah, he is the one who was coming in to see me the day of the blizzard."

She held her hand in front of her mouth as if to hold the news from him. "He was lost down the Sioux Coulee road and was found only twenty feet from his car."

"Oh God! No!" Tom half stood. "I talked with him only a couple of hours before I left town. He was coming in to do some shopping and said he would stop by the Elevator. What happened? Did they say?"

Janet sat heavily in a chair by the table. "They haven't been able to get to his family, but they seem to think he was on his way to town when the storm hit and his car ran into the ditch. Evidently he got lost and went across 13 down Sioux Coulee road. One of the Indians found him. His poor family! What they must be going through!"

They fell silent. The blizzard had claimed its first neighbor and the news was a source of thoughts about others who might be among the victims.

Tom broke the silence. "If only he hadn't talked to me on the phone. We had a contract that needed signing and he could have waited 'til later on to do it."

"It's not your fault." Janet put her hand on his shoulder. "You didn't know the storm was coming. Anyway, he planned to go into town for his own errands."

"No, I guess not, but I could have figured it out if I had been paying attention to the weather." Tom felt responsible for Ernie's decision. If he had tended to Elevator business weeks ago, the contract would have been signed and there would have been no need for Ernie's trip to town. Every time he made a mistake in his dealings with others, the consequences were unbearable. He could never treat others as acting, deciding individuals; instead he saw everyone in need of support, advice, or help from him. Even today he should be doing something productive. Sure, playing with Chrissy was important, but he ought to be thinking about the Elevator's problems. He should be looking at post-holiday markets to see if the Christmas Eve run-up in price had leveled off.

With a sigh of resolve, he went over to the couch where Chrissy was listening to her radio. "Honey, let me use your radio. I need to see what's happening today." He tousled her hair with his other hand as he reached for the radio.

"Sure, Dad, but give it right back." She drew the sleeping bag around her shoulders and smiled up at him.

He took her radio to the card table and dialed while Janet brought him coffee. Between the blasts of country-western music, there were announcements about the storm and its consequences. For several minutes he searched for some indications of the market situation.

"...try the Valley Restaurant for those wonderful steak and lob ..."

"...country roads, take me home to the place I belong, West Vir..."

"...days, hindering the clearing of roads in the Dakotas and Western Minnesota. Blocked roads and impassable railroad tracks have made it impossible for farmers to take advantage of the runaway market in feed grains and it looks as if this is a real bonanza. Today, the Minneapolis and Chicago markets opened limit up in all grains and it looks like the same will be true tomorrow. The big Russian purchase, coupled with rumors of Chinese interest, comes as a mighty fine Christmas present to area farmers. Hopefully, the trend will continue, so that all growers can benefit when transportation is restored. Well, folks, that about wraps up the .."

Tom twisted the radio control violently. "What the goddamn hell! Those bastards told me the Russians weren't coming in!"

Janet stood up, frightened at his violence. "What is it? What's wrong?"

"Christ! Gotta cover that corn!" He pushed his chair back from the table and pounded up the stairs to the kitchen. He slipped across the snowy floor to the wall phone. In the cold receiver, silence told him that the line was still dead. He jiggled the hook violently with no response. He banged the handset back on its hook and swore with frustration.

"Damn! Damn!" He hit the wall with his fist and leaned his forehead against the cold plaster.

Janet came up from the basement, her face white with worry. "Tom, what's the matter? Please tell me."

"It's the goddamn market! I sold a bunch of corn a couple of weeks ago and they told me that the price would be coming down. Now the Russians come in and the market's going wild. If I don't buy some futures right now, I'll take a bath and have a hell of a time finding money to buy back the corn I sold."

He paced the floor, his rage increasing as he lost his footing occasionally in the snow.

"I got to get to town or to a phone before the market closes this afternoon." He looked at his watch. "And that's only two hours away. If I can get to the highway, it might be clear, and I can catch a ride to get there on time." He ran down the basement stairs, two steps at a time, and flung on his outdoor clothes.

Janet followed him, pleading. "Please. Don't go out in the cold. It'll take you too long to walk to the road. Let Pete take care of it for you. He'll think of the problem." She put her hand on his arm. Angrily, he shook it off.

"Can't rely on that. He may be snowbound, too. Even if he gets to work, he hasn't been close enough to the deal." Striding up the stairs, he called back, "If I get to town, I'll probably stay there until the roads are clear."

He banged his way out of the kitchen and waded through the snow-packed porch. At once, he was assaulted by wind, now noticeably colder than it had been earlier.

"Damn! Shit!" He cursed to himself. "What horseshit luck!" He began to run in the clear spaces between snowdrifts in the yard. At the end of the row of evergreens, the storm had piled a drift nearly five feet high across the driveway. He lunged at the barrier and clawed his way to the top. There the smooth hard-packed snow stretched away in rolling waves across the fields. Ahead of him, about a half-mile away, was a higher drift with a trace of blue color showing. This was the Fury, now almost completely buried. He climbed to his feet and began running again. He had gone several steps when his feet broke through the crust and he fell heavily, his knees gouging deep holes in the snow.

"Dirty bastard!" he hissed through clenched teeth as he staggered forward on hands and knees until his momentum was spent. Again he got to his feet and tried to run; this time he took no more than a single step before the crust gave way and he broke through, now to a level above his knees. "Goddamn, what awful crap!"

Obscenities took his breath away as he tried to get a foothold on top of the snow. Each lunge led to his breaking through the crust. Carefully, he crawled onto the firm upper layer of snow and made his way on all fours to the top of one of the drifted swells. There he was able to stand and walk. However, the crest of the drift did not lead to the highway, but went off at almost a forty-five degree angle to the proper direction.

Tom walked for a time, looking for cross-drifts or for snow that would carry his weight. He was drawn increasingly away from his goal and the raw wind began to numb his left cheek. He drew off his left glove and massaged his face. The biting tingle of thawed flesh was a warning that he could not stay exposed to the wind for any length of time. He put on his glove and looked toward the buried car. If he could force his way between the drifts, he could walk on packed snow for about a third of the way and reach the shelter of the Fury before continuing on.

He pulled back his sleeve and looked at his watch. Already fifteen minutes gone! He would have to hurry like hell and be extra lucky to reach town in time to make the call. Well, he thought, at least I can be there for the opening tomorrow morning and cover the corn before the price rises again.

He started off the snow ledge and immediately buried himself to his waist in deeper snow. Slowly, he slogged forward, lifting each foot high only to have it sink out of sight in a white morass. Now he headed into the wind. His forehead ached with cold and his lungs burned. Each breath shocked his system and caused an overpowering urge to cough. Once or twice each minute, a spasm of coughing interrupted his breathing as his body attempted to warm the freezing flood of cold air.

These halts in Tom's progress resulted in fits of swearing and frustrated wild surging effort. Each time he surrendered, often falling forward, burying his hands to the elbows in frozen snow. The sub-zero crystals cut like sandpaper on his wrists and ankles where clothing was forced back by plunges through the crust. His struggle was overcome by a growing feeling of weakness and a numbing acceptance of defeat.

Finally Tom stopped, turning his back to the wind. With the falling winter sun behind him, it was easy to see his route. An erratic path marked with gashes in the smooth snow led only about half the distance from home to the end of his driveway.

His watch, snow-covered, gleaming on his red-chapped wrist, showed that he had been gone from the house nearly a half-hour. At this rate, he wouldn't reach the highway before dark and, by following some lead in drift-covered fields, he might be hopelessly lost before that time.

Surrender and dejection won out and he began to stumble back along his track. The wind at his back instantly cut through his sweat-soaked clothes. Now his falls were complete. He did not try to break them with his hands, but simply resigned himself to burial in the snow, each time sobbing with weakness and frustration.

"God, why do this to me? Damn! Damn! Damn! Why didn't I stay in town? Please give me a break!" The pleading went on, a flood of self-pity and accusations against his fate. Tom was now shivering uncontrollably and beating his arms at his chest.

When he was nearly to the entrance of the farmyard, the back door of the house opened and Janet stood in its frame, shielding her eyes. She swept the snowfield with her gaze, her body tense with anxiety. Then she saw him silhouetted against the setting sun and she gave a cry.

The sight of her brought total defeat home to him. He began to sob with a mixture of rage, frustration and submission that dominated him.

She came running toward him, only a thin sweater over her shoulders and no covering on her head or hands. As she mounted the first drift, she fell through the snow. Surprised by the fall, she disappeared completely from his view as she rolled into the trough of the drift.

"Janet!" he called. "Are you all right?" He tried to hurry forward, only to be held back by the snow.

She raised her head and crawled to him. "Tom! Tom!" Over and over she repeated his name until they came together.

He helped her to her feet, holding his arms tightly around her, to protect her from the cold. They both sobbed wildly, she with the worry of the past hour, he with failure.

"Come! Quick, inside!" She drew him back down the drift and across the clean, wind-swept yard. Even the ice-cold porch was a relief to both, the hard floor a secure platform, the quiet a respite from the steady force of wind.

Together, they went through the kitchen and down the basement stairs. His clothes cracked when they were forced to bend as he lifted his feet from one step to another.

"Quick, change your clothes. There are warm ones over by the fire." She helped him with the zipper on his coat.

She whispered continually to him as she bundled him into dry clothes and wrapped a blanket around his shoulders. "I love you. Oh, what is it?"

He could not respond. As warmth returned to his feet and hands, he bit his lip to hold back groans of pain.

On the couch, Chrissy stared dumbly at her parents, frightened by this display of emotion and by actions she had never seen and did not understand.

Janet left him sitting next to the stove and went to the table for a cup. She picked up a half-filled bottle of Jim Beam from the floor where it had sat since Christmas Eve. Quickly, she splashed liquor into the cup, and to this she added hot coffee from the stovetop. "Here, drink this. It'll warm you up." She handed the full cup to Tom.

He caressed the warmth, concentrating on controlling his shaking hands so as not to spill the drink. He raised it to his lips, taking in the pungent odor of the mixture. He sipped at it slowly, allowing warmth to work its way down his throat. His shivers gradually diminished. His sobs became less violent and further apart. By the time the cup was empty, he had gained control of the physical signs of emotion. Depression overcame him as his failure to escape the trap sank in. He held out the cup, a mute request for a refill.

"Tom, are you sure …," she began, but relented at the look of misery in his eyes. Less quickly this time, she went to the table and poured a smaller amount of whiskey into the cup, then added more coffee to make this mixture warmer than the first.

With deliberate movements, Tom took the cup from her and drank off the entire contents at once. Then, holding the blanket tightly around his shoulders, he stood up and walked to the table. He sat with his back to Janet and Chrissy and refilled the cup with the last of the whiskey.

"Mommy, what's happened to Dad? Why is he so sad?" Chrissy raised her eyes to Janet with an anxious look.

Janet sat down beside her and held the girl closely. "It was cold, honey. He tried too hard to get to the road and got so exhausted that he had to cry."

"Will he be all right?"

"Oh, yes. As soon as he warms up he will." The reassurance was belied by anxiety in her voice. She tucked blankets around Chrissy and went to Tom, now bent over the table, head in hands, elbows propped on table top.

"Are you all right?" She knelt beside him, leaning to see his face. For more than a minute, there was no response, and then he slowly stared down at her.

"No, I'm not all right. I've made a hell of a mistake and unless I get out of here tomorrow, I'll be in such deep shit that I'll never get out."

"But, what is it? What did you do?" Her voice caught.

"I sold a hell of a lot of grain a couple of weeks ago. Thought I could buy it back cheap from farmers. Then this goddamn market turns around. I'll lose thousands of dollars every day that I'm stuck here."

He shook off her hand and reached for one of the full bottles of Beam beside the table. Roughly, he tore off the paper seal and filled the cup with raw liquor. He drank deeply and set the cup down.

"Tom, please don't drink. Talk to me. Maybe there's a way we can solve the problem." She rose from the floor and drew her chair close to him.

"Nothing we can do," he barked, and drank the balance of the cupful.

Tom stared at Chrissy as she watched them from the sofa, gradually hugging blankets around her until only her round, frightened eyes were visible above the encircling folds.

"There has to be a way," Janet pleaded. "Don't do this to yourself. The Elevator isn't worth it."

"Don't you understand?" he turned to her in a rage of self-incrimination. "I sold grain that doesn't belong to me. That's a crime. I could end up in jail if I don't replace it before the next federal inspection."

"Oh, isn't there some way you can put things back in order?"

"Yeah," he filled his cup again, carefully, so no drops were wasted. "I can either cover the sale in the futures market, or I can buy grain from farmers with money from the sale. Fat damn chance of doing either, trapped in this place."

He drank again. Janet's pleadings and false solutions went on for the next hour, as he kept drinking. By the end of the afternoon, the last of the second bottle of whiskey was in the cup and both had been overwhelmed by the problem. There was no way to correct the situation until the roads were plowed, or the telephone worked again.

Throughout the evening Janet continued to check the phone and to look out of the upstairs windows for lights of snowplows. The quiet of the night was mute evidence of the security of their prison. When she tried to feed Tom supper, he only shook his head and continued to drink from the third bottle of Beam, now in smaller amounts and more steadily.

After supper, Chrissy went to the sofa and crawled into her blankets. Later, she began to cry softly. At first, Janet didn't hear her. Then the sound became audible over the crackling of the fire. She went to the child. "Chrissy, honey, what's wrong? Don't cry. Tell Mom what's the matter." She smoothed hair from the child's eyes.

"Mom, is Dad going to jail?" Chrissy sobbed.

"No, no, no," Janet reassured her. "Try to stop crying and go to sleep." She held Chrissy, bowing over her, gently kissing her forehead. Gradually her sobs stopped and she fell asleep. Janet lowered her to the couch and covered her.

Janet then stood up, brushing her hair to one side, and looked at Tom. He was lying with the full weight of his head and shoulders on the table. Whiskey had won the contest over mind. No more trouble for him this day; only the delusions of alcohol remained.

She eased him out of his chair and onto the sleeping bag on the floor. She tucked extra blankets around him and spread her own bag over him. After blowing out the lamp, she replenished the logs in the fire and sat with a blanket over her shoulders, peering into the leap of flames. Only then did she allow the last of her reserves to weaken. Sadness possessed her body with a tensing of muscles in her chest and neck. Tears spilled over her staring eyelids, then long, uncontrolled sobs emerged as she gave in completely to the sorrow of the afternoon. Finally, she bent her head to her knees. When the initial spasm had passed, she simply stared into the fire as if searching for the happiness that had filled the room the night before. Only cold despair was left where once the day had danced.

CHAPTER FIVE

One Hundred Thousand at $3.05

They were snowbound for the next three days. The first day, Tom lay in his sleeping bag, recovering from whiskey. Janet spent the day with Chrissy, trying to divert her attention from her father's condition by playing games and reading quietly to her. The diversion was only partly successful. Each time Tom sighed in his sleep or turned from one side to the other, Chrissy grew quiet and a look of fear and sadness returned to her eyes.

On the second and third days, Tom moved to the couch, his back turned to them—silent and outwardly asleep. For him, these days were broken into intervals of restless sleep interspersed with waking hours filled with mental computation and anxious totaling of financial consequences of the trap in which he lay.

In late mornings and early afternoons, Janet and Chrissy were outdoors, shoveling snow out of the entryway and rebuilding Chrissy's snow cave, which had drifted full. Late each afternoon, Janet climbed into the attic and looked across the prairie to the freeway, five miles south of their home. She could see some evidence of activity. Snowplows and then, later, a long convoy of cars and trucks were being shepherded through some sort of path by the flashing lights of police and emergency vehicles.

News of the opening of the freeway did nothing to raise Tom from his despair. He only grunted and swung his head away from her to stare at the back of the couch. She could begin to appreciate his feelings. Each noon, she took Chrissy's little radio up to the silent kitchen and listened to market reports. These were uniformly optimistic—continual upward trends in demand coupled with a shortage of grain occasioned by the storm, and limit-up moves each day in price. Every day, there was an additional ten-cent loss on each bushel that had gone east on the unit train. Her feelings of frustration grew and she considered plans for reaching a telephone or the highway—only to reject each because of the depth of snow and wind chill.

On the afternoon of the third day, she was sitting with Chrissy at their little table with a make-believe coffee party to pass time, when she became aware of a distant buzz that rapidly grew louder. Soon it became apparent that someone was coming to the farm on snowmobiles.

"Tom! Tom!" She raised her voice in excitement. "Somebody's coming! Tom! Wake up!"

He raised his head to listen. When he heard the engines, now very loud, he swung his feet to the floor, feeling for slippers.

"Who it is?"

"I don't know, but it sounds like a couple of snowmobiles outside."

He went quickly to the steps, taking his jacket from the chair where it had hung since his abortive trip outdoors three days ago. When he reached the top of the stairs there was a sound of knocking at the kitchen door.

"Hey! Tom! Janet! You in there?"

"Yeah! Pete? That you?" Tom called as he climbed the stairs. "We been living in the basement. Roads open yet?"

"Nope." Pete and Andy came in and took off their helmets. "I just got into town today. My snowmobile was on the blink and Andy came by with a new plug. Roads are still all closed except for the freeway, and that's only open with one lane."

"God! What a storm!" Tom drew them into the kitchen and motioned toward the basement stairs.

"Janet!" he called. "Pete and Andy are here. We got any coffee?"

"Sure, bring them down." She peered up the stairs. "Hello, Pete, Andy. You both look frozen! C'mon, stand over here by the stove and I'll pour you some hot coffee."

"Hey! This looks pretty cozy!" Pete peered around the room, his glance passing over the empty whiskey bottles. "Looks like you had a good Christmas. How was Santa, Chrissy?"

"Just fine, Uncle Pete! Look! He brought me these new games!" She showed the boxes to Pete, her happiness returning at the talk and movement of her father.

"Say, Pete," Tom asked, "how are things at the Elevator?"

"Nothing doin'. We stopped there on the way out and the place is drifted shut. There's a drift completely over the office—two stories high! Nothing's goin' on in town either."

"Is there any telephone service?" Tom asked anxiously.

"Yep. Sheffield was connected this morning," Andy answered. "No service for any of you country folk yet."

"I got to get to the phone right away," Tom said. "You suppose I could ride back with you?"

"Sure," Pete grinned. "You can come with us and we can run you out again. You need anything, Janet?"

"No thanks," she answered. "But Tom, you could bring some milk and eggs when you come back."

"…uhh, OK," he answered absently as he ranged around the room looking for his shoes and outdoor clothing. "Where are my cap and mittens?"

"Right here." She picked them up from a chair near the table. "Be careful, you three! Don't go too fast!"

Andy grinned and pointed to Pete's shoulder patch—Fences are Hell—"With that kind of advice, we don't have to worry!"

Pete laughed and put on his helmet. "C'mon, let's go. We can be in town in a half-hour."

They went up the stairs and out into the cold. The two snowmobiles started easily and Tom gripped the seat rail behind Andy as the machines accelerated. Soon they were riding the crests of snow waves, two ice bugs skittering across the surface of a frozen pool.

Pete's prediction of the trip to town was accurate. Within twenty minutes, they reached the crest of the river hill and slowed in their descent into the drifted landscape of Sheffield.

On Main Street, the city bulldozer and front-end loader were at work bucketing snow into trucks. Already, several blocks had been cleared and the work was proceeding up the street toward the Elevator. The snowmobiles made their way carefully around the machinery and climbed the unworked snowface to enter the Elevator parking lot.

Tom looked over Andy's shoulder. The whole yard was filled with snow, grandly sculptured by wind so that each concrete silo wore a train of white. Dryer towers were spectacular monuments, sculpted in snow and crusted with frost. The office was entirely buried in a mantle cast from the old elevator house. Only one side was visible, the back door half-buried in the general level of snow in the yard.

The snowmobiles pulled to a stop near the door and the three kicked at snow blocking their entry. Tom fumbled for his keys and they forced their way into the office. Inside, it was faintly warm; supplementary electric heating must have started with the restoration of power.

Tom turned on the lights, dispelling the grey twilight coming through snow-covered windows.

"Why don't you two check the house?" he asked. "I'll look things over here and make a couple of calls."

"Sure thing," Pete answered. "C'mon, Andy, let's see how much snow's piled in the driveway."

Tom waited for them to leave, then almost ran to his desk. Frantically, he rummaged through the center drawer looking for the number of the commodity broker he had called last month. He picked up the telephone and dialed a Fargo number, hoping he would be able to reach the man—and that there was still time to do business.

The phone rang in Fargo several times. Finally an answer, "Hello, Triangle Commodities."

"Hello, this is Tom Cooper in Sheffield. Is Gene in?"

"No, sorry," the voice answered. "We haven't been open for business. We will be tomorrow, though."

Tom considered a moment.

"Hmmm, well, I need to take a position in corn. Can I call somebody in Minneapolis to do that?"

"Yes. Our Minneapolis office will be open for another half-hour. Call 612-786-9900 and ask for Jack Stuart."

Tom hung up and dialed the new number.

"Good afternoon, Triangle."

"Connect me with Jack Stuart, please."

After a moment a second voice came on the line.

"Hello, this is Jack. Can I help you?"

"I hope so. This is Tom Cooper at Farmers Elevator in Sheffield—out in Dakota. What can you do for me in corn futures today?"

"Well, corn closed limit-up again, but I think that it will soften some tomorrow and I believe we'll be trading again by afternoon. What do you want to do? Buy or sell?"

"I have to buy about 100,000 bushels."

"That's a hell of a lot of grain! Do you have an account with us?"

"Yeah. We opened one last month."

"Just a minute, I'll check your account status on the computer." The clicking of a keyboard came over the line.

Tom held the phone between his ear and shoulder and lit a cigarette from the pack on the desk. Soon the voice returned.

"I can't find any Sheffield Elevator account. Are you sure you opened one?"

Tom thought. "Damn! I'll bet it's still in my name. I opened it one day when I was in Fargo and we haven't transferred the listing to the Elevator. Try Tom Cooper," he advised.

Again the phone was silent for a time. Then Stuart came back on the line. "Yes, we do have an account for you, Mr. Cooper. Currently, you have 10,000 bushels of beans on futures and have made a good bit on them."

"Great!" Tom paused. "Sell those beans and use the money as a part of the margin for 100,000 corn. Can you get that on the March?"

"Just a minute. I'll get the March update."

Tom jotted some figures on the corner of his desk blotter. With the bean futures gains, he should have enough current cash to meet margin requirements on the corn contracts. If he could get a good March price, he might work out of the jam yet.

"Mr. Cooper?" Stuart's voice returned. "I've got a notion that I can get you about $3.05 basis Minneapolis tomorrow or the next day."

"Well, that's pretty close…," he quickly penciled the figures. Four days at limit-up was forty cents. He had sold the train load at $2.70 delivered Minneapolis, so discounting for the freight, he was covered against any further upturns in the market. "Okay, Jack, let's do that. You better keep an eye on this one. I'll want to unload as soon as there's any downward pressure on price. Or, you can get me out if the market goes up over a dime."

"Don't worry. For an account like yours, I'll watch it plenty close. I think we'll get some more movement up, but there will be profit taking pretty soon. We may have to weather a short down move before you get the gains you want."

"By the way," Tom said, "this is a hedge account and I'm covering shipments in transit." The lie came easily. He wasn't hedging—he was speculating. Hedgers owned grain and were taking offsetting positions to lock in price. Tom had nothing and was simply trying to establish a price for the replacement corn he still had to buy.

"I'm glad you told me," Jack responded. "It doesn't say so on the account. Shouldn't this be in the Elevator's name, though?"

"Yeah. I better get that done the next time I'm in Fargo. Well, I'll be talking to you, Jack. Try to get that order off, huh?"

"Will do, Tom. So long."

Tom hung up the phone and switched on his desk lamp. He took out one of the yellow legal pads on which he did his scratch work and pulled his chair closer to the desk. He began to fill the pages with figures, talking to himself in a steady monologue. "Let's see—45,000 bushels with the market up 40 cents means I'm out $18,000 on the last train…and, now…I was about half-sold on the first cars…that was, hmmm…30,000 bushels…yep, that's right…10 cars times 3,000 per car and half sold…that would be about 15,000 bushels and 40 cents lost on each was…," he calculated, "about $6,000 more…$24,000! Goddam! That storm! Shit! Just when things were lookin' up!"

Now he was out at least twenty-four grand, and the bank note that Ben Waters would be calling soon was for $60,000, so he had to come up with almost a hundred grand pretty damn quick. And, he would need to replace the sixty thousand bushels of farmer-owned grain that had gone east.

Tom sat back in the chair and ran various plans through his mind. How could he do this with the limited supply of ready cash on hand? Well, now, Ernie Larsen's corn was priced before the market ran up. Ernie wouldn't like the licking he would take, but he was pathologically honest and would insist that their verbal agreement was a deal. "My God!," he mumbled, "Ernie's dead! The storm! Jesus! I hope he told his boys about the sale!" Tom began to write on the pad again. "Ernie…20,000 at…What was the price? He looked at the scribbled notes on his desk blotter. There in the corner was "Larsen—20K—$2.55." Good! That would mean about thirty-five cents profit in the current market, allowing for freight. A big help!

He sat back. "Better get to Ernie's boys as soon as the road opens. I sure as hell need that corn bad!" Profit on the Larsen corn would cover part of the bank note and he could assign warehouse receipts on the corn to secure the note. Now he was making some progress. If he could get to some of the other farmers while they were excited about the market runup, he should be able to buy one hell of a lot of corn. Then he'd need only a steady price gain into spring and the loss would be covered.

He tossed his pencil down and swiveled the chair to look at the snow-covered lower window pane. The winter sun was setting fast. He probably wouldn't be able to get home tonight. Better stay here and do some work on the books. Maybe he could identify prospects for corn sales and set up some kind of schedule so he could start calling farmers as soon as the phone lines were back in order.

He got up and walked through the outer office to the door of the main elevator. He opened it and went out into the frigid air.

Pete and Andy were shoveling snow into the Bobcat loader and pushing back a drift from the entrance to the elevator driveway. Their breath mingled with the Cat's exhaust vapor, giving an underworld look to the scene in the fading light.

"Hey! Pete!" he called.

Pete came over, sweat running down his forehead. "Yeah?"

"Better knock off for today. The rest of the boys will probably be in tomorrow and we can get a crew to work on this snow."

"Okay," Pete replied. He motioned to Andy to shut down the Bobcat.

"Andy!" Tom called. "Will you run some milk and eggs out to Janet? I got to stay in town tonight and get after some book work."

"Sure, Tom. Glad to do it. It won't be much out of my way." Andy pulled on his snowmobile helmet and soon the rattle of his machine faded as he turned on to Main Street.

"You goin' to stay in town?" Pete asked. "Where?"

"Haven't thought much about it. Guess I'll just sleep in the office. There's a hell of a lot of work to do with the big market change. We'll have a lineup of farmers here unloading grain as soon as the roads are open."

"Yeah, I guess so," Pete answered, looking down at the floor. Then, slowly, he raised his head. "Say, we okay on that last trainload? Our stock in balance?"

"Sure, Pete," Tom responded quickly. "Why do you ask?"

"Oh, just wonderin'. If we're oversold, we could catch it from the inspectors. They'll probably be comin' in pretty soon."

"Yeah, I suppose so. We're into our stored grain a little." About 60,000 bushels, he thought. "But the first few truckloads of new grain will clear that up."

"Won't we take a lickin' on that grain?" Pete asked.

"Sure, but we'll make it up on the good freight break I got on the last trainload. I also had some beans in our hedge account. Sold 'em this afternoon and made about a buck on ten thousand bushels." But that money had gone as margin for his new corn contracts. The calculations raced through his mind.

"Great! I hope that account works like this all the time." Pete seemed relieved at the explanation. "Well, I got to go by Helen's house and check her furnace. It just got workin' this afternoon. She had to go next door to the Johnson's, where they have a fireplace."

"Okay, Pete, I'll walk over to town for supper later. See you tomorrow."

When Pete had gone, Tom sat for a long time at his desk staring at the jumble of figures on his blotter and totals on his yellow pad. All this juggling, he thought, all of it at the very edge of the rules of the game. All of it brought on by the everyday demands of running a big elevator and all of it done by others in positions like his. How many of his buddies had been caught in this run-up?

He remembered managers who had fallen out of favor with their directors for not reading market signs correctly in past years. Every manager at one time or another had sold into farmer-owned grain in the hope that a dropping market would permit profitable replacement. Some made this decision because they had the soul of a gambler and couldn't resist the temptation to predict swings of price, others because they were in short cash positions where the only hope of recovery was in some kind of speculative miracle. Tom had fallen into this trap because he saw the opportunity offered by the freight break on the unordered unit train, and because his beliefs about the market were reinforced by opinions of acquaintances in the trade.

But this system wasn't right. Nobody could function under these uncertainties. He recalled bitterly the spectacle of his breakdown and his binge. There was no need for him to give in to the unspoken pressure from the Board of Directors to make ever larger profits each year. He should just concentrate on moving grain as a service to farmers and getting the best possible deal for them. The Co-op didn't need to be a moneymaker to do the job for its members. Many other co-op managers felt the same way. The original idea of the cooperative movement was being short-circuited by wires of big business. In larger co-ops, net profitability for the Central Office was the rule—not service to farmers. Jesus! Sometimes it made him so angry! He had often spoken out at area meetings. The word came back in no uncertain terms from big co-op suppliers that he had better change his tune, or else his allotment of scarce supplies would be cut. That would be one hell of a fix, especially if the rumored fertilizer scare became a reality this spring!

Always between these two pressures. Do the work legally and honestly—and get fired for not fattening the bottom line! Or, cut corners and walk the tightwire of price and win the applause of Directors at the annual meeting. That approval, along with the support and advantages big central co-ops provided, were damn near impossible to resist.

Tom sighed and leaned forward, opening the desk drawer and drawing out the heavy black account book that listed grain brought in by farmers for storage. This Assembly Book was now the key to making up the shortfall. He had to guess which of the farmers would sell to him, and he had better guess right. He didn't have much time to make the contacts necessary to get his house in order for possible inspection.

The Book was heavy with last fall's work. Each load brought in by farmers for sale or storage was listed on a page of the Book under the patron's name. As he turned the pages, Tom drew on a mental image of the farmer and considered the likelihood that he could be persuaded to take advantage of the price run-up. Many of the smaller farmers he rejected with little thought. They didn't have enough grain in the Elevator to make any sizeable dent in his obligation to cover the trainload sales.

Slowly he turned the pages. ...Anderson, Baird, Benson...then Arnie Carlsen's page came up. Arnie, now there was a possibility. He recalled a conversation of a week ago, when Arnie had mentioned his intention to sell as soon as the income could be declared in the next tax year. Yes, Arnie was definitely a possibility. Tom switched the small desk calculator on and added the loads Arnie had hauled in. Lucky this stuff was in open storage. No warehouse receipts had been issued.

Tom remembered a conversation last fall. "Say, Arnie, want a warehouse receipt for this grain?" "Hell, no. Why should I? You gonna steal it?"

They had both laughed at the idea. Now he had stolen the grain. It was gone and the Elevator had the money—but no price had been set with Carlsen. This one had to be settled! He punched the Total key on the calculator. The machine ruminated and offered its assessment on its paper tongue: 20,250.32. Good! Twenty thousand! That would make a good start on replacing the shipped grain.

Tom went on studying the Book. Donnelly, Dugan, Eriksen, Frederickson, Jacobs. Barney's entries took up several pages in the Book. This was the first year that he had brought his grain into the Elevator for storage rather than keeping it on his farm. Now it, too, was gone—shipped, and had to be paid for sometime. Might as well be now.

He scribbled Barney's name on the legal pad next to Carlsen's. Again he went through the computation. This time the calculator tape slithered across the desk and ducked over the edge—a total of more than 40,000 bushels. "God!" he whispered, "I didn't think he had that much in here!" He compared the tape with the pages in a rough estimate. "Looks like he does, though."

Adding the 40,000 bushels to the total on the pad, he penciled in a running sum on the margin. With Jacobs and Carlsen, he would have replaced 60,000 bushels. The only problem would be Barney's reluctance to be stampeded into doing anything that wasn't his own idea, plus the fact that Jacobs might not need the money. He had come off some excellent cattle markets in the past two years and might be carrying a tax problem that couldn't take another hundred-twenty thousand dollars in income.

The thought of that amount brought Tom upright in his chair. A hundred-twenty thousand dollars! That would be one hell of a lot of cash to come up with in one payment. He wondered if Barney would take, say, fifty thousand, and leave the rest as credit against his spring fertilizer bill. Wouldn't hurt to ask. That would give him a nice balance in his operating account and would take care of Ben Waters at the bank. The thought cheered Tom and, at the same time, made him sweat in anticipation of the rough reaction that a proposition like this would get from Barney.

He could imagine Barney saying, "Why the hell should I let you use my money?", his eyes glaring under those frosty brows. "Don't try to put anything over on me, Cooper!" Not the kind of reaction Tom would have expected a year ago, before Barney had gotten pissed off at him. Was it the success of last year at the Elevator? Or was it the booze? Then he remembered—he had given Barney a check for $80,000 almost a month ago! And hadn't Barney left the eighty grand as a deposit for spring fertilizer? Better ask Bob.

Tom stared across the room. A big white calendar from the Sheffield Production Credit Association stared back. It was a symbol of the tidy rules of money and the precise way it was doled out by the same people who controlled the Bank and Elevator, the people who had it made, with farms paid for and businesses neatly tied into the agricultural prosperity of Sheffield. Not like him, a newcomer on the fringe, manipulating a short supply of cash and farmers' grain.

He looked down at the Assembly Book again and continued his search…Jacobs…Knutson…Ernie Larsen's name stood primly in blue against the white page. "Ernie!" he exclaimed. "Corn in here? Damn, I thought he only had corn on the farm!"

Eagerly, he began to add the entries on Ernie's page in the Assembly Book. Total—ten thousand five hundred forty. This was a big step in the direction of correcting his position! He checked his notes again. The price he and Ernie had agreed on was $2.55 per bushel. He noted the total of entries in the book and wrote the sale price and date of their conversation. Now this was better! After he had cleared this deal with Ernie's boys, he could arrange for delivery of the balance.

As he made these computations and entries on Ernie's account, Tom thought back to a conversation the previous summer with the manager of the Grandview Co-op, Al Newsom. Al had been in a bind like this last year and had managed to gloss over the problem during a federal inspection by marking some of his open storage accounts as 'sold' or 'priced'. Through these entries in his Assembly Book, Newsom was able to suggest that the Grandview Co-op had paid for more grain than it had actually purchased. The Book then showed that the Co-op owned grain that had been oversold.

Tom paused, pen in hand, for several minutes, studying Ernie's account and thinking of the bookkeeping consequences of following

Al's example. If he marked some of these sure sales with today's price, he would cover a lot of the shipped grain. Then all he would have to do is correct for the final price when the farmers agreed to sell. He paged back in the Book. When he came to Jacob's account, he paused only briefly. "Better not do this with Barney—he could ask to see the Book, and then I'd be in real trouble!"

He went on. Finally, at Carlsen's page, he penciled in the words "Priced–$2.85." He mentally added the figures of Carlsen and Ernie. "Hmmm—about forty thousand bushels covered—that'll help."

In an optimistic mood, he paged to the back of the Book, looking for other accounts where a sale might be probable. As he tried to predict the psychology of his patrons, Tom heard the clatter of an approaching snowmobile. Maybe Pete was coming back! He tossed a legal pad over the Assembly Book and went to the office door.

As the snowmobile's engine died, the door was flung open and two masked figures stormed in.

"Hey! He's here!"

"Tom! You old fart! What the hell you doin' here?"

Instantly, Tom penetrated the disguises. "Bob—and Star! How the hell are you guys? Star, you made it through the blizzard! Where did you land?"

Star pulled off his helmet. "Yep," he gave the usual confident grin, "had to shack up in the old Kenworth for two days, but we made it!"

"Yeah, I'll bet you did! But how did Kate survive?"

Bob interrupted, "Made it is the word!"

Tom laughed, then asked, "Seriously, how did you do? Didn't you run out of fuel?"

"Yep, but I got a little fish house stove and my propane tank was full, so it was okay, but wasn't that one hell of a storm?"

They moved into the inner office and sat down, Tom behind his desk. They talked for a time about the storm and the experiences of each. Star gradually drew the conversation around to his adventures, with several sly references to the housekeeping arrangements he had devised. As he talked, Bob stood up and clomped around the desk, his boots leaving a trail of snow.

"Say, Boss," he asked, "you got any of that hooch in your desk? We sure could use a couple of belts to cut the chill."

"Probably," Tom replied. He opened a lower drawer of the desk and took out a half-empty bottle of Jim Beam. As he was opening the paper bag that enclosed the bottle, Bob rummaged through papers on the desk.

"What you doin' here? Tryin' to balance the books?"

"Oh, nothin'—just lookin' for some new prospects to get some corn in here."

"I see that you priced Carlsen's grain. Didn't know he sold it."

"Hasn't yet," Tom said confidently, "but I think he's goin' to with this price boost."

"Yeah, might as well get it on the books. You probably need some with that trainload gone."

By this time Star had returned from the washroom with three paper cups. "Beam and water for you, gentlemen?" He mocked the role of the maître d'hôtel with a checkered Purina feedsack draped over his arm, looking more like a table than a waiter.

"But, of course!" Tom responded in a mock French accent. "Put zee drinks on zee table!"

Bob laughed in his coarse deep-throated manner. "Great! Let's drink to the Elevator. May the goddamn thing pull in cash for all of us!"

They drank.

Bob put his cup down and hitched his leg over the corner of Tom's desk. "Seriously, how you doin' on replacing that trainload of grain?"

Tom paused in raising his cup. He slowly lowered it and stared at the Assembly Book in front of him. "Well, to be honest, I'm really in a bind. I thought I could make the Elevator a bundle by selling that corn in a down market and farmers would come in willing to take almost any price to get their crop sold. When the Russians came in, I was way out in left field."

"Did you cover the sale?" asked Bob.

"Not 'til this afternoon. My phone was out of order and there was no way I could get into town until Pete and Andy picked me up."

"Jesus! You poor bastard!" Bob drank from his cup again. "Can you get enough of these birds to sell now to cover the shipment?"

"I think so. I got Ernie Larsen to sell me twenty thousand before the storm and it looks like three or four others might be ready to move this week."

"Ernie?" Bob asked. "Wasn't he caught out in the blizzard?"

"Yeah, but I don't think that'll be a problem. He probably told his boys about the sale last week."

"Those sonsabitches!" Star exclaimed. "They can't do business with nobody, let me tell you. I hauled some sunflowers to Fargo for them last summer and had to dig up a Highway Department weight ticket I got at the Interstate weigh station to prove I wasn't stealin' from them. Good luck if you think you can deal with those pricks!"

"That's right," Bob added, "they're real assholes! I hope you can convince 'em. Sure would be nice if you had a signed contract though."

"I know," Tom sighed. "Ernie was comin' in to sign on Christmas afternoon. He never got here."

They drank in silence for a minute, then Bob spoke. "Well, what you got to do is shape up the books and, you know, keep workin' on the farmers to get the grain in here."

"I know," Tom agreed. "Maybe you can give me a hand and try to buy some grain when you make the rounds to line up spring fertilizer."

"Sure. No problem. I can think of five or six farmers who have some corn on the farm and aren't in your Book. Let's see…there's Frank Morgan, Pete Jackson, Jack Banazak…"

"Who the hell are they?" Tom asked. "I never heard of those guys."

"Oh, they farm up to Grandview. We'll probably be able to expand our fertilizer trade over that way this spring. In fact, I've made some good contacts and we'll sell a hell of a lot of material; and, along with that, buy some grain at the right price."

"But, I don't see how we can add any new customers. We're already committed up to our allotment, and you heard Jim Leach a couple of weeks ago. He said there wasn't gonna be any loose fertilizer this spring."

115

"I heard him," Bob said, "but I got to talkin' with him, and he thinks that there'll be plenty of cars of product on track around the Midwest that can be sent our way, especially if we can find cash customers to sell it to."

"Hell, I don't believe him!" Tom stopped to finish his drink. "Why should we be gettin' any of the stuff that's on track. Everybody else will be short. Those cars ought to fill allotment shortages in other elevators."

"Well, they won't!" Bob raised his voice. "Those other elevators have always been rippin' off the free cars and we've never got our share! Now it's time to do it to them! With Jim on our side, we can move a lot of product in here and I know that I can sell it! Shit, if we don't find a way to pull in some new customers, you ain't gonna cover that corn sale and we'll be in a hell of a bind!"

Bob slapped both hands on the counter. "Lemme say that again! It's new customers we gotta have! And, I know I can get 'em in here!"

Well, thought Tom, that sure was right. It was beginning to look as if he didn't have a line on enough corn stored on farms to cover his sale. If he could offer a sure fertilizer supply, he'd have a hell of a bargaining edge in coming to terms with farmers.

"Okay, Bob, you're probably right. But I don't see how we can cut any kind of deal with Leach. What's in it for him?"

"Good thing you asked." Bob leaned forward in a conspiratorial way. "I've talked with Leach about gettin' up an independent fertilizer company in this area. He'd like to leave Farmhand and go into business as a fertilizer broker. If we can help him get a small business started this summer, you and me could join him next year and maybe go into grain."

The bait lay on the table and Tom recognized it for the enticement it was. A grain business! Freedom from the Elevator and, maybe, connections to do the job right! The hook was, of course, the uncertainty about the ethics of fertilizer dealing. Maybe those cars were surplus. Somebody had to take them. And farmers would be needing the product. If he could help farmers, he would do the area a favor, part of his job as manager. He took the hook.

"Sounds pretty good. Let's talk to Jim about it one of these days."

Tom began to clear off his desk and put the Assembly Book in a locking drawer. The business problems and Bob's opportunity were also locked away in his mind.

"Say," he asked, "is the Club open? We ought to celebrate the end of the storm."

"Think so," Star said. "There was lights there when we came by."

"Let's go!" Bob added. "This bottle is empty anyway." He held up the paper-covered flask.

"Better throw that away outside," Tom said. "Pete would have a fit if he knew we were havin' a party in the office."

They dressed for the outdoors. Star and Bob zipped their snowmobile suits and covered their heads with helmets and face shields. Tom pulled on his heavy coat and set his cap round his ears. When Star and Bob had the machines running, he turned out the office lights and locked the door.

"C'mon, Tom!" Star shouted. "You ride with me!"

Tom jumped from the Elevator dock into hip-deep snow and floundered to a seat behind Star. No sooner had he boarded, then they were off. No tame starting like Pete and Andy. This was Star—the professional racer! They took a turn around the Elevator at high speed and leveled out in the street—a straight run to the VFW Club.

Bob was already fifty yards behind. By the time Star slid his machine to a halt in front of the Club, they had gained another thirty yards.

"Jesus Christ!" Tom gasped. "What you tryin' to do? How the hell am I supposed to hang on? Look at Bob. He's still a block back!"

Star laughed and struck a pose as if to receive the victor's laurels. "These little toys got to go! You ride with the Star and we'll make one hell of a team!"

They both smiled, then laughed as Bob tried to mimic Star's slide stop. His weight was too much for that graceful maneuver. He and the snowmobile finished left-side-down in a cloud of snow.

"Nice goin', Evel Knievel!" Star called. "You could jump a couple of beer cans as your next trick!"

"Or you could do a wheelie!" Tom added. "Just set them 250 pounds on the back and the thing'll go right on over!"

Bob picked himself up and set the snowmobile back on its track. "Okay, you bastards! Just for that, we'll play a round of pool for drinks!"

They laughed again and crowded into the Club. A round of pool with Bob was a 'gimme'. Nobody could beat him with a cue anywhere in the Dakotas.

Inside, the dim lights gave the impression of an animal den. The bar was lined with men and women in snowmobile suits, all dark in color, and the air was heavy with moisture from melting snow. It looked like a surrealistic painting of people with bear-like bodies, dark and sensual with the overtones of sweat and pleasure.

"Hey, Bob!" "C'mon Star!" " It's Cooper!" People recognized them as they pulled off their headgear. "Over here! Some of these Grandviewers are buyin'!"

The three gathered around a large table where several local people were entertaining an adventurous party of Grandview snowmobilers who had made the thirty-mile trip.

"What you havin'?" Kate asked, her hand resting lightly on Star's shoulder.

"Hi, Kate," Tom said. "Glad you're back?"

"Yes, I am." She was serious for a moment. "We were very lucky."

"You bet!" Star confirmed. "Let's drink to our good luck!"

Kate brought their drinks and they all agreed with liquid votes that they were lucky. Luck was cemented with additional toasts and drinks.

"Hey, you Norwegians from Grandview hear 'bout Lars and Sven and their wives?" Bob hollered.

"Hell no."

"What about 'em?"

Bob, now the center of attention, dropped into his story-telling role, dialect ready, and the story commenced. "Well," he paused waiting for all eyes to turn his way, "Lars and Inga and Sven and Helga went to this picnic in Grandview Park." He paused again for local color to sink in. It did, with half-hearted threats and curses.

"Well, they were in this park, see, and Lars says to Inga, 'Say, Inga, yeu hear 'bout dot svappin?' She says, 'Ya.' Then Lars says, 'Vell, vy don't ve try dot vid Sven und Helga?' And Inga says, 'Ya.' Well, they all go off to a motel next to the Park and about two hours later, Lars wakes up and sits up in bed and says, 'By golly! I vonder vat does odder teu are doin' over dere, Sven!'

For a moment, silence, then a roar of laughter as the joke was understood.

"Bob," said a Grandviewer, "that's pretty good. You hear about the Norwegian accountant?"

"Hell, no. What'd he do?"

"Well, he skipped town with the accounts payable!"

Groans and some puzzlement among those not initiated into the mysteries of accounting.

The stories and drinking went on. Tom and Bob were seated on either side of Star, who, as the evening wore on, became more animated and began to tell trucker stories, drawing the attention of the entire table.

While this banter was going on, Tom and Bob gradually drew their chairs back from the table until they were seated just behind Star's range of vision. Carefully, they upended Star's snowmobile helmet on an empty chair and began to fill it with surplus beer.

Finally, the Grandview visitors got up from their seats and began to dress for their return trip. Star, by now deep in exchanges with them, offered to ride along to show them a shortcut out of town and up the north bluff. Tom and Bob edged closer to the door, not wanting to miss the fun. Star was talking earnestly to a small blonde woman from Grandview and holding his helmet in front of him, ready to put it on.

Tom and Bob were now laughing uncontrollably. Suddenly, with a flourish, Star flipped the helmet onto his head. The beer, suspended an instant by the sudden movement, released and cascaded down his hair and onto his face. The entire crowd erupted in laughter and Star wheeled to spot Tom and Bob, now stumbling over one another in haste to get outside.

"You bastards!" Star shouted. "You better get goin'!"

Outside, Tom and Bob jumped on Bob's machine. It started immediately, and they were off down the street with Star in hot pursuit. In their first attempt to dodge off the track, they were upended and buried in snow. Star slid to a stop beside them and pounced on the two larger men. They rolled over and over in the snow, laughing and cursing.

Drunks at play.

CHAPTER SIX

The USDA Shall Inspect

The next week brought a rise in temperature frequently experienced on the prairie in January. Like early December, the temperature was above freezing during the day and strong winds reduced snowbanks in the Elevator yard. As soon as roads were open, a steady flow of grain moved into the Elevator, and with it, a steady outflow of cash to farmers. Once again, Tom was caught in the delicate balancing act of an inadequate cash flow. No matter how many phone calls he made to Twin Cities buyers to hasten payments for shipments made, he was always at a near-zero balance in the Elevator grain account.

It if weren't for the help Bob gave him by talking several farmers into leaving their cash on account as credit for anticipated spring fertilizer needs, Tom would have had to tell several patrons that he could not issue checks until payment was received from Minneapolis. That would turn a steady customer into a foe whose grain would be hauled to Grandview, Hazel Creek, or another nearby elevator.

Along with cash juggling, Tom talked almost every day with Ben Waters or his Assistant Cashier at Citizen's Bank. As soon as the Elevator account balance fell below five thousand dollars, he received a call and had to collect any cash in the till and head for downtown to allay Waters' suspicion. During these days, the market trend was steadily upward and the loss sustained on his trainload shipment remained with him. The only consolation was an accompanying increase in March futures price, which increased the value of his holdings in his account at Fargo. His position in the futures market was now that of a speculator, since payment for the trainload of grain had been received. And, each time the market rose, he received a margin call from Triangle Commodities. These calls invariably resulted in hunts for cash in Elevator accounts in the hope that gains on speculation would offset the losses of December.

When these calls came in, Tom asked Stub to write an Elevator check to him personally, with the explanation that he would have to get the Triangle account shifted to the Elevator next time he was in Fargo. Then, with a feeling of martyrdom, he wrote his personal check to Triangle. Here he was, using his own account to help the Elevator and nobody on the Board knew the risk he was taking. By using his Fargo checking account, he gained a two-day float in the exchange of checks. In this way, he could bring some small help to the cash balance on hand. The fact that each check he wrote was an overdraft, and a fairly large one, did not enter into his management strategy.

The pressures of this balancing act kept him close to the phone and on duty behind the counter every day. He couldn't leave to comb the country for replacement grain. Without his hand on the till, there would be no telling what checks might go out and what reaction the bank would have.

He tried several times to call the Larsen boys to bring in the corn Ernie had promised. But they didn't answer, or else Mrs. Larsen told him that the boys would speak for her now that Ernie was gone.

Finally, on the fourth day of the thaw, he left the Elevator in Bob's charge and climbed into the Fury to try to settle the Larsen problem.

"Don't let those bastards buffalo you!" Bob called as he drove the Fury out of the Elevator yard.

"Don't see why they should," Tom hollered back. "I had a deal with Ernie."

"Didn't I?" he murmured as he rolled up the window and turned down Main Street. So what if the boys were tough to deal with? They had to be honest in recognizing the commitment Ernie had made before he lost his way in the storm. Tom mentally tested several approaches to the topic as he drove up out of the valley through pools of water covering low spots in the highway—not yet icy in the afternoon sun. Say, boys, Ernie made a sale with me before…No, that wouldn't work…too much like a con man. Now, Mrs. Larsen, Ernie and me…Nope, no good. The boys wouldn't let their mother have anything to do with the business end of the farm.

He maneuvered the car down the township road toward the Larsen place, fighting the pull of ruts in half-frozen mud. God! This weather would make it tough to haul Ernie's grain. Sure a hell of a change from the blizzard. Ernie would be pleased to see the moisture working its way into the ground if he were alive. How could a sensitive, honest guy like him have sons who were so mean and suspicious?

Tom turned into the graveled drive of the Larsen farm. Obviously, the boys hadn't taken time to blade the drive; it was a mass of muddy ruts. If Ernie were alive, he would probably be piloting an ancient road grader while one of the boys served as an unwilling teamster on one of his smaller tractors.

He drove along the curve of the drive around the house and into the farmyard. It, too, was a mass of ruts and puddles filled with snowmelt. On the far side of the yard, the two Larsen boys were at work augering corn from a storage bin into a truck.

"Dammit!" he said aloud. "They're moving corn! This isn't gonna be easy! Either Ernie didn't tell them about the sale, or else they're ignoring it. Goddamn!"

He stopped the car and worked his way out of the door, stepping across the mud to a verge of brown grass beside the drive. He walked along the grass toward the bins. Jim, the younger boy, looked up from an auger where he was scooping spilled corn into a pile.

"Hello, Jim. How's things?"

"Umm, yeah, Cooper. Pretty damn muddy for workin' outside." He went on with his shoveling, Tom standing uneasily, hands in pockets, as the auger ground on, and the level of grain began to appear over the sides of the truck box. He stood watching the progress of loading until finally Jim signaled to his brother by banging a shovel against the tin sides of the bin. The flow of grain stopped, and when the auger ran empty, Jim threw a switch to disconnect its motor.

The sudden silence was broken by an exclamation from the roof hatch of the bin. "Cooper! What's on your mind?"

"Hi, Frank!" Tom tried to be cheerful in the face of evident hostility. "Just thought I'd drop by to see how things were. Sorry to hear about your Dad."

"Yeah, he should have known better. We told him not to go out that afternoon."

Tom broke the silence that followed this remark. "I talked with him earlier that day. He said he was plannin' to come in to the Elevator—but he never made it."

"So that was who he called." Frank scowled. "Been better if you'd told him to stay the hell home!"

Tom began to grow angry and made a conscious effort to control his temper. "Well, I had to talk to him. We had a deal on some corn and he wanted to get it on paper."

"That so?" Jim blurted. "I suppose you're gonna tell us that he sold a pile of corn to you just before the price increase."

"Well, that's exactly what he did. We had a deal for twenty thousand bushels at $2.55, and I know that he would want to go through with the agreement."

Frank snorted, "Shit! I can imagine that you'd want to keep a deal like that goin'! Well, piss on it! We're haulin' corn now to Hazel Creek and gettin' $2.95 for it!"

"Yeah," said Jim, stepping so close that Tom could see spittle at the corners of the man's mouth, "and we know that Pa had corn in the Elevator. Either you're gonna buy it at the goin' market price, or we'll haul it out of your crummy joint!"

Tom could see that a fight in the muddy yard was only a remark or two away. He turned from Jim and spoke to Frank. "Frank, I don't want to quarrel with you boys. I'm tellin' the truth when I say that

Ernie had a deal with me, but I'll be fair. I want to continue to do business with you and I'll negotiate a new price. Just give me a chance."

"I'll bet you'd like a chance! Tell you what, Cooper," Frank spat tobacco juice so that wind carried drops cross Tom's face, "I wouldn't deal with you if you was the last grain man on earth! You better clear the hell out of here before we mop up some of this water with you!"

Jim was now standing beside Tom. "That's right, Frank! You tell the bastard! Now clear out of here, Cooper, if you know what's good for you!"

Tom could feel his face redden with anger. He walked slowly back to the Fury, retorts running through his mind, all of which were likely to make matters worse. As he left the yard, he heard Jim's parting shot through the open window.

"Get out of here, Cooper! You fuckin' crook!"

When he had negotiated the muddy drive and was on the township road out of sight of the farm, he stopped the car. He was shaking with anger. The open window allowed wind to evaporate the sweat on his body, and he shuddered with chill. He rolled up the window and lit a cigarette with trembling hands. He considered several responses he might have made, and ways he could have handled the boys physically. These were all might-have-beens.

As his anger subsided, he became more realistic. The only thing that would have helped was to have a signed contract from Ernie. Time and storm had cheated him of that advantage. Now he was in a hell of a fix. The twenty thousand bushels he had counted on as a sure thing had disappeared. Not only was he short the grain, but now he had to find replacement for it at the going market price, rather than at the price he and Ernie had agreed on.

He finished his cigarette and flung the butt out the wing window of the car. With a sigh of frustration, he put the car in gear and drove back toward the main highway. *God! This will put a crunch on my cash—unless I can space out the demand for payment. I'm gonna have a hell of a time keeping this from the Board and the bank!* He would have to go on the road to try to find corn still on the farm and persuade some of those holding grain to sell at current prices. He drove slowly, making a mental list of farmers to visit and rejecting those who had a history of conservative marketing—talking to them would be a waste of time. They would just take an opposing position out of stubbornness.

By the time he descended the hill into Sheffield and turned into the Elevator yard, Tom had a plan of action. He would begin immediately with phone calls, following up with visits to specific farmers. He shut off the Fury's engine and began to write the list of prospects in his pocket notebook. He had written only five names when Bob came out of the Elevator office, running through mud and water. He opened the door on the passenger side of the car and levered his bulk into the seat.

"By God! I'm glad I caught you before you came in! The federal inspectors are here and have got us tied into an inspection!"

"Jesus Christ!" Tom exclaimed. "What the hell brought those bastards here now?"

"I don't know," Bob replied, "but I got a call from Newsom up to Grandview. He told me that the Feds were leavin' there and on the way to our place!"

"Sonofabitch! I wish I had been here! There were some changes that should have gone into our books!"

"Yeah, I know. When the call came, I went through the Daily Position and saw that we need to own a hell of a lot more grain than we do. So I went through the Assembly Book and finished the work you were doin' last week. I priced enough grain to put us okay with the books."

"Great! I'm glad you thought of that. Ernie Larsen's deal just fell through and we'll be short too much to pass inspection."

"Don't worry, Boss. I priced all of Barney's grain too. That's more than enough to carry us over."

"Holy shit! If Barney finds out, he'll have our balls!"

"Fuck! I can handle him. Leave him to me!" Bob grinned confidently. "We'll lick this thing yet! I know where I can lay my hands on plenty of grain. You handle the inspectors and I'll get the grain in here!"

"I appreciate what you're sayin'," Tom put his hand on Bob's shoulder, "but we don't have the cash to make any buys from farmers, especially if they want any advance."

"No problem," Bob smiled, "I'll find a way to get the grain we need without runnin' us out of cash. Just watch my smoke!"

Bob guffawed, slid out of the Fury and tiptoed across puddles to his four-wheel drive pickup.

Tom stood beside his car, watching the pickup disappear around the corner onto Main Street. The confidence he felt in Bob's prediction of new sales helped him decide to enter the office rather than leave for the day, something he had done in the past when the Feds were on hand.

He mounted the stairs to the office, stamping mud from his boots. Inside, Stub and Helen were talking with Joe Carson, the Chief Inspector for the Fargo section of the Department of Agriculture. Carson turned to greet Tom.

"Hello, Cooper. How've you been?"

Tom advanced to shake the offered hand. "Hi, Joe. Time to give us the once over again?"

"Yep. Your checkup was about due and we were in Grandview anyway, so we thought we'd get it over with. But I suppose it's not much of a surprise," he added, with obvious reference to the elevator grapevine that followed the movement of inspectors with the accuracy of radar.

Tom laughed. "Didn't know you were coming, Joe. I've been out visiting customers." He pointed to his muddy boots as confirmation. "And a hell of a dirty job it is."

Joe smiled. "Good. Then we won't have to worry about last minute changes that sometimes crop up in the books when the inspector is on the way."

He half-turned and motioned to another man seated at Tom's desk. "Cooper, this is Alex Johnson. He's new in the Fargo Division and will be workin' with me until he sets up his own route."

Johnson rose from the desk chair and shook Tom's hand. "Hi, Cooper. Glad to meet you. People in other elevators have told me that you're doing a first-rate job here."

"Thanks, Alex. I guess you'll know more about that in the next couple of days."

Johnson broke off the handshake and addressed Carson. "Well, Joe, I've totaled the books as to Daily Position. Let's look at the Bin Board and we can get moving on measuring the house."

Stub led the inspectors to a blackboard on the office wall where the forty-six different bins used by the Elevator for grain storage were drawn in a rough plan view. Contents of each bin were noted along with an estimate of the number of bushels.

The inspectors studied the board for some time. Then Johnson asked over his shoulder, "Cooper, my rough guess says that you don't have quite enough grain on hand to square with my calculations of your position. Do I read this right? Or am I missing something?"

"No, you've got part of the picture." Tom walked over to join the inspectors. "We've got quite a bit of grain bought and it's still on the farm. The price run-up has lots of farmers cashing in on grain they had planned to store. That and the bad weather has us holding more grain on the farm than I like."

"Hmmm," Johnson murmured, "that's not so good. You know, of course, that you must hold the grain in approved warehouse storage space. We may have to cite you if you're too far off in the inventory."

Tom did not answer, but he noted the uneasy way Joe Carson watched Johnson. Maybe their relationship was different from his first impression. It seemed like Johnson was in charge and that Joe, too, might be under observation. This reversal could sure gum things up. In the past, Joe had been an easygoing inspector who, even if he ferreted out some irregularity, would listen to reason and would bend regulations over a beer at the VFW. Johnson probably would be a stickler for the rules and a hell of a problem to deal with.

The two inspectors had now moved to the coat hooks near the door and were donning heavy coveralls and mittens in preparation for the lengthy job of measuring the depth of grain in each bin. They would also take samples to determine the grade in storage. This grade would be compared with the grade listed in the Elevator record books to reconcile the inventory of the house with the actual quantity on hand.

Tom tried to lighten the mood by offering some helpful advice. "With the nice weather today, it probably would be a good thing to handle the silos first. If the weather changes and the wind comes up, the catwalk can be a pretty scary place."

"That's a good idea!" Carson agreed. "The ride to the top is plenty cold, Alex."

Johnson frowned. "I don't mind the cold, Joe. Guess we'll start with the wood elevator today."

Tom nodded in agreement, while his concern increased.

Behind the counter, Helen and Stub were standing close together as if to draw support from one another, sensing a possible problem and very much aware of Johnson's behavior. As the house door closed behind the inspectors, Helen asked. "Tom, is everything okay?"

"Huh? Oh, yeah. I guess so."

"Are you sure?" Stub asked. "That shipment that went out of here before Christmas cut into our stored grain pretty bad. Have we been able to buy enough of it back?"

The seeming innocence of the question was belied by a knowing look in Stub's eyes.

He knows damn well that we didn't buy enough back, Tom thought. "I think so, Stub. Of course, we haven't paid for most of it yet. With the cash position where it is, we couldn't buy back more than half and pay for it."

Stub paused, sighed and continued. "Well, I suppose we'll be okay if the market turns round. Do you think we have enough priced grain on the books to cover our position?"

Stub had hit the key issue. The Elevator records showed grain on storage that was receipted to farmers. If they had a total stock short of the receipted amount, they would be guilty of fraud and in danger of losing their Federal License, and could be prosecuted, as many elevator operators had been across the Dakotas in recent years. What Tom and Bob had done by 'pricing' grain was to reduce the size of storage obligations. They had made 'paper' purchases of large amounts of grain. The fact that it wasn't paid for was not of concern to the inspectors. All they cared about was the reconciliation of records with inventory. The measuring and grading that would take place in the next several days would involve a cross-check between book inventory and actual bin contents. So long as the inspection did not coincide with a formal audit of all Elevator books, there should be no problem.

Tom gave an involuntary shudder at the thought of the elevator manager's nightmare—simultaneous audit and inspection.

Helen came around the counter and walked past him on her way back to her desk. She stopped for a moment beside him and held out her hand as if to give him support. While not quite touching his arm, she voiced her feeling. "Tom, don't worry. I think everything's in shape. We'll be okay once the market steadies and the weather gets back to normal."

Tom felt the sincerity of her remark. "Thanks, Helen. If it weren't for you and Pete, I really couldn't make this thing go."

She murmured a denial of his statement, but her glance assured Tom that he had their support and that they would back his judgment as long as he tried his best to make the Elevator work for farmers. As Helen walked on, Stub motioned to Tom to take the phone. He went into the inner office and sat on the corner of the desk.

"Hello, Farmer's Elevator. Cooper speaking."

"Hi, Tom. This here's Arnie Carlsen. What's corn doin' today?"

Tom swung his head to look at the chalk board where Stub had posted the day's grain prices. "Down a little, Arnie. We're payin' $2.85 cash today."

"Dammit!" Carlsen swore. "I knew I should have hit you when the price was way up!"

Tom held his breath and sank into his desk chair. Here was a chance for him to close one of the sales he had priced, and at the amount he had planned!

Carlsen sighed. "Okay, Tom, guess you'd better sell me out. What I got in there?"

"Can't say exactly, Arnie. The federal inspectors are here and they have the books for the next couple of days. As I remember, it's right around twenty thousand bushels, though. Tell you what, I'll mark down the price, you come by and sign a sales contract and we'll square it up when the Feds leave."

"Okay, Tom. I could use some cash now, but I imagine it won't hurt to wait a couple of days for it. Say, how you doin' on settin' up spring fertilizer?"

Here was a chance to get some of the money back! He waited a moment, "Well, Arnie, we're bookin' orders now and can lay out some awfully good prices for advance payment. When Bob comes back in, I'll have him call you to set up your program."

"Good, Tom. Better have him call me soon. I hear the stuff's goin' to be plenty short in spring."

"That's right. We have pretty good supplies in now, but it'll go fast. Lots of elevators in the country haven't laid in enough and there'll be slim pickings two months from now. I'll be sure to tell Bob to give you a ring first thing in the morning, okay?"

"Yeah. And, Tom, if he's comin' out this way, have him bring along a check for part of that corn."

"No problem!" Tom's hearty response contrasted with the grimace that crossed his face. Any cash out now was painful, but a small payment might pacify Arnie for quite a while, and Bob just might persuade him to apply the bulk of the payment to spring delivery of fertilizer. "Bob'll be there tomorrow…cash in hand!" He laughed.

Arnie returned the chuckle. "Say, you guys are okay. Hell of a lot better than the run-around I used to get before you took over!"

"Well, glad to hear it, Arnie. We try to do our best. We'll be seein' you, and thanks for the business."

Tom hung up the phone and swiveled his chair to look out over the muddy yard. The sun now was low in the west. It would be quitting time soon and he had forgotten lunch. He was hungry for food and for somebody to talk to who wouldn't bring business into the conversation.

Deciding he'd better check on the inspectors before taking off for the day, Tom pulled on his work coveralls, yellow hard hat, leather mittens and a heavy coat.

"You goin' out in the house?" Stub asked as he walked out of the inner office.

"Yep. Better see how the Feds are doin'. Won't hurt to check their measures."

"Good idea! I don't like the way that Johnson was eyeballin' the books!"

"Don't worry, Stub," Tom said curtly, "everything is in order. How many times do I have to tell you that?"

"Okay, okay. Like you said, it won't hurt to check up on 'em."

Tom wheeled and clomped his way across the office to the house door.

"Helen," he called, "anybody phones, tell 'em I'm up in the elevator and won't be down before dark. I'll call back in the morning."

"Will do, Tom. Be careful." Her warning always suggested that she sensed his fear of heights and the mysterious impact the old house had on him. He walked to the manlift and began his passive ride to the upper floors. This trip would end, not at the very top, but on the third-highest floor where a cluster of spouts delivered grain to the wooden bins, each some eighty feet deep.

As the lift neared its destination, he could see lights over the bank of bins where the inspectors were at work measuring and sampling the contents. He stopped the lift and made his way to the men. They were kneeling, as if in prayer to some being that resided in the nether regions of the bins, peering into the access hatch in one of the wheat storage bins.

When Tom approached, Carson looked up. "Well, about time you joined us. No reason why the manager shouldn't suffer with the inspectors."

Carson's attempt at humor didn't square with the worried look on his face. He was obviously uneasy with Johnson's presence.

Johnson, too, looked up. "Hello, Cooper, looks like you have some wheat that's goin' out of condition!"

"How's that?" Tom asked.

"These last two bins have weevil in them and that'll be a problem when we total up the grades on your report."

"Weevils! Damn the little shits!" Once they got a start, they could spread like wildfire. The Elevator would have to be shut down and the dangerous process of fumigation begun. More cost and a loss of business--unless he could persuade his men to use their Sunday for the job. Tom knelt beside the inspectors and scratched his fingers through the pan of wheat Johnson was holding. He held the pan under a flashlight. Sure enough, several of the small insects scurried for cover among the kernels of wheat–a hell of a crop of bugs!

"How many of the bins got these?" He looked into Johnson's face.

"The last two. The corn looks as if it'll make grade so far and the CCC oats are okay, but your wheat will have to be treated to bring it back up to grade."

"Dammit! That means the weekend is shot for the boys. We'll have to fumigate right away!"

"I figured you'd want to get goin'," Johnson replied. "The bugs could get into your corn in nearby bins."

They continued talking as they moved to the next hatch cover. Carson went down on one knee and raised the lid. All three men looked involuntarily at one another. The odor from the bin was unmistakable—weevils had been at work in that bin for several weeks.

"Sonofabitch!" Tom exclaimed. "Here's one that I gotta get to right away!"

"Sure smells like it," Carson agreed.

Johnson lowered a plumb bob on its cord, following its descent with his flashlight. When the bob touched the wheat, he read the depth on the marked cord.

"Twenty feet. Got that, Carson?"

"Yep. Want me to get the sample?"

Johnson shook his head. "Nope. I better probe this one." He wiggled his way into the hatch and reached back for the brass probe. As Johnson climbed down the inside ladder, Tom looked over at Carson.

"How you think we're doin'?" he asked in a soft voice.

Carson turned his head to keep his voice from carrying down into the bin. "So far, okay, except for the weevils, and that sort of thing happens all the time."

"Good," said Tom. "But who is this Johnson guy? I don't think he's got a very good opinion of me and our position."

"Aw, he's just givin' you the treatment that all regional people feel they have to put on local boys. When you square up the books, you'll be okay."

Tom glanced down into the bin. Johnson was busy pulling up samples and dumping them into a cloth bag attached to his belt.

"I hope you're right. Tell you what. I'm goin' over to the VFW for supper. Why don't you drop in later on and I'll buy you a drink?"

"Sure thing!" Carson smiled. "If I can get away, I'll do just that!"

Tom punched Carson's arm, then leaned down and called to Johnson.

"Say, I'm goin' down now. I'd better get on the phone before quittin' time and order some Tetrafume so we can clean up these bugs."

"Good idea, Cooper," the voice answered from the gnome-like figure hunched over the wheat. "We'll be talkin' to you sometime tomorrow when we got an idea of how you're shapin' up."

Tom looked back at Carson, shrugged his shoulders and made his way back to the manlift. As he swung himself aboard a platform, he mentally reviewed the men he might be able to coax into a Sunday session with fumigant. The problem, because it required immediate action, submerged the fear that usually rode with him on this trip. He was only barely conscious of the dark well under his feet and the ease with which he could fall off his perch to plumb its depths. By the time he stepped off at the bottom and pulled the stop cord, he had decided to prevail on Pete and Andy to join him in attacking the insects. They could always be counted on as willing helpers.

"Tom!" Helen called to him as he came into the office. "There are three phone calls for you."

"Yeah. I suppose so. Any of them important?" He bent over the notes on his desk as he shrugged out of his jacket.

"No, I guess not. Two of them are from farmers…Probably want to get your ideas on prices. The other is from Bob. He seemed like he wanted to talk to you. Probably better call him. He'll be at that number for the next half-hour."

"Wonder what's on his mind?" Tom mused as he dialed the number. The phone rang several times. Finally, a breathless voice answered.

"Hello. Jim's Service."

"Say, this is Tom Cooper. Is Bob Clausen there?"

"Yep. Guess he is. Hang on."

Bob's booming voice came over the wire. "Hi, that you Boss?"

"Yeah. What you doin' up there? Ain't this a Grandview number?"

"That's right. I've been hittin' some farmers up here for corn and wheat and have just come up with a couple of good buys. Now get this down. Gerry Ryan—R—Y—A—N—just sold us 25,000 bushels of corn for $2.85 and he'll deliver it."

"Great, Bob! That's a hell of a price! How'd you do it?"

"Listen! That ain't all! He's goin' to leave the whole amount with us as a deposit on spring fertilizer! What do you think of that?"

"Jesus!" Tom sat down heavily in his chair. What a break in cash flow. "But, we won't have anywhere near enough fertilizer to take on another new customer as big as Ryan."

"Just leave it to me, Boss. I'll be meetin' with Jim Leach at the Agri-Dealers' Convention and we'll be right at the head of the line for extra material this spring."

"Boy! You'd better be right, or we'll have so many farmers after our asses that this inspection will look like a Sunday school picnic!"

Bob laughed. "How's the inspection comin'?"

"There's a problem with the new boy, Johnson. Looks like he's keeping an eye on Carson. They sure are being careful with measurements this time. No sitting at the desk and eyeballing the Bin Board."

"Hmmm…well, this corn we just bought is ours. Better put it on the books in case you need it. I got to get goin' now. The roads are so muddy up here that I won't be able to see more than a couple of guys today."

"Okay, Bob. So long—and keep it up!"

Tom put the phone back on its cradle and entered the purchase on his Temporary Position record. God, what a help! Twenty-five thousand bushels and no cash required! He would look pretty good by the time his monthly report to the Board was due, especially if Bob could bring in a couple of other purchases like this one. He scanned the day's trading. Several farmers were selling steadily in small amounts. It was beginning to look like he would work his way out of the corn problem, but only at the expense of making some fertilizer commitments that would be very hard to meet. Unless Bob could make good on his promise of additional product through Jim Leach, they would have to find cash to repay farmers who had left corn dollars on deposit. While he ran these problems through his mind, Pete came in to punch his time card.

"Say Pete, can you and Andy spare a couple of hours this weekend? We got to do a job on the wheat bins…got a hell of a lot of weevils in there."

Pete put his time card in the rack. "Well, I was kind of figurin' to run up to Helen's folks. But I guess that could wait if we're in a jam." He looked at Helen for confirmation. She nodded her approval of the postponement.

"Tell you what, Pete. You talk to Andy, and we'll all meet here early Sunday. Maybe we can get done so you can still take that trip."

Another weekend gone. How many times had he given up plans like Pete just did? How many promises to Janet and Chrissy had been broken? It was no use thinking that he was doing this work for his family. He was doing it only for the Elevator. He must do it for the Elevator. It was his to run.

As the door closed behind Helen and Pete, the Elevator settled into the quiet of off-business hours. The last gleam of sun through the west window of the office glinted off dust particles moving in eddies of air. Tom leaned forward in his chair, drawn by the sparkle of each mote's movement. He drew his fingers through the dust accumulated on the polished surface of his desk. Dust was always with him. In spring it came in through open windows, expressive of the promise of the prairie. In dry springs, it flew thick and grey, whirled by wind from parched fields. When rain came, dust settled onto every surface, ready for the impregnation of seed.

Summer dust was occasionally ripped from the earth in the violence of pre-thunderstorm winds, but was usually brought in on farmers' clothes when they sought air-conditioned refuge in the Elevator office.

Fall and winter brought dust home to the Elevator. All the rattling weight of harvest moving through the Elevator brought with it tons of dust, seeping into every opening, building in little drifts wherever direct traffic did not flow, marking the well-trodden paths of commerce in and around the office by tiny banks cast aside by hurrying feet. No matter how careful clean-up crews were, dust silently moved in behind them.

While he sat, Tom was enveloped in dust. He could almost feel it fall on his shoulders, each tiny molecule adding its bulk to the weight of responsibility bearing on him. He stirred uneasily under the burden.

Whenever possible, Tom, and others like him, used dust. When grain was moved out of the Elevator, dust was carefully shoveled into each carload, adding its useless weight to the mass of grain. Masked men worked on each floor of the house, coaxing the grey piles into open chutes or directly into the clattering buckets of the elevator, always conscious of the explosive power that could reduce the entire structure to its own elemental dust.

Tom sighed. Taking his handkerchief from his pocket, he blew dust from his nose. The blackness on the cloth was evidence of the cancerous penetration of dust into his body.

The whining of the manlift drew his thoughts back to the inspectors. He looked at the clock—6:00 p.m.—later than any had ever stayed in the Elevator in the past. The lift clicked to a stop and the house door opened to admit them. They stamped their feet and beat dust from their clothing.

"Man! It's cold up there!" Carson rubbed his red hands and held them to the office stove.

Johnson dropped a collection of small sample bags on the floor. "You still here, Cooper? Good! Looks like we'll be able to wind this thing up tomorrow. You don't have a hell of a lot of grain in the house so our measures went pretty fast."

"Yup," Tom replied, "we're pretty well shipped out now, but I've been talkin' with Bob and we'll be movin' in quite a bit of our priced grain in the next couple of days."

"That's good," said Johnson. "The way I see it, you are plenty short over what you should have. You know that priced grain has to be in the house, but maybe we can make allowances for the blizzard."

"I sure hope so. We really drew ourselves down with recent shipments. I hoped to have all that grain in last week, but you know how tied up we were and how bad the roads have been."

Carson shifted his feet—finally he interrupted to change the subject. "Hey, Tom, we'll be going to supper. How about joining us at the VFW?"

Johnson pre-empted Tom's reply. "I don't think I'll be going out. Too much work to do. But why don't you and Cooper go along without me?"

"Okay, Alex," Carson said. "Why don't we go now, Tom, then I can give Alex a hand later?"

"Suits me," said Tom. He came around the counter and followed the inspectors out of the office. It was now dark and he hunted the key into the lock while Joe waited for him. Johnson had the federal car running and called to them. "See you soon, Joe!"

He drove off though a light, sifting snowfall that had begun just before sundown. Johnson's federal car swirled the fluffy flakes into twin vortices behind its fenders and swept a pathway for Tom. All of Sheffield was being gently covered by a slowly building white mantle that masked the grey dust fanning out from the Elevator. Like Tom, Sheffield was sinking ever so slightly under the weight of dust and snow, bowed down by the already-hard winter of freeze and thaw. In its own way, nature was pressing Sheffield into the ground to force it under the prairie on which it depended. Whether by dust, rain or snow, this was a place where the power of nature was absolute, a power to raise man to ecstasy in the limitless beauty of emptiness—or a power to crush him in its freezing grip.

The neon sign of the VFW Club was the only bright spot in the white of the street. As Tom and Joe approached, the door swung open to let another patron in and a shaft of light illuminated the falling snow, just as sunlight had lit the dance of dust in Tom's office. For a moment, Tom's mind held a clear picture of the meaning of time. The small rays of light cast by men into the gloom of the past or their searches down the corridors of the future were tiny extensions of the self—explorations into the meaning of the relationship between the individual and nature. When the door of the Club closed, he was again seized by an unreasoning fear of being totally alone.

The quiet scrunch of Carson's footsteps alongside his own helped him to suppress his fear. "C'mon, Joe," he said, "let's get with it! It's starting to get a little on the cold side."

"Damn right!"

They walked quickly into the red pool of light below the VFW sign and through the door into the warmth and hum of conversation inside the Club.

"Hi, Cooper!"

"Hello, Tom!"

"Hi, Kate," he responded. "Glad to see you're back on the job. All recovered from the blizzard?"

She blushed and set her tray on the bar. "Yes, everything's fine now. Did you know about my good news?"

"No. What's that?"

"Star and I are engaged! We're going to be married next Christmas as a celebration of the blizzard!"

"Dammit! Kate, that's good news! But what about the rest of us? What'll we do now that you're taken?"

She smiled at the flattery and its underlying sincerity of congratulations.

"You'll just sit down and have a drink on me!" She pointed Tom to an empty table in the corner of the room and Joe joined him, elbows on the table, looking expectantly for his drink. When it arrived, they toasted Kate and she went on with her work, leaving them to study the menu.

After they had ordered, Tom gathered the loose ends of conversation and directed it at the inspection.

"Just what's goin' on with you Feds? How come you have this fellow Johnson along with you?"

"It's a long story." Carson drank deeply. "There's been a lot of talk about grain inspection all around the country, you know."

"Yeah. I hear about the port inspectors and how they change the grades on grain to make the overseas shipments look better."

"That's just it!" Carson paused again and drained his glass. Tom signaled to Kate for a refill, while Carson continued. "You see…what happened is that the General Accounting Office got interested in all of the federal grain inspectors and they found some problems. We had been a little too easy on a couple of elevators and they really laid down the law. Then, this fall, Johnson shows up from the GAO and starts to make the rounds with every inspector in our region. Jesus! That guy sticks to the letter of the law! He fired two of our boys on the spot! Said they were takin' bribes from elevator operators to falsify reports. Shit, they were only takin' a couple bottles of whiskey at Christmas time…but Johnson wouldn't stand for it." He stopped the story as their drinks and food arrived.

When Kate had left, Tom asked. "But, Joe, all of us know each other and it's not unreasonable to be friendly."

"Sure, I know." Carson took a mouthful of food and washed it down with whiskey. "But that kind of talk won't cut any ice with Johnson and the GAO. In fact, I think I'm really under the gun. I've been pretty good friends with a couple of you operators. Sometimes I've let you get by with off-grade grain or some shortage against warehouse receipts when you've been in a bind."

"Well, why not? There's no way in hell that we can always be square with our books. If we knew when you were comin', we could get our cash in hand and pay off farmers as we shipped grain. This way, we load out a big order and have to wait for the cash before we can pay farmers. Most of us are short all the time."

"I know. I know." Carson pushed his plate away, his dinner only half-eaten, and emptied his glass. "This has really been gettin' to me this fall. That sonofabitch Johnson has made all of us nervous wrecks. Me, I'm drinkin' too much. Been loaded half the time these last two months. Now I'm right up against it. Johnson has me measured for the high jump. I figure this is the last elevator I'll ever inspect. If I'm lucky, I'll get a scale job in Minneapolis. But the way he's been actin', I'll probably get the axe by the end of the month." Carson's eyes lost their steady gaze and there were traces of moisture at their corners.

Tom looked away and motioned to Kate for another round of drinks. "Cheer up, Joe! You never did anything wrong. All of the boys you've worked with will swear to that!"

"Tom, you don't know how big this thing is! The Feds are gonna look at everything, and I mean everything in the grain trade. There's even a chance that they'll pull some kind of audit on all the Federal License holders. Think what that would mean! How many times in the past couple of years have your books been out of joint? How many times have you sold—even a little—into stored grain? How many times have you watered grain when you've shipped it out? All of us are in for a big hassle, and lots of us are going to be out of work. And, for the really big freewheelers, maybe even jail!"

Tom stared at Carson. For the first time, he began to understand Joe's helpless feelings. Nobody could survive a comprehensive audit. There wasn't an elevator operator in all the Midwest who hadn't violated one or more of the many regulations. The ones who hadn't weren't in business anymore. But, Jesus! An audit! His thoughts pursued many avenues…none promising a path for escape.

"But, Joe, what if we get by this inspection? Won't that keep them off our backs?"

"All depends on the pressure the politicians bring on the bureaucrats to clean up the trade. I hope, for your sake, that this purge ends with us inspectors. If it don't, the whole grain business is in big trouble. Sure, there are some who really take advantage of the slippage in the system. But most of you are only trying to do a job for the farmers with little enough cash to buy and sell at the pace necessary in any big elevator. You are the guys we can't do without in this part of the country."

They fell silent. Alcohol was clearly affecting Carson. He grew sad and began to reminisce about his family and the problems they would have in accepting the loss of his job and the prospect of a move to another part of the country.

"Joe, I'll try to help in any way I can. Maybe I'd better get you back to the motel so Johnson doesn't have anything special to complain about."

He helped Carson to his feet and, for a moment, they looked into one another's eyes. Tom found there a depth of despair as one would expect to find in a person condemned, at the ragged edge of suspense and oblivion. In Carson's eyes, Tom saw a reflection of the empty fear that was his own constant companion. In that instant, he and Joe Carson were the only people alive, alone at the border between ordered society and empty cold.

BOOK 2

DAKOTA FERTILIZER COMPANY

CHAPTER SEVEN

Dakota Fertilizer Company

The evening with Joe Carson was a low point in Tom's climb out of the trading loss. The balance of the inspection had not gone badly. He was thankful that his books showed grain obligations that were covered by the storage records that Bob had altered. While Johnson had been adamant about the need to move purchased grain into the Elevator immediately, he had grudgingly admitted that Tom was 'long' and that he had more than enough grain to cover his obligations to farmers. This was a debt now owed to Bob. Without Bob's ability to bring in new accounts and to trade promises of spring fertilizer for immediate grain, he would never have passed the inspection and would likely have lost the Elevator's license, or at least had a probationary citation against it.

Now the problem had been pushed off into the future and its shape changed. Where he had been pressured to find additional grain, he now had to find fertilizer to back up promises made by Bob. Each time Tom brought this problem up to Bob, he received a confident assurance that there would be 'plenty enough' for everybody or that 'we'll have so much fertilizer that we won't have room for it'. After several of these conversations, he too began to feel that there might be a potential for solving his problems. Now everything hinged on Bob and his connections with the fertilizer trade.

Against this background, Tom made plans for himself and Janet to attend the Northwest Agri-Dealers Convention in Minneapolis early in February. This annual event was a gathering point for retail grain traders and for those who worked with them at the wholesale level. There he would meet with fertilizer suppliers and negotiate allotments the Elevator needed to meet its commitments. Thus, the convention promised its usual blend of business and fun. This year, though, the convention had a sense of finality about it. Either find new allotments of fertilizer, or face some legal actions from farmers whose deposits had already been spent and could not be recovered by spring.

The convention was also a reprieve. Drinking and socializing with other managers and suppliers would be an opportunity to forget the reality of his problem and to share in a sort of boisterous communion. Beginning with operators in Montana and picking up revelers as it ran, the Burlington Northern Railroad would send its special chartered train, an arrow of high spirits aimed at the Curtis Hotel in Minneapolis, convention headquarters.

The week before the convention was one of phone calls among elevator operators throughout the upper Midwest and Canada, making plans for celebration. Most of these conversations showed that operators were coming off a high resulting from the boom in grain prices. Only a few were like Tom, trying to overlook the past and seeking opportunity in spring and a new crop year.

"Hey, Cooper! You old sonofabitch!" This call from Marv Sorenson in Billings. "Remember last year? How the hell did you ever get back to Sheffield after we dumped you off the train in Fargo?"

Tom recalled. Yes, it had taken a day before he had felt well enough to drive home. He hoped that Janet's presence this year would avoid that sort of problem. "Guess I remember. Seems to me that was about as much a miracle as your gettin' back from Hennepin Avenue with your virginity!"

Laughs and obscenity on the phone. Sorenson was a jovial giant of a man whose appetite for whiskey and women was legendary among prairie grain people.

"Yep, me and my wife," Tom said, followed by groans from Sorenson, "will be waitin' for the train at Fargo. Let's get together in the bar car. I'd like to hear your views of the spring season shapin' up."

"Hey! Let's do that." Sorenson said. "I'd like to meet your wife. Ain't this goin' to be a hell of a spring? These high grain prices are settin' my farmers wild. I've already sold more fertilizer than I did the last two years put together."

"My folks are the same way," Tom replied, "but I'm goin' to have some problems findin' enough product to fill all the orders. Looks like the supply will be tight."

"That's so, but I've found quite a bit of stuff off the normal channel. Say, maybe you better buy a couple of drinks for Leach—he'll be on the train and he's done a couple of real favors for me already."

"How's that?" Tom asked.

"Old Jim, he got me a couple of carloads and I had already got all the allocation I had comin'. But, man! Did I have to pay through the nose for it!"

"What did you give?"

"You won't believe this, but I had to pay $250 a ton for 18-46-0!"

Tom whistled. "No shit! Why that's damn near a hundred dollars a ton more than the going price! Where you gonna sell that?"

"Well, I figure I could sell five or six more cars at that price. I'm gonna buy it if I can. Then, when it's time to settle up with farmers, I'll have to come up with an average price. That way, I can lose the high-priced stuff in the allocated material and my boys will have the fertilizer they want."

"Sounds fair." Tom thought for a moment. "Guess you're right. I'll have to talk with Leach on the train. Be seein' you in a couple of days. So long."

"See you," Sorenson replied. "I'll save a seat for you in the bar car!"

Other calls were repetitions of this theme. Managers were uniformly concerned with the upcoming fertilizer shortage and were talking about a two-price system. One price related to product allocated to each elevator by suppliers and another, higher price, for free-floating fertilizer waiting to be found by men like Jim Leach. As Tom listened to these conversations, he heard the name of Leach frequently. He was coming to be known as a person who could get the job done and not be limited by the red tape of fertilizer suppliers.

"Guess I better get next to Leach," Tom mused as he penciled his projections of fertilizer demand. "Yeah, I better talk to Jim."

On the day they were to take the train, he and Janet got up early to take Chrissy to stay with Helen for the week they would be in Minneapolis. Then, shortly before sunrise, they met Bob and his wife Doris at the Elevator. Bob, as usual, was a few minutes late and roared into the parking lot in a new Blazer with well-marked Desert Dog tires.

"Hey, Tom, Janet! Let's get goin'!" Bob's ruddy face beamed out the car window.

"Hi, Bob! Where did you get that rig? You want us to drive?"

"Nope. This trip's the first for this baby and we won't have to worry about gettin' caught in the snow." He pointed down to the craggy print of the wheels.

They climbed in and made the big step to the raised back seat of the Blazer. Janet and Doris greeted one another with some reserve. Doris was a good companion for Bob, flashy and loud at parties, bored and somewhat sullen at other times.

"No kiddin', Bob, when did you get this outfit?" Tom asked as they sped out of the yard.

"Just last night," Bob grinned. "Ain't this better than that old pickup?"

"Sure, but the pickup was brand-new last spring. You sure didn't need a new one."

"That's just what I told him," Doris whined. "He's always spendin' money and we don't put it into the house!"

"Don't worry, woman!" Bob trumpeted. "There's plenty more where this came from. I can't drum up new business for the Elevator by goin' round in an old truck. Got to have style!"

Miles passed and the conversation gradually diminished to infrequent comments about the scenery and an occasional exclamation about the features or cost of the Blazer. Finally, Janet and Doris began to doze. As the sun came through the side window, Doris's cheap perfume made Tom's eyes ache. He stared out of his window. Why couldn't he manage his own money at least as well as Bob? There was no way that he and Janet would be buying a new car for the next couple of years.

Bob broke into his reveries as if he had been talking aloud. "You know, Boss, you ought to get yourself one of these Blazers. Be a hell of a help when you're out in the country."

"You, bet. But I couldn't raise the cash for a down payment."

"Hell, there has to be a commission or two in the grain trade. There's always a few dollars floating around among the fertilizer boys."

"Never had the chance. All us grain buyers are poor."

"Well, we get some action in fertilizer and we'll both be able to live a little higher on the hog."

"What do you mean?"

"Oh, I been talkin' with Jim Leach and we got a couple of ideas we'd like to talk over with you. He'll be meetin' us on the train. Should be real interestin'."

Tom took up the thought. "Yeah, I talked to Sorenson over at Billings. He says that Leach got him some 18-46-0 at damn near double the market price."

"Figures." Bob was silent for a moment as he hauled the Blazer around a slow-moving truck. "That's the way it works. Some elevator had more than they could hold in storage and turned a neat profit."

"That so? But why didn't Farmhand take the profit?"

"Well, it's kind of complicated." Bob considered. "Here's how I see it. The elevators are all gettin' allocated fertilizer, right?"

"Right."

"Then…in order to sell that extra stuff, Farmhand would have to reallocate it and couldn't hardly charge more than the goin' rate for allocated product—or else we'd all be on their ass. They would just as soon see the elevator with the extra fertilizer sell it and not be bothered with the red tape of taking it back and finding another home. 'Specially if they don't make nothin' on it."

"But, Bob," Janet broke in, "what sets that high price? Isn't this just a kind of black market?"

She's right, Tom thought. God! I didn't know she was listening!

"Yeah," he asked, "isn't Janet right? Doesn't seem that there should be a higher price. That material should be passed along at cost to get the stuff to farmers who need it."

"You don't do that for nothin'," Bob grumbled, his neck getting red around his collar. "Somebody's gotta pay for freight and phone calls and for credit."

"Sure," Tom agreed, "but it doesn't cost double the price per ton to get those things done."

"Look at it this way. The elevator that ordered the fertilizer went out on a limb with a cash deposit. They got some right to a profit on their risk!" The Blazer was gradually accelerating as the argument developed.

"I suppose so, but $250 a ton seems awfully steep to me."

"I know Tom's right," Janet added. "There has to be a fair price without profiteering."

"Janet," Bob said with a sigh, "there's a lot you don't know about the fertilizer trade. See, there's an allocated price based on commitments the wholesalers made way last summer. This price is a lot lower than the goin' price on the world market. It's this last price, the world price, which has to be on the label for anything that ain't allocated."

"Maybe so," she said with just a trace of exasperation, "but I don't see how fertilizer allocated to one elevator gets to be world market stuff just by turning the car around and sending it out of town."

"Think of it this way," Bob turned to face her—the Blazer responded by darting off the side of the road.

Doris woke up. "Hey! Watch out! You tryin' to kill us?"

Bob wrenched the wheel and slowed the Blazer as it returned to the road. He drove for a bit, then resumed his education of Janet.

"Suppose you bought a farm last year on contract for deed. Say you paid $600 an acre for it. Now the guy that sold you the farm has to perform on that contract. But you turn around and sell the farm on the goin' market for, say, $800 an acre. How did the farm get to be worth that much more? It didn't even turn around—it just sat there!"

"Oh, Bob!" Janet exclaimed. "That's not right! Here we have some elevator people who are supposed to be helping farmers. They can do somebody a favor and lose nothing by sending fertilizer along. That's the right thing to do!"

Tom listened closely to the argument. While he could follow Bob's reasoning, it just didn't seem right. If elevators were in business for farmers—and wasn't that what the word 'co-op' meant?—maybe they should do something to hold down prices. The trouble was that he couldn't think of a single elevator manager who wouldn't jump at the chance to make extra dollars to improve his cash position.

The argument between Bob and Janet ranged back and forth. Occasionally, their voices rose and Doris stirred in her sleep—causing Bob to speak more softly. The longer he listened, the more convinced he was that Janet was right, but that Bob had a better grasp on the reality of trade and on the behavior of managers who would be buying and selling.

It was Tom who finally changed the subject and set it to rest by saying, "Well, it sure seems complicated, but I bet we can sort it out in a couple of hours with Jim Leach. Let's leave it be until we can get some expert advice."

Both Bob and Janet quickly agreed, each glad to derail the confrontation that had been building for the last fifty miles. A few more comments on the scenery and a half-hour of driving brought them to the outskirts of Fargo. Bob leaned over and shook Doris.

"C'mon, Momma! Here we are! Time to get yourself ready for the party special!"

"Dammit, Bob!" she exclaimed, then remembering their riders, "Oh, yeah, honey." She stretched, the stir of her movement sending eddies of perfume through the car.

Bob looked at his watch and pulled the Blazer to the curb in front of a Country Kitchen restaurant. "What say? It's about an hour to train time. Let's have some coffee and stretch. We'll be sittin' plenty long before we get to the Twin Cities."

Janet agreed, and the other two murmured assent.

As they got out of the back seat, Janet took Tom's arm and held him close. "Please, don't you get involved in any of these dealings," she whispered, looking up at him. "There will be trouble!"

"Don't worry, babe, there isn't much of a chance for us. We'll be lucky to get what we need for our farmers, let alone have some to sell to other elevators."

This assurance seemed to lighten the mood of everyone. Bob could sense an easing of tension and Doris immediately lost her anger with the arrival of coffee.

"What you girls gonna do in the Cities?" Bob asked.

"Oh, we'll do some shoppin'," Doris replied, "and get ourselves ready for parties in the evening."

"I'd like to buy some books and take some time to see what's new at the Walker." Janet said. "It isn't often that I get to see anything but flat ground."

Tom could sense another potential disagreement and turned the conversation to the train ride.

"Let's see. We get on in another half-hour, and we'll be gettin' into Minneapolis about seven tonight. That'll give us plenty of time to rest up before the opening meeting."

"Well, better get goin'," Bob said. "We have to get our suitcases checked before the train comes in."

They paid their bill and went out into a dazzling sunshine that strained their eyes after the dark of the restaurant. A short drive to the station got them there in time to make arrangements for baggage and tickets. While Bob and Doris checked their luggage, Tom walked with Janet out to the station platform.

"Are you going to visit your mother in Minneapolis?" he asked.

"Yes. I thought that you might get away from the convention for an evening and we could both go out to her house for dinner."

"Golly, honey, I don't know. A lot depends on how the meetings go. I have to be sure to see all the people I need to deal with this spring and…" His voice trailed off.

"I know that she makes you nervous, but she really wants to see you."

"Okay," he agreed. "You try to help me find the time and we'll see."

She took his arm again. "This convention sounds like an important one. Is there any way I could hear some of the arguments on the price issue? Bob was talking about decisions on the handling of unallocated fertilizer."

"Gosh! hon, I don't see how. No member's wife has ever been at any of the meetings. In fact, that lady who ran an elevator in Iowa made everybody real uncomfortable last year!"

Janet frowned and tightened her grip on his arm. "You must see how important these problems are to managers' wives. We all have a stake in your decisions and need to know the reasons for some of the directions the trade is taking."

"Hmmm…well, maybe… I can see what you mean. Let me kind of ask around. Maybe there's a way we can get you in." They walked to the end of the platform and retraced their steps. This was a new development. Janet was making a case for involvement in business decisions that had an impact on both of them. For him, her request only built greater tension between a normal family life and the bizarre pace of agribusiness.

When the Special rolled in, it looked like a long trailer court. Paint on the coaches told the story of the demise of rail as a major passenger carrier. Each coach had a different paint and a style harkening back to days when the Empire Builder was the lifeblood of prairie commerce. In those days, the giants of grain and investment used it for leisurely commuting between their Minneapolis offices and the country towns where their fortunes were being made. Now the train had an air of decay about it.

"Hey! Cooper!" Marv Sorenson called from a half-opened window in one of the rear coaches. "We got a seat for you! And who's the handsome gal with you? Bring her along—the party's waitin'!"

"Oh, Tom," Janet whispered, "they must already be drunk! Please don't you get involved in that!"

"No problem, Jan. I have a couple of business deals to discuss, then I'll be back at our seat and we can talk about visiting your mom."

They boarded the train and worked their way to an empty seat on the shady side of the car.

"Say, honey, what's in that basket?" He pointed to the hamper she had been guarding during their boarding.

"That's a surprise for you. When you get back from your meeting, I'll show you what it is."

"That'll bring me back in record time!" He leaned down and kissed her lightly on the cheek.

She pulled him, almost desperately, toward her. "Tom, I love you."

"Me, too, babe." And he turned to make his way to the bar car as the train accelerated out of Fargo. As he swayed through the partly-filled cars to the rear, he stopped from time to time to exchange a greeting or engage in a conversation concerning weather or trade with people he had met at other meetings. In the bar car, the volume of talk drowned out the click and rattle of the train. Through the haze of smoke, he could see Sorenson, Leach and Bob holding a table, drinks balanced against the movement of the car.

"How the hell did you get down here so fast?" he asked Bob.

"Nothin' to it! I made a beeline for the juice as soon as I dropped the old lady off!"

"Hi, Tom." Leach extended his hand. "Long time, no see."

"Hello, Jim. You talkin' business with this old whoremaster?" He took Sorenson's hand and roughly clapped him on the shoulder.

"Nothin' doin'," Sorenson replied. "We were just drinkin' your health before you got here. You're the one who can get this business under way."

They all laughed and Tom signaled the waiter for a drink. Sun was shaking spears of shadows of trackside telephone poles across the tiny table as the train gathered speed, leaving the outskirts of Fargo. Sorenson reached over and pulled a plastic shade across the window as their drinks arrived.

"Well, here's to Minneapolis! Watch out Hennepin Avenue!"

Bob chuckled and the others raised their glasses to this toast. Leach sat back in his chair. "Glad you two boys are here. We have a lot to talk about before we get to the Cities."

"That's so," agreed Tom. "I hope you can help us find enough fertilizer to meet what looks like double last year's demand."

"Hell! No problem with that!" Leach smiled. "I can slip you a few extra cars and nobody will know the difference."

"But won't that cut back on somebody's allocation?" Tom asked.

"Sure," Leach replied, "but one car here and there ain't goin' to make the fur fly when you look at how much fertilizer Farmhand handles."

"Glad to hear you say that," Sorenson said. "If you can get me a couple more cars of 18-46-0, I'll be your friend for life."

"Hell with that!" Leach exclaimed. "I don't want friendship, I want cash! Those cars will be on the way next week and they'll cost you another $50 a ton over the last ones!" His tone and the italics in his voice made it clear that there was no friendship in this deal.

"Fifty bucks!" Sorenson snorted. "Why, you old fart! That's robbery! What the hell will the farmers say when I try to average that kind of price into our charges?"

"I personally don't give a shit!" The grin widened on Leach's face. "They got to pay if they want the product. And, if they don't, there are plenty of farmers in Minnesota and Iowa who'd go another $25 above that to get the stuff for spring."

Bob leaned forward. "What I hear tells me that we'd better get our oar in if we want to get anything like a decent price and more product for our patrons. That right?"

"Yep. Give me the word now, and I can plan for a steady flow all through spring plantin'. And, if you back that up with a written order and deposit, I may even be able to hold the price against the run-up that's sure to come."

"I don't know about Tom." Bob paused, glanced at Tom over his glass and went on without waiting for a response, "But I know that we can sell about 600 tons of 18-46-0 over our allotment and another 500 tons of potash."

Tom almost dropped his drink. He stared at Bob. "What the hell you sayin'? Six hundred tons! My God! There's no way we could move that kind of volume!"

"Hell, Boss, don't worry. I'm bringin' in a couple dozen new customers and they're big boys who'll have to be treated right or they won't be back. I got to have the product to do it."

"I sure can understand that!" Sorenson grumbled. "I lost two or three of my best customers this month to that new outfit over to Havre just because I couldn't answer their demands right away."

Tom considered this reasoning. True, Bob had brought in several new patrons whose corn sales and money on deposit had to be taken into account. If they could expand business, maybe it would be good planning to lay in as much scarce material as they could.

"Ummm—yeah, that's right. Bob did come up with some new accounts. But how can you be sure that they want to take that amount of product at those prices?"

"That ain't how it works," Sorenson said. "Like I said, you don't give them the high price. Instead, you average out your price and then you charge all the farmers who buy it the average price per ton. That way, they all share in the added cost."

"But, Marv," he said, leaning forward and looking directly at Sorenson, "that ain't fair to farmers who have already booked orders at a lower price. You're cuttin' their throats to give some new boys a break!"

"No. That ain't the way to look at it," Sorenson answered—giving the table a light thumping with his huge fist. "There is a cost increase so you got to raise the price to everybody. And new customers make the co-op stronger so that old-timers ought to help bring them aboard. Takin' a piece of the fertilizer cost is the way to do it. Besides, if you spread, say $150 a ton for six hundred more tons across your total—which was what?…about twenty-four hundred tons?"

Tom nodded.

"Then you get a per ton increase of about, say, thirty seven dollars over the old price. When farmers hear some of these new prices, they'll thank God for old Tom Cooper who can hold costs down to less than forty bucks increase!"

"Yeah! Here's to old Tom Cooper, the farmer's friend!" Bob struck a pose of mock seriousness and he and Leach raised their glasses to the savior of farmers.

"Tom," Leach argued, "you got to see the point! There's goin' to be a hell of a demand for product this spring and the elevators who can deliver the goods are gonna corral a lot of grateful customers. And that can be a big plus when the goin' gets tough."

Tom nodded and reflected on how valuable several of these loyal farmers could have been in bailing him out of his overshipped position, had they been on board in January. "Suppose so," he said, "but how do we get this goin'? We haven't the cash to lock in an order now."

"Just write it up. I got my books along and we can sign up the tonnage when we get to the Cities."

"But I can't do that, Jim. I can't commit the Elevator to that kind of order without informing my Board. I'll be raising prices and they have to back me or there will be hell to pay!"

"Don't worry about that, Boss," Bob said earnestly. "You will be doin' them a favor and if you don't move now, there might not be any extra stuff to take advantage of. That right, Jim?"

"You bet!" Leach sat back in his chair, fingers hooking over his bulging waistline. "Got to have the orders this week. You boys don't want any, I can move all I can spare at the convention."

"Count me in for about four hundred ton more of 18-46-0," said Sorenson. "I have to take the plunge, and I'm sure you're right, Leach. The demand is out there and the sky's the limit on price!"

"Okay, Sorenson, you're on. Stop by my room at the Curtis and we'll do the paper work. How about you Sheffield boys?" He looked at Tom.

"Well," Tom mused, "maybe we can go along with a couple of hundred ton of 18-46-0. That's about it so far as our cash goes. What do you think, Bob?"

"Boss, I say take the whole six hundred ton and the potash and anything else Leach can spare. We can always move the stuff to other places where it'll be short. Maybe even into Minnesota and Iowa. Right, Jim?"

"Sure can," Leach fired back. "I don't care if you resell the stuff. Just meet our price and it's yours."

Tom took a deep breath and slowly exhaled. "Okay, if you think you can move it Bob, I guess we can go along. What are the terms, Jim?"

"Got to have cash in thirty days after invoice. We can do some jugglin' of shipment so you get the cars about when you're sellin' the product."

"That's pretty tight," Tom frowned. "Can you go forty-five days?"

"Well, maybe on a big order like that. So long as your credit's good. Can you give me a good line?"

"Sure. We'll have our overline from the Bank for Co-ops later this month and I'll be able to show a letter of credit for about eight hundred grand." He scribbled these numbers on his drink napkin.

"That's good enough for me." Leach said. "Say, how's about that truck drivin' fool? He ready to do some haulin' from the potash mines?"

"Hell, Star's always ready to roll—one way or another!" Bob raised his glass to the absent trucker. "He can move a couple of truckloads a week for us and maybe more. He said he'd like to put another rig on the road. One of our boys, Andy, got his license this month and could go to work right away."

"Hey, Bob!" Tom interrupted, frowning at the turn in the conversation. "I didn't know that Andy was thinkin' of leavin' the Elevator. When did he get that idea?"

"Oh, I been talkin' to him about his future and showin' him how he could be better off by drivin' than workin' on the house crew. Couple of years with Star and he could finance his own rig."

"Maybe he could, but I sure hate to lose him. Just got him where he could back up without steppin' on his tail."

They all chuckled at the image and a waiter brought another round of drinks, appearing as if by magic at a slight nod from Leach. "You just tell that Superstar that the haulin's definitely there and he can start soon as he's got some kind of company and credit rating that'll let him buy direct from the mines."

"What do you mean by that?" Tom asked. "I thought you were talkin' about him haulin' just for Farmhand."

"Hell no!" Leach responded. "Ain't no money in that! What he's got to do is get himself a little company and buy direct from the mines. Then he can get the whole profit himself!"

"But won't that cut Farmhand out?" Tom asked, frowning at the complexity of the scheme.

"Sure, but the main thing is to get the stuff to farmers. No reason why a big co-op has to get its cut on every ton." Leach peered at Tom over his glasses, like a gambler raising the ante.

"Maybe so," said Tom, "but where is Star goin' to get a company, much less the kind of credit he needs to buy any product?"

"I been thinkin' about that," Bob said. "Me and Sorenson here are ready to co-sign a note with Star to do the job. If we could get one more signature we'd have the credit to buy a couple of loads. With the profit on those sales, we could get enough to pay back the loan and Star would be on the way."

"I suppose I could go along with that. Be good to see Star get a leg up on that truckin' company he always talks about." Tom swirled his drink and sipped. "We can have a meeting with him when we get back. Maybe you can stop over a night, Marv?" He looked at Sorenson with the question.

"Sure, glad to help." The big man grinned. "Star's a good guy and he ought to be in charge of a bigger operation."

"Okay," Leach said, breaking into the discussion of these details. "You go ahead and set the thing up, but I got to get an order in this week or there won't be any potash available. I can't wait for no new company to get off the ground."

"Geez!" Bob exclaimed. "Ain't there no way you can hold the product? I know that Star's already talked to the bank at Sheffield and they'll go along with some credit."

"Maybe," said Leach, "the best way to do it is for you two elevator managers," he looked at Sorenson and Tom, "to give me an order for the stuff you think Star can sell—then you move it to him at a profit for your elevators when he gets his company goin'."

"Sounds okay to me," Sorenson agreed. "How about you, Tom? You can always use the stuff he can't sell. Seems like no risk to me."

"Sure. Well, at least I think so," Tom considered, rubbing his chin. "If I put the Elevator on the line for a couple of hundred ton, I got to be damned sure that there's a place where it can be sold if Star can't get his plan to work."

"I can guarantee that," Leach said. "I'll be talkin' to some Minnesota and Iowa boys this week and I can let them know that they can expect to hear from you or Star pretty quick. They'll be happy as hogs in the mash to know that there's gonna be some product and they'll snap it up damn quick!"

"Okay, then," Tom agreed, "I guess we can do it. Bob, you think Star's ready to go through with this? You talked to him. Do you think I'm goin' out on a limb?"

"No way," Bob said in a relieved tone. "We'll all … there's money to be made here and Star can smell it out. Besides with the three of us behind him, he can't lose!"

"Shit!" said Sorenson. "He's already got a name cooked up and the paint ordered for his trucks—Dakota Fertilizer Company—ain't that a bitch?"

The jokes flew from one to another as each found a way to draw comedy from Star's choice.

"Suppose he'll hook one of them John Deere shit spreaders on that Kenworth, and zowie! There goes Dakota Fertilizer!"

"He's got an edge on the competition, that's for sure. He can sling it better and farther than anybody I know."

"Imagine! A whole fleet of them Kenworths, each with a Star kind of guy in it. That'll keep the morals squads from every prairie town on the jump!"

Gradually levity diminished. Sorenson left to keep a dinner date. Leach and Bob turned their talk to details of the fertilizer market and new products that might turn up in spring. Tom listened closely for a while, but he couldn't concentrate. The swaying car and rapidly fading light as the train sped from prairie day into Minnesota night with its dots of light and blurs of towns created a psychedelic play of color that dulled his senses. Shortly after the train left Willmar, Tom got to his feet and unsteadily groped his way forward toward the car where Janet was waiting. He moved carefully so as not to upset his delicate balance. Each unpredicted lurch of the car over poorly set switch points cannoned him into a wall or table—"'scuse me," "sorry about that." Between cars, cold opened his nose and brought a sharp pain to his lungs after the heat of the bar car. He paused for a moment to restore his equilibrium and make ready for a bumbling passage through the coaches—hand over hand, in a swimming motion from one seat to the next.

When he finally reached their seat, he found that he had stayed too long. Curled in one corner, an open magazine pinned by a relaxed hand, Janet was fast asleep. Next to her, on his seat, was the picnic hamper carefully opened and stocked with his favorite wine, sausages, herring, crackers and all the things they used to celebrate with in the old days when they were alone and in love. Gulping back a wave of drunken emotion, he carefully closed the hamper and slid quietly into his seat.

The picture of Janet sleeping reminded him of other train trips. Years ago, when he was a small boy, he and his mother had traveled to the Cities by train from the small town where they lived. Then the train rolled along with its crew of adventurers on their way to unfamiliar territory. As they had traveled, night had come and gone and, in the early morning, they came to the city. There, the rush of the train was slowed by acres of ruin and decay that had to be crossed. The engine was no longer majestic, but apologetic in huffing its quiet way through disappointment—no adventure, no color, no image of the city as he had imagined. Only wreck, dirt and the smoke of industry.

Now Tom knew that he would find the same sight waiting for him on this approach to Minneapolis. First they would cross acres of splendor in the suburbs. Even though masked by darkness he would be able to imagine the refuse of unwanted homes and stores as they approach downtown. The city hiding decay from the freshness of the prairie.

Like the city, the outside shell of the train only hinted at the real condition inside. Now the fresh paint of an Amtrak logo covered worn-out upholstery and the smells of long-overused coaches, and the husk of the train enfolded people who were, in many ways, worn out by living and used up by the pace of business.

CHAPTER EIGHT

Night on the Town

The arrival of the Special at the Minneapolis Depot was an anticlimax for all travelers. They were almost an hour late and the station was virtually deserted—a large, echoing hall—cold from the comings and goings of the day. At this hour, janitors were busily herding small mounds of rubbish into manageable piles. The new arrivals, confused by the light and emptiness of the station, were gathered into little groups, each looking for leadership to move from the cold of the station to the comfort of a hotel. The late hour made this transition far from easy. No taxis were available and calls to local cab companies were met with offhand promises—'a cab has been dispatched'. These assurances did little to dispel the sense of frustration and confusion which was in marked contrast to the confident levity of their trip east.

Tom and Janet stood near their luggage, making small conversation with Doris, while Bob used his bulk and bluster to commandeer a taxi. Janet hunched her shoulders in her coat, her eyes barely emerging from the upturned collar. "What time is it?" she asked. "How long will it take for us to get to the Curtis?"

"If the goddamn train had been on time, we'd be partyin' already!" blurted Doris.

Tom half-turned, as if to shield Janet from Doris's rapidly cracking social veneer.

"Bob'll have a taxi in a few minutes," he promised.

"God! I sure hope so!" Doris snarled.

Tom and Janet moved off a little distance, as if stretching their legs, glad to be free of Doris's complaints.

"Honey, I'm sorry that I didn't get back for our party. There was just too much business to talk over and, when I was done, you were asleep."

"That's okay, but it always seems that way. We never get to be together like we used to. The Elevator is always standing between us."

"… I guess so, but what can we do? If I don't give it the time it needs, I'm not doing my job."

"Maybe that's the key," she stopped and looked up at him. "Maybe you should find something different where you can have time to be with us."

Tom looked at her, seeing the unspoken prayer in her eyes. God! Quit the job! There was no way he could do that. His job was a good one and could lead to some major opportunities with one of the grain companies. But Janet was right. There was no time for her and Chrissy. They were virtually strangers to him now. By the time he arrived home on a typical day, they were both asleep. And in the mornings, he was gone before they awoke. When he could find time to be with them, he was usually too tired to take any part in family activity. His home hours were for eating and sleeping—and not much of either. The idea that he was growing apart from his family sent a spear of loneliness through him. To lose contact with Janet and Chrissy would leave him at the brink of an empty existence of work, a feeling now accentuated by the cavern of the train station and the insecurity of his fellow travelers.

"Honey, you're right. But there's not a chance that I can change jobs now. Where would I go? I haven't been at the Elevator long enough to use the job as a stepping stone to something else."

"You can do any other kind of work you want to. You could come here to the Cities and get a normal trade job and we'd be happy for you."

She put her arm through his and hugged him. As he looked over her head, he felt the uncertainty that city competition always brought on. In Sheffield, he was in control of decisions that shaped his life—at least insofar as the Elevator gave him that freedom. In the city, he would be in constant competition with others. Confidence left him in a wave.

"That really wouldn't work. I would have to start at the bottom, and we'd never get back to the level we're at now. We'll have the farm mortgage down in another couple of years and we can start to live a little."

"But Tom, those are the years we can't afford to lose. Chrissy will be grown and gone before you can break away from the Elevator. Remember, the reason we bought the farm was to have a place where we could be a family in the way we wanted."

Lose Chrissy! He felt his throat tighten at the thought, a feeling of desperation. In that moment he knew that Janet had hit on the key issue. Time was a flow, like grain through the Elevator, and had to be shaped to each person's use—or it was gone forever.

It took a conscious effort for him to turn his thoughts back to Janet's questioning look. He had to find a way to reconcile these impossible demands before it was too late. "Honey, we have to figure out a way to get through the next couple of years," he said. "I'll try to cut down on the job enough so we can do things together. You can help me by reminding me when I'm not keeping my part of the bargain."

She frowned, biting her lip. "It's more than that. You're killing yourself with work. You don't take care of yourself. In the last year, you've been drunk at least two nights a week, and I smell liquor on you every night when you come home!"

Now the real issue was out in the open. Dammit! He wasn't a drunk—just a person who needed help with the everyday problems of doing his job. Anybody would drink if he was running the Elevator!

"No! That isn't right! I drink, sure. I have to do a little of that to keep up the business. But I've been drunk only a couple of times—just at parties…" His voice trailed off, knowing the lie, but resisting the acknowledgement.

"Tom, don't hurt yourself. You must see that, whatever it is, it's too much. Your eyes are always puffy and your feelings are so different. You don't even seem to love me anymore. You never hold me in bed and we haven't…" Her face collapsed in a swell of emotion that halted her speech.

He stopped, wanting to hold her and affirm the bond that had joined them over the years. Instead, he put his hands in his pockets, touching the bar car napkin on which he had noted Leach's fertilizer prices. His emotion turned off neatly, as with a switch. He looked over Janet's shoulder to see Bob—victorious!—beckoning from the station entrance.

"Hey! I got a cab!" Bob's announcement broke the tenuous thread of concern, and the shared knowledge of their common problem was lost.

The relief this brought for Tom was evident in his eager response. "That's great! It's about time!"

He moved toward the suitcases, almost at a trot, leaving Janet to stare at another slide in the downward course of their relationship. They collected luggage and wound their way through the envious travelers who hadn't yet found a means of escape from the terminal.

Outside the air was sharp with cold. Their cab was huddled under a white cloud of vapor, a minute envelope of heat in a city of chill. They forced their bags into the trunk under the uncaring eye of the driver and took their places in the vehicle, Bob beside the driver and Janet between Tom and Doris.

As they drove away, each stared ahead seeing nothing of the city, seeing only the result of the day's experience.

For Doris and Bob, this was a typical end to any party—one angered at the way things had developed, the other looking optimistically ahead to the next event.

Tom leaned his head against the curved window of the taxi, his mind alternately flooded with worry and relief. Janet's unexpected confrontation about his drinking was past. It left, however, a new load of care that tied the problems of work to the basic fabric of his personality. Was he really an alcoholic? Had he actually changed so much in the eyes of his family? *No! They just didn't understand!* He was no different from other elevator managers—everybody had to give part of his life to the job. And everybody needed a drink now and then to relax. Anyway, a few drinks didn't make you an alcoholic; they just lubricated the wheels of trade.

Now, let's see...tomorrow he could get on with building a base for a whole new look in Sheffield. A fertilizer and commodity service! That's it! His mind raced with the thrill of a new challenge and the heady drug of a problem solved.

Janet could not hide her disappointment and despair. These familiar emotions were beginning to wear thin—penetrated by a small puzzling question about the shape of the future. Her love for Tom and the memory of their relationship was as strong as ever, but it was taking on some of the same tone as the feeling young people have always had for their parents and their childhoods—a bittersweet foundation on which new emotions must be built.

Check-in at the Curtis was routine. They were processed along with other convention arrivals. "Mr. and Mrs. Cooper? You will be staying in room 1066. Three nights? Okay, please follow the bellhop; he'll show you to your room. Next please."

They fell obediently in step with their ancient bellhop and forced themselves into an already-crowded elevator cage. As the door closed, Tom was recognized by one of their fellow passengers.

"Cooper! By God! You prairie dogs finally got here! Where the hell you been?"

Tom looked awkwardly over his shoulder. "Uhhh ... Frank? Hey! Glad to see you! We just got in and had to wait for a cab at the station. What's goin' on?"

Frank Becker was well known for his convention skills. His was the suite where the wildest parties took place, yet he was always the first person to arrive at breakfast the next morning—eyes bright and optimism unbounded. Like Bob, he was an embodiment of the total integration of personality and agribusiness. Friendly waters without depth.

"We're havin' us a little seminar up to my room," Frank roared. "Better come along so we can catch up on the latest Dakota jokes." He laughed in anticipation of new twists in themes heard at countless conventions.

Tom responded. "Sure. Let me get settled and we'll be there." He glanced back at Frank as the elevator door opened for the tenth floor. "Where you at?"

"1230," Frank answered with a small shake of his head. The message was clear—wives were not welcome at this seminar. The door closed on the party-goers, but not before their conversation began again. "Who's the chick?" "Cooper's wife." "Oh, I thought he'd already scored!" The narrowing gap in the doors cut off the more off-color remarks that were likely to follow.

The bellhop sighed and grappled with the impossible combination of suitcases. "Follow me, folks." He led off to the right. A few doors down, they watched in silence as he turned the key in the door of 1066, reached in, turned on the light and led them into a bright, fresh sanctuary. "I'm sure you'll be very comfortable here. Is there anything I can bring you?"

Tom pressed a tip into the outstretched hand in exchange for the room key. "Nope, everything's fine. Thanks for your help."

When the door closed behind the bellhop, Janet sat on the bed and looked up into Tom's eyes. "Now what? Are you going to party with the boys, or will you be staying with me?"

The unexpected question caused him to hesitate between anger and puzzlement. "Jeez! What gave you that idea? I thought we'd relax a little and maybe go down for a cup of coffee."

"I'd love that." Janet's desire was clear in her voice. "But are you sure that's what you really want to do? The boys in the elevator sounded like they expected you to come to their party." She offered this alternative hesitantly, afraid that its temptation would be too much for him to reject.

He reflected on her question. Sure, he would like to meet with the boys in Frank's room. After all, that was the accepted thing to do on the first night of any convention. Besides, he might be able to get some ideas about the direction business would take in the spring. That made sense. He was here on business and had better tend to it.

"Gosh, honey, you may be right. Tell you what let's do. You order some coffee and rolls and I'll check in with Frank's group and be back here in a jiffy. Once I see what's on the docket for tomorrow, I can forget the convention for the rest of the night."

She looked at him in silence and her voice shook as she responded. "Don't go. We need to be together—more than ever. We need to work this out now."

He stood, arms hanging loosely, a preoccupied look on his face. This problem was too much for him at this moment; escape was easier than facing her concern. "Jan, you just don't understand. I've got to make the contacts I came for, and tonight is a part of the convention. If I don't show up, I may be cut out of a deal I can't afford to miss."

She stood up and stared at him, her arms folded. "Are those deals really more important than us? We are coming apart and you have to make an effort, or there's no telling where this might end."

"Aw, honey, it ain't so bad." He moved toward her and took her in his arms. Not gently, like a lover, but awkwardly like a stranger. He felt her stiffen at his touch—no soft response as always in the past, instead a reserve that shielded her emotions from the injuries of his rationalization. Her lack of response only made him more nervous and anxious to avoid the situation that was developing.

"Hey! Don't let's argue on our first day of vacation!"

His forced cheerfulness sounded artificial even to him—his real reactions were crying out in need. His throat constricted with the intensity of these emotions—they welled up in him, but could not find their way to expression. "Ummm…well…honey, guess I'd better be going if I don't want to be up all night. You give room service a call, and we'll have a little coffee party when I get back."

He released her and picked up the room key from the dresser. With his hand on the door knob, he looked back at her. She stood still, staring at him. Neither could speak. For different reasons, they were mute in the face of impending disaster—held immobile by the enormity of the alternative that had surfaced in this room. They looked over the rim of emptiness and drew back, appalled at the prospect of a future alone and apart.

He broke the silence. "Let's not get too excited about all this. You relax and I'll cut this short so we can talk."

His voice trailed off in the face of her silence. He shrugged and slipped through the door, closing her and the problem out of mind. Now, what the hell brought that on? He shook his head as he walked down the corridor toward the elevator. She was probably just tired from the trip. Nothing was bad enough to cause problems with their marriage.

He pressed the elevator button for 'up'. Let's see, Frank was in 1230. They probably had a hell of a party going already. God, but it would feel good to have a drink and relax.

The elevator arrived and Tom stepped into the empty car. As the door closed, he pressed the button for the twelfth floor. The instant he took his finger from the control panel, he became conscious of the emptiness lurking below the thin floor of the elevator cage. Nausea and cold fear swept him into another dimension, where his grip on the thin railings of the car was his only hold on reality. He stood poised for a plunge, supported on a flimsy trapdoor of technology designed to oppose the leveling force of gravity. The insignificance of his own personality in the face of these truths nearly drove him to his knees. He gritted his teeth and clamped his eyelids shut.

In his mind, he was a small boy again, sent to the top of his father's farm silo to help position the metal pipe that would convey cut forage from the ground over the silo rim. A partly rotted wooden ladder, nailed to the wall of the vertical chute, carried him to the top. At the end of the ladder, two planks were laid over the top of the empty silo, a pathway to the other side, where a rope for lifting the pipe was to be threaded through a pulley. He set out on the planks, moving on all fours toward the pulley. Midway across, he became aware of the empty pit below and of the pull of gravity that bowed the planks. He froze, motionless with vertigo, hands gripping the gently swaying planks, eyes riveted on the clouds moving across the window in front of him.

The soft warning bell signaling the twelfth floor brought Tom back from the past. He pushed himself from the corner of the cage and staggered through the opening door into the safety of the corridor. He sank gratefully onto one of the benches in the elevator alcove and hung his head while the vertigo slowly left him. As the minutes passed, he became aware of his surroundings and the noises of Frank's 'seminar' down the hall. He pushed himself to his feet and moved in the direction of the sound. At the open door to 1230, he was greeted by the familiar cries of agri-cronies.

"Cooper! You old fart!"

"Hey, Sheffield's here!"

"Set 'em up! Cooper's buyin'!"

Frank offered a more explicit invitation. "Here, Tom, let me pour you a double. You look like you could use it!"

He took a brimful glass from Frank's steady hand. With only a slight tremor, he raised it in salute and downed the contents. Wiping his lips on the sleeve of his shirt, he acknowledged the praise of the revelers for his undiminished prowess. The second drink was a pillar to hold onto as his fear receded into the background and he became increasingly attuned to people around him.

Marv Sorenson was there, in earnest conversation with Leach. Al Newsom, the manager at Grandview Co-op, stood next to Carrie Johns, the Cargill representative, guarding her from the approaches of other would-be suitors. In these glimpses, Tom felt at home among familiar faces, a circle of support that was superficial but ever-ready.

He drifted toward Sorenson and Leach and came into their conversation gradually.

"…then we could make it go?"

"Sure, no reason why not. All we need is the company to front for the trades."

Sorenson looked over Leach's shoulder. "Hi, Tom, how's it goin'? You get settled in?"

"No problem." He sipped at his drink and nodded at Leach. "You guys still talkin' business? Thought you got that done on the train."

Leach laughed. "Nope. There's just too much to worry about this season. Every time I get with elevator people, we get to talkin' about spring. A lot of us won't be around unless we understand how agriculture is changin' and find new ways to do business."

"That's pretty serious talk," said Sorenson. "You mean to tell me that it ain't goin' to be business as usual next spring?"

"Yer damn right! A lot of elevators will be losin' trade because they got their heads up their asses and can't see change when it's right in front of 'em!"

"What does that mean?" Tom asked.

"Just this." Leach pulled at his bottle of Miller Light. "Farmers will be wantin' fertilizer—remember my figures on the train? Well, them elevators that don't have the product will be out of it and the suppliers who have the guts to go out on a limb now will have all the business."

"Sure, you went over that before," Sorenson interjected, "but what's that got to do with us? You already got us to commit to extra product."

"Yeah, that's the point. You got the product and, suppose all your customers are satisfied and there's still fertilizer left in your bins. If you ain't got a way to sell that to new people, you ain't takin' advantage of the changes I'm talkin' about!"

Tom scowled, trying to follow the argument. "But, Jim, you just said that we already sold all our own people. Where are the new customers comin' from?"

"I'm talkin' about wholesale accounts. You move any surplus you got into wholesale channels, and you all of a sudden got access to big dollar markups in addition to high volume. That makes your elevator profitable and gives your patrons the dividends they need to stay in business."

The clear logic of this reasoning seemed, all at once, to clarify the web of transactions for Tom. He could not only supply his patrons at good prices, but he could also enlarge his base and tap a lucrative market that he had never even considered. All he had to do was convince his Board that the Elevator needed a wholesale division.

Tom exclaimed, "Why, that means that something like a truckin' firm—say, like Star's—could become a wholesale outlet for the Elevator and do my members a good turn!"

"You got it!" Leach exclaimed. "With a move like that, you've got the best of both worlds—guaranteed supply for your retail customers and the flexibility and profit of wholesale tradin'."

Sorenson agreed. "Now I see it, Jim. We got to think bigger if we're gonna stay on top of this thing."

Tom considered. "But, Jim, there's still the problem of allocation. Where's the surplus gonna come from? You said that you are gonna be all sold out and that there won't be any unallocated material available through Farmhand."

"That's right, as far as it goes. But some of you good customers can up your orders now—and, what you can't sell at retail is yours to do what you want with. There's also the stuff that gets lost in the system—remember, I told you about cars building up demurrage—they can be bought right and resold at wholesale, and can get the higher unallocated price."

Leach clutched Tom's arm and drew him to a cluster of chairs in the corner of the room. When they were seated, Tom returned to the problem Janet had identified.   "Sure, I remember, but I still can't get the idea of two prices straight. Why should the unallocated stuff bring a higher price? Seems it all ought to be the same."

"That's just supply and demand," Sorenson said. "Jim's right. There's gonna be a shortage, and elevators will pay what they have to in order to get the product. The wholesaler is just getting paid for taking the risks of ordering now and payin' interest on the money."

Leach reached over to bottles on a nearby dresser. "Well, I finally got it through your thick skulls. This calls for a drink! Here, Frank's buyin'!"

As he poured drinks around, Frank joined their circle, his arm possessively around Cargill Carrie. "Now, you boys stop swillin' my booze. What say we split this place and see the uptown lights?"

"Great idea!" boomed Sorenson, as he emptied his glass. Leach and Tom seconded the proposal, and they gathered at the door to put it into action.

Frank called to the others in the room. "Hey, you freeloaders! We're movin' this party uptown! Anybody stayin' here, be sure to turn out the lights and shut the door when the booze is gone!"

"Go ahead!"

"It's warm in here."

"Have one for me!"

"Watch out for them whores up on Hennepin Avenue!"

They gathered in the Curtis lobby and exploded through the hotel doors into Minneapolis. Their passage through its nightlife was a kaleidoscope of impressions for Tom: a distorted mix of reality, cold and alcohol that grew ever more confused as the night continued.

Their first stop, a mistaken venture into a gay bar, was a wake-up call as to the nature of city life. "Hey! What the hell kind of a place is this?" Sorenson frowned as they looked around their table.

"Holy shit!" Leach's jaw dropped. "These broads are really guys! We're with a bunch of queers!"

They guffawed at their ignorance and sat back to enjoy the unfamiliar spectacle as their drinks arrived. Tom was silent as he drank—the distorted love exhibited by the customers was a sobering counterpoint to his own experience. He thought for a moment of his promise to Janet. "Say, I forgot that I told the wife that I'd be right back. That was an hour ago. I'd better drink up and get goin'."

"Aw, Tom," Frank protested, "she'll understand. When she finds out that you been around all these fairies, she'll know that you were safe. Or will she?"

The laughter following this aside broke the spell of concern and Tom reentered the exchanges of the party. "Why, you old queer, did you see how that fat guy at the end of the bar was lookin' you over? We'd better get outta here or they'll have you up on stage!"

A few more remarks like these—delivered in whispers, with covert glances at the painted patrons—increased their uneasiness. Their drinks disappeared more rapidly than usual, and they left, crowding together toward the door, each not wanting to linger behind.

Once outdoors, their party mood returned and they plotted a course that would insure an adequate sample of city entertainment. Leach emerged as their leader. "Let's walk northwest. We can hit a couple of places and end up on Hennepin Avenue."

They voiced agreement at this proposal and set out with somewhat more care in selecting the next bar. With each stop, the talk grew more slurred and profane and Tom's impressions of his surroundings were only fleeting glimpses. At the fifth stop, only Sorenson and Leach remained with him, Carrie and Frank having disappeared somewhere along the way. Tom was very close to being sick and often left drinks unfinished; he was dimly aware of the effect of his behavior on his two companions.

"We better get this guy home Jim, or we're gonna have a problem on our hands."

Leach agreed. "Yep. Let's drink up and slip back to the Curtis—maybe Tom'll sober up on the way."

The journey back to the hotel was a nightmare for Tom. A light, freezing wind penetrated the superficial warmth of alcohol, and he shivered violently. Each curb was a trial of balance that could not be passed without help from Sorenson. Swift passage of cars and the glare of their lights were like fingernails drawn over the surface of his brain—irritations to the very core of consciousness.

Finally, he could no longer contain his nausea. He leaned against a parking meter and expelled the alcohol violently. Leach and Sorenson stood well back, waiting with some embarrassment for the problem to pass.

Now he was even colder. He could hardly walk, and both men had to support him for the last two blocks. Fortunately, the Curtis lobby was nearly empty and Tom's companions were able to get him into an elevator with no trouble. Once inside, they felt through his pockets for a room key. Then Sorenson remembered.

"Say, Jim, it just hit me. His wife is in his room. We better not wake her up with this guy. Let's take him to my room and we can pile him into the extra bed."

"Good idea, Marv. He's probably not done being sick. If we laid this on his wife, he'd be in big trouble tomorrow."

Tom heard these protests and thrashed around the elevator cage with unspoken thoughts driving in on him. He had to get home. Janet was waiting with coffee. He had promised he wouldn't be long, and they would talk about real important things. But none of his thoughts were able to overcome mute drunkenness, and the elevator passed the tenth floor.

Tom tried to reach the control panel as the number ten lit up, but his arms would not respond to his dim will. Their arrival at twelve was a replay of the lobby scene. Sorenson and Leach each took an arm and carried him around the corner to 1250. He stood outside his body, a disinterested observer watching his drunken self. He had been in this place many times in recent years, as if he were merely living in a body that had no value expect as a temporary home.

Inside Sorenson's room, they took off Tom's jacket and shoes and laid him on one of the two double beds. They covered him and then discussed his future.

"Let's leave him sleep it off." Sorenson looked down with pity in his gaze. "He sure had a load. Must have had something on his mind. Can't remember when I've seen him this drunk."

"Sure, Marv, but what are we gonna do about his wife? She's gotta be told."

Yes, please tell her. Don't leave me here! I've got to get back to her. We have to talk now, or it'll be too late! His mind formed the words, but none of these cries were audible to Leach and Sorenson—they only heard the labored breathing of his alcohol-soaked system.

"You know Marv, you can call her and she'll be up here in a flash. Then we'll really have fireworks. Better let things go. She'll know he's on the town, and everything will be okay in the morning."

"Well, maybe," Sorenson deliberated, "but I don't like leavin' her worry. Just don't seem right."

"Okay, tell you what. I'll go. You crawl into the sack and keep an eye on him and I'll give his wife a call when I get back to my room. Maybe I can smooth it over so that she doesn't get too upset."

"Sounds good," Sorenson agreed. "Tom's probably gonna be sick again and I can better be watchin' him than talkin' to his wife."

In his stupor, this solution satisfied Tom's conscience. The pressure to voice his concern diminished. He was aware of Sorenson's bedtime rituals and final turning out of the lights before he lapsed into a deep, drunken sleep. There was no sense of the passage of time before he was awakened by the insistent ringing of the bedside phone. The efforts of his mind were, however, futile. Finally Sorenson answered the phone, groggy with sleep.

"Yeah—hullo–who's this?"

The noises in the instrument were not intelligible to Tom. Nevertheless, he was conscious of the urgency they communicated. As he listened, Sorenson awakened fully and turned on the light near the phone.

"Yep, this is Marv Sorenson. Slow down! Who is this?" Again the receiver echoed with the caller's frantic pleas. "Sure, sure, Mrs. Cooper. He's here with me. Didn't Jim Leach call you to let you know that Tom was sick?"

Oh God! Why hadn't he gone back to Janet last night? Why hadn't Jim let her know where he was? *Please let me tell her how sorry I am.* All these protests went unsaid. Tom was a drunk without a voice.

"Gosh, I'm sorry about that, Mrs. Cooper. We just thought that Tom was too sick to bother you. He just had a little too much to drink, but he'll be fine in the morning."

Janet, Janet, can you hear me? I'll be alright and this will never happen again. Please don't be angry—don't give up on me. His mind-struggle was so violent that he stirred on the bed and gave audible groans of despair.

"Mrs. Cooper, please settle down! Tom's gonna be okay—you can depend on me to have him ready for breakfast in the morning."

Sorenson was speaking to a dead line. "God!" he muttered. "You wouldn't think she could be so mad. We only had a night on the town."

CHAPTER NINE

And That's a Promise!

"Tom! It's time to get up!" A voice penetrated the fog of drunkenness. "Tom! Tom! Can you hear me?" The voice went on—insistent, growing exasperated with his lack of response. His feeling of guilt caused him to turn in his sleep and to groan audibly. Then he slept again.

"Tom! Honey! It's almost five thirty and you've got to be at work by six. Remember, it's your first day and you don't want to be late! Tom? Tom?" This voice was sweeter, gentler, but pleading for an answer. It was, however, no less guilt-producing. This time he had the added weight of family responsibility pressing on him and he involuntarily struggled against the covers to try to get his feet to the floor—without success. Sleep came again.

These dreamthoughts continued, each with its own set of demands—followed by his failure, until the load of guilt was so great that he raised himself to consciousness and answered the most recent voice.

"Huh? Yeah? What is it? Who? What time..." He lifted his head and looked around the room, trying to place himself. He was alone.

Another bed showed that someone had slept there. Little shafts of sunlight were prying aside the blinds on the window, making the room a twilight of confusion for him. Where the hell was he? How had he gotten to this place? Where was Janet? He sat up in bed, noticing that he wore his clothes of the day before and that his jacket was hung carelessly over a chair near the television set. He reached up and turned on the bedside lamp, making the narrow confines of the room clear and bringing remembrance to the front of his mind. The night before! Jesus! He had been out on the town with Frank and the boys! He hadn't gotten back to Janet! She must still be waiting up for him—and what about the convention? What time was it? Shit! He had probably missed the opening conference and…his thoughts trailed off as he fumbled for the bedside clock. God! Eleven o'clock!

He tipped the phone off its cradle and swung his legs over the side of the bed. The sudden movement made his head swim. He sank back on the pillow and closed his eyes, holding the telephone tightly to his chest. As weakness passed, he stared up at the ceiling. Should he call Janet? What would he say? Maybe it would be better to go to their room and face her directly. These alternatives brought home the magnitude of the mess he was in—one that couldn't be resolved by any ready excuses. He had to face the facts—he was a drunk and unless he could do something about it, he was likely to lose both his family and his job.

He sighed, and, more carefully this time, slid his legs over the side of the bed and gradually sat upright. The waves of pain in his temples forced his head into his hands and his elbows to his knees. Pain, guilt and self-pity coursed through his mind, driving the last confusion of sleep away. He was caught in a net of his own making, a snare where any attempt to escape only held him tighter.

No, trying to fix the problem by phone wouldn't work. He had to face Janet, and, somehow, convince her that this was the last of his drunken failures.

He rose slowly to his feet, supporting himself on the edge of the dresser, and worked his way to the wall mirror. In it, he saw the consequences of his behavior—red blotches on his face, a stubble of beard and deep lines where the pillow had pressed its shape into his cheek.

He scowled at the apparition and looked down at his clothes. His trousers were stained with vomit and the odor of stale sweat and alcohol almost drove him to nausea again. What a mess—he certainly couldn't convince Janet of anything looking this way.

He staggered into the bathroom and splashed the small sink full of water. By holding his hands cupped, he soaked the caked sweat from his face and the crusted matter from the corners of his eyes. He began to recover his balance and the pain in his head subsided to a degree. He turned off the water and walked back into the room with a relatively steady tread.

Standing in the center of the room Tom surveyed the disorder, as the phone beeped accusingly at him from the floor. He bent to pick it up and was instantly struck with a shaft of pain behind his eyes. The stroke was so sharp that it drove him to his knees and he gripped his temples to hold his mind in place. He fumbled the phone to its cradle and carefully raised himself until he was seated on the edge of the bed with his head again in his hands, squeezing his eyes shut against the light of the bedside lamp.

He sat for several minutes. He thought of himself as others must see him—drunk, dirty and out of control. It was a picture he could not accept. How could he, Tom Cooper, sink this low? Good job, great family, strong friends—everything going for him. He rationalized. Everybody expects too much of you. They don't know how tough it is to carry the whole Elevator and all the customers on your back. Besides, everybody in this business had a drink or two. After all, drinking was the way you got to really know the people who counted.

This familiar voice had the unpleasant sound of whining, childish excuses. They just didn't stand up to any real examination of his condition.

He was coming around to the certainty that he was in serious trouble. Self-control was a myth that deserted him whenever problems or opportunities came his way. He spoke aloud to his ebbing confidence. "I got to get this thing licked. If I go ahead this way, I won't have a job to worry about. I won't have Janet or Chrissy. What can I do? Where's the way out? God! How can this be happening to me?"

The questions clamored for attention, each crowding on the previous and adding to his despair. He swiveled his body and lay back on the bed, arm folded over his eyes. Gradually quiet overcame his headache and he breathed more deeply until finally, he fell into a fitful sleep.

Sleep was only an extension of the debate within him. On one side, the arguments of guilt and conscience demanded changes in behavior. On the other came the litany of excuses. These fought for domination, causing him to toss and murmur as his body was pulled from one to the other.

"C'mon, Tom old buddy! Let's hit the VFW for a couple! We been beatin' this Elevator horse too hard lately."

"Listen, Tom you're supposed to be at Chrissy's school conference. She's counting on you."

"Give me a couple of bottles of Beam. I got some company comin' this weekend."

"You promised that you'd take us to the lake this weekend. Just the three of us. You promised!"

The phone abruptly ended this subconscious struggle. This time he reached out for it carefully and pulled it gingerly to his ear after the fourth ring.

"Hullo. Who's this?"

"Well, Goddamn! You finally up and around? This here's your roommate. How you doin'?"

"Umm, hi. Not too bad. What's goin' on down there?"

"Oh, not too much," Sorenson replied. "We just got done listenin' to somebody from USDA. Head up his ass, as usual. You comin' down?"

"Pretty soon. I got to check in with Janet first and get cleaned up. What time is it?"

"Little after one. We'll be goin' into the general meeting soon. Take your time; you won't be missin' anything."

Jesus! After one! This drunk was turning out to be one of the longest he'd been on recently.

"Say, Tom," Sorenson ventured into his silence, "let me send up a pot of coffee. That'll help you get the motor runnin'."

"God! Yes! That's just what I need. Hey—and thanks!"

He hung up the phone and sank back on the pillow. Now that was the kind of friend a guy ought to have. Covering for him at the convention and thinking enough of him to help him out. What would he do without people like Sorenson, and Bob too? He was probably taking care of the Elevator's interests at the meeting. No need to panic now. Better get things straightened out with Janet first.

The knock of the room service waiter drew him out of bed. The fragrance of hot coffee on the waiter's tray whetted Tom's hunger. He hadn't eaten since the snacks of last night, which hadn't stayed with him long enough to be of much value. When the waiter left, he lifted the silver cover on the tray—hot rolls! What a great guy, that Sorenson!

He wolfed the food, letting the flavor of fresh coffee drive the last taste of sickness from his mouth. As he finished, he paced deliberately around the room, finally letting in early afternoon sunlight by drawing the window blinds. Outside, the glare of a winter day was diminished by long shadows of the hotel falling like barriers across the freeway below. The press of cars waiting to enter 35W told him that the afternoon was getting on. He had better clean up and convince Janet of his determination to control himself.

He sat back on the bed, coffee in one hand, the phone wedged against his ear, and dialed their room number. The phone rang and rang.

"Must be out," he mumbled. "Good thing. Maybe I can get myself organized before she gets back."

He put the now empty cup on the tray and pulled the bed covers into some semblance of order before letting himself out into the hallway. Instead of using the elevator, he entered the stairwell and hurried down to the tenth floor. A quick glance through the fire door convinced him that no one could see him on ten. He scurried to his room and slipped through the door with a fluid motion.

Inside, everything was clean. Only his unopened suitcase showed that the room was occupied. Where was she? Her clothes should be hanging—he turned to the open closet. No clothes there and no makeup in the bathroom. Worried now, he looked around the room. An envelope with his name was propped up on the desk.

He ripped the seal on the letter and moved to the window to read its contents.

"Tom: I've gone out to Mother's. Please don't call me unless you are ready to deal with your problem. Janet".

No mention of love, no softening of the message. Just straight from the shoulder. If you can't sober up—don't bother to call.

Christ! Did he have a problem now! How was he going to convince her that he really was ready to give up alcohol and come back to their marriage? Was he ready? More importantly, was he able? The familiar uncertainty enveloped him and he felt the urge for a drink.

No! That wouldn't work. He had to halt the slide of their lives. It was up to him, and not Janet, to bring them back together. What if he couldn't do it?

He broke off the reverie—using his emerging resolve to force him to take the next step. First, he had to get presentable. Then he could call Janet and try to make amends for all the times when he had let her down. He strode to the shower, removing his soiled clothes on the way. As water cascaded over his head, the shame of yesterday drained away, replaced by a sense of purpose.

By the time he had finished his shower and was working on the stubble of beard in front of the bathroom mirror, he was humming to himself, confidence growing. He studied his face. Good! Already better! Just little circles under his eyes. His gaze followed the contours of his body and he tried to draw in the bulge of stomach that two years of partying had produced. "Uhhh," he grunted, "got to get this belly worked off. How the hell could I get so out of shape? Enough of this crap. I'll go on a diet and work with the boys in the yard and be in good shape by spring."

With this vow made, he dried himself and dressed in slacks, turtleneck and sport coat before sitting on the bed with the phone. He dialed and held the phone expectantly to his ear. After two rings, he heard his mother-in-law's voice.

"Hello, Esther Gunderson."

"Hi, Mom. This is Tom. Is Janet around?"

"Oh, Tom." She paused as if uncertain how to answer his question. "Yes, she's right here. Let me call her."

He waited, nervous as a teenager, running his free hand through his hair. Finally he heard her indrawn breath.

"Hello, Tom. Are you okay?"

"Honey… Honey, I'm…" He swallowed on the emotion and could not find the next words.

"Tom? Are you all right? Tom?"

Her anxiety came through to him as if she was standing in the room and he could picture her frown of concern and could almost feel her hand on his shoulder.

"Sure—sure, babe. I'm fine. Listen, I have to see you. You're right. This has got to stop and I'm ready to change. But I need to have you with me. I can't do it alone."

The words bumped together as he tried to show her the conviction he felt. Emotions made a mockery of the smooth presentation he had rehearsed moments ago. His voice trailed off.

"Tom, I know. And I want it to be right again, but this time it must work. We can't keep on trying without any hope of success. Do you really want to give up drinking?"

He took that question, which he had only now begun to face, and it brought back the eternal debate—endless and self-destroying. It isn't drinking, but only the load you have to carry. She doesn't understand. And, that's the problem—you've got to want to stop. You had better want to stop, because that's the only way to keep your family together. But, if she really wanted you to stop, she would offer to help. Maybe she doesn't care anymore.

He blurted his fear into the phone. "Honey, do you still love me? Enough to help me change my life back to what it was?"

"We can't go back, but I do love you for what you were. If you really want to try, I'm ready to help in any way I can."

Relief flooded over him. "Honey, please let me. Can I come over so we can talk about it?"

"Okay. Mom will be going out in an hour or so and we'll have the house to ourselves."

"Great! I'll get a cab and see you soon. Babe, I love you."

"Please come."

She hung up and he set the receiver on its cradle. A whole hour to wait! Although he had seen her only yesterday, and she had been a part of his life for fifteen years, he felt the emptiness of life without her—a bottomless pool of sorrow in which he could easily drown.

He stood up and paced the narrow corridor between bed and desk, his mind tossing up trial versions of the approach he would take. *Honey, I'm sorry and I'll never do it again…*Too superficial. Better to bring the problem out where they could deal with it. How about…*I know that I'm an alcoholic, or close to it, and I have to kick the booze or else.* That, too, wasn't right. Sure, it was true that he was hooked on drink, but the problem was bigger than him. It was a part of the life they had chosen and only together could they make their marriage a shield against the confusion outside.

I need you and I want you to need me. Together we're strong. I can't be anything without you and Chrissy. Please, let's try to be what we were—that's all I can ask. There, that was better. That was the way he really felt. He drank whenever he lost sight of their common strength and tried to handle the world by himself.

He made a cup of coffee using the Mr. Coffee provided by the Curtis and sat, staring at the movement of sun across the room. "It really started at Peavey." He spoke the thought aloud, the memory of days of travel and corporate expectations he was barely able to meet. Taking the Sheffield job was his attempt to return to the rural life he had known as a child.

Tom did not see the changes in agriculture clearly, but he sensed them as his life stood in counterpoint to that of his childhood. The everyday work of his parents' farm was always punctuated by meals and rest periods when they all gathered to discuss the day. Although none of these conversations stood out in memory, they nevertheless added together into a powerful contrast to the life he now led. At a moment, he could picture them clearly, seated around the old kitchen table, his father joking over some small happening at morning chores or his mother finding some beauty to share in the tracery of cloud or in the sweep of snow in their farmyard. The content of these conversations disappeared in the fog of time, but the unity they represented shone brightly out of the past.

He stood and moved to the hotel window. Holding the flimsy curtain, he experienced a sensation of suspension over an abyss of despair. For a long time he stood looking out of the window—turning the fabric of the curtain in his hands, considering the net he had woven around himself and his family. His job and his behavior had bound the three of them in a mesh that drew them closer in misery—where their efforts to escape or change only tied them tighter with bonds of anger and despair. This was no cloth of love; it was a cocoon of pain with no springtime of release in sight.

During their years in Sheffield, he had become a slave to circumstance, an important cog in the machine of agribusiness. Despite his importance, he was generally helpless in determining the course of his own life. Instead, he was battered by the swings of success and failure and totally owned by the business he was hired to manage. The change in him was easy to see from his new perspective. He had given up meaningful relationships for the quick pleasures of party. Promises to his family were always subject to change, depending on the demands of the Elevator. And, in a very substantial way, his personality had changed.

Before Sheffield, he had been a quiet, almost shy person, an individual whose sincerity was obvious in the attention he gave to friends and those who came to him for advice or for just casual conversation. When he came to the Elevator, he had a clear sense of purpose and could easily see the links between his values and his behavior. To his friends, he was known for the 'rightness' of his decisions and the concern he felt for those who would experience the consequences of his actions.

Now he was preoccupied. So much so, that he rarely heard anything but the economic content of conversation. Now people never came to him with personal concerns, and few really trusted his judgment when questions of right and wrong were at stake. He did not know these changes in detail; he only felt their impact on him and his family. It was obvious that he had changed and that the new Tom Cooper was ill-suited to maintaining the total oneness of family. Something had to change, and that something was him. His job. His behavior. His life.

But Janet had said they couldn't go back—shared confidence was gone and the kernel of love had to be nurtured to grow again. It had to be protected from the elements of life in Sheffield that would destroy it.

He dropped the curtain, letting it swing back to cover the day outside. Standing, he looked in the large desktop mirror and spoke to his reflection.

"Now you know what has to be done. Find a way. If she's with you, you can make it."

Tom sighed, straightened his clothes and left the room.

Once he reached the lobby level, he was immediately pulled into the flow of convention goers.

"Look! There's Cooper! How's she hangin' after last night?"

"Heard you really hung one on! That's the way to get somethin' out of this convention!"

He elbowed his way through the crowd, murmuring responses to the jibes. The lack of real concern in the comments of his associates was an impressive counterpoint to his own feelings. How could life be so empty? Why was there no real understanding among the businessmen he knew?

The chill of winter almost turned him back at the front door of the hotel, back to the warmth of the lobby. How easy it would be to stay here and let her come to him.

He took a deep breath and signaled for a taxi. The cab moved up and he dived into its heated environment.

"Where to, buddy?"

"Need to go out to the suburbs. On Eighty-fifth Street, west of Met Stadium."

"No problem at this time of day."

They moved off toward the freeway ramp and were soon southbound facing the afternoon sun. Tom turned his head to the east to lessen the glare and tried to ignore the dancing shadows cast by cars on freeway embankments.

"You in town for the convention?"

"Yep. Got in yesterday."

"Pretty active crowd you got. I been hauling party folks around town all last night. Well, I go off at four so I can get a break before it happens again."

"Yeah, I suppose so." Tom's brief answers gradually silenced the driver and they were soon westbound on Eighty-fifth.

"Right along here, driver. Stop at that brick house. The one with the pine tree on the lawn."

He paid the fare and stood, hesitant as the cab drove off. He reviewed approaches in his mind. Should he be sorry? Behave as if nothing had happened? Start over?

The house door opened and Janet called to him. "Tom! You came!" She ran down the walk and they hugged as if a long absence was finally over.

Holding tight to each other, they walked up to the house. Inside, Tom took off his jacket and turned to hold her close. "Jan. I'm so sorry. Please, I want to change and I'll do everything I can to make things better."

The rush of words was stemmed by her lips. She pressed tightly to him as if to weld them together. She spoke softly in his ear. "Let's not worry about what's past. Let's go on from here. We have to—for us and for Chrissy."

"We will. Oh, Jan…" He drew her to him, his hands pressing her hips against him.

Her response was immediate. She began to move against him. She murmured as her lips brushed his.

He hesitated. "Is your mom home? She'll…"

"She's gone for the rest of the day. Come!" She led him up the stairs; he followed the swing of her hips, stumbling, eager.

She pulled him into the room they had shared on their honeymoon, college posters still in place, the picture of him in his football uniform, their wedding picture and the little snapshot of them, grinning, mounted on plastic horses at Rapid City.

She moved away and began to undress deliberately in those direct, provocative moves that he could never resist. Her uncomplicated approach to sex was a compelling mystery to him.

As she bent to remove her pantyhose, he marveled at her never-ending youth. Her breasts were firm, upright as they had been fifteen years ago. And, as she straightened, she drew her stomach in tightly, accenting the loveliness of her form.

They kissed, straining against one another, his hands roving over her body. Finally, she pulled away and lay on the bed one leg straight, the other folded beneath her knee. She looked directly into his eyes.

He struggled out of his clothes. Conscious of his extra weight, he moved to the bed and knelt over her. As they came together, he rolled her on top of him. She pressed herself to him, moving slowly, then faster.

When the rush of their passion had passed, she pillowed her head on his shoulder and held him with both arms. For a long time they were silent.

She brushed his hair back from his forehead. "It's been so long. How I've needed you!"

"Me too, honey. How could I have let all this happen? It just can't be…"

She kissed him urgently. "Stop it! All that is past. Now we can start over and make things even better than they were."

"God! I surely hope so. I'll do everything I can to make it work. And that's a promise!"

CHAPTER TEN

Lay, Goose! Lay

Tom's promise made the convention irrelevant. There was no point in staying on in Minneapolis. He made arrangements for their return to Fargo and for Pete and Helen to meet them. The return to Sheffield was like their first days that spring three years ago; they were filled with a sense of shared opportunity. Their hours on the train were a blur of conversation, plans and laughter.

They could see the results of their resolve when they arrived in Fargo. Chrissy stood on the station platform, holding tightly to Helen's hand, uncertainty evident in her posture. As Tom and Janet stepped out of the railcar, Chrissy's eyes opened wide and she smiled. She ran to them, throwing herself into their arms.

Pete's car was parked next to the station platform and he loaded suitcases into its trunk. He slid into the driver's seat and looked expectantly at Tom. "C'mon, climb in and we'll get goin'."

Tom hesitated. Then he took Chrissy's hand. "Guess I'll ride in back with Jan and Chrissy. Here Helen, you sit up front with Pete."

Breaking the prairie pattern of 'men in front, women and children in back' puzzled Pete. His attempts at engaging Tom in a discussion of Elevator business were limited by this arrangement and he soon gave up.

Rear seat conversation was monopolized by Chrissy. "Mom, you'll have to read the neat story Helen helped me write! It's all about growing up on the prairie. I made our place just like the Little House on the Prairie!"

"That's great," Janet said. "When we get home, you can read the books Dad gave me at Christmas."

'Yeah," Tom added. "We can all sit round the Franklin tonight and you can read to us."

"Oh, Dad!" Chrissy laid her head on Tom's shoulder. "That would be great!"

When they pulled into the Elevator parking lot, Pete said. "Want to come into the office? There's a lot of stuff you should look at. Helen can run Jan and Chrissy out to your place."

"Nope," Tom replied. "We'll move on home. Plenty of time to get back to business tomorrow." He transferred their luggage to the Fury while Jan and Chrissy climbed in.

As they drove out of the parking lot, Janet took his hand. "That was just the right thing to do. Let's go home."

"Right!" Chrissy exclaimed. "We need to feed the cats and…"

Tom laughed. "Take it easy! I'll give you a hand. Maybe that old three-legged tomcat is back for a visit."

That evening around the Franklin stove was another Christmas. Chrissy's reading of *Little House* held Tom's attention and he responded to her interpretation of the story with references to their house and its prairie.

At the end of the evening, they watched the fire die and Chrissy fell asleep on the basement couch. Tom lifted her and carried her upstairs as he had done when she was a child. "Sleep well, honey," he murmured as he tucked her into her bed.

Peace remained his companion throughout most of the night. It wasn't until four a.m. that he awoke, sweating and anxious. What was he to do in order to balance family and Elevator? How could he replace the grain that had been shipped? Where was the cash to be found that could pay for it? These questions were too much for Tom. He arose and dressed in his work clothes.

In the kitchen, he filled the coffee maker, positioned the paper filter and added coffee grounds. While he waited for the brew, he peered out of the kitchen window. The night was totally dark and all he saw was his worried face—staring back at him.

"Gotta get this thing solved," he whispered to the image in the window. "Can't take time away from home. Better be the first one on the job." He swiveled, poured a cup of coffee and drank it off with a gesture of finality.

The note he left summarized his decision. "Thought I'd better go to work early. If the Ford won't start and you need the Fury, give me a call. Will be home about 6. Love, T".

Janet awoke at the sound of the outside door. "Tom? What…..?" She stood and looked out the bedroom window. The lights of the Fury swept over the snowy yard as the car turned to leave. She ran down the stairway only to see Tom's final turn onto the township road.

Then she saw his note. *Would he keep his promise?* She poured a cup of coffee and hugged herself as she drank. *Would he keep his promise?*

Tom's promise was also on his mind as he drove down Highway 13. It had to be kept. The Elevator would have to take second place to his family. That was all there was to it. He coasted through the deserted streets of Sheffield and turned into the Elevator parking lot.

"Nobody here. Good. Maybe I can figure a way out of this mess." Tom switched off lights and engine and climbed the steps to the Elevator office. Inside, everything was in its familiar place. The few chairs for customers were against an outside wall. The counter had its customary layer of dust and advertisements. Yesterday's coffee was a brown crust at the bottom of a still-heated pot.

He sighed as he looked at his desk. Just as it had been left five days ago. Yellow pads with impossible figures scrawled at random angles. Stacks of "While You Were Out" demands for call backs. And a weight of responsibility. He sat at his desk and sighed again.

Tom studied the notes he had made prior to the convention. Then he recalled his conversation with Jim Leach on the train. Fertilizer could be the way out. The shortage and the two-price system seemed made to order for him. If he could shape product flow to his sales, he just might make enough to cover all the December loss, and build a new line of business in the process. However, juggling fertilizer was not as simple as grain trading. He could not insert himself into the fertilizer system with a few phone calls. Instead, he had to re-enter the social exchanges of Bob, Leach and Sorenson.

Supply, orders and cash churned in his mind. Yellow pads were filled and discarded as he waded through the complex balance of fertilizer and grain. At seven a.m., Bob burst through the office door.

"Hey, Boss! Where the hell did you go in Minneapolis? Anything wrong back home?"

"Hi Bob." Tom looked up from his desk. "Come on in and close the door."

They stepped into the inner office and Bob sat in the extra chair.

"Bob, you know how smashed I got in Minneapolis…"

"I'll say!" Bob grinned. "You were so far gone I thought you'd never get back!"

"I'm serious! I got to quit drinking and tend to my family—and to this business. I hope I can count on you to help."

Bob stared at him. "Jesus! You got to be kiddin'. Hell, a little partyin' never hurt nobody!"

"It's hurting me. If I don't lick this, my family's going to leave me."

"Damn! You're serious! Take it from me, it ain't easy to quit cold turkey."

"I know, but there's no other way. I'm just not tending to business, and I got to lick this by spring or quit my job."

"Now, don't talk like that." Bob twisted his cap and leaned forward. "We need you here. There's no way we can run this place without you in the driver's seat!"

"Thanks. I'd like to think that's the way it is. But I know better. The place has been running in spite of me these past few months. Now I got to take hold of it and shape it up."

"Sure, but what's that mean? You ain't changin' any of the plans we made, are you?"

Tom considered the question. No, he didn't want to withdraw from the deals they had identified in Minneapolis. He simply wanted to put them in their proper perspective—and to get them under control as manager in charge, not as a drunken victim. "No. I think we're on the right track with the idea of increasing our fertilizer trade. There's no other kind of business that would give the Elevator anything like the profit margin in fertilizer."

"Sure, but you don't owe the Elevator the rest of your life. Remember, we want to build a business that can carry us both in the future."

Tom frowned. "That's what we said on the train. But now it's the Elevator first and any other business second. After all, that's what I'm being paid for."

"Maybe, but I sure ain't gonna bust my ass for this place forever." Bob leaned back and lit a cigarette. "I got to think about the future and my wife. We can't get by on what I make here."

"That's so. And I've got your salary increase up for the annual meeting. The Elevator can't afford to lose you. You've made the difference between red and black ink this year. Especially after the corn disaster, and I haven't forgotten that."

"But, Boss, you gotta understand where I'm comin' from. Even if you don't come along, I've gotta get a piece of this fertilizer action. I'll never get another chance."

Tom toyed with his pencil. This was a tough call. He could see Bob's point. Overwork with no bonus or salary increases would be a poor combination to hold a person with Bob's sales ability. But the Elevator had some legitimate claims on Bob and he would have to watch this closely to make it work to the advantage of both.

"Well, maybe you're right. This could be the time when we try to work a special deal for you. Maybe some free time to work your own business, but we got to be sure that the Elevator comes first."

"Shit, that ain't no answer." Bob waved his hands. "Without the Elevator directly in line, there's no way I can get my hands on any product."

As that analysis penetrated Tom's thinking, he saw the flaw in the plan outlined by Jim Leach on the train. "If that's so, there's no way I can let product pass through here without the Elevator taking the profit."

Bob stubbed out his cigarette in Tom's ashtray. "Sure, sure. The Elevator's gotta come first. But remember how the tax men were goin' after you and the Board last year about your tax exempt status?"

The interview with the Internal Revenue Service was easy to recall. Too much profit on the bottom line and the Elevator would be taxed just like any other corporation. No longer would it enjoy the tax advantages accorded the co-operatives that apportioned their earnings to members.

"Yeah, I remember. But what's that got to do with this fertilizer idea?"

"Just this." Bob moved his bulk forward on his chair, his frown intensifying. "You make too much on fertilizer and there's more than a little chance that you'll lose the exemption. Then where would you stand with the Board?"

"That's true. Maybe what we ought to do is order just what we can sell to our patrons and forget the rest. That way we'd…"

"No! No! No!" Bob exploded. "This is the opportunity of a lifetime and we can't afford to let it get by! We gotta move fast and…" His voice trailed off, the argument dragging itself down of its own weight.

They were getting nowhere with this discussion. There was a basic conflict of interest here, one that would take a lot of thinking to resolve.

"Maybe so, Bob, but right now I'm leaning toward cutting business to serve only our own people and any new accounts you can bring in. That's enough to get rid of our red ink."

Bob stood up and growled. "Think it over, Boss. You don't owe this place nothin'." He moved to leave the office, his hand on the doorknob. "Tell you what. I'll have Leach give you a call. Maybe he's got the answers to your questions. After all, he sees hundreds of elevator managers just like you. He would be sure to know some with your problem."

"That's a good idea. Let's try to take care of it this week, though."

Bob nodded and pulled the door closed behind him, shutting the problem in the office with Tom.

It wasn't a problem that could be put off very long, however. Phone calls from customers later that day made this evident to him.

"Hello, Farmers Elevator. Tom speaking."

"Tom, this is Gerry Ryan. Remember me?"

"You bet! How could I forget that big corn sale? How's she goin' up there? Ready for spring?"

"That's what I'm callin' about," Ryan responded. "We're tryin' to line up fertilizer for a couple of farms we just rented. Can't seem to get a corner on product anywhere. Thought I'd call to see if you can help."

"Maybe. It's awful tight here, but I've got a line on some extra cars. What you got in mind?"

Ryan considered. Tom could hear uncertainty in Ryan's voice as he made an impossible demand.

"Well, Tom, we'll need about two hundred ton of 9-23-30 and one hundred fifty ton of N."

The numbers actually made Tom speechless for a moment. "God! What you plantin' up there, the whole county?"

Ryan laughed. "Nope, not really. But we got these farms from another operator and there's about two thousand acres in the package, and we can't up our allotment at Grandview."

"Gerry, I'll be straight with you. I don't have that much extra. I'd have to go into the high-priced market to get it."

"Tom, we committed ourselves to this ground and I'd pay a premium to fertilize it right. What you talkin' for price?"

Tom did a quick calculation based on the markups Leach had described. When he quoted the figures to Ryan, the response was an indrawn breath on the other end of the line.

"Holy shit! That's damn near double last year's price! But I got no choice. Put me down for the two hundred ton of 9-23 and I'll get back to you on the N. When will you know for sure?"

When would he know? It had better be damn quick! These demands were real and farmers had to know the answers to them.

"Gerry, I'll call you just as soon as I can. By the middle of next week at the latest."

"Okay, but don't forget. We're really up the creek on these farms."

He hung up and added Ryan's demands to those already penciled in a small pocket notebook. When he added Bob's estimates of new customer needs, the Elevator was committed for all of the tonnage he had ordered from Leach. If these sales remained firm, the Elevator would turn a neat profit, and make some new friends among local farmers. The potential increase in business of all types would insure that the Elevator would have the customers needed to weather storms of future shortages and price fluctuations.

When he closed the office at six o'clock, thoughts of fertilizer accompanied him on his drive home. Fertilizer demand gave him confidence in the Elevator's financial strength, but it was also a source of growing concern. What if the new orders didn't come through? What if Leach had given up on him after Minneapolis?

He remained preoccupied with fertilizer through dinner and only mumbled incoherent answers to Janet's attempt to start a family conversation. After dinner, Tom sat with Chrissy staring at a television program. There was no *Little House on the Prairie* reading that evening. Nor in the next nights. Although he kept his promise and returned home every evening, Janet and Chrissy did not see the person they hoped for.

Another week went by with no confirmation of the order he had mailed to Farmhand. It was as if the giant co-op hadn't opened their mail. The lack of response began to get on his nerves and he finally called Leach to trace his order.

"Hello, Jim? Tom Cooper. How are things going?"

"Fair to horseshit! Where the hell have you been? I ain't heard nothin' from you since the convention!"

Tom caught his breath—hadn't heard? What did that mean? What about…

Leach went on. "Where's your order? And the cash? I can't hold the product forever you know."

God! No order! And all those farmers counting on his word. "But, Jim, I mailed the confirmation and our check over two weeks ago! That's what I'm calling about. We haven't heard from Farmhand since!"

"What do you mean, you mailed the order?" Leach shouted. "Where did you send it?"

"Why, I sent it to Fertilizer Supply, same as usual."

"Jesus Christ! That order should have come to me personally. Supply will think you're crazy! They haven't any stuff that isn't already allocated!"

"But, I thought…" Tom faltered, at a loss for words.

"Shit! You weren't thinkin' at all. Now you stay by that phone and I'll try to intercept that order."

The line went dead and Tom hung up. He swiveled his chair to look out the office window across the Elevator yard. Already the winter snow banks were shrinking, their size a promise of the imminence of spring, and a warning of the beginning of the race to sow the prairie.

What was Leach talking about? Why didn't his order follow the normal channels? Was his order too late? Jesus! The farmers! Gerry Ryan! If he had to back down on his promises…

Thoughts tumbled through his mind, lurches of concern that paralleled the erratic progress Andy was making across the slush of the yard, a bag of seed on his shoulder. A tentative step forward—*maybe the fertilizer would come through*—a slip—*but maybe it was all committed to other elevators*—then a steadying step—*Leach would help him out*—the weight of the sack shifted—*but more farmers were calling each day*—progress stopped to restore balance—*after all, he was doing his best.*

These ramblings were arrested by the telephone. He reached for it quickly.

"Farmers Elevator. Tom speaking."

"Okay, Cooper. Now listen to what you got to do." Leach's anger was evident in each word, grudgingly given—almost like a stream of curses.

"The fertilizer boys had your order on top of the desk and were gonna talk to Jessup about it. If I hadn't got to it, we'd be up shit creek! And I don't mean just without fertilizer! I been cuttin' some of the allocation procedures to supply you and some of our other good customers. And it boils down to this. If you want the product, you'll do it my way!"

Tom cut in as Leach paused for breath. "Okay. Okay, Jim. Calm down. Just what do I have to do to make this work?"

"Cut me a new order today for the number of tons of each analysis you think you can move. Be sure to check with Bob to find out what he's got committed. Then send me a check for the total on the price scale we agreed on."

"That kind of money's hard to come by. Can't we be carried on a thirty day account?"

"Nothin' doin'! This has to be cash on the barrel head. You'll have to collect from your buyers or float this on your own account. Be sure the check is in the mail!"

Leach hung up and Tom replaced his phone. Why would it make any difference how the order was processed at Farmhand? And why cash with the order? Well, maybe the shortage was changing lots of old ways in the trade.

He wheeled his chair to Helen's desk and flicked on the switch for the yard intercom. "Hey, Bob, you out there? C'mon in for a minute."

Back at his desk he turned pages in his fertilizer notebook and added the totals of orders he had from farmers. God! He had firm orders for twenty five hundred ton more than he had sold last year! That added up to a lot of customers who would be on his neck if he didn't deliver—a lot of customers who would be going to another elevator with their business. But the money! Where was that going to come from?

Getting up from his chair, he walked into Stub's cubby. "Say, Stub, what's the status of our cash on hand? I got to get some money to Farmhand this week."

Stub opened the Cash Journal and ran his fingers down the column of entries. "Well, right now we have about $250,000 in the bank. But we owe right around $200,000 of that to farmers for delivered grain."

"Better hold on writing any grain checks for now. We can pay the farmers as soon as we move some fertilizer."

"Okay, Tom, but some of these guys are countin' on those checks to cover their planting expenses."

"Don't worry," he said, turning away from the accusation, "they'll get their money. We only need coverage for a few days."

As he was striding back to his office, Bob bounced in from the yard. "Hi, Boss, what's up?"

"C'mon in and close the door."

When Bob was seated across from him, Tom recounted his conversation with Leach. "Just what does this mean? Is Leach cuttin' some corners that will get us in trouble?"

"Naw—no problem. It's just that the allocation procedures at Farmhand can't keep up with the two-price market. We're lucky he's sittin' in the right place to help us out."

"Well, I sure hope you're right. I'll have to dip into our cash pretty far to cover these orders. And that's money we owe to farmers for grain we already sold."

"Hell, there ain't one of those boys who would squawk at waitin' a few weeks for their money knowin' that you're usin' it to get them the product."

Tom leaned back in his chair and clamped his pencil between his teeth. He was silent as he studied the figures he had scratched on the desk pad. Then he leaned forward and, taking the pencil in hand, underlined the totals he had written earlier.

"If I figure this right, we're goin' to move about three times the product we sold last year. Most of that's new business. But if all the orders we've placed with Leach come through, we'll be up to our ass in fertilizer. What'll we do with all that stuff?"

Bob stood up and paced the office, waving his arms as though to help the fertilizer on its way.

"Don't you worry about that. Every elevator in the Dakotas is cryin' for product. Hell, I can move three, four carloads a day. Only thing we've got to be careful of is to balance our sales so we don't make too much profit."

"Yeah. That's what you said before. If we show too much black ink, the IRS will be wonderin' about our tax status."

"You bet, Boss. Just last week I sold a carload of 18-46-0 to Pine Creek Co-op and made a hundred dollars a ton!"

"A hundred a ton!" Tom exclaimed. "Jesus Christ! That's almost ten grand a car! We can't sell at that kind of profit. It just ain't right. And we'll be in deep shit with the feds if we run that through our books!"

"You still don't get the picture. Look, if we were short on product, we'd pay what we had to in order to satisfy our customers. And they'd ante up and be damn glad to get the stuff. That's the way the two-price system works. The ones that are short get to pay."

Tom frowned, the logic still confusing him. "But what about our tax status? We've got the product coming and we can't use it all. How can we pass it on then?"

"There's only one way. We got to find wholesalers who can give us a good profit and let them handle the deal. That way, we provide the service and make enough to be well in the black on our fertilizer division."

"I suppose so." Tom looked across the yard. "But that means that you have to find some solid accounts who can finance some pretty big purchases. Can you get the job done?"

"No sweat," Bob beamed. "People like Star will be happy to help us out. Shit, he can take the bulk of our surplus!"

"Star? Has he got the money to handle this kind of deal?"

"You bet!" Bob grinned. "I been workin' with him and he's leased two more trucks and got the bank in Grandview behind him. Don't worry, he'll be able to take the product off our hands."

Bob paced excitedly around the office as if to take a run at an obstacle. Then, abruptly he stopped and leaned against the opposite side of Tom's desk, his face shiny with sweat and eagerness.

"Boss, this is a hell of a deal for all of us. We got the chance to help out the Elevator and put together a wholesale business that'll work hand in glove with us."

Tom looked at Bob, puzzled by the plan. "I see how Star can work with us, sure. But what's that got to do with us? We have our jobs to do."

"That's just it," Bob agreed. "You and me carry this Elevator and we make a livin', no more. This opportunity is a once in a lifetime chance to build a real business where we can call the shots! Remember last year when you wanted to quit? When the Board wouldn't go the big line of credit?"

Tom rested his chin in his hand, elbow on the desk. Yeah, that had been a big disappointment. The chance to make the Elevator a really significant business was bungled by conservative farmers on his Board. He had been ready to quit. Maybe he *should* be running his own business.

"That's easy to say, Bob, but I don't see how we can benefit from Star's company. We can't be part of that and still hold our jobs."

"Not directly," Bob agreed. "The thing we can do, though, is to get on his Board of Directors and set us up a place to land when we decide to get outta this place."

Tom considered this proposal. Wouldn't that just be good planning? After all, he didn't have any savings or another business to fall back on. Then too, the Elevator would profit by having a wholesaler it could work with—especially this year.

"Maybe you're right, Bob. But this is just wishful thinking. Star probably has his business all set up the way he wants it and we'd just be extra baggage for him to carry."

"Nope! It's just the opposite! He's got to have some outside directors in order to set up long-term credit with the bank. In fact, I've got the papers out in my Blazer!"

He wheeled toward the door and Tom could see him lumbering across the Elevator yard toward his vehicle. He had never seen Bob move so fast; the slam of the outside door on his return made Tom wince.

"Here's the whole thing!" Bob held a flat, oblong cardboard box. While Tom watched, Bob drew out a book with black binding and the gold lettering "Dakota Fertilizer Company" etched on its cover. "Ain't she pretty? This here's the Corporate Record Book for Star's company. All set to go with the three of us as Directors!" He placed the book on Tom's desk with it open for inspection.

Tom gazed at the book, a beautiful, professional thing, speaking at once of business, quality and a promise for his future. Here was tangible evidence of what would be possible with Dakota Fertilizer working together with the Elevator. A new set of possibilities for farmers and new opportunities for him and Bob.

Tom opened the book. "Articles of Incorporation—Dakota Fertilizer Corporation. Incorporated under the laws of…" There followed pages of detail as to the manner whereby the Corporation would conduct its business and make decisions.

As he turned the pages, his mind raced with possibilities. Here was a new experience; he was looking into the future with optimism. If he could be a part of Dakota Fertilizer, he would be able to follow his ideas and make those moves he knew to be in tune with the directions of agribusiness. Why he could…

"Well, Boss, what do you think of it?" Bob stood with hands on hips, a triumphant smile on his face.

"Bob, this is really great! You guys have sure been busy and the whole thing is ready to go!"

"You ain't just a-woofin'. Why, Star's got the office set up too! He's hired Sally Knutson, you know, the one who used to keep the books for Super Valu. He's got invoices and bills of lading and stationery, and…everything!"

"Hey, slow down!" Tom laughed at Bob's sputtering enthusiasm. "Looks like it's on the way. Now where do we come in?"

"Just you keep turnin' them pages!" Bob reached down impatiently and flipped the record book open to the section entitled "Corporate Officers." There in crisp black print were their names: "President: Theodore Schultz; Vice President: Robert Clauson; Secretary-Treasurer: Thomas Cooper." There it was! A solid business role for the first time! He sat back grinning.

"Bob, this looks really great! Now all we have to do is check this with the Elevator Board and we're ready to go!"

Bob greeted this comment with silence. He frowned and cleared his throat. "No, Boss. That wouldn't be a good idea."

"But why? If we're going to be working and dealing with the Elevator, the Board should know what we're doing."

"That's right. But I talked with the lawyer who did the incorporation and he said that we should get this off the ground first and then let the Board know that we've got a new business that's makin' them money." Bob was more earnest than usual. There was a kind of intensity about his argument that was out of character, something like his behavior when he was on the verge of losing a very large sale.

"That just doesn't seem right, Bob. We are going to be involved in a business that's pretty much the same as the Elevator's. They need to know and to approve of what we're doing."

"Sure. But remember, we are just in the fertilizer wholesale business. That's somethin' the Elevator can't do. In fact, we're helpin' them get the product for their customers and makin' them some nice money while we're doin' it. Besides, we gotta move product right now, and you know that Chris Odegaard would chew on this one all summer."

"Hmmm, well…you sure the attorney knows what he's doing? I agree that the Board wouldn't move very fast on this idea, and we wouldn't be able to handle the commitments we've already made."

"You bet! Now, what we gotta do is sign these papers. Here, let me show you what to do."

Bob found the page in the Record Book where their signatures were needed and handed Tom a pen. "Now, sign here…and here." His finger guided Tom to the proper spaces where his signature was to be added to Bob's and Star's.

When Tom had signed, Bob flipped to the back of the book and proudly displayed the Stock Certificates. These gaudy instruments drew Tom's attention from the issues of his involvement. He gazed at them in wonder. "My God! These look like the NATO Charter! You sure that this sort of thing is necessary?"

"Boss, we got to do this first-class! Now what you do is give me a check for $1,000 made out to Dakota Fertilizer Corporation for your shares in the Company. Then I'll…"

"Hey, wait a minute! I don't have a grand in my checking account. And if I did, there are a hell of a lot of bills I need to pay!"

"Don't worry! I got a check here from Dakota Fertilizer for you. It's for a G and you can cover your check right away!"

"Why do you need my check then?"

"It's this way. The lawyer said that we all gotta ante up some cash for our paid-in capital. Now, the check back to you is for your Director's salary for this month. So there's a wash!"

"Director's salary? What for? I haven't done anything."

"Just listen! That's just the way business is done. Directors get paid for givin' advice and support to the company. You got this comin' for the time you spent with Leach on the train and in plannin' this Company."

"Well, if the lawyer says so, I suppose it's okay, but I want to be sure I earn anything I get from the Company."

He took out his checkbook and wrote a check to Dakota Fertilizer Corporation, marking it for 'stock' on his check stub. At the same time, he entered the deposit of $1,000 as 'director's salary'.

"Bob, this all looks pretty complicated. I sure hope you and Star know what you are doing."

Bob swept the check into the record book and placed the book in its cardboard box.

"Don't you worry none! This here Company is on the road and there's gonna be plenty more in it for all of us!"

Bob waddled to the door. As he was leaving, he poked his head back into Tom's office shouting, "Lay, goose! Lay!" and slammed the door.

CHAPTER ELEVEN

A Time for Sowing

The first signs of prairie spring came in the last slushy days of March, when a combination of sun and strong winds liquefied the packed covering of ice on the streets of communities throughout the Dakotas. In Sheffield, merely to walk across the street on those days was a mighty effort resisted by clinging mush and tiny hillocks of ice built by the passage of traffic and the footprints of citizens. Most people managed those days very well. The promise of spring found in sunny spots sheltered from the wind, coupled with lengthening daylight that lingered in the afternoon, was a tangible indicator of the weakening grasp of winter. A holiday atmosphere of optimism minimized the inconvenience of travel.

Not all days were promising. Often clouds covered the sun and wind rapidly turned cold. Crusts of ice then formed over water-filled ruts in the streets and people visibly hastened their pace and covered themselves as they went about their business. On some days, the promise was crushed under a weight of March snow, heavy with moisture—and spirits fell as if winter held the land under its dominion again. The short supply of heat easily gave way to blasts of Canadian cold air.

At the Elevator, optimism lightened even the dreariest day. The phone was constantly alight with signals for spring supplies, and several times each week rail cars pulled in to add their contents to stock in the fertilizer sheds, product that would be needed shortly. For Tom, slush and mud were the focus of a constant battle. Each day, the Elevator Bobcat and Ron made short running leaps at the day's accumulation of loosened ice and snow to force it into heaps where it slowly shrank, to find its silent way under snow-covered fields between the Elevator and the Thoms River. At the railway siding, ice and snow had to be chipped away to slide a fertilizer unloading belt under the hoppers of railcars. Invariably, this maneuver had to be done with the car in place, as nobody could persuade the engineer to deposit his hundred-ton load anywhere near the holes so laboriously chipped the previous week.

Loading ramps on seed and chemical sheds became treacherously slick with a mixture of frozen moisture and chemicals, a coating with an oily consistency and the coefficient of friction of moist ice. When temperature fell, heaters had to be started in the sheds to keep expensive chemicals from freezing. Each fertilizer spreader and anhydrous tank received its annual tune-up despite the sea of mud and ice in the Elevator yard.

All these activities were carried out under the press of call after call from farmers trying to secure scarce supplies or to set plans in motion for spring planting. Never before, in Tom's experience, had the rush been so demanding. At the end of each day, he tipped back in his chair and raised the slant of his cap, putting the pencil it had held on the desk.

Just as Tom relaxed, invariably another farmer broke in with a phone call and typical questions.

"Say, Tom, you got any good ideas about what I ought to do for my corn fertilizer program this year?"

"Well, Sam," Tom answered, "what's your soil test recommend?"

"Oh, yeah, that. Well I looked for it today and can't seem to put my hand on it. You got a copy of it over there?"

"Let me look." He put the phone down, cursing the carelessness of farmers who just couldn't 'put their hands on' important information, to look through his files for a copy of the university print-out of test results. "Sam? I got it here. It says that you ought to put on about 150 pounds of actual nitrogen, 'bout 80 pounds of phosphorous and 60 of potash."

"That sounds okay to me," Sam replied. "You able to give that to me?"

"Well, I guess so, but you better get an order in pretty soon. The supply's gonna be tight and we don't have any too much left that ain't committed."

"That so! Well, put me down for enough of that program to cover 'round 500 acres. And, say, what's that gonna cost me?"

Tom ran his current price numbers through his desk calculator and mentally checked his calculations to make sure he was spreading the increased product costs among customers. "Let's see. The orders I get this week will be quoting actual N at 18 cents a pound for anhydrous ammonia and about 24 cents a pound for dry—that's 35-0-0. Then, phosphate will go for about $234 a ton and potash for $90."

There would be a sharp intake of breath on the other end of the line. "God!" Sam said, "That's damn near double what I paid last year. You sure you're right?"

"No question, Sam. These are the best prices I can give, and they're only good for today. Any new product I get in tomorrow is sure to be more spendy. I'll have to add any increase into the quote."

Another series of short breaths, then, "Well, I'm sure goin' to take the stuff. With corn way up there, I got to plant all the fence rows. Say, what's new crop doin' today?"

Tom looked at the chalkboard where current and future prices were displayed, then reported, "For December corn we're buyin' at $2.60, but I think it's gonna go higher. The shortage of fertilizer is makin' them doctors and school teachers who play the futures plenty nervous. I'd say we could see damn near three-dollar corn before plantin' time. It all depends on how much fertilizer gets onto the fields."

"OK," Sam said, his voice indicating resignation to reality. "You better put me down for the fertilizer and sign me up for ten thousand bushels of corn for December delivery if the price hits $2.80."

"I'll do that. Better stop by tomorrow to sign this fertilizer order."

"You bet! See you."

With variations, this conversation repeated itself at least ten times each day for larger or smaller amounts of fertilizer, reflecting the size of the caller's operation and his level of optimism. Even though the pressure was exhausting, Tom felt a growing sense of accomplishment as the volume of business soared. The word was out that the Elevator could get fertilizer and that Tom wasn't jacking up prices like some suppliers. This news brought in farmers within a fifty-mile radius and added to the volume of trade in seed and chemicals. Profits in this new business began to reduce the losses of the blizzard. These successes, along with the promise of a huge volume of grain to be bought and sold in the fall, would bring the Elevator back to its feet by summer, and well into the black by next winter.

In the middle of the month, Bob brought in a note from a Grandview bank to the Dakota Fertilizer Company for Tom's endorsement. The loan provided Star with the capital he needed for setting up his new business. Tom had been busy that day and hadn't paid much attention to the note, simply scrawling his signature across it. Later, during a lull in Elevator business, he asked Bob about the note.

"Say, Bob. That note for Star—wasn't it for two hundred grand?"

"Yep!" Bob rocked back on his heels scratching his back on the door jamb.

"Isn't that a lot of money? Does he need that much?"

"Sure does," Bob answered. "When you think that a car of 18-46-0 costs upwards of twenty five grand right now, and he has to move lots of cars to make his operation pay."

"I suppose that's right." Tom said. "Anyway, how's it goin'? Does he have access to product?"

"You bet! Leach has put him onto potash haulin' now. The margin's good, but he has to haul a lot of tons in the next month. That's comin' direct from the mines and he won't be into the carload market until we get in the field around here."

"How's he comin' on the extra truck?" Tom asked. "Star told me he was gonna hire Andy away from us to drive it."

"Star said that he would put on another truck in April—he has the rig picked out. Sure looks like we've—I mean Star—has got himself a goin' thing."

Tom often thought of that conversation and how good it would be for Star and for the Elevator. Now that Leach was ready to work closely with them, the flow of fertilizer was unbroken. Already they had received much more than their allocation, and several times other elevators had called Tom to complain of their problems and to question Sheffield's good fortune. He always told these callers that all he did was order what he could sell and that Farmhand made the decisions. This response invariably resulted in some enthusiastic cursing of the big co-op and thinly veiled threats of action to be taken with its management. While Tom often felt guilty for his good luck in dealing with Leach, he was restrained from sharing it with his competitors by the knowledge that he needed every dollar he could earn in order to get his books back in the black.

April came in with a promise of rain and by the end of the second week, all the traces of snow were gone, and frost was working its way out of the ground. This gave the Elevator employees a short quiet period, as restrictions were posted on secondary roads so that farmers couldn't move grain, nor could supplies be hauled into the country. Finally, as in every past year, an early bird farmer would make the call everyone dreaded.

"Say, Tom, can you bring out a spreader of potash? My field is ready to go."

The first two or three of these callers were wrong and the heavy spreaders were dispatched to sure graves in the muck of unready fields. This meant that Tom would have to organize a rescue crew and hire a local contractor to drag the Elevator's property to high ground with one of his crawler tractors. These early birds were well known and it was common practice to load their spreaders lightly and to wait at the farm for the inevitable wheelspin, stalling and cursing before calling the rescue squad.

Eventually the weather improved, so fields were actually ready and the mad rush of planting began. During this time, Tom turned the phone over to Pete and spent his days finding trouble spots in the flow of work and checking the quality of service given farmers. He liked nothing more than to be out in the fields and to stop by a patron's farm to wait for a tractor to complete its path across the prairie. While he waited, Tom sensed spring and the sleeping power of earth. Bending to his knees, he ran his hand through the mellow soil—feeling its texture and squeezing it to test its moisture content.

This spring, the ground was warm, moist and ready for seed. The distant sounds of tractors were symbolic of the vast pattern of coordinated effort unleashed on the prairie and the power of farmers to change its shape. At times like these, Tom felt a close relationship to the land—a rhythm of men and machines that he helped to orchestrate. He did not feel the press of his job, rather the enjoyment of playing a role in a great game. Here, he was part of the environment, in tune and sensitive to its slow changes and immense potential.

While Tom watched, the farmer would arrive at the end of a field and throttle back his clattering diesel. Then Tom would spring up the steps into the heated cab. There, the farmer would tune down his radio with its country themes and ask, "How's it goin' Tom?" or "Hi, Cooper, ain't this a hell of a day?" Tom would shelter briefly in the cab, enjoying the part he played in the drama of planting. "Just checkin' up. Everything okay? You getting all the fertilizer and seed you need?"

When he had been assured, or when he knew of new needs, he jumped down and waved as black smoke poured out of the tractor's exhaust. In a few minutes it was silent again and he was alone, now with fresh-turned earth at his feet, a part of the landscape. A man with his feet in the dirt.

Back at the Elevator, the pace was frantic. Calls for supplies constantly came in and unexpected shortages and problems showed up. These were usually dealt with speedily by Bob or Pete and rarely required Tom's personal attention. Instead, his hours behind the counter were used to speed the flow of seed and fertilizer. All the while, he remained conscious of the balance in his accounts.

This spring fertilizer was the source of most problems. Not too little, but too much. Day after day cars arrived on the rail spur, quickly filling Elevator bins despite the record volume being delivered to farmers.

"Say, Bob," he asked after an unusual number of cars had appeared, "the depot agent tells me that we're goin' to get another five cars of 18-46-0 this week. What the hell we gonna do with them? We're full in all the bins aren't we?"

"Sure, but we better keep the stuff comin'. I'd like to go into summer with the bins full. This shortage will keep on pinchin' 'til fall."

"Well, we better divert a couple of cars. I'll call up to Hazel Creek to see if they can use the stuff."

"Hey! Don't do that! We better pass any extra cars along to Star so he can keep those trucks rollin'. Just run them along to the Dover siding. He can use that track to unload."

Tom hesitated. "…I suppose that'd be okay. But be sure to take at least ten percent over our cost when you bill them out."

"No problem!" Bob grinned. "We could take twenty and Star could still make a buck on the product."

This conversation, or variations on it, repeated several times during April and into the first weeks of May. Each time cars were sent along to Dover and billed out to Dakota Fertilizer Company.

The volume of fertilizer business was not apparent to Tom until the middle of May. One day, he and Stub were going over accounts. It was Stub who brought the fertilizer trade into perspective.

"Say, Tom, do you know, we're runnin' more than double last year's retail fertilizer sales this spring?"

"No! Really? I knew we were movin' a lot of material, but I had no idea it was that much."

"Yeah. And not only that. We've done almost $500,000 of wholesale business—somethin' we never done before!"

"What? Let me see those figures!"

He pulled the account book to face him. "Hmmm…" He paged through the entries. Many were sales to account number 0730.

"Stub, who's the customer for code 0730?"

"That's a new one, Boss. Dakota Fertilizer Company. The checks we get are always signed by Ted Schultz."

"Is the account current?" Tom asked.

"Sure, right on time, but we don't bill them as soon as we should. It only works because most of that product comes from Farmhand, and they extended our credit another fifteen days this year—so we aren't in a pinch."

"Yeah, I know. Leach said they would do that for us. But, Stub, what kind of a margin is Bob takin' on these sales?"

"Oh, nothin' to worry about there," Stub said, looking at his Inventory Control. "He's makin' anywhere from eight to fifteen percent on each sale. That's almost as good a margin as we take on the retail trade. That Schultz must have a good market somewhere in order to make anything on that kind of cost."

Tom ran his finger down the list of sales. "The way it looks, he must have cars stacked up all along the Dover spur. Well, no problem so long as he's payin' us on time."

"What you mean 'Dover spur'?" Stub asked as he closed the Inventory Control book.

Tom started. "Isn't that where the cars are goin' for Star?"

"No," Stub replied, "only a couple went that way. The rest are invoiced directly to other elevators in Minnesota and Iowa."

"Hmm…that's funny." Tom tipped his hat back. "He must have been able to get a delivered price on rail that meets his cost."

"Suppose so," Stub said. "Some of them cars don't even stop here. Bob just invoices them straight through."

"Guess he knows what he's doin' in order for us to get these kind of profits. You be sure to keep an eye on the receivables, Stub. And be sure that Star doesn't get behind in his payments."

As Stub went back to his office, Tom thought about the fertilizer movements. Funny that Star could make the contacts for direct rail sales. Well, no problem for the Elevator. The increased volume and the attractive profits would sure as hell add to the black side of the ledger. That and the fact that farmers were able to pay cash at an unprecedented pace due to high grain prices meant that he would be able to show a solid profit at the annual meeting in June.

The next few days after his meeting with Stub were busy ones and his plan to question Bob about details of fertilizer transactions slipped his mind. In the few moments when he was free of phone calls and problems, he reflected on how the pace of agribusiness had changed life at the Elevator.

Tom recalled his first spring at the Elevator when several of the regular hangers-on had been waiting out a rainy afternoon under the loading dock canopy looking across the glistening wet of Elm Street, staring at stores and houses on the far side. That was the day that Harold Christopherson noticed the sign in front of Baker's service station. The Bakers were new to Sheffield—a couple in their late thirties and evidently not happily married. Their frequent shouts and quarrels were commonplace, and nobody paid much attention. A group of regular customers still bought their gasoline from the Bakers and a few groceries when other stores were closed on weekends or evenings.

That day, rain had started early, and Harold had been sitting under the canopy for several hours, long enough to have heard one of the Bakers' arguments and the angry roar of Alvin Baker's car engine as he stormed out to River House for a day of drinking. Harold, normally a very deliberate person, had been studying the station for several hours when he observed, "Say, don't that sign move around a lot?"

"What you talkin' 'bout, Harold?" asked one of the other loungers.

"Why that little 'Open For Business' sign in the window of Baker's station over there."

"Yeah—so what?"

Much discussion followed, but it wasn't until a blue pickup belonging to Mark Nerenson pulled up at the pumps that the mystery was solved.

"Well now, I wonder." Harold mused. "Don't suppose that old Mark, he got himself a new woman over there?"

Nerenson was known for his womanizing in Sheffield, which was a surprise to many residents. His timidity and slight build did not give the impression of great sensuality or virility. The assembled loafers studied the situation carefully. Several volunteered that they had seen Nerenson's pickup there in the past. Others added that they were sure that Ted Baker was gone at the time.

Gradually, a plot began to take shape.

"I imagine the sign's the signal," Harold concluded. "Wonder what would happen if that sign got in the wrong corner of the window when old Ted's at home?"

The chuckles that followed were indications of endorsement for the emerging joke. It incubated for the next week and a half, with casual but regular checks on the movement of the sign and disposition of the players. The directors decided that they had the ingredients of a first-rate drama that could be played to an audience in the front-row box of the Elevator platform.

The next rainy day, the crowd on the platform was the largest Tom had ever seen. Farmers and townspeople were lounging around casually, stealing glances at the Baker station–now on center stage. During a lull in the shower, Harold rose and strolled across the street to enter the station. Watchers could see him through the window—ordering a pack of cigarettes from Mrs. Baker, and the quick shift of the sign in the window when her back was turned to get cigarettes from a shelf behind the counter.

Conscious of his role in the play that was unfolding, Harold stepped out of the station, paused in its doorway to open his purchase, and lit a cigarette before walking back across the street. A director about to see his masterpiece develop.

The audience sat and smoked, talking quietly in anticipation.

"Think he's gonna come?"

"What if them Bakers have a fight before he gets here?"

"Where was Ted when you went in Harold, in back?"

"Bet he's in the sack. Won't that be a hell of a jolt for Nerenson? Think three's a crowd?"

When the blue pickup appeared at the far end of Elm Street, the house grew quiet. The curtain was going up.

Nerenson drove slowly past the station, seeming to look straight down the street. He nodded confidently to the group on the Elevator platform, then turned his head quickly to catch a glimpse of the station and the telltale sign. The pickup disappeared down the street, turning right to circle the block.

"Think he saw it?"

"What if he missed it and's goin' home?"

"Look! There he comes!"

The blue truck reappeared at the Main Street end of the block and slowed to pull up beside the single gas pump at the Baker station. Nerenson swung himself out of the car and strode through the screen door of the station, whistling. The watchers leaned forward, now openly laughing and nudging one another.

"Think it'll be long?"

"I'd like to see their faces!"

Then, the screen door of the station exploded! Nerenson raced out without his hat and scurried around his pickup. Behind him came Ted Baker, swearing.

"You bastard! Thought you could come sneakin' 'round here eh? Well, I'll show you!"

Just as he caught up with Nerenson, the audience stood with wild laughter and applause. To a man, they remained standing, clapping for encore bows from the performers.

Ted stood with Nerenson's shirt in one hand, the other drawn back to strike. Nerenson's mouth gaped, as they both stared at their fans. Baker's wife, standing in the station doorway, covered her face with her hands and backed offstage. Baker slowly released Nerenson's shirt, and Mark leapt into his pickup and sped down the street, never again to take a major part in the drama of Sheffield townlife.

These jokes and the free time for them were, each year, more constrained by the pressure of farming as economics—rather than farming as a way of life. Now, each of the patrons had to be more sensitive to cash flow and to an increasingly narrow margin between profit and loss. As the result of good crops last year, many farmers had refinanced their farms to buy additional land, whose price was inflated in a seller's market, with the anticipation that everyone had for good grain prices this coming fall.

As time went by, there were fewer smiles and more anxious faces around the Elevator. Friendly conversation was replaced by a brusqueness that precluded the kind of easy interaction of another time. Nobody was more under the pressure of farm economics than Barney

Jacobs. In every way, he represented the direction farming had taken in the 1970s and his way of dealing with both suppliers and neighbors was a sign that many others recognized and followed. When Barney bought from you, he always had at least two competitive bids in hand and you were conscious of being evaluated as a potential victim when he called.

In the middle of spring rush, Tom had an opportunity to out-guess Barney's information about the fertilizer market. One Wednesday afternoon, just as the wind was drying out a morning shower and the few hangers-on at the Elevator were leaving, Pete called Tom to the phone.

"It's Barney," Pete whispered, handing over the phone. "I think he's gonna jack you around on some more fertilizer."

Tom took the phone, mumbling to Pete, "Oh, shit! Just the guy I need to make my day!" Then he shifted gears. "Hello, Barney. How's things?"

"Well, those of us who gotta work are hittin' the ball. I suppose your office is full of those lazy bastards as usual?"

"Nope, Barney, we're all pretty busy getting the last of the spring order out. What can I do for you?"

"That so, Cooper? OK, I got a couple of new farms up north of the River and I need some 9-23-30 bulk spread tomorrow. You got any?"

"Yep. We're in pretty good shape on most of the analyses and could get one of the boys out on the job…how's 7 a.m.?"

"Not so fast, Cooper!" In the background, Tom could hear the creak of Barney's chair protesting under the two hundred and fifty pounds it had to bear. "I ain't givin' you the go-ahead yet. First, we got to talk price. What you gonna do for me?"

Tom paused and pushed papers on his desk to a corner to expose a clean section of the large legal pad centered in front of him. *Let's see. We pay about $160 a ton for 9-23. Hmm…If we take 10%, we should get…* He penciled the numbers that tracked the flow of product…*$160 + $16 +…delivery…$4…that would be, $180.*

"Barney, guess we could put it on your farm for $175 and spread it for another $4 a ton."

Silence, broken by the squeaking of Barney's chair and some labored breathing.

"You're close, Cooper. Tell you what. Make that $170 and I'll take about 300 ton."

"Dammit, Barney! I can't go that low! But I could spread it for the $175 and give you a cash discount of another $3 per ton for thirty-day payment."

"Okay, Cooper, you got a deal. You must have a hell of a good supply to get the price that low." Barney laughed. "Be sure your boys are here on the money tomorrow. And don't send one of those idiots like the guy that let the spreader run all the way out here last year."

As Tom hung up the phone, he silently cursed Barney's sharp trading ability. "That bastard! I bet he couldn't get within $15 of that price anywhere else. I sure blew that one! By the time we haul the stuff and spread it, we'll just about break even—and on a whole damn 300 ton!"

Leaning back in his old swivel chair, Tom doodled on his blotter. The deal could have gone the other way too. He could remember times when there had been a verbal agreement only to have Barney cancel it when another elevator came up with a better price. Other times, Tom had waited months for payment that had been promised, when Barney used the Elevator as a bank where loans could be obtained in the form of fertilizer, chemicals or seed. Tom tolerated this practice because Barney represented a large account and a powerful force on the political side of Elevator management.

The next Monday, Barney arrived at the Elevator and stomped directly into Tom's office where Tom was talking to a customer.

"Cooper, you got a minute? I want to talk about this fertilizer business."

The customer who had been sitting across from Tom rose hurriedly. "I better be goin', Tom. I'll be back later this week and we can close the deal."

"Yeah, okay," Tom said, "but maybe Barney can wait a minute and we can finish now."

"Can't do it," Barney interrupted. "I got things to do and this is important."

The other farmer's face flushed and he abruptly got up from his chair and brushed past Barney out of the office.

Tom motioned Barney to a seat and said angrily, "Barney, you just cut the Elevator out of a big feed contract. I've been workin' on that guy for the past year, and I think I had him ready to sign. Your problem better be important."

Barney squeezed himself into the facing chair. "Cooper, this ain't my problem. It's yours. I been keepin' an eye on the cars comin' in here, and there's a hell of lot of them that don't get unloaded. Stub tells me that you're sellin' a lot of fertilizer to the wholesale market. What's the idea? You know we need the stuff here this spring."

"Barney," Tom sighed. "That isn't a problem. We have plenty of product and you know that we're pricing at the bottom of the market to farmers. Any of our wholesale business is what we can't use here."

"That so?" Barney peered out of narrowed eyes, masked by folds of fat. "Well, what kind of profit you takin' on them cars?"

"We're getting ten to fifteen percent above our cost, and we don't have any handling charges. Plus, we'll get a dividend rebate from Farmhand, so the net to us will be more like twenty percent."

"…now…that's nice. But if there's such a hell of a demand, why don't you take more profit? I been lookin' for fertilizer around the area and I don't mind tellin' you that you are way low in price."

"Barney, there's two reasons why we don't. We're makin' a good profit on these sales and we'll be pretty close to exceeding our tax exemption status as a co-op if we make too much on wholesale trades. Also, I don't believe in screwing farmers who have to pay for the product at the end of the line."

"Piss on them!" Barney snapped. "If they don't know enough to line up their stuff when the price is right, they shouldn't be in business!"

"I can't go along with that," Tom retorted. "Some of these guys are milkin' cows and workin' all day, so they just don't have time to look for deals. It's my job to keep on top of the situation and give them the best deal I can."

"Two things wrong with that, Cooper." Barney grinned. "You can't watch out for those dummies. If they want to bust their ass workin' cows, they deserve to go broke. And..." Barney paused and the smile faded. "If you're all so red hot at givin' the poor farmers a break, why don't you sell all them carloads of fertilizer direct to them other elevators and take the profit. Then you can cut the prices you charge here." With that he got up to leave the office. At the door he paused. "Say, by the way, some of the bigger farmers are askin' me to run for the Elevator Board. Think I might. Wouldn't hurt to have some decent businessman keep an eye on you."

Barney wheeled out of the door and a few moments later Tom heard the rasp of Barney's CB radio—always turned to full volume—and the scratch of pickup tires as he left the Elevator parking lot.

Tom stood looking out his office window at the dissipating cloud of dust that marked Barney's exit.

He spoke to the dust. "Runnin' for the Board. Wonder what that means?"

CHAPTER TWELVE

King of the Road

West of Sheffield, where Highway 13 crested the bluff and the prairie began, there was a sweeping curve, the last turn of climbing switchbacks before the highway shouldered its way toward the horizon through ranks of wheat and corn. At the center of the curve there was a graveled parking area and an illuminated plastic sign proclaiming the location of the Sheffield Knights of Columbus Hall.

The tidy steel-shrouded building that locals called 'Agribusiness Modern' was completed the year Tom and Janet arrived in Sheffield—the culmination of a long fund-raising campaign by St. Stephen's Parish. When finished, the Hall showed Sheffield that its Catholic minority was no longer an invisible newcomer, but a mature economic force equal to the Lutherans. The location of the Hall, overlooking Sheffield, where its lights could be seen from Main Street and its silhouette by the worshipers coming out of the doors of Our Savior's Lutheran Church, was evidence of the confidence of its builders. The fact that the Hall was the newest, largest and best-appointed in the area aided in the ecumenical kindness of the Knights, since they made it available to many community groups for social events and meetings.

The most important of these events was the annual meeting of the Farmers Elevator patrons and stockholders. This was an opportunity for farmers and invited guests to share in the confidence that another planting season had produced. Everyone looked forward to the meeting, especially now that an air-conditioned hall could hold the July heat outdoors. The local Bishop had even relented to allow non-Catholics the luxury of a cash bar.

Planning and arranging the annual meeting took a large part of Tom's time in the final weeks of June. Hiring the Hall and arranging for St. Stephen's Ladies Circle to prepare and serve the meal were lesser chores. Of primary importance was the choice of prizes to be raffled and the selection of an entertainer who was spirited enough to get applause from banqueters without offending.

Tom, Pete and Helen spent several afternoons at the Elevator going over prize lists of past years and recalling the reactions of winners. In these conversations, Helen had the most penetrating insights and a keen ability to identify precisely what the majority reaction would be to a given prize. Tom and Pete deferred to her judgment, reserving only the right to suggest ideas for her approval or rejection.

"Tom, you remember last year when the Swensons won the freezer?" Helen asked as she brought coffee and doughnuts into Tom's office.

He remembered the looks of Mr. and Mrs. Swenson. "Yeah, they both looked pretty depressed. Wonder why?"

"Just think," Helen said. "For Ole, that freezer meant hoeing in the garden and some butchering to do when he'd rather be playing cards at the VFW. For Inga, the freezer was a lot of afternoons and evenings in front of her stove. No wonder they were depressed. That freezer was no fun—it was work!"

Tom grinned. "I see what you're sayin'. Things like that won't do the job, but…"

Helen interrupted. "People see this meeting as a party and if you're going to give expensive prizes, they had better be fun—and for everybody in the family, not just the man."

"I agree," Pete nodded, leaning back in his chair. "We had a much better response to the boat and motor we gave for first prize the year before."

"Well, if you two are right, that shoots the snowmobile—especially the Brute I had a deal on. That ain't a lady's machine."

"No," laughed Helen, "and it isn't a machine for a lot of the men either. Can't you just see Cora and Felix Peichack on that? Why, they'd be so scared they wouldn't stop 'til they hit Minot!"

They all chuckled at the thought of the conservative, overweight Peichacks grimly hanging on to the racing sled. As they grew quiet, Pete suggested, "Say, if you're gonna spend that kind of dough, why don't we fly the winners to Las Vegas? That way they can really party it up—or at least get away from the snow next winter."

"Why, Pete," Helen said, "that's a swell idea! I'll bet even the real straight-laced folks would like that. They can suggest that they have been close to sin, and everyone will know that it really isn't so. What a great prize!"

Tom agreed. "That's not bad! It'll really pull people into the meeting. Everybody can see themselves in the middle of one of those Las Vegas billboards in the middle of February."

"But how do we follow that act?" Pete asked. "What can we give 'em to carry away? We got to make the other prizes good enough so the winners won't feel left out."

Helen smiled. "Yes, it wouldn't do to send the Peichacks to Las Vegas and give one of the Board members a picnic cooler."

Tom started, at that unhappy circumstance. "Hell, I'd better save enough for a ticket to Wolf Point if somethin' like that happens. I could end up dumpin' trucks at some scale in Montana for the next five years." He reached into his desk for a collection of prize catalogs and laid them out for inspection.

Each of the prizes in the spread-out catalogs was analyzed and jokingly accepted or rejected, usually with clever matches to certain Elevator regulars. By the end of June, they had a list ranging from the Las Vegas trip and a trailer camper that Pete claimed as 'ours' while Helen blushed, to several barbeque grills that represented ten consolation prizes.

At their final meeting, Tom sighed and stretched. "That's some list of loot. This ought to be the best bunch of prizes these people have ever seen."

"Yeah," Pete agreed, "but we've spent a hell of a pile of money to get it. Maybe we went a little too far."

Tom punched the 'total' key on his desk calculator. "That's $7,600. And this is the best way to let stockholders know that we've had a good year. Can you imagine what they'd say if we were givin' away a dozen of those picnic baskets?" He pointed to one of the prizes in an open catalog.

"But, Tom," Pete protested, "we haven't had all that strong a year. If it weren't for the fertilizer crunch and our wholesale sales, we'd probably go into the annual meeting in the red."

Helen bunched the prize order forms and stared at the pile in her hands, averting her eyes from the two men. The room was now very quiet and the ticking of the old Regulator clock could be heard above the hum of the air conditioner.

"That's right, Pete." Tom said. "We aren't out of the woods yet, but I have to get the support of the Board now if we are goin' to have any chance at a good year this fall. If I don't get a couple of new Board members in the election at this meeting, I won't be able to float the line of credit we need to operate. Prizes are a part of the picture and we had better do it right."

Pete's protests about the prize list were mild compared to the violent reaction he had to Tom's choice of entertainment.

"Stormy Skye! My God, Tom! You can't be serious! Why, she's one of the top ten country-western singers this year, and her show don't come for peanuts!"

Pete was marching around the office waving the promotional samples Tom had received from Stormy's booking agent. "Hell, people will think we've cracked up—blowin' our money on that kind of main line act! We sure better cancel this right away and pick up one of them New Ulm polka bands!"

"No they won't." Tom said. "They'll be tickled as hell to see Stormy here. They'll go wild when she gives them that 'Rose Garden' number."

"You're damn right they'll go wild! Seeing their dividends go down Stormy's blousefront!"

They both grinned in spite of the argument as they visualized the outstanding components of Stormy's act.

"Look, Pete," Tom reasoned, "you and I know that this kind of act will really stretch the miscellaneous budget and we'll have to do some switchin' around to cover it. But Stormy is a lot of votes in our pocket, and the best way I know of getting some of the swing voters to the meeting."

"That's buyin' votes!" Pete exclaimed. "They'll be supporting you because they've had a good time and not because they think the Elevator is in top shape!"

"Sure, you're right. But that's beside the point. There ain't no way anyone can step in here now and turn this thing around by fall unless the Board comes through with a bigger line of credit and gives in on futures trading."

The argument continued for the next two weeks, always with the same points raised and no agreement. In spite of Pete's concerns, Tom held to his plan. Announcements of the annual meeting headlined both the Las Vegas raffle and Stormy Skye. Tom knew that he had guessed correctly as raffle ticket sales began to come in.

"See, Pete!" He waved the most recent day's results against Pete's scowl. "We'll sell enough tickets to pay for all the prizes and the Hall rent to boot. Not only that, we're pullin' in people from some of the other towns. These are the new customers we got this spring and this show will put them right in our corner."

"Maybe so," Pete shrugged, "but that don't make it right. We're not drawin' these people because we've got the best prices or the greatest service. They're comin' to a goddamn circus!" He turned and stomped out.

Tom stared at the empty doorway for a time, then looked again at the ticket summaries. He added several totals, mumbling, "Let's see. Two hundred registered. If I can pull in another twenty five new customers, I'll have the votes to back me with a couple of new Board members who will do what we need." He thought of the Board members who would be retiring at the meeting and their opposition to futures trading and the balky way they had dealt with his credit proposal of last year. "…just one up-to-date Board member…then I can trade the Elevator back into the black by Christmas." But no matter how he rationalized his actions, he couldn't pretend that Pete's criticisms hadn't hurt. He had respect for Pete's honesty, and he knew that his use of prizes was a trick of a fairly low order—and that the carnival atmosphere of the meeting would carry him along over reasonable but unanswerable questions that some stockholders would ask about the balance sheet. In the end, he always dismissed these misgivings by a sure knowledge that he was doing what was best for the Elevator.

He was supported in his plan by Bob, who saw the situation in identical terms.

"Sure, Boss, we got to give them somethin' to keep their minds off our problems, and that's a good show, prizes and a positive shove into next year."

"But do we have the right mix?" Tom asked. "I'm satisfied with Stormy and the Las Vegas trip, but it just doesn't seem as great as when I made up the list."

"Tell you what. Let's make that camper trailer a motor home!"

"Bob, are you nuts? That would add at least ten grand to the prize cost, and we don't have that kind of loose change!"

"No problem! What we'll do is take it out of the fertilizer profits. We are just rollin' in dough now and ten grand's peanuts. Hell, I can still get that out of a couple of wholesale carloads."

"But that's profit that should go to all the patrons." Tom could almost hear Pete agreeing with his comment. "It wouldn't be right to spend it on a prize for the raffle!"

"Don't worry! Here's how we'll do it. I'll just jack up the price on a couple of cars of urea another five grand each and we can use the money for the motor home."

"Well…okay…but how will we ever get this idea past Pete and Helen? And what'll the Board say?"

"Leave 'em to me. The Board will be so happy with the meeting that they'll forget the cost of the prizes. That's your job—make sure they don't think about any of the problems we had, just about a good future."

Somehow, Bob fulfilled his promise. Pete and Helen came around to grudging support of the motor home prize, especially when Bob explained that it came out of profits the Elevator couldn't take under its tax exemption.

Tom was able to get the prize list past his Board chairman with some discussion of how the meeting would be used to build business. However, Bob's use of the fertilizer money was constantly on his mind.

On one of the last afternoons before the meeting, Tom was poring over a list of stockholders when he noticed an entry for 'Theodore Schultz'. He puzzled over this for a moment, then called Helen.

"Say, Helen, I noticed Star's name here on the list of stockholders. Shouldn't he be on the list of business guests? There must be a mistake."

"No, Tom. I noticed that too. But I checked with Stub, and he says that Star has earned his stockholder position. Something about Dakota Fertilizer being one of our biggest accounts."

She returned to her typing as Tom digested her report. *One of the biggest accounts! My God! I thought Star was just goin' to move a few loads of fertilizer. Guess that makes him a stockholder—so long as he's current on payin' his bills.*

He got up from his desk and walked back to Stub's cubby. "Say Stub, how we doin' on the Dakota Fertilizer account?"

"Fine. There's always a big cash flow, but we've been making good profits and Star always pays cash at the end of the month."

"Hmmm…let me take a look at his account." He took the Accounts Receivable Ledger from Stub and opened it on his desk. Dakota Fertilizer entries made up several pages with most of the trades being in carloads of standard fertilizer analyses. "Jesus!" He mused, "Over a million dollars worth of business! I sure the hell hope that Bob's been leveling with me on the profits on these trades." He got up again and called to Stub.

"Stub! Bring me the Inventory Book. There are a couple of these carloads I need to follow through."

Stub brought the requested ledger. As he put it on Tom's desk, he said, "I know what your thinkin' Boss, but every one of these sales is a profit for the Elevator. Here, let me show you."

He opened the ledger to one of the analysis headings. "See, here's 0-0-60. Now, the sale to Star on April 23—here's our price and here's what we charged him." Stub pointed to the entries.

"I see what you mean," Tom observed. "We made ten dollars a ton on that sale. Are the others the same?"

Stub considered, "Generally, yes. Except on 18-46-0 where we're makin' more like sixty dollars a ton. But you got to realize that we could have turned around and sold the stuff ourselves at wholesale to another elevator and taken maybe another fifty to seventy a ton profit."

"Yeah, but we couldn't do that more than a couple of times or we'd lose our tax exemption as a co-op. Remember when I came, the IRS was in here for two months. We had a devil of a time convincing them that the profits we made—I think it was on wholesale feed—were in line with our co-op status."

"Yep. I remember," Stub nodded. "They gave me a real goin' over and I don't want that to happen again."

"Maybe a ten percent markup will sit all right with the IRS," Tom concluded and turned to leave.

"That's what I told Chris last week," Stub said.

"Chris Odegaard?" Tom asked from the doorway. "What's he want to know?"

Puzzlement and worry sharpened the question. Why would the chairman of the Board want to concern himself with details of daily trading?

"Oh, nothin'," Stub waved his hand. "His boy had seen some cars on the Dover siding and heard that they came from here. He was just checkin' to see what the price was to Star and how much we made. Something about not wantin' to see Star get a price that farmers couldn't match."

"Well…I guess that's OK," Tom said slowly, "but next time Odegaard asks questions, send him in to me. I want to be sure the Board gets the right picture of our business. Won't do to have them try to figure out the books."

"Sure thing, Boss. I didn't think you'd mind. There's nothin' to hide in the account books."

The emphasis on the word 'account' did not escape Tom. Stub was obviously referring to pricing of grain in the Daily Position Book at the time of the last federal inspection. Damn him! Wasn't he ever going to let up on that? Didn't Stub know that without his Elevator job he would be keeping books for about ten little businesses out of his living room instead of making a good salary for steady work. Dammit…

These issues dominated conversations with Bob over the next several weeks. When Tom shared these discussions with Janet, she raised many of the concerns voiced by Helen and Pete.

"Tom," she said, "the Elevator is taking control of you again. You have less time for Chrissy…you are almost on the schedule of last winter. What's the problem?"

"I know. I know," he mumbled. "This Annual Meeting is always on my mind. We are making progress on our grain shortage, and fertilizer sales are going through the roof. But any opposition from the Board will put me right back in the hot seat."

She stood behind his chair and hugged him. "Please don't worry. Everyone knows that you are the right manager for the Elevator. Everything will come out fine at the Meeting. You'll see."

"Sure hope you're right. This is the big one!"

The night of the Annual Meeting was a relief from a week-long hot spell and there was a promise of rain, so everyone arrived at the KC Hall in a good mood.

"Hey, Tom! Ain't this a nice night?" "Hi, Cooper. We gonna to get rain?" "I'll turn in my raffle ticket right now for two inches of the wet stuff."

"I'll take that," Tom replied. "Go in and have two inches of bourbon on me."

Everyone laughed. For this one evening, all tensions of farming and making ends meet were forgotten. A night for a party.

In Tom's agreement with Stormy Skye, there was a short pre-banquet warm-up when she would sing a couple of numbers and her band would play through the cash bar period. This was an instant hit with the crowd. The farmers' sedate, careful, almost-furtive approaches to the bar became blurred as the noise level rose and, when Stormy appeared, there were cheers.

"C'mon Stormy, let's Walk the Line!" "Hey gal, give us that Tallahatchee Bridge!" Stormy smiled and eased into a throaty version of the Johnny Cash number. By the last verse, the crowd was clapping and a few people were singing along.

Tom watched and knew that he had a hit on his hands. Now, all he had to do was pull off the dinner speech and the formalities of the Annual Meeting and he would have the crowd with him when the evening ended with votes for new Board members.

"Too bad I couldn't get Jim Leach here for the main speaker. He could really add to this country act with his jokes." Tom recalled the cool reception he had received when he called Farmhand for Leach and received Leach's supervisor instead. The conversation replayed in his mind:

"Hello, this is Tom Cooper at Sheffield. I'm lookin' for Jim Leach. He's supposed to speak at our Annual Meeting."

"Has Jim promised to come? What was he supposed to speak about?" the supervisor asked.

After answering these questions, Tom was told that Farmhand would send somebody to the meeting, but it wouldn't be Leach. Yesterday, he had discovered that Frank Jessup, Leach's supervisor and a Farmhand Vice President, would attend. Now, he looked across the noisy hall to where Jessup and Barney Jacobs were in earnest conversation. "Wonder what they're talkin' about?"

Then he put the question out of his mind as Stormy ended her pre-dinner numbers with the Blue Skirt Waltz, an obvious attempt to help older members recall their youth, and a smooth way to quiet the noisy crowd.

"C'mon everybody!" Tom yelled, "let's eat!"

Animated groups moved toward tables at the other end of the Hall and the St. Stephen's Ladies Circle went to work. Although the ladies offered the usual ham, peas and mashed potatoes, the meal was one of the best Tom had eaten at a community gathering. Extra plates of food were heaped in the center of each table and farmers made sure that none was sent back to the kitchen unless empty. As the meal drew to a close, there began to be questions about prizes, especially from tables of younger farmers.

"Hey Tom! Let's get the drawin' on the way. I got plans for askin' one of these ladies to go with me to Las Vegas!"

"Drawin' time! You better get me somethin' fancier than that blanket I got last year! Used the damn thing just once and Jean got pregnant! If that happens again, the Elevator's gonna get a bill from me!"

Smiling at these comments, Tom took the microphone. "Welcome, everyone, to the Annual Meeting of the Sheffield Farmers Elevator. Before we get under way, I think we should give a hand to the St. Stephen's ladies for their fine dinner and service."

The Hall instantly filled with enthusiastic applause and the ladies lined up near the kitchen doors to take their customary praise. Each smiled a little nervously and all blushed to be the center of attention.

When applause died down, Tom spoke. "You all have been so good that we'll draw for prizes now—and not wait for the end of the business meeting. I won't worry that you'll leave, because there will be more from Stormy after our main speaker. So there's a lot of fun ahead of us. Say, that reminds me." He paused and the expectant laughter rushed around the tables.

"The other day, Paul and Axel Olson came in with a problem." Everyone looked around for the two brothers who were notorious for playing tricks on Elevator hangers-on. "They told me that they were havin' problems raisin' chickens. Seems that last spring they got a couple of hens and decided to grow a whole flock. So they took the birds out in the garden and dug a hole for each one. Then, they put the chickens in the holes and covered them up so just the heads were stickin' out. They watered them every day, but it didn't do any good. The birds died in a couple of days. Well, Axel, he thought about it and figgered that they had done something wrong so he tried it again. Only this time they planted the birds upside down so the feet were stickin' out of the ground. They watered the birds and kept the weeds down—but, no use, the birds died.

"When they told me about their problem, I got right on the phone to the University and told them the whole story. I went out to lunch and when I came back the guy from the U called and told me he couldn't figure out the problem. The only way he could help was for the boys to send in a soil sample."

The crowd was silent for a moment, then the laughs came.

"Yep, By God! That's the way with the U."

"Hey Axel! You probably used too much lime!"

When the crowd had quieted, Tom looked to the side of the Hall and moved up to the plastic drum that came with the supply of raffle tickets.

"Now, folks, the time you have been waiting for has arrived! I'm gonna stir up this drum real good and ask Stormy to draw out the winners. Remember, the first ticket is for the trip to Las Vegas and the last for the camper. Okay—here goes—I'll give this a little spin." He whirled the crank, and the drum revolved, a blur of anticipation. As it slowed, Stormy reached as if to draw a lucky ticket. "No Stormy! Hold it! Carl's ticket is on top!"

Again, a wave of laughter licked at the head table. "Round she goes! Okay Stormy, let's hear the lucky number."

She reached into the drum, captured a ticket and read the number in a deep voice.

"36765."

"Wow! That's my number," came a jubilant call from one of the side tables where the new patrons from the Grandview area were gathered.

Tom pointed to the winner. "Congratulations to the Las Vegas trip winner, Ray Dickerson! Ray is one of our new customers from Grandview and will be a regular face around the Elevator in the years ahead. Let's all give him a hand!"

Enthusiastic applause from the Grandview contingent was gradually joined by Sheffield locals whose good manners covered their disappointment at seeing an outsider capture an attractive prize. Only a few disgruntled people like the Larsen brothers were openly angry at this turn of luck.

Tom continued, "It's probably right that one of our new patrons won this trip. They have added more than half of our new business and are the main reason that we're lookin' forward to a great year."

This remark restored the party spirit and the drawing proceeded with a sprinkling of smaller prizes distributed at random around the room. As the drawing progressed, excitement grew. The crowd began to clamor for the grand prize.

"Where's the Winne?"

"Yeah! What about the Winnebago?"

"Me and the missus are gettin' ready for that Black Hills trip in August!"

Tom made a show of whispering to Stormy, their heads together as if conspiring to steal the camper for themselves. Mounting tension finally burst in cries from the gamblers.

"Cooper! Let's get this show on the road!"

"C'mon! Who's got the lucky number?"

"Stormy! Give us a break!"

Tom walked to the center of the floor, his arm around the singer's hourglass waist. "Now for the big one! Who'll be the lucky family to drive off in the Winne?"

At his question, big doors at the end of the Hall opened and a shiny Winnebago rolled in, Bob at the wheel waving out an open window and blasting on the horn.

Cheers and applause broke like blasts of prairie wind all around Tom and he was carried along in a rush of enthusiasm. Stormy, too, let her entertainer's face break for a moment as she drew out the winning ticket.

"Number 45230! Who's the lucky winner? Let's find him so we can all go for a ride in the Winne!"

Three hundred heads swiveled, looking for that unimagined turn of fate. 'If only my ticket ...' Then one of the front tables erupted.

"By golly! It's Phil's ticket!" Chris Odegaard exclaimed. He stood and clapped his nephew on the shoulder. "Stand up, Phil, and let them see you!"

Phil Odegaard, his earnest manner forgotten, waved the ticket above his head. "Here it is! Number 45230! I can't believe it! But Stormy's right! You're all invited for a Winne vacation! Just sign up with Agnes." His arm encircled his wife and they hugged in the joy of good fortune.

Many people left their tables to inspect the camper and to discuss its merits with Phil and Agnes, who were acting like Winnebago sales representatives should, giving authoritative answers to questions of performance and equipment. The answers were probably incorrect, but nobody cared.

Chris Odegaard was basking in the reflection of his nephew's happiness. It was clear to Tom that the prizes were a reservoir of good will that could be drawn upon in the future.

Seeing the mood, Tom whispered to Stormy. "Now's the time, baby! Let it go!"

As her band swung into the familiar tune, Stormy surprised the crowd with lyrics that pictured the prize winners.

"Three bedrooms, kitchenette."

"How homey can you get."

"Hot dish to go, you all know."

"Queen of the Road!"

Everyone laughed and began to provide a background rhythm of clapping as Stormy went on.

"Two bushels, pinto beans."

"Buys new stonewashed jeans."

"Ten gallon hat, a smart cat."

The band stopped playing. With a sweep of her arms, Stormy directed the stockholders of the Farmers Elevator in the finale.

"King of the Road!"

CHAPTER THIRTEEN

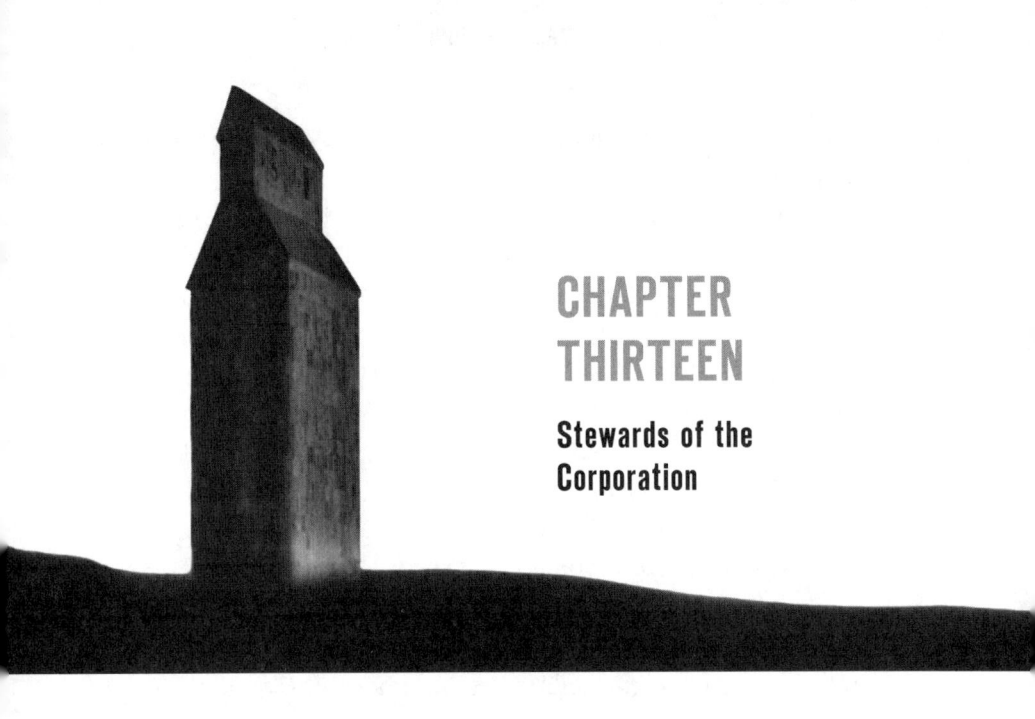

Stewards of the Corporation

After the excitement of the raffle, proceedings of the annual meeting were an anticlimax. Several members, especially those accustomed to other annual meetings, were on their way out when Chris Odegaard called the meeting to order.

"Ladies and gentlemen!" He paused to mop the sweat from his balding head. "Sure is hot in here...anyway..." he struggled on, a pioneer making his way into the unknown. "We got to get our annual meeting goin'. I'm sure glad you all came and are havin' a good time."

Applause and whistles from the crowd.

"But now we better get down to business. I'm gonna ask Sam to give us a report from the Secretary-Treasurer."

Sam Lofthus was one of those persons who were called, by God or Mammon, as custodians of community resources. He was treasurer of the Elevator, the Lutheran Church and the Sons of Norway. For each organization, he charted the comings and goings of money, much as he might watch the progress of water down an irrigation ditch, ready to dam up the flow or divert it where he thought it could be put to better use. You could be dying for water, or money, but unless Sam thought you had it coming, you were likely to dry up before a trickle found its way to you.

Sam rose and positioned his bifocals on his sunburned nose. Whatever neighbors might say about his stinginess, nobody disagreed with his honesty and hard work. When Sam cleared his throat, all of Sheffield listened.

"Now, I'm real happy to say that we are in pretty good shape at the Elevator. Our capital stock grew by thirty percent, mostly due to new patrons. And, thanks to our manager for that." Sam nodded at Tom and waited for the applause that followed. His gaze lingered on two tables of new members and they came in for a special blessing, a kind of dispensation for good economic behavior.

Sam went on. "We also more than doubled our sales from one and a half million dollars to three point eight million. We also went from five million to eight million in grain trades. This makes us one of the four or five biggest elevators in this part of the Dakotas."

Sam continued, supporting these summaries with detailed accounts of cash on hand, liabilities, and net worth. As a part of the report, he addressed the grain and fertilizer trades of the past year.

"You all know that Tom had a little tough luck in the storm last winter. But you'll be glad to hear that he's nearly covered his losses with profits in fertilizer. And nobody's had to go without the products they need at a price they can live with."

These statements brought approving comments from several patrons.

"Yeah, that's right!"

"Boy! Without Cooper I'd be shovelin' cow shit on my fields this year."

Sam raised his voice over table talk. "To wrap it all up," his glasses came off and he peered into the future, "we have a fine business here and most of it is due to Tom Cooper!"

The earlier murmurs of support grew more audible until Tom could hear several comments clearly.

"Damn right! Cooper deserves the credit!"

"He got me top dollar for my wheat and I ain't goin' nowhere else with my business!"

"Tom's a square shooter, and that says it all!"

Blushing, Tom got to his feet and took over the podium. "Thanks, Sam, and all the rest of you for making this a good year." He stopped, not knowing what to say until Pete whispered.

"Tell them where we're goin'. Give them a look at next year."

"Huh… oh, yeah…" This was another one of those times when he stood alone, not in danger, but the object of too much attention, when everyone expected more of him than he felt he could deliver. Why should he have to spell it out for them?

Gradually, his vision became clear. He could see how his future and that of the Elevator were joined. It became easier to explain the possibilities that faced them. "Your Elevator has changed a lot this year. When our new silos were completed, we became one of the largest elevators in the Dakotas. Our six hundred thousand bushel capacity makes it possible for us to load unit trains so that we can take advantage of volume pricing. I see a pretty bright future for the Elevator. We are bringing in new business, mainly because our prices are very competitive and our services better than anywhere else. We buy right and pass the savings along to our customers."

Now he had everyone's attention. Only Barney Jacobs was ignoring him to whisper to Frank Jessup, the night's featured speaker.

"This is going to continue to be a full service elevator, one where farmers can get good deals and the products and advice they need to compete in today's agrimarket. I hope that I can continue to be a part of Farmers Elevator and work with all of you who have become my friends during the past years."

He sat down to applause. It grew in volume until he had to stand and wave his acknowledgement—shy in the face of emotion.

When clapping had subsided, Chris took over.

"Now, ladies and gentlemen, it's my pleasure to introduce our guest speaker. When we planned this meeting, Farmhand was gonna send us Jim Leach. Well, Jim couldn't make it. But we're goin' one better—we got his boss. Let me introduce Frank Jessup, Vice President for Marketing at Farmhand. You all know how Farmhand works with us and helps us make the co-op idea real. Frank, why don't you tell us about it?"

Jessup stood and nodded at Chris's introduction and stepped to the podium. He arranged the speaker's light and microphone to suit his five-foot-eight stature. Placing his notes on the stand, he looked slowly around the room.

"Directors, patrons and guests," he began. "This is a happy night for all members of the Farmers Elevator family. You have a growing, thriving business that has every prospect of success. And, it looks like you have the leadership and management to make this a first-class organization."

Jessup's tone and delivery were those of rural evangelists who had led countless similar gatherings over the years. Many of the farmers sat back, prepared for a sermon on the virtues of cooperation, several relaxed to a point where sleep was not far away. Then Jessup abruptly changed his tone to one used for casting out those demons opposed to co-operative orthodoxy.

"But, let me tell you. Your Elevator is in trouble! If you patrons and directors don't do your part, none of the predictions made here tonight will come true!"

Tilted chairs came down and faces frowned.

"What!"

"The Elevator in trouble!"

"What's he talkin' about?"

The whispers became louder in Jessup's pause. He looked over his attentive flock and continued.

"I'm glad that shook you up! No, the Farmers Elevator isn't broke, but the whole co-operative movement is at risk, just as sure as I'm standing here. The risks result from poor management, and patrons and directors who don't realize that co-ops are only as strong as their members. Let me tell you a couple of true stories."

Jessup stopped and drank deeply from the speaker's water glass and shuffled his notes. Now every person in the room was leaning forward to hear what was to come.

"Not too many miles from here there's an elevator that looks a lot like yours, about a half-million bushel operation. The only difference is that it's empty and in the hands of a Chapter Eleven receiver."

Knowing looks flashed from table to table. That had to be the Severance Elevator. Didn't they go under last year? Or was it Griffin Co-op? Something about grain contracts.

Jessup read these thoughts accurately. "I can see that you have some idea of what I'm talking about. The fact is that more than twenty going businesses in the Farmhand territory went under last year. Most of these weren't ripped off by criminal management; they were done in by the very people who were supposed to prevent failure: by directors who didn't watch operations closely, by managers who hadn't kept up with changes in agribusiness, by patrons who took their elevator for granted. In fact, there's no surer prescription for bankruptcy than the notion that elevator business is business as usual. I can prove that to you."

As he spoke these lines, Jessup strode away from the podium, his voice rising so that no microphone was needed. Now he had everyone's attention and was able to manipulate their feelings to his theme.

"Does the Farmers Elevator have a policy on open grain accounts?" he paused, waiting for an answer that did not come.

"It's obvious from your Treasurer's Report that you don't. If you had a policy that stated that all purchases and sales had to be immediately covered in the futures market, you wouldn't have lost a dime in the December storm. But you wouldn't have had the opportunity to make big money that way. Well, you shouldn't. The Elevator isn't here to speculate with your equity. It's here to give you fair prices and good service—that's all!"

Tom could feel his face reddening. He reached for his coffee cup and managed to raise it to his mouth with only a faint rattle as it left its saucer. He was aware of a few sidelong glances. They amounted to nothing in the isolation he felt under Jessup's eyes. He knew that Barney had his laser-like gaze turned full on him and that it was up to Jessup whether this line of argument would turn into an inquisition in which he had the lead role. Open accounts! Losses on speculation! These phrases crossed his mind like the computer-controlled messages on the new Citizens' Bank sign.

Jessup went on. "How many of you have gotten good deals at your Elevator? Gotten a better price for your grain or cheaper fertilizer or chemicals than your neighbor?" He looked closely at each table and several eyes were hastily busy in other directions.

"That one struck close to home, didn't it? Well it ought to make you think. Every good deal you get raises the price to somebody else and hikes the general level of prices for next year. But you aren't the only guilty ones. Co-ops are trying to find their good deals, too. Fertilizer allocation has been a happy hunting ground for bagging good deals."

Tom had been following Jessup with a mixture of relief and interest. Despite the focus on his management, Jessup had given him some useful ideas. Good policies and fair trade only made sense. Well, maybe he had been a little too generous with some customers—there was that big lot of poor corn he had bought from Barney.

Fertilizer allocation! Now there was something he'd like to have explained to him. Too bad Leach wasn't speaking—he was somebody who knew what it was all about!

In the best country-revival tradition, Jessup had saved the Word until every parishioner was receptive. This year the Word was Fertilizer—from Beginning to End.

"We have an allocation program at Farmhand—one that we thought would give everyone a fair shot at a limited supply. Well, it didn't work. Every elevator got on the phone to ask for special treatment and a lot of you got it. So many did that we have a two-price market—one with standard prices and another with true black market prices where anything goes!"

Tom nodded. That's right! Just what I always said! Black market! How was Jessup going to explain the deals Leach had made this spring? The answers weren't long in coming.

"At Farmhand, we've been taking a real close look at our allocation program. Right now we've relieved a couple of our top fertilizer supervisors of their responsibilities until we can get to the bottom of their decisions. They appear to have given some co-ops better deals than they should have. And, there may be more to it than that. I'm talking about the menace to co-operatives—insider trading!"

What did that mean—insider trading? Tom's mind raced. Was Leach one of those 'relieved'? Had he read the whole thing wrong? Were the deals he had made any part of this problem? God! All he needed was to have the fertilizer business slide out from under him! The confidence he had felt during his earlier speech deserted him, taking away more than it had given. In its place was the specter of guilt, now personified by Jessup—whose emphatic gestures seemed to point directly at Tom.

He stole a look at Star, who was sitting at a corner table. There was no expression on Star's face, and he did not meet Tom's gaze. What was Star thinking now?

Jessup continued. "My point is this. Co-ops are big businesses. They have all the opportunities of big business—and all the problems. What you make of your Elevator is up to you. You directors and patrons hold this co-op for a short time. If you want to pass it along to your children and grandchildren, you must understand your responsibility. You are stewards of the corporation; its vitality and existence are in your hands!"

Jessup snapped off the speaker's light abruptly, nodded and strode to his seat. The silence that followed finally gave way to neighbor-to-neighbor discussion of the speech.

"Maybe he's right!"

"Yeah, I know that Griffin Co-op went under speculatin' on soybeans."

"I'd sure like to see somebody nail those black market fertilizer boys!"

These phrases flickered across Tom's mind as he glanced around the room. The nods and serious faces at each table told him that Jessup's remarks had hit home, planting a seed of worry that mocked the harvest of optimism expected minutes ago. If the meeting couldn't be pulled back on track, he'd have one hell of a time persuading the Board to back any of his ideas. He was almost physically ill with doubt, but somehow he managed to rise to his feet and make his way to the podium.

"I'd like to thank Frank for making it clear to us how important the Elevator is to our community. I'm sure you all agree that we've only started to build our business and that we have a long way to go."

The crowd was watching him, open to suggestion and waiting to hear what Jessup's speech meant to them. Their attention was a small sign that he might be able to shape opinion.

"I hope you keep his warnings in mind when we turn to election of new Board members. Be sure to pick your directors carefully. Choose men who will give the job the time and effort it requires, and pick the people who want to make the Elevator one of the best co-ops in the area."

He returned to his seat, perspiring with effort and worry. Had he turned the meeting in a positive direction? *God! I hope so!*

Janet squeezed his arm. "That was great! You said just the right things. I could see them change from suspicious to concerned. A lot of people were nodding at the end."

"I hope you're right, honey. The next half-hour will tell. If I get the right people on the Board, we're home free, if I don't..." His thoughts surged and covered possibility with a wave of potential disaster.

"Try not to worry," Janet said. "You've too many friends here who want the same things you do. See, that Ryan fellow is winking at you."

He followed her gaze. Gerry Ryan caught his eye and gave a knowing nod. There, at least, was one vote of confidence.

Chris Odegaard was back at the microphone. "Now, all you patrons be sure to stick around for the nomination and selection of directors. All visitors are invited to stay too. Some of you will want to leave, so I'm callin' a fifteen-minute break, and we'll ask the St. Stephen's ladies if we can have a refill on coffee."

When Chris had returned to his seat and talk was bursting out at tables, Bob tapped on his glass with a spoon.

"For those of you who want a little somethin' in your coffee, the bar will be open too. For the next fifteen minutes the drinks are on the Elevator boys!"

The announcement brought both cheers and frowns. The old time Board members showed their disapproval by glaring at Bob, but they were outvoted by newcomers and younger farmers who began an immediate drift to the bar.

Tom whispered to Janet, "What does he think he's doin'? Doesn't he know how Odegaard feels about drinking? And the employees are buying!"

"It doesn't seem right," she agreed. "It's coming at the wrong time!"

These reservations were overcome by the numbers who voted with their feet. Bob and Gerry Ryan led the charge to the bar, arms around each other's shoulders.

Tom's concern was mirrored in the determined look of Odegaard as Chris worked his way against the crowd to confront him.

"I hope this wasn't your idea, Tom. Remember, I was against having an open bar at our meeting."

Tom tried to diffuse Chris's anger. "No, Chris. This is all Bob's doing. In fact, I was just going to ask him how we'd pay…that is… gonna tell him to tone it down."

"You had better! And did you hear what Jessup said about the fertilizer black market? I know you been resellin' some of the extra fertilizer you've bought this spring. Isn't that goin' into the black market?"

Tom hesitated, the possible answers and new questions fighting for domination of his thoughts. *No, the Elevator was just doin' business. But what about Chris checking the books? Anyway, which is more important, drinks or fertilizer? Chris could go to hell! No, you got to have him in your camp at the meeting.* He realized Chris was waiting for an answer—about to repeat his question.

"Tom, I said…"

"Yeah, Chris. I heard you. I was surprised by Bob's idea myself. I'm on my way to close the bar. We got to remember we are guests of St. Stephen's."

"So—get crackin'. We can talk about the fertilizer thing at our next Board meeting."

Chris dismissed him with a wave of his hand—a minion sent to do the master's bidding. *Like a Goddamn puppet! Why can't I face up to these hypocrites? If he feels so strong about liquor, he should do his own police work!* He wove his way through the eager beneficiaries of Bob's generosity until he was standing next to Gerry Ryan and Bob.

"Bob!" Tom exclaimed. "What the hell's goin' on? Chris is mad as a hornet about opening the bar again. Who's gonna pay for this?"

"Hold your horses, Boss! Don't worry about the cost. The Fertilizer Division's buyin'. These people…" he waved his arm to embrace the bar crowd. "…are my customers and we gotta let them know that we appreciate their business!"

"Sure, Tom," Ryan agreed, "we like to know that we're wanted. You guys are doin' real right by us and we'll be back this fall with our crop. Anyway, a little fun don't hurt none. I'll bet old Odegaard's only pissed off that he can't likker up with his old lady around."

Tom laughed in spite of his worry. "That's probably right, but don't make it too hard for me. Remember, I gotta face them the next time the Board comes together."

Bob drew Tom aside and gave Ryan a gentle shove toward the bar, then whispered. "Boss, I've got Ryan all set up to run for the Board. And I think he's got the votes to get on. If he does, and we get another good local member, we can swing some of the deals we planned."

The scheme seemed reasonable. After all, Chris and the older patrons were probably setting up their own candidates—or had already done so. If he had two solid members in his corner…that would make for a two and two split on the Board with Chris the deciding vote. Not perfect, but better than the five to zero he had received against his requests last fall.

Like any other party, the gathering at the bar began to assume a life of its own. Small groups of farmers formed—some in earnest discussion.

"Prices look pretty strong for new crop."

"Yeah, I sold some yesterday at $2.75."

"Hey, you hear about the land sale at Grandview? Some of that hilly shit went for $1,100 an acre!"

Others were celebrating—like those surrounding Bob and Ryan.

"Goddammit Gerry! Where you puttin' them drinks?"

"Hell, I got a hollow leg and it ain't no more than half-full!"

"I always thought you were a couple quarts low!"

Tom stood a little apart from this group. He saw clearly what alcohol had hidden from him in the past. Being part of these good times looked much better from the inside. Star detached himself from the revelry and raised his glass to Tom.

"Well, Cooper. You finally made it! You're number one here tonight!"

"Don't gimme that! When the food, booze and prizes are forgotten—tomorrow probably—I'll be back to bein' number one on a lot of shit lists!"

Star laughed. "Always the optimist! Well, you can fall back on D.F." He drank, sparingly as usual when he was among his farmer customers.

"What the hell is D.F.? That some kind of disease?"

"Dakota Fertilizer, dummy! The way business is goin' we'll be the ones who come out on top after all the co-ops go under. This week I traded twenty thousand in corn at a fifteen cent margin. That's three grand clear profit!"

Tom gasped. "When did you start movin' grain? I thought you were only in fertilizer."

"Got the buyer's license in June. Have to do somethin' in the off season if I'm gonna keep the trucks movin'. Way I figure it, if we can start to build a grain trade, you could leave the Elevator and come to D.F. full time."

"Jesus! Not so loud! Chris will hear you. Look. He's watchin' us now. Barney too."

Star peered at the watchers over the rim of his glass. "You know, that sonofabitch Jacobs has been snoopin' around my warehouse at Dover. Andy says he's been askin' all kinds of questions about the business."

"That's a mystery to me, Star. Barney used to be one of my best friends. Now he can't pass up a chance to needle me about the Elevator or the way I run it."

"Then let's hope the new Board will give you the muscle to shut him up. Who's runnin?"

"Let's see…the holdovers are Odegaard, Arne Carlson and Lofthus. That leaves two vacancies. The two outgoing directors aren't elgible to run again. Ryan is my number one candidate, and I hoped that Ernie Larsen would be another—too bad he didn't make it home in that storm."

"I agree that Ryan would be great for us. But who else?"

"I been after Ray Dickerson to run. With this bunch of newcomers here, I think he'd get on."

Star thought for a moment, then looked directly at Tom with rare seriousness. "Tell me, was that drawing rigged? How come Phil Odegaard and Dickerson won the big prizes?"

Tom was silent and gradually his eyes drifted away from Star's gaze. "Ummm....noo...What makes you say that?"

"Just wonderin'. If Phil could put a little pressure on Chris and you got both Ryan and Dickerson on the Board, you'd have the Directors in the bag."

That sure was true. But would Phil be able to sway Chris' thinking? And what about Ryan and Dickerson? They were unknowns who were pretty friendly now....

"Well, we'll see." Tom said. "The election's got to go my way before any of this talk makes sense." He turned abruptly away from Star and crossed the room to the Odegaard table—Star's gaze following thoughtfully.

As Tom approached the group around Chris, he was conscious of an entirely different conversation. Here, the mood was one of business, not party. Barney and Jessup were dominating the discussion.

"What I say is that we need directors who are in the agribusiness mainstream. No bunch of two-by-four farmers can understand big business." Barney was shaking his meaty fist to make his point.

Jessup nodded. "That may be so. But remember it was the two-by-four farmers who built this co-op and Farmhand too, for that matter."

"Huh!" Barney snorted. "That's all in the past! This is now, and we need new thinkin' on the Board!"

As Tom came up, the conversation dwindled and everyone looked at him. "Sounds pretty serious over here. You folks ready for the election?"

"You damn right it's serious, Cooper," Jacobs exploded. "We better get some businessmen on the Board or you'll run the Elevator into the ground!"

Stunned by the viciousness of Barney's tone, Tom shifted his attention to Odegaard. "Well Chris, should we get this meeting on the way?"

"I think it's about time," Chris responded. "If we're going to have a serious election, we'd better do it before your new friends are too drunk to vote!" He stalked to the podium.

The others moved away; only Tom and Barney remained. They looked after Odegaard, and finally Tom spoke. "Barney, what's the problem with you? For the past year, you've been on my case, and I don't know why."

"That's easy, Cooper. You're sittin' on a big moneymaker and I don't like the way you're runnin' it."

"But what about our friendship? I thought we were in this thing together. You've always got much more than a fair shake from me."

"A couple deals don't do it! I want control of this Elevator and I think I'm gonna get it tonight. When Jessup showed up instead of your buddy, Leach, I knew I had it made."

Tom paused—this was new information. *Jessup and Barney! Why hadn't Leach shown up? Control of the Elevator. God! What next?*

"Oh, I don't know, Barney. Jessup's just sayin' what all the ag magazines have been writin' about. Good management is all we need."

"Goddammit Cooper! That's just the point! Good management's just what we ain't got! But it's what we're sure as hell gonna get!" He tramped off to a group of farmers near the rear of the room.

As always when he was under stress, everything in the room receded from Tom's perception. He stood in the middle of the room—voices became muffled through an aura of isolation. Intolerable pressures bombarded him from all sides, and emptiness at his core allowed them sway over his being. He was a shell, only lightly protecting the tiny embryo of self.

Isolation emptied him—the resulting void filling with the anxieties of the moment. Who would be elected? Where was Leach? Would he survive the financial crunch at the Elevator? Would he…

Janet came up to him, touching him carefully—feeling his pain through his public shell.

Then she asked, "What was that? Barney seemed so mad! Is something wrong?"

"No—no—," he began. Then the truth forced its way to the surface. "Yes. It sounds like big trouble! He wants control of the Elevator. He's somebody I've never seen before."

"What are you saying? You mean Barney is openly against you?"

"That's right. He made it pretty clear. If he gets on the Board, there'll be hell to pay."

Janet thought for a moment. "So that's why Jean Jacobs has been so distant these past months. Why, she isn't even here tonight. And that's the first time she's missed one of the annual meetings since we came here."

"Too bad—there's nothin' we can do about it, Jan. We just have to see how the election comes out." He put his arm around her, feeling the strength of her support as they found a place at one of the rear tables.

"Patrons and friends," Odegaard began, the center of attention. "Our Annual Meeting is reconvened and nominations are open for new directors."

After a short silence, one of Ernie Larsen's boys stood up. Frank Larsen stared at Tom as he spoke. "I nominate Barney Jacobs and I'd like to say that he's the kind of director we need to see that things are on the up and up." He sat down and the crowd stirred—Jacobs clearly had some significant support.

The Jacobs nomination was seconded—then one of Tom's regular patrons, Sam Pedersen, rose. "I nominate Gerry Ryan. He's the sort of new blood we can use on the Board."

This line of thought, too, was greeted with a murmur of agreement. Tom looked around, hoping that the ideas he had planted over the past month would take root now.

"Are there any further nominations?" Odegaard looked around the room. "If not..."

There was a movement among some of the younger farmers. Finally, one of Ryan's neighbors stood up.

"Umm...I...I nominate Ray Dickerson."

A quick second by another new patron and some additional table talk followed.

Chris Odegaard waited for the conversation to subside, then he spoke. "Hearing no further nominations, I ask for a motion that nominations be closed." This proposal was immediately approved. "Now, each of you patrons got a blank ballot when you registered tonight. Please write in the names of two nominees and pass your ballots to the front of the room. I'll ask two of you ladies to work with Sam to tally the results."

The next minutes of ballot counting were agony for Tom. He wavered between optimism and despair. *If only Barney didn't make it...* He only needed another couple of years to get things on an even keel to make the Elevator a tower of strength in Sheffield. *Please, let this be my...*

He was interrupted by Odegaard's announcement. "Ladies and gentlemen! Here are the results. Ryan: 185 votes." Applause from the younger contingent. "Dickerson: 155 votes." Further applause. Tom clenched his fists in anticipation. He had it made with those two!

"And Jacobs: 210 votes." Our new directors are Barney Jacobs and Gerry Ryan. Let's give them a hand!"

Tom's heart sank as he recalled Jessup's challenge: Stewards of the Corporation.

After the election, the Hall emptied quickly. Most members were well pleased with the event and took special pains to see that Tom knew it.

"Great evening. Best Annual Meetin' ever!"

"Can't remember when we've had so much fun!"

"Hell, I'll never forget the look on old Odegaard's face when Phil won that camper!"

"Let's do it again next year!"

All these comments went a long way to restoring the confidence Tom had brought to the meeting. A slightly positive feeling grew slowly, building on the obvious joy he had engineered. Only the cold stares of Jessup and Barney fenced in his pleasure. They were still deep in conversation and appeared to be directing it his way. His tide of confidence ebbed and he turned his gaze from the two.

Janet broke the spell. "Oh, Tom! They loved it!" She held his arm close to her side, her fingers moving slightly as if to share his thoughts. "I'm so proud of you!"

"Guess that's right." He looked down at her, conscious of the bond they shared—now, two alone in the crowd. "C'mon, honey, let's go home." He put his arm around her shoulders and led her outside to the Fury. In the parking lot, a line of cars pressed their way onto Highway 13 with a good deal of happy horn blowing.

"Sounds like the junior prom!" Janet giggled.

He joined in. "Doesn't it though!"

They took their place in the exit line and turned west. They were almost instantly alone—one spot of light thrusting into the prairie. Night surrounded them, pulling their thoughts into the timeless song of summer. Crickets in unison, thrilling at limitless warmth. Stars without number, no longer faint above the lights of town, were overwhelming in the vast depth they gave to the night.

As they drove along, Tom and Janet's hands reached out to make a oneness, transported back to the beginning of their marriage when their future was only dimly sensed and all their energy focused on the emotional wealth of now.

These days, such moments were rare. When one had the experience, the other was caught up in the pressure of living. The future was still dim, but no longer cloaked in promise, covered instead by a brooding uncertainty. Love, though still warm at the core, did not burn with the fire of fifteen years ago. When it flickered into life, as it did now, it required careful tending or it would expire to smolder beneath the surface of more powerful emotions.

It was as if they were seated on an over-long bench—one at each end. Between them sat the principal figures of their lives–Jacobs, Chrissy, Odegaard, Bob, and now Jessup—so that their reaching fingers could barely meet. Even now, the magic of the night was veiled by the ambivalence of the meeting outcomes. And each loving expression was shouldered aside by the blunt surges of power and business.

"What do you think of the Board, hon?" he asked.

"Oh, it'll be fine. Once Barney sees how difficult the Elevator is to run, he'll come over to your side." Janet tightened her grip on his hand to emphasize her conclusion.

"Boy, I hope you're right. But I still can't see why he's so rotten. He and Jean used to be so close to us." He shook his head and released his hand from hers to drive–both arms stiff with tension.

"They've changed." She sighed, folding her hands in her lap. "It seems that they have grown away from us. The bigger their farming operation gets, the less they have to do with us."

"Guess that's so. Why, remember when we first came to town. That night they came over with a picnic hamper. . ." His voice trailed off in recollection.

"Two bottles of Annie Green," she finished his sentence. "We all drank to the future that night."

Tom rested his left elbow on the open window, learning his head on his upturned hand. "Those sure were the days! Remember how we could hardly keep up with the way things were going?"

"I remember. You and Barney were so optimistic about farming. He'd tell you about the way he planned to expand his operation, and you were right there with another idea about the grain business."

"Sure—that's part of it. But we were up on our future, too. That was the summer we bought the farm. When Barney offered that eighty dollars an acre rent, we could see payoff in ten years."

They were silent for almost a mile. This past spring, Barney hadn't been around for their annual rental conference. At the time, the omission had made no difference. Another neighbor came across with a fifteen-dollar boost in rent and a five-year contract. It was, however, a sign of change.

"Well, I'm sorry that Barney isn't like he used to be…," he mused.

She moved closer to him, taking his hand again and holding it in her lap. The figures between them on their mental bench faded and they were close again.

When they turned off Highway 13 and headed south, Tom slowed the car. The song of insects flowed through the open windows of the Fury—a harmony symbolic of the unity of country life in another time.

Theirs was the last innocent generation—an anomaly positioned in time when the pace of life and its institutions came together to create an idyllic environment, where order smoothed the rough edges of living.

In the communities where they had grown up, security came with the end of war and the beginning of economic good times. The rituals of school, church and home blended for a brief instant to give youth a sense of purpose and opportunity, channels for restless desire along with generous support for achievement.

They were firmly locked into a well-defined path of development, always achieving goals within their reach, adored and envied by their peers. Theirs was ordained success. They were expected to realize life-long benefits for the talents it was their right to possess.

While these conditions made for integrated personalities, they did not equip for challenge and possible failure. They left, instead, an unstable structure that could stand tall if unshaken; but one that was empty of confidence and lacking in emotional strength. Without easy success and continuous praise, such personalities could crumble under the press of small reversals.

This defined the difference between them. She had an inner strength that had repeatedly risen to new demands. Each challenge was carefully weighed and those within reason accepted and mastered.

His reservoir of confidence was, by contrast, virtually empty. It had never been filled by conquered failure. It was an emptiness walled off by the tokens of past triumphs. As these receded in time, the nothingness at the center of his life was always ready to expand—to engulf any potential he might have available to master the moment.

Their reactions to this night were evidence of the depths of this difference. He could not suppress his anxiety over the future. The fundamental conflicts of business remained unresolved, an oozing darkness pushing at memory to cover the few glimmerings of opportunity.

Hers was a soundness based on the healing power of time—days added together to bury trouble and provide a clear field on which new life could be seeded. Forces that were monstrous to him were of human scale to her—understandable—within coping range.

Janet reached to the dash of the Fury and snapped the radio on. A few aimless turns of the dial brought in WAYL, a summer evening companion that had entertained them many times.

"Hey! There it is again!" Tom slowed the car to a near stop and leaned forward to catch the familiar rhythms of swing.

"Yes. Isn't it funny. We can't ever get WAYL during the day."

"They say it has something to do with some layer in the atmosphere…" He left the sentence unfinished as the station came in more clearly.

He pulled the Fury to the side of the road. When the engine stopped and the headlights turned off, they were steeped in summer. The outdoor music was tuneless, elemental, soothing. The radio provided a melodic counterpoint to the sounds of nature, weaving memories on the woof of time.

She leaned her head on his shoulder and he drew her closer.

"Say. Remember the time…." They both spoke at once. Identical words—identical thoughts. They laughed.

"Pretty sentimental, I guess." He hugged her.

"Oh, I don't know. That's what music is for. Kind of a memory builder. You hear it when you're having some experience. Then, everytime you hear it again, you can't help but remember all the other times…" She stopped and chuckled at the confusion in her explanation.

He laughed along with her. "I know what you mean. I still remember the music of *My Fair Lady*. That was sure playing a lot when we were in college."

The radio had been filled with the Lerner and Lowe tunes, competing with rock 'n' roll. They had met during their second year at Concordia College. Both had returned early that fall—he for football and she for a special choir concert. They had been thrown together by their dining schedules and were drawn to one another by their mutual enthusiasm for college life.

Each evening, before their scheduled activities, they had walked over the campus—busy discovering one another. At first, only their minds touched in a superficial way—brushing lightly against one another—searching for a match of belief and expectation. As their compatibility became apparent, they walked closer together—a preliminary physical touching. A promise of future fulfillment.

Their early love was one of hands. Holding gently, with occasional grips of emotion. Their fingers searched—and found—like bundles of charged wires locking together in a circuit of feeling. Apart, they were only components—together they found new energy and new dimensions of self, reflected in the eyes and gestures of the other.

They became ever more interdependent over the years, and their decision to have Chrissy confirmed the strength of their relationship.

They had been sitting over a Sunday breakfast in the little kitchen of their Bloomington apartment. Each was holding a cup of coffee with both hands when their eyes met across the table.

"I love you, Mrs. Cooper."

"Oh, Mr. Cooper! This is so unexpected! Whatever will Mother say!"

They had laughed and reached across the table, their hands confirming unity.

He reached into the pocket of his robe with a free hand. He brought out the round blue container that held the measured regimen of her birth control pills. With a casual flick of his wrist, he spun the disk into a nearby waste basket.

"I think it's time, don't you, Mrs. C?"

She looked directly at him, then she smiled, her face lighting the morning.

"I sure do, Mr. C. In fact, I haven't been taking them for almost two months."

His jaw dropped—a parody of comic double-take.

"You haven't…What?…But…"

"Oh, T. I've known for almost a year that you wanted a child. Haven't you?"

"Well…yes…But I didn't really see it until last week when I was alone in Minot. You know, I saw this family in a restaurant. They looked so complete, you know…"

Four hands reached out—linking them in a oneness of belief and desire. Then, she spoke again.

"Now, don't get too excited! I didn't have my period last month."

"You…do you mean…?"

"I hope so. It would be so right for us now."

It had been so right. When Chrissy was born, she was the final piece in their lives. Tom became conscious of this fact when he picked Janet up from the hospital in their little Volkswagen. She was holding the tiny bundle on her lap. When the door of the car was closed by the nurse, Janet grinned at Tom.

"Look! Isn't she just the most precious little thing you've ever seen?" She unbundled Chrissy's blanket, revealing a little pink face, eyes closed, serene and secure. Her tiny hands were tightly clenched, holding on to life.

"She's a lot smaller than she looked in the hospital. You sure we should be taking her home? Shouldn't we wait a few days?"

"Oh, T! Don't worry!"

There had been no need for worry. The three of them were a perfect fit.

They slid out of the Fury now and stood together, she leaning back on the car's fender and he gazing over her thoughtfully.

"Aren't they beautiful," she whispered, her head thrown back, staring into the depths of the night sky.

"Ummm…you bet." He held her hands and let his mind project itself in a half-shared flight.

They stood quietly, listening to the muted music of the radio. When the song finished, he reached into the car and turned the radio off. Quiet flowed back, covering the small ripple of their presence.

"Hi, Cat Eyes." Tom smiled into her upturned face, the glint of reflected moonlight a reminder of a wild creature caught in the headlights of emotion.

"Hi, Tom Cat." She laughed, the old exchange coming easily for them.

Closer now, their hands sliding down the curves of shoulder and muscle, they kissed.

"Purrrr." Her quiet rumble of pleasure stirred him, and he pressed tightly to her—forcing her hips firmly against the car.

Her response was a smooth sliding back and up so that she was partially sitting on the Fury's hood. Gradually, her legs parted—drawing him in.

As her tongue touched his, his hands pressed her against him, guiding the motion of her hips. Her legs hooked around him.

Their mutual desire moved them apart so that their hands were free to explore. Her fingers raced over his belt, unfastening, gracefully, quickly caressing him. His hands smoothed her thighs under her dress.

He stood on tiptoe to reach for her. She slid slowly down the hood to mesh with him. They moved in unison, slowly, savoring the delight of two persons accustomed to one another.

Her murmurs became little cries until their mutual convulsion. Then she relaxed against him, tiny spasms representing the aftershock of love.

"Oh! It's so perfect!" she murmured.

He kissed her forehead. "Cat Eyes, I love you."

They held one another, letting the night breeze cool their passion.

"My God! What a night!" he exclaimed. "Just like a couple of teenagers!"

"Oh, no! Teenagers never had it like this. Tom, darling, I'll love you forever!"

He hugged her, flexing his muscles to feel the soft yielding of her body, glorying in the exquisiteness of this woman.

After a time, they went back into the Fury. Tom started the car while she dialed the radio. It was Ella.

"Blue Moon. Now I'm no longer alone…"

"Say, that's too much! My favorite song, my favorite woman and…"

Janet interrupted. "That's it. The word. Favorite. That's what you are!" She cuddled against him as they drove the last miles home.

Their hands rested now—his holding hers. Safe and secure.

CHAPTER FOURTEEN

Area of High Pressure

The next three weeks brought the hot, dry weather that was a Dakota trademark. The prairie burned—withered—and cracked. Drought and its consequences were a constant topic of conversation at the Elevator.

"Jesus H. Christ! It's hotter than the hinges of hell!" Bob plunked his already sweaty frame into his desk chair. "Why in God's name do we gotta sit here on a Saturday mornin' like cooked turkeys?"

"Hey! Who you callin' a turkey?" Tom laughed. "Besides it's been hot before. Just wait 'til fall and you'll be bitchin' about the cold."

"Can't come too fuckin' soon for me!" Bob reached up and focused the small video monitor where Minneapolis grain quotations were displayed. "Holy shit! Look at that! The goddamn market closed limit up on Friday! If this keeps up, corn'll hit four bucks by September."

"Yeah, I been watchin' it pretty close. I figure that some of the Dakota counties will be declared disaster areas in another week."

They mopped their faces. Even though the office was in the shade of the giant silos, it was already very hot. The afternoon sun of yesterday was still trapped in the fabric of the Elevator. No air moved anywhere.

If this day ran true to form, the temperature would climb rapidly into the high nineties and a furnace-like wind would blow from the south. Every living thing would then seek shade if it could.

"Did you look at that big field of Barney's down on the flats this morning?" Bob plied a toothpick to finish off his breakfast.

"No, but I'll bet it's hurting."

"Damn right! I drove past it just after sunup. Half the plants already looked like pineapples. Hell, there are some sandy spots where the whole crop is dead. Not a plant standin'."

"Looks just as bad up my way," Tom said. "Even the fields with good reserves of moisture are showin' stress."

"What do you think this means for us this fall?"

Tom chewed nervously at his pencil for a moment. Then, pushing his cap back on his head, he focused on the implication of Bob's question. What would they do? He was still short on quality corn—and there sure wouldn't be anything but sub-grade crop this fall.

Nevertheless, he put a positive spin on his answer. "No problem. We'll just go long on the futures. Each week this dry spell goes on, we stand to make another twenty to thirty cents a bushel on our contracts."

"Sounds pretty complicated," Bob said. "You sure it'll work?"

"Hell, yes. All I do is call my broker and buy a couple of contracts for fall. Then, when the new crop fails to come in, I'll be able to sell those contracts for a fat profit."

"Ain't that just speculatin'?" Bob frowned owlishly at the complexity of the transaction.

Tom wandered over to the window air conditioner and began the morning ritual of button pressing and selective beating. "Might as well see if this mother is gonna work today."

Some squeaks and rattles from the unit predicted that it would provide a few wisps of tepid air, until it would finally give up and pop its circuit breaker.

He turned to face Bob, arms folded, and leaned back on the wall. "Let me explain it to you, Meathead. Here's how it works."

Bob too, sat back—hands clasped behind his head—ready for the lesson.

Tom began. "See, now we got corn that's open. If we don't sell it, we're speculating, right?"

"Sure, but..."

"Hold your horses! If we want to, we can sell enough on the futures market to cover what we paid for and a little besides."

"Yeah, then we can't..."

"Goddammit! Shut up and listen!" Tom laughed at Bob's confusion. "That's pretty simple," he went on. "Now it gets complicated. Suppose a farmer walks in here and sells us a couple thousand bushels for delivery this fall. We aren't out any cash, but when his trucks roll in this fall, we'd better be ready with the check."

"Suckin' aye!" Bob nodded.

"Well, if we guess wrong on our new crop price, we could be holdin' the bag."

"Jeez! Remember the time..."

"Not yet! Not yet! Instead of takin' that risk, we sell the same couple of thousand on the futures market. Then, when the farmer comes in with the crop, we pay him off and sell the corn for cash."

"But—wait a minute! We still got the futures."

"Sure, dummy! We use the cash we get for sellin' the real corn to buy back the futures."

"Sounds to me like a carny shell game. How do we be sure nobody pees on us?" Bob guffawed at his pun.

"That's the beauty of hedging. Every time we take a cash position here, we take an equal and opposite position in futures. Then, if the cash market goes up, we'll make money sellin' the product and lose money on the futures. The idea is to break even."

"Seems like a hell of lot of fuckin' around to cover our ass."

"You got it! Coverin' our ass is what it's all about." The lecturer straightened up and took his place at his desk, eyes bright with the successful outcome of the lesson.

"But what about the open contracts we been writin' on new crop? They covered?"

"Well...nooo. But with this drought there's no way corn is goin' down before next year."

"Shit! This whole thing's a lot like a condom. It ain't as much fun when you use it and it sure don't do no good to wish you had one when the party's over."

Tom laughed. "Guess you got me there. But this is one time we don't need birth control. The poor farmer is on the pill. Anytime he comes in to sell new crop, I can give him the best price he's ever seen and know that the run-up isn't near over. In fact, any time I think we've seen the high—all I got to do is make a phone call and we're covered."

"Okay. Okay. You convinced me. But just remember how hard it is to quit when you're havin' fun." Bob winked and rolled his chair to the desk where fall fertilizer orders were beginning to accumulate.

Tom looked at Bob's back. The blotches of sweat reminded him of his own anxiety. Was it a good idea to be open on all the grain he had purchased for fall delivery? Maybe, but he was also plenty long in the futures market. He was speculating on both ends of the market—equal positions—but not opposite.

Here was a growing dilemma of the country elevator manager. In order to make a viable organization out of the slim profits in trade, managers had to be expert in playing the market. Unfortunately, there just wasn't enough time to give to marketing. Management of the day-to-day affairs of these multi-million dollar businesses was far too demanding, and the load generally fell on a single person. The result was speculation—the notion that an informed guess was as good as serious study. What the typical manager did was pit his limited knowledge against sophisticated traders who had accurate data and computer models of production and demand, an unequal contest in a very high stakes game.

Tom turned on the radio and searched the dial for a weather report. The Grandview station obliged.

"…with local record highs in the low 100's. Cattlemen are warned of unusually high livestock stress. Special precautions for adequate water and shade are in order. And, folks, there is no relief in sight. An area of high pressure is dominating the weather picture. We can expect little or no relief for the next three to five days. This means trouble for local farmers. Crops are already damaged and…"

Tom cut the news short and stared out the window. At least he was on the right side of the speculation. If everything came in, he'd...

"Cripes!" Bob threw his pencil at the invoices on his desk. "If this weather don't break, there ain't no crop and no money to pay for these orders. Wish I could hedge fertilizer."

No crops. No money. Jesus. That would bring down the house. Suppose nobody came in with grain. Sure, he'd be okay on his futures contracts but...

"Well. Dammit! We just got to hope that this thing don't go on too long." Bob retrieved the pencil and went back to checking his orders.

The air conditioner hummed. Would the drought break? Would the price rise persist? Tom recalled the storm of last winter when he couldn't cover his sales. These worries buzzed through his mind, rattling like the loose fan on the laboring appliance.

Pete broke into this reverie and the cool air along the floor escaped his attempt to trap it with a quick slam of the office door.

"Well, you two sure got it made. Here I am, boilin' in that damn house while you sit here like a couple of queens."

"Watch it," Bob grinned, "you talkin' 'bout our sexual preferences?"

"Could be," Pete replied. "You sure spend a lot of time together in this closet. Anyway, I got bad news for you guys. We got some hot spots in silo six and I think we better turn the stuff now."

"Oh, shit!" Tom blurted. "How bad is it?"

"There's a crust on top and she's beginnin' to stink." Pete said.

"Okay." Tom moved to the blackboard that showed the contents of the various bins and silos in the Elevator. "Let's run the crust into bins three and four in the house. They've got some air and maybe we can save the bulk of it. Then let's draw about half and shift it into silo four. When the stuff comes out cool we can stop. Okay?"

"Yep," Pete agreed. "Should work. But it'll play hell runnin' that shit through the old leg."

Tom considered. The elevator leg Pete was referring to was an ancient one. Driven by obsolete flat belts, it was very sensitive to overloading and once the belt began to slip, it quickly jumped its pulleys. The following reversal of flow in the leg resulted in a mess in the underground pit that fed the leg.

"Hell, Pete, we gotta try it. The only other way is to auger the stuff into trucks. That'll take all week."

"Right," Pete said. "I'll get the boys on it. Remember, it's Saturday and we only got a couple of hours before they head home. Once that crust moves down in the silo, we got to keep goin'."

Pete was right. Bins and silos had their unloading spouts at the bottom. However, the material moved down from the top. Thus, spoiled crusts on the bins had to be pulled down through the entire mass before a problem could be considered solved. If the process stopped with spoiled grain in the middle of the silo, a good deal more could be at risk.

"I know, I know. But me and Bob will help babysit this thing so we can keep it goin'. Just get her set up and runnin'."

"Hey. Speak for yourself," Bob growled. "I got a heavy date with the old lady for a trip to Fargo where they got factory air in them blackjack parlors."

"You stayin' in some kind of factory over to Fargo?" marveled Pete. "Why that's a new kind of escape. Hell, I bet…"

Tom cut the banter short. "All right, Pete, give it a go, and we'll work it out."

Pete turned and grinned his way out of the office, satisfied that he had planted a seed of reality among the uninformed.

"Dammit, Bob. I was hopin' to take Chrissy and Janet swimming this afternoon! Now we've got this problem!"

"Piss on it! You should let it wait 'til Monday. That corn ain't gonna get no worse. And you can bet your ass that nobody on the Board, not even that shithead Jacobs, would be down here in this heat!"

Tom thought for a bit. "You're probably right. But we better get on the problem now. Don't worry. Between Pete and me, we can work it out. Maybe one of the other guys…"

"Suit yourself!" Bob stood and stretched, his eyes flitting nervously—a caged bird ready for flight. "Guess I'll check on these orders. Probably take me 'til afternoon, so I won't be back. Be seein' you on Monday." He scooped up a random sheaf of invoices and was out the door.

Tom was torn between anger at Bob's escape and admiration for the speed and resolve with which he had carried it off. Once again, he was alone with the Elevator. Thank God Pete was willing to share the responsibility.

He studied the bin board, considering how to accomplish the move of spoiled corn. If everything went well, they would dispatch the crust by sundown, and he could spend all day Sunday with his family.

His thoughts faded with the gradual slowing of the rumble of the elevator leg. Everyone who worked at the Elevator was in tune with this sound. If the leg wasn't unloaded right now…He sprang up and ran for the door into the house.

"Hey!" he yelled. "Shut off the feed auger! She's…"

The rumble became a squeal, and the flop of the leg-drive belt punctuated the sudden silence. Then the leg began to run backward and the heavy upward-bound buckets of spoiled corn reversed direction. The mad race was short. The corn was now packed tightly in the underground feed pit and the leg wedged in a mass of rotten goo.

"Sonofabitch!" shouted Pete from the tunnel under the silos. "The goddamn gate on silo six broke. We're up to our assholes in corn in the tunnel!"

"Well, we sure as hell are plugged solid," observed Tom. He opened the trapdoor to the leg pit. It was normally a ten-foot deep, dusty hole surrounding the leg hopper. Now it was a sea of moldy yellow, at least six feet deep.

"Fuck!" he gasped. "That's the worst mess we've ever had!"

Pete climbed out of the tunnel containing the feed auger from the silos. Coughing, he peered into the pit.

"Jeez! That sure as hell is a mess! Well, we better get the little auger and a couple of trucks over here if we're gonna get this thing runnin' again."

Tom rocked back on his heels. This afternoon, only two hours from now, he was supposed to pick up Janet and Chrissy at the farm.

How could he possibly get this problem under control in time? Pete's questioning gaze contained the only solution.

"Suppose so. I'll get the GMC. You wheel the portable auger around, and let's give it a try."

They assembled the equipment and carefully worked the portable auger into the pit trapdoor. When the truck was under the other end of the auger, they were ready to begin.

Tom threw the switch on the auger's electric motor and the first of the spoiled corn thudded into the truck box. Soon, however, the flow stopped. The auger had eaten its way into the spilled grain; now shoveling must begin.

"Well, that's the easy part. You want to go first or second?"

Pete sighed. "Probably don't make no diff. We'll both get our fill of shovelin'." He sat on the lip of the trapdoor and slid off into the pit, clutching his shovel. Sinking into the stinking mess nearly to his waist, he began shoveling corn into the auger intake. The heat and poisonous fumes of spoilage soon sapped his strength and he struggled up the short ladder to ground level.

"Better not stay down there too long," Pete gasped. "That mold is somethin' else. Wait a minute and I'll get a respirator."

"Go ahead. I'll get started and you can hand it to me." Tom swung down the ladder and began his turn at the shovel. The heat of the spoiled corn immediately penetrated his shoes and trousers. Sweat rolled off his face and nausea came and went as his shovel released clouds of spores. It was a bare five minutes before he groped his way to the ladder and sucked in the clear air above.

Pete and Tom repeated this nightmare over and over again for the next two hours. Despite the respirator, they grew progressively ill. They had no sense of time. Tom's promised holiday faded into the routine of shoveling, climbing and retching.

By early afternoon, they had emptied most of the pit and reached the cover plates on the bottom of the leg. Working together, they stacked the covers against the wall of the pit.

"Goddammit! The fuckin' thing's plugged solid!" Tom poked at the packed cube of corn. Only a little fell away. He refastened his mask and dug at the corn to uncover the belt and buckets of the leg. Gradually, the machinery emerged and, as they dug, the remaining weight of corn-filled buckets rotated the belt. A mass of corn grew around them and the auger and shovel process resumed.

Another two hours and there were no more filled buckets in sight. Pulling together, they were able to rotate the belt enough to make sure it was free. Like automatons, they replaced the covers and cleaned the last of the spoiled corn from the pit.

When they finished, they pulled themselves to the level of the house floor, letting their feet dangle over the edge of the trapdoor. The superheated air of the scale house in the afternoon was chilling in their sweat-soaked clothes.

Neither spoke for several minutes. Then Pete sighed. "Looks like the worst is over. Guess I'll mosey upstairs and see if we can get the old bitch runnin' again."

"No, hold it a while," Tom said. "We better get dried out first. I think there's a couple sets of clean coveralls in the office. Let's change and cool down before we try to run this thing."

They staggered to their feet, carefully straightening sore backs and stretching muscles that were already contracting.

Entering the office, they shivered in what felt like arctic air. They wasted no time in shedding their soaked, dirty clothes and pulling on clean coveralls. They sank into chairs, relaxing in the luxury of escape from the drudgery of the pit.

They had been sitting for some time, nearly asleep, when the office door swung open and Star bounded in. He vaulted to the top of the counter, and landed—legs dangling—smiling, a cold six pack of beer in each hand.

"Hey, you jokers! Here's the Star with the fixins! Let's have a party!"

Like an accomplished shortstop, his hands performed the illusion that floated two cans into the grasps of Pete and Tom.

"Here's lookin' at you kids!" Punctuated with the 'Busssch' of the opening brew, Star raised his can in salute.

Pete followed suit, his broad grin matching the joy that Star wore as his customary mantle. Tom clutched the icy can, and moved its moist caress over his forehead.

"Hey! Old Star! Where the hell you been these last weeks?" Tom said. "We been wonderin' if the morals squad finally caught up with you."

"No way! I been so damn busy truckin' that I ain't even had time for any real fun!" He paused and drew at his beer. "C'mon Big T, drink up. There's another six in the cooler out in the old Kenworth."

"Nooo.. not now. I'm tryin' to stay on the wagon. But I'll have a Coke on you. Gimme a couple quarters."

"Say, you weren't kiddin' us when you quit. Probably a good idea, but I sure hope I never get one like it." He tossed the coins to Tom.

When the vending machine had served him, Tom leaned on the counter next to Star.

"How's business?" he asked. "You makin' the fertilizer racket go?"

Star glanced at Pete, then replied. "Sure. It's still goin' good. But the hot spell is puttin' the clamps on sales and I got to rustle up some grain haulin' if I'm gonna keep the boys on the road."

"How many trucks you runnin' now?" Pete asked.

"Let's see. I got one on grain and two on fertilizer. Almost put on another in June, but the product wasn't movin' to suit me. Sure glad I didn't sign anymore lease papers."

Tom digested this answer and the scope of Star's operation. "Say. That's three times what you were doin' last year. Andy workin' out OK?"

"You bet! He's on the road all the time. Super reliable. Another guy from what he was when he was workin' at the Elevator."

"We sure as hell could use him here today," Pete commented. "Hot corn, leg plugged and all."

"Yeah," Star said. "I ran into Bob over to the VFW and he sent these beers along for you guys."

"Why, that sonofabitch!" Tom exclaimed, awed by the completeness of Bob's escape. "He ran out of here on his way to Fargo. Guess he couldn't pass up the Club."

Star popped another can and took up the defense of the accused. "Aw, don't be too hard on old Bob. Just think—he's gotta ride all the way to Fargo with his old lady. Bet he'll wish he was shovelin' corn before he's halfway there."

They concurred. Time with Bob's wife, especially in a closed car on a hot day, was an assignment from the devil.

"Guess you're right," Pete concluded. "Well, I'm gonna try the heat and see if the leg'll start." He placed his empty can neatly in the broken six pack, a subtle hint for the others.

"Stick around, Pete," Star invited, "no hurry to get roasted. Better fuel up on the cool stuff first."

"Nope, I want to be out of here by sundown. So I better get crackin'." He pulled on his hard hat and slipped through the house door.

"Hell of a worker, that guy." Star raised his can in praise.

"You said it!" Tom replied. "Without Pete, there's no way I could run this show. Just look at the difference—here he is sweatin' his balls off while Bob's off partyin'."

Star laughed. "Sure. Bob got away on you today. But remember, he's set us up to make a bundle off this fertilizer business."

"Whaddya mean, a bundle? Hell, I don't expect to make anything off your business. I'm only in it to build a wholesale trade for the Elevator."

"Mr. T, it's doin' a whole lot better than that." Star slid to his feet across the counter from Tom. "The reason I dropped by is to bring you a dividend from the Company." He reached into his shirt pocket and flipped Tom a folded check.

"What's this?" Tom asked.

"Just what it says on the bottom. Fresh-killed money! Our first quarter dividend—number one in a long line, I'll bet."

Tom opened the check. "Jesus Christ! Ten thousand dollars! I haven't earned any ten thousand!"

Star's grin widened. "You sure have. Why, I couldn't move ten pounds of product without you guys from the Elevator. No allocation—no fertilizer—as the guy says." He drank, eyes bright as twin suns rising over the rim of the can.

"But..." Tom was overwhelmed at the size of the check. Ten thousand dollars! For what? He hadn't done anything. Allocation—what did that mean?

"I thought you just needed another person to incorporate the Company. I didn't…"

Star interrupted. "Look, old T. For a long time I been watchin' you work your ass off for damn little pay. Now, when you got the chance to do a good piece of business, you better expect to make some dough."

"Sure—that'd be OK, if I earned it. Hell, all I did was to help you with the company paperwork."

Star studied him, thin clouds of concern covering his eyes. "If you mean that, you ain't payin' attention. Without you, there wouldn't be any fertilizer to trade. As a newcomer, I couldn't have bought a hundred pound bag this spring. Instead, I traded almost a million off your allocation."

"What're you sayin'?"

"Just this. You opened the door for this business by sellin' me your surplus allocation. Now, you get your share of the profits. That's the way business is done."

Tom frowned. "Hmmm…just doesn't seem right. Ten thousand for doing business with you."

"All I got to say to that is that you're a damn fool if you don't take what you got coming. And a double idiot if you don't see the potential for the future."

They sipped in silence, Coke and Bud, each puzzled by the other. Tom awed by the magic of work-free money. Star amazed by Tom's ignorance of the most basic business principles.

Finally, Star straightened and held out his hand. "Here—gimme the key for the Coke machine."

"What you want that for?" Tom asked as he rummaged in the center desk drawer.

"Never mind—just gimme."

Key in hand, Star opened the machine and carefully mixed the remaining cans of Bud with the columns of Sprite, Coke and Mountain Dew. "This'll give the patrons a lift on Monday," he chuckled.

In spite of his worry, Tom grinned at the joke. He could imagine one of the customers spellbound by the caprice of the Coke machine.

"That's more like it. We haven't had a good laugh around here since we were at River House last fall."

"Yep," Star agreed, "we got to do that again soon. Now, I'm on the road to pick up a load of hay in Missouri. Some of these hay shakers around here are sure enough dried out."

"That's a hell of a way to go empty." Tom said.

"No way! I got a load of used tractors I bought at fire-sale prices from a couple of dealers in them dried out counties 'round Minot. Got 'em sold in southern Iowa. They got plenty of rain there."

"Say," Tom said, "when you're toolin' along, take a close look at the crops. Be nice to know what to expect this fall."

"I'll do that for you, good buddy. See you in a week or so."

When Star had gone, Tom sat at his desk, idly fingering the check. In the background, he heard the steady rumble of the leg. Pete had finally got it running.

What would be the right thing to do? He had helped launch Star's company, and the Elevator had made a good profit on all the trades with Dakota Fertilizer. But…a million dollars of new business! God! That was nearly as much as all the Elevator's retail sales put together!

The ringing of the phone interrupted his musings. Absentmindedly, he drew it to him.

"Hello, Farmers Elevator."

"Dad! Where are you? Is anything wrong?"

"Oh—hi honey. No, nothing's wrong, why?"

"But you said you would take us swimming. We've been waiting since noon!"

"Honey, I'm sorry. There's a big problem here and I can't make it home until tonight. But, don't worry—I'll make it up to you. Let me talk to Mom."

"Oh, Dad," she sobbed, "we were planning this for so long. We've packed our lunch and your suit and…"

There was the clatter of a dropped phone. Then Janet came on.

"Tom! What's the matter? Chrissy just ran out of the house crying."

"It's one of the usual things. Hot corn and the leg's plugged and…"

Her voice cut in. "You can't keep on doing this. The Elevator has to take second place to us. Can't you see what you're doing to Chrissy by never keeping promises?"

He sighed. "I know, I know. But what can I do? Nobody else will solve these problems."

"Then they have to wait. Please come home as soon as you can."

The line went dead. In exasperation, he returned the phone to its cradle. More of the same! Why couldn't they understand?

Tom picked up the check again. At least this was something he could do for his family. He tore a deposit slip from his checkbook and entered the total—ten thousand dollars. He endorsed the check and put both check and deposit slip in an envelope, addressing it to Citizen's Bank, Sheffield City. After stamping it, he tossed it into the mail tray on Helen's desk.

God! How frustrating it all was. He had been turned into a money-making machine, totally at the whim of the Elevator, his only purpose to dance to its mindless tunes.

CHAPTER FIFTEEN
Manlift

That evening was difficult. They were three people circling a problem, each on a separate orbit. Chrissy's disappointment was magnified by the fact that she was growing up. A mood that would have been momentary a year ago was now a tragedy to be played out to its climax. Janet was quiet and reflective. Tom was, more than ever, helpless, torn between guilt and responsibility.

Chrissy went to bed early. By the time Tom had thought to say goodnight to her, she was asleep. In the semi-dark of her room, he could see the outlines of her face—framed by her teddy bear and a poster of June and Johnny Cash. He looked at her thoughtfully for a long time, seeing in this image the tensions of her life, that she needed him constant and caring—and, at a deeper level, knowing that she needed to reject him and find another focus for her affection.

He left the room with a new emptiness, holding old feelings—jealous of change. There were only stirrings of an emerging relationship between them that tugged at his emotions. He was conscious of the press of time and the way it gnawed at the edges of his life.

Sunday was better. Chrissy's mood had swung back to normal. She was almost childlike in her enjoyment of the simple activities of a country Sunday. Breakfast and barnyard chores were an opportunity to share the day on neutral ground. While Chrissy had not completely forgiven him, he was gradually reintegrated into familiar patterns of behavior and Saturday receded into memory.

Janet's accommodation puzzled him. On the surface, she was very much the same cheerful organizer of the day. There was, however, a reserve in her interaction with him. He felt her considering him in a clinical way. Her responses were not spontaneous; they were perceptibly delayed—analyzed before she put them into words.

By mid-afternoon, they could discuss Saturday with some objectivity. Sitting in the shade of the porch, they watched Chrissy riding down the driveway on her bike.

"Tom, we need to talk about what happened." Janet moved her chair near him and laid her hand on his arm.

"Sure, but what's to say?"

"Chrissy's coming to an age where she needs both of us very much."

He considered. "You're probably right, but it doesn't look like it sometimes."

"Don't worry. That's just the way it has to be. She has to rebel against us and we have to accept it. Our support is really important to her. That's why your unpredictability hits her so hard."

"But, honey, I can't help it! Yesterday everything went wrong and I just couldn't get away."

"Bob did," she observed.

"Sure. And he should have stayed to help. But he didn't. That doesn't change anything. I'm still the manager and it's my responsibility."

"Couldn't you have left it to Pete or postponed it until Monday?" she asked.

"No! You don't understand! Monday's too late! When grain is rotting, it can't wait. And if I left things to Pete, pretty soon he would be the manager, and there would be no need for me."

That was the fundamental problem. Tom couldn't delegate his authority with confidence. He personally took on the whole complex maze of a busy elevator. The result was aimless lurching from one problem to another, while a stack of unresolved issues grew and grew.

"Tom, listen to me! You can't be everywhere. You must share your job with the others who are paid to help you. Otherwise you have nothing left to share with us. Can't you see that?"

"It's just not that easy!" he protested. "Take yesterday. That was a two-man job. If I had come home, Pete would have had to quit, and we'd have a worse problem Monday. Why, the corn in the leg would be even more rotten..."

"Please," she interrupted. "You're drifting back into the Elevator. We need you here now. Please look at me."

He shook off the impossible net of management and slowly raised his eyes to hers. Tears streaked her cheeks and she blotted them with the backs of her hands.

"Aw, don't cry, honey. This'll all work out. You'll see."

"You must stop promising. Not unless you really mean it. Every time you choose the Elevator over us, you say the same thing –'it'll never happen again'. We are losing confidence in you."

"Dammit Jan! You don't understand! We need this job. I just gotta do what's necessary to keep it!"

She was silent, her eyes squeezed tight.

He went on. "Yesterday, when I was shoveling that corn, don't you think I felt bad about not being able to get home? Sure I did! But coming home wasn't the answer. You and Chrissy got to understand that there are times when..."

He looked over at her. Tears were now flowing freely and the character of her face had dissolved into a crumpled tissue of grief. She sobbed.

Paradoxically, this angered him. "Oh...dammit!" He got up and marched into the house.

Janet sat alone and watched Chrissy through a wavering film of tears. Riding to and fro—turning in ever-widening circles—reaching for a tangent. Now shooting off down the driveway, becoming dimmer in the distance. Now racing back.

She wiped her eyes and the image sharpened. But the message was the same. The moments of family life were winding down and their quality was diminishing at the same time.

When she and Tom finally overcame their upset and reaffirmed their commitments, it was already evening. Like similar disputes, the path to reconciliation was exhausting. It was a path that, taken too many times, led always to the same unsatisfactory result. They agreed to change, but each knew that these were empty resolutions. The immediacy of Monday penetrated their agreement and exposed its weakness. In a few hours, business as usual would be under way and a setting recreated where family would give way to economic crises.

When Tom arrived at the Elevator on Monday morning, a brown car was waiting outside the office. Its two occupants were sitting, arms on open car windows, drinking coffee. The U.S. Government license plate on the car spoke of a range of impossible problems.

Tom pulled the Fury alongside the federal car and forced a smile.

"Well, you boys are sure up early. I got 6:30 a.m. Time for another inspection, I guess." He raised himself out of the car and gazed down at Alex Johnson, his nemesis of last winter.

There was no answering smile.

"We have to tell you Cooper, that we're here on an official audit. Your Board has been informed and is cooperating with a comprehensive review of your business. You know that means that we have to catch you before you open the books for the day."

Tom stretched, using the movement to consider the meaning of this announcement. Hadn't the Board changed the audit procedure at its organizational meeting? After all, they wanted to take their job seriously. Even Barney had slackened his criticism to support this new direction.

"No problem," he stated. "You boys got a job to do. I know you'll find everything in order here."

No sooner were these words spoken than doubts began to emerge. Did he have enough grain of the proper grade to cover his warehouse receipts? Did he show sufficient 'priced' grain on the books to account for grain that farmers owned, but was not recorded as paid for? God! If only he had known the inspection was coming!

While these thoughts caromed across his mind, he led the way to the office and unlocked the door for the inspectors.

"Say, where's Joe Carson?" he asked. "Thought he was our regular inspector."

Johnson stared at him. "Guess you didn't hear. Joe took early retirement at the end of March. The job probably was too much for him."

The prophecies that Carson had made last winter in the VFW had come true all too soon. Evidently the General Accounting Office audit of inspections was serious business.

Johnson continued. "This here's Frank Burns. He's taking Carsons's place on this audit. Frank's been working the elevators in the western Dakotas for the last ten years."

"Hello. You must be Tom Cooper." Burns offered his hand and smiled at Tom in an uncertain way.

"Hi, Frank. Gee, I'm sorry to hear about Joe. He was a good friend to all of us."

"Maybe too good a friend," growled Johnson. "Well, let's see those books."

"Sure hot in here," Frank added.

"Yeah," Tom agreed. "We were runnin' most of the weekend to clear a hot spot in one of the silos. A real bitch! Can't remember when it's been worse."

Johnson eyed him suspiciously. "Got stuff goin' out of condition? How much?"

"Oh, not a lot," Tom said confidently. "We're on top of the problem and got it under control."

"We'll see about that," Alex scowled and strode over to the bin board. "Where's the problem?"

Tom pointed to silo six. "Right here. This mother's got a crust on it. No air in that silo, so we had to pull the crust through. The low grade stuff is in bins three and four in the house, and we're using air to clear it up. That reminds me, I better swing up and check on the fans. Won't do to let them shut off."

"First give us the Daily Position Book and your Warehouse Receipt Book, Cooper," Johnson commanded. "Then we can get down to business."

Tom unlocked the old safe, splitting the faded image of Mount Rushmore that was painted on its ornate door. He removed the specified books and laid them on Bob's desk for the inspectors.

Johnson sat and began leafing through the records. "Frank, I'll do the paper chase, you follow Cooper and size up that spoilage problem. Then we'll decide how to get measures and grades on all the grain in storage."

"Okay. C'mon Tom, I might as well go up top with you."

They walked into the relative coolness of the cavernous scale house, and Tom turned on the master switch for the manlift.

"There she is, Frank. You go first."

Burns stepped onto a platform and jerked the control rope. The click-whine of the drive motor raised him up the dusty shaft.

After a short interval, Tom swung onto a platform, gripping the handhold, hugging the belt. The upsweep of the lift gave him the usual sensation of a loss of control over his fear of height, a sensation strengthened by the lack of control over the events of the day. When he reached the seventh floor, he stepped over bottomless space, landing smoothly on the secure roof of the wooden bins—his hand simultaneously stopping the lift.

Frank was standing nearby, leaning on a roof support.

"Tom, I don't know how to say this, but I think you and I have to talk about what's comin' in this inspection."

"Oh, how's that?"

"Well, Joe Carson didn't really take early retirement. He was canned. And I'm probably the next one on the block. They don't like the way I was handlin' my territory, so they put me with Johnson to let him decide what to do with me."

"That bastard!" Tom exclaimed. "What the hell is the government thinkin' of in cuttin' off you boys? Why, you've been good friends…"

"That's it. Too good, I guess. This thing has developed to the point where everything has to be done by the book. That means that most of you operators are in trouble."

"Shit! They can't close all of us down. There wouldn't be any way to market the crops!"

Frank shook his head. "They don't care about that. They're on a witch hunt, and somebody's gonna get burned."

"Just what do you mean?" Tom asked.

"Today we're starting a full-scale audit on the Elevator. A regular audit firm will come in here at the same time and look over the total business picture."

"Hell, that's no problem," Tom said. "The Board does that every year."

"This is different. We're using a Minneapolis auditor who knows the grain business inside out. A guy named Bill Weber, not one of your local CPAs who just gives you the once over."

Tom frowned. "How's that any different?"

"This guy's an expert in agribusiness. He has a hell of a record in uncovering fraud and doctored accounts. You better hope that everything's in top shape, or you'll have some tough questions to answer."

Tom strode around the cramped area, his shoes scuffing the windrows of dust.

Burns went on. "What's happenin' in this crackdown is that every transaction has to be justified. If you really have agreements to buy farmers' grain, okay, but any scale tickets marked 'priced' without a sales contract are gonna be treated as violations of the law."

Goddamn! He had nearly a hundred thousand bushels of 'priced' tickets and no contracts.

"But you know most farmers don't sign paper," Tom sputtered, "they just…"

"Sure, sure." Burns said. "That's the way it was. Now every ticket marked 'priced' is gonna result in a phone call to the farmer to see if he agrees with your records."

Sonofabitch! No more than two or three farmers would go along with his pricing. Tom's head reeled with the possible consequences of the records he had created.

"Another thing, Tom. You shouldn't have been on our schedule for at least another two months. It's almost as if somebody on your Board asked for this audit. Anything going on here?"

"No. Nothing," Tom answered. "The Board is takin' its job seriously. I sure can't complain about that. I've been tryin' to shape them up for the last couple of years. Maybe they just got the message."

Barney! How else would an audit be called for without his knowledge? That asshole sure knew how to twist the knife.

"I sure hope you're right, Cooper. Johnson is really on the cases of all you managers, and he'd like nothin' better than to hang one on you."

"Why's he got a hard on for me?" Tom asked, shifting his weight—arms folded to hold in his worry.

"Nothin' personal. He has this personal investigator image of himself and he's gonna find somethin' wrong with every operation." Burns paused and straightened, ready to begin his tour. "Let's hope everything's under control—like this hot spot—where's it at?"

Tom pointed to open bin hatches halfway along the dusty floor where currents of air were visibly stirring. "Over there. All the covers off and the fans on high."

They moved to the openings. As they approached, the odor of mold and spoilage became overpowering.

Frank stopped, wrinkling his nose. "Jesus! It sure stinks! You sure you got this under control?"

"No problem," Tom blurted. Then he stopped. The smell was ample evidence that there was a good deal wrong with the corn in these bins. "Well, it sure doesn't smell too good," he admitted. "Maybe the fans haven't had enough time to take effect."

Frank stared at him. "C'mon. Don't fool yourself. This stuff's obviously done for. How much you figure is shot? And can you cover it in your total position?"

The shock of this announcement made him speechless for a moment. Of course the stuff was rotten. How could he have thought that air would cure it, especially in this heat? "Guess you're right! Should be no problem though. We been long this summer, lookin' for price increases. Probably we'll have to use some to cover this."

Luckily he had accumulated Elevator-owned corn in June when the first signs of drought appeared. Still, he had sold quite a bit over the last two months to get enough operating cash. But there should still be plenty—these few loads of spoiled corn wouldn't put much of a dent in the total picture.

Frank continued, "Lucky for you. Lots of elevators have had big spoilage problems, and they weren't long enough to cover. We've issued at least ten citations in the last month. Even pulled the license over to…"

Tom shut his ears to this litany of failure. Why couldn't Frank shut up? His mind raced ahead, calculating the amount of the loss, and the amount of Elevator-owned grain, less the few loads he had sold.

The complexity of these calculations grew exponentially. Soon his grasp of the total was lost. If only he could sit down with the Position Book.

"C'mon, let's take a look at the silos. It's already getting' hot up here," Frank said as he turned back to the manlift.

Tom followed and joined in the step, jerk, click-whine of the lift, and they stepped off the lift at the ninth floor. Here the slight morning breeze was magnified. A hot wind howled through the opened windows of the catwalk tunnel over the silos. Pigeons clattered out the windows, beating against one another into open space.

"You gotta get these birds under control!" Frank exclaimed. "Better put some of your boys to work on these windows."

They moved out on the catwalk. Everything was okay in numbers one and two. They were nearly full, one with Commodity Credit Corporation oats, held ready for a launch against overpricing of what had become a worthless commodity. Like other government missiles, the oats had been shifted from elevator to elevator over the years for obscure reasons. At least no enemy of agriculture would ever find them.

As Tom approached silos three and four, he became aware of sickening depths. Four was empty, but three should have plenty in it—why, there should be—he stole a glance down and to his left. The yawning depth nearly pulled him over. He staggered. *Jesus God! The thing was nearly empty! It should be half-full. Where the hell had all that grain gone? Shit! He'd sold only a few loads!"* He stopped—hanging on to both railings, his face streamed with sweat.

Frank peered at him. "You all-right? You don't look so good. Why don't you go back and I'll just take a quick look around."

"Yeah, sure…" he stammered. Carefully he reversed his direction, hands clawing at the wavering railing. His feet slid along the catwalk, one after the other, until he was safe above the full silos.

He wiped his face with the outside of his cap, the relief a physical thing. However, the enormity of the possible shortage in silo three soon came coursing back. He'd better check that out and …

He called back to Frank, "I'm going down now. See you in the office." He waved and walked quickly to the manlift. Gritting his teeth, he pulled the control rope and stepped onto a sinking platform. Holding his face close to the shiny belt, he tried not to think of the immensity of his height above solid ground. If the belt should break… a wave of nausea raced through his body.

Finally, the painted shaft told him he was nearing ground level. His hand slid over the control rope and he stepped back just as the guiding knot touched his hand. Down, but not safe.

He stood for a time in the scale house considering his options. No way could he work the books while the inspection was in progress. How could he create a reserve of grain to cover the spoilage?

Suddenly he brightened. A sales contract! He'd need only one big one that showed a recent purchase—too recent to have been entered into the accounts. How about one last Saturday? Everybody too busy with hot corn. Stub on vacation! The perfect solution! He snapped his fingers.

Who could it be? Ryan. A big operator. He'd be sure to have some corn on the farm. And, he was a good friend so he'd back up the deal—at least temporarily—to make sure the Elevator kept its license. That'll do it.

He opened the office door, the wash of chilled air a tonic reinforcing his decision. Almost joyful, he sat at his desk and switched on his work lamp.

"How's it goin', Alex?"

Johnson looked up from his work. "You back already? Just lookin' over my rough figures, I think you're playin' it real close. If you got any amount of spoilage, you'll be outside the three percent limit."

Tom slid the Sales Contract Book out of his desk drawer and arranged it in the center of the blotter.

"Oh, I don't think we'll be short. When Stub comes in, we can check on the trades we made while he was on vacation. Most of those won't show up in the Position Book yet."

"What do you mean? The Book is supposed to be kept up daily," Johnson growled.

"Sure, I know. But I don't like to fool around with Stub's books. Anyway, you'll see that we've got things under control when he gets here." Tom looked at the clock. "Should be in any minute now."

Johnson grunted and returned to his study of the books. Tom quickly filled in a Sales Contract. 'Seller: G. Ryan—Grain/Grade: No. 2 Yellow Corn—Quantity: 25,000 bushels–Price: $3.25.' There—that looked OK. Now, to put it into Stub's work folder.

He rose and went over to Stub's cubby. Glancing at Johnson's back, he slipped the contract into a folder of trades to be posted. Picking up a yellow tablet from Stub's desk, he walked briskly back to his desk. *Made it!*

No sooner had he sat down, than Stub came waddling in. Right on time.

"Mornin', Tom. How's things? I see we got company."

"Yep, just a routine inspection. This here's Alex Johnson. Alex, Stub Thompson."

They nodded.

"How was the vacation, Stub?" Tom asked.

"Great. But there's too many tourists at the Black Hills these days. One afternoon…" Stub rambled on as he arranged his desk for the day's work. As he rummaged through the accumulated paper, Tom held his breath. *Let him—just this once—do his job.*

"Hey, Tom. How do you want to handle this Ryan contract? Should I issue a check or what?"

Tom clenched his fists. What could you expect from this idiot?

"No, let's wait until he comes in and we can pay him then. Might as well leave that corn at his place until we get our spoiled stuff cleaned up."

Conscious of Johnson's attention, he pivoted away from Stub and picked up the telephone. He dialed Bob's number. After several rings, Bob's sleepy voice came over the wire.

"Bob, sorry to call you at this hour, but we've got inspectors here and I'd like for you to work with Pete today. Okay?"

"I suppose so. What the hell they after now? Any problems?"

"Sure, that'd be fine," Tom laughed, hoping that Bob would get the message. "See you soon." He hung up, still aware of Johnson's presence.

"Cooper, I'd like for you and Thompson here to lay out your records as they are. You show me which transactions were made during Stub's vacation and I'll work them into your position."

"Well, sure—," Tom replied. Then, turning to Stub, "Stub, bring me that work folder on your desk and any other stuff that needs to be posted."

"Coming right up." The relief in Stub's voice was obvious. Now Johnson would be doing his work and he'd be free of any pressure during the inspection.

Johnson added, "Oh, and Thompson, we'll want to see your General Ledger and checkbook. Might as well get those ready."

Stub peered over his glasses. "But why? You guys don't pay no attention to our financial accounting."

"Nope, not usually," Johnson said. "This time we'll be bringing in Bill Weber from Minneapolis to do an audit."

"Weber!" Stub exclaimed. "No kiddin'. That guy's hell on wheels with the elevator business. Any special reason why he's puttin' the finger on us?"

Johnson paused, "No, nothing special. Just part of a general audit."

Tom was surprised by Stub's reaction. "What do you mean, Stub? What's the scoop on Weber?"

"I only know what I heard. He came into Hanley Springs Co-op like a dose of salts. Found all their books in a mess and put them right into receivership. It's like he's out to teach us all a lesson in accounting."

"You got that right, Thompson," the inspector grated. "Too many of you guys been playin' fast and loose with customers' grain and money. Well, that's all over and it'll be guys like Bill Weber who'll get the credit for clearin' up your mess!"

Tom stared at his blotter. What a fucking day! He could handle the juggling of grain, but making sure that these manipulations matched the financial accounts was a task for a computer, not for an idiot like Stub Thompson.

The idiot was rattling on. "Well, Mr. Johnson, I'm sure Bill Weber will find all my stuff in order. Every dollar is accounted for." He deftly laid the real burden at Tom's feet. "Sometimes our grain accounts are a little out of line, but Tom always clears that up."

Thanks, you motherfucker! Tom thought. Then with a confident grin. "Right, Stub. No problem."

Stub nodded and began assembling the required slips, memos and records, humming to himself, giving the impression of a willing worker who wasn't responsible for anything.

Tom watched Johnson methodically analyze the data. He systematically cross-checked scale tickets, sales contracts and warehouse receipts against entries in the Daily Position Book.

Mentally, Tom followed the flow of grain.

30,000 corn bought from Jim Arneson at $3.10.

27,000 wheat sold to Cargill at $4.78.

5,000 wheat bought from Sam Lofthus at $4.25.

Usually he was able to add these complex transactions in his head, a running set of totals like pinball machine counters in the front of his thoughts, but the speed and size of trades in recent months couldn't be grasped so easily. The counters were coming up with question marks rather than numbers in an alarming way.

The phone rang.

"Farmers Elevator, Cooper speaking."

"Mr. Cooper, this is Bill Weber. You may have heard that I'll be doing an audit along with the federal inspection."

"Sure have. Frank and Alex are here already."

"Good. Let me talk to Alex."

Tom pushed the 'hold' button on his phone and called out to Johnson.

"Alex. It's for you—Bill Weber on line one."

Johnson picked up the call. "Johnson here…Yep. We've got the books. Frank's up getting ready to measure the house."

Noises from the phone.

"What? You think so?"

There was a long pause while Johnson listened to Weber's answer.

"Well, okay. It's pretty irregular though."

More noises—these emphatic in tone.

Then Johnson spoke. "Yeah, sure. See you when you get here."

He hung up and looked over at Tom. "Cooper, we want to close the Elevator for a day or so. Want to be sure we get an accurate reading on your business."

"Close the Elevator!" Tom blurted. "Christ! You can't do that! It'd cut the hell out of our business!"

Johnson stared at him, his eyes boring into Tom's mind. "Sure, it'll be a little problem for you. But let me tell you Cooper, you had better cooperate on this or we'll just suspend your license for a couple of months."

"A couple of months! W…what the hell you talkin' about?" Tom stammered.

Even Stub was shocked at this prospect. "But, Mr. Johnson," he pleaded, "we all got jobs and…"

Johnson held up a hand. "Now you guys listen to me. When we get a Board request for an audit from a co-op, we take it very seriously. This isn't only farmer grain, it's a farmer business. And we'll do exactly what's needed to be sure everything's in order. Get it?"

"Yeah, but …," Stub stammered.

Tom interrupted, "Hold it, Stub!" Then he spoke to Alex. "Okay, Johnson. If we shut down today, how long will it be before we can open again?"

"That's better, Cooper. Shouldn't be more than a day or so. Now what I want is for you to stay here, Thompson. Cooper, you clear out. Stub can answer the phone." He thought for a moment. "Thompson, you call the employees and tell them to stay home for a couple of days."

"…Sure…" Stub groped for the phone, fumbling at the receiver.

Tom sat back in his chair, stunned by the speed of Johnson's action. He was completely out of the picture! For the first time, an inspection and audit would be conducted without him. He wouldn't be able to explain. He sat up and began to formulate an argument for Johnson. He never made it.

"I know what you're going to say, Cooper. So I'll save you the trouble. We don't want your help and explanations. We just want the records to tell the story. Now you better hit the road. We'll call you when we're done." He turned back to his desk. "Thompson, bring me the Warehouse Receipt Book with numbers from 1030 to 2065."

Tom stood up, dizzy with anger and fear. He pulled on his cap, and strode toward the door.

"Don't forget to turn out the fucking lights!"

BOOK 3

END OF TRACK

CHAPTER SIXTEEN
Bull in a Ring

The rest of that week was worrying days and sleepless nights—and heat. On Monday afternoon, Tom tried to call Ryan several times to confirm the grain sale he had posted that morning. There was no response to his calls.

Finally, he called Bob as one of Ryan's close friends. "Bob, you know where Gerry Ryan is hangin' out? I'm tryin' to confirm a grain deal with him."

"Didn't you know?" Bob asked. "Gerry and his wife went down to the Ozarks for the week. They won't be back until next weekend."

"Dammit! I really need to get hold of him. Got to get his corn on hand for these fucking inspectors."

"What's cookin' with those guys? I went over to the Elevator this morning and the place is all locked up. Finally got Stub to answer the door. He looked like death warmed over!"

"I'll bet he did," Tom said. "That Bill Weber guy is probably workin' over his books and…"

Bob broke in. "Did you say Bill Weber? That sonofabitch?"

"Yeah, why?"

"Let me tell you, Boss. If Bill Weber is into our books, we got real trouble. Why, that fucker is a whore's dream when it comes to findin' problems. You heard what happened over to Hanley Springs?"

"No," Tom responded, "I just heard that they went into Chapter 11."

"Well, it wasn't as simple as that. Weber kept worryin' at the books until he found enough to hang both the manager and the bookkeeper. No wonder Stub's got a wild hair up his ass!"

"Jesus Bob! I think we're OK. We'll sure get our fingers slapped for some of the ways we account for our trades, but the bulk of the work should be fine."

Bob hesitated. "Yeah…maybe…but we better hope that Weber don't get onto Dakota Fertilizer!"

They were both silent for a moment. Then Tom raised the question they were both pondering. "What's wrong with Dakota Fertilizer?"

"Nothin' in particular," Bob said, "but D.F. has made too many trades with the Elevator this spring."

"So what? Every one was at a fat profit to the Elevator. And Star always paid right on time."

"That ain't it, Boss. Weber's gonna ask why the Elevator didn't make all them sales at inflated prices."

"No problem," Tom said. "Remember, the co-op can't make that kind of profit if it wants to hold onto a tax exempt status."

"Sure, sure—that's right. But we don't want them pryin' into our business and findin' out just how much we been makin' on them trades."

"Are you sayin' that we've done something wrong?" Tom gripped the phone, sweat making it like a freshly caught fish—slippery—almost ready to wiggle out of his hand.

"No—no—no. It's just that we don't look good playin' both sides of those deals."

"I know what you mean," Tom said, "but we've been careful to set a good margin on the trades so that we're dealing at arm's length."

"Arm's length!" Bob exclaimed. "That's a good idea! Let's be sure that we talk that way from now on. Well, I gotta go. Talk to you later." The line went dead.

Tom's other attempts to get information on the inspection and audit fared no better. On Thursday, he called Chris Odegaard, chairman of the Elevator Board.

"Hello, Chris. Tom Cooper. Just thought I'd give you a call to see what you know about the inspection."

"Well now, Tom," Chris said. "Can't say as I like what's going on. What with the Elevator closed and all. Every time I call, they got questions about our policies and what we decided to do at different Board meetings. Don't sound real good to me."

"Gee, Chris, I'm sorry to hear that. Can't see what the problem is. All our accounts are in shape and…"

Odegaard cut in. "Yeah, but they seem to be saying that we haven't been doing anything right these past few years. No policy on hedging. No real audits of the books and so on."

"Now, Chris, don't worry," Tom said with a confidence that didn't ring true. "They got to find fault somewhere. I'm sure that this will all turn out fine, once the audit is done."

The conversation went on for several minutes, and Tom had the growing feeling that he wasn't convincing Chris. It was like struggling against waist-deep snow; slow and exhausting with the track filling in behind him so that progress couldn't be measured. Finally, he gave up and left Chris to his worries.

Tom's own concerns were more than enough for him. As the week ended, he was aware of a growing conviction that something fundamental was wrong at the Elevator. No amount of review of the past could reassure him. The more he examined the little he knew, the more anxious he became and the more Bill Weber dominated his thoughts.

At seven a.m. on Sunday, the air in the upstairs bedroom was perfectly still. The heat of Saturday remained trapped in a layer above the level of the open window like a blanket that physically glued Janet and Tom to the mattress. Thoughts of the Elevator kept him awake, proposed solutions leading only to more impossible problems. As he tossed in the heat, he reviewed other options that resulted only in failure.

Finally, he gave in to the inevitable.

"Honey! I can't sleep. It's just too damn hot!"

He swung his legs to the floor and reached for his trousers.

"Me, too," she said. "Too much on my mind. I'll go make some coffee." Janet pulled her robe around her and left.

He grunted agreement and continued the hopeless discussion he had been having with himself for the past week.

Okay. Now the first thing to do is to call Ryan and get him to back the sale.

But what if he won't?

Don't think about that. He's got to. After all, it's just for a few months. When fall comes, there'll be plenty of profit to offset the losses.

But what about being oversold? Where can that money come from?

Wait! Wait! The profit on the futures accounts! They'll more than cover that!

Sure, but those were supposed to make up for last fall's losses.

Here was the dilemma. Tom had rolled last year's losses into this year by manipulating his commodity accounts. By showing ownership of grain he didn't have, he'd balanced last year's books. The unexpected inspection had called this solution into question. With insufficient grain on hand and not enough money, he was short on both ends of a dangerous stick.

"Well," he whispered, "the Board will see how far I've been able to correct things. And it'll be obvious that we're on the mend. And Weber will just have to listen to reason. Same with Alex Johnson."

"Tom, coffee's ready," Janet called to him from the open stairway.

"Coming!" He changed into a dry shirt and a clean pair of jeans, trying to put off his worries with the old clothes he threw in the corner of the bedroom. He ran his fingers through his hair and clattered into the kitchen.

"Hey, that smells good!" He turned a chair and leaned his arms on its back.

"Oh, T," she said, "it's great to have you here."

"What do you mean, honey?"

"Just that this week you've been going around mumbling to yourself. That inspection has really been on your mind."

"You bet it has! But I've done the right things and the Board will see that there's light at the end of this tunnel." He grinned and toasted her with steaming coffee. "Why is it that we still want hot coffee in the summer?"

She laughed. "I suppose it's the contrast between temperatures. What I mean is that the coffee's so hot that the weather seems cool—or something like that."

They sat together, letting time run on as they waited for Chrissy to wake up and close the family circle. Tom remembered how his parents had turned off the outside world to center on their family. His father often said, "Tom, nature will be here long after we've gone. It doesn't need us to survive, but we need each other, and we can't let anything stand in the way of that."

No job or position could take the place of understanding—no rules could offer the support found in the mutual commitments of family. When that circle had been complete, he was confident and cheerful. Now he was lost, a seeker that struggled to maintain a durable family circle of his own.

The telephone interrupted these melancholy thoughts. Janet walked to the wall and answered.

"Hello, Coopers...yes, he's here." She handed the phone to Tom, ducking under its long cord.

"Hello, this is Tom."

"Tom, this is Chris Odegaard. We'd like for you to come down to the Elevator."

"Okay, I guess. When?"

"Right now. How soon can you get here?"

"Well—I suppose fifteen, twenty minutes."

"Good. We'll be waiting."

Tom handed the phone to Janet, a puzzled look on his face. "That was Chris. He wants me to meet him at the Elevator. I wonder…"

"Oh, no, Tom!" she cried. "We were hoping to be together today!"

"Don't worry, hon. This won't take very long. I'll just run down and be right back. Won't be more than a couple of hours. Tell Chrissy I'll be back for a picnic this afternoon." He gave her a brief hug which she returned with an unusual fierceness.

"Don't go! This isn't right, you giving up everything for that place!"

"You're right! This will be the last time." He grabbed his cap and waved from the doorway.

On his way to Sheffield, he mused about the purpose of Chris' call.

Probably got the final results of the inspection and wants to plan how we'll respond to the report. Should be pretty simple. I'll just outline a couple of policies and a budget for the next six months. Then, we'll have the crop in and everything will be okay again.

He crested the hill above Sheffield and let the Fury surge around the sharp, descending curves. Rush, brake, glide—and repeat. How easy when the road was clear and empty. He coasted through town and pulled into the Elevator parking lot.

It was nearly filled with cars and pickups. Odegaard's Buick, Jacobs's pickup, and wasn't that Ben Waters's Cadillac? The drab government cars were there too.

"What the hell? Looks like a Board meeting. God! I wonder if..." In a daze, he stopped the Fury and got out—images flashed through his brain and he had to hold onto the car door to let it pass. "Jesus!"

The Elevator office door opened and Chris called to him. "Tom! C'mon in! We're all waitin' for you."

He staggered up the steps and into the office, where the stale odor of tobacco smoke and sweating men sent another spasm through his stomach. They were all there, perched on desks, leaning against walls, and sitting in the few chairs around the office. Only one chair was empty, in the middle, reserved for him.

"Hello, everybody. Didn't realize I was interrupting a meeting. Chris, I can wait outside until you're through."

"No, Tom. This concerns you. Please sit down." Chris gestured toward the empty chair. Then, wiping the sweat from his forehead, he hoisted himself onto an edge of the counter. An elderly hawk perched—waiting for a movement of his prey.

An athletic younger man stood next to Odegaard and looked at Tom. "Cooper, I'm Bill Weber. The Board has asked me to conduct this meeting. We'd like to hear your answers to some questions."

"Fuckin' aye!" Jacobs snarled. "And, I'd like to…"

"Mr. Jacobs! That's enough!" Weber raised his voice and emphasized each word. "I'll do the talking here, and don't you forget it!"

In amazement, Tom saw Barney clamp his mouth shut and lean back against the outside door. Weber in charge, he thought. What'd that mean?

Weber rested one arm on the counter beside Odegaard, leafed through a yellow legal pad, then looked at Tom.

"Now, Mr. Cooper, let me give a general background to the problems of this Elevator. Then, we'll ask you a few questions."

Tom stared. *This was just like a goddamn trial! Opening statement! Holy shit!*

"Umm…yeah…go ahead," he mumbled.

"The problems of the Sheffield Farmers Elevator aren't unique. They are the results of using old-time business practices in a brand-new agricultural economy. In the past five years, grain prices have more than doubled. The volume of trade has increased by forty percent. The result is a cash flow nearly triple in size."

Damn right! Tom thought. *Why, this guy may be on my side after all.*

Weber went on. "This means that any elevator could easily be exposed for several hundred thousand dollars on a given day—if proper hedging doesn't take place. And, let me tell you, hedging just isn't done in most elevators like this one."

Great! Tom brightened. *That supports my opening the hedging account!* He opened his mouth to add to Weber's story.

"Just a minute, Mr. Cooper. Let me finish. In addition to volume and dollar growth, we've seen unprecedented swings in market price. When traders have failed to protect themselves, they have lost fortunes."

Weber looked around the room and turned a page of his notes.

"Then, this year, we've seen a runaway price climb on fertilizer. Many products were three times their price of a year ago."

Right on! Why, that's where I did a major favor for patrons! By holding prices on fertilizer! Thank God for Dakota Fertilizer and the solid profits of their trades!

The story continued. "As a result, there has been a thriving black market in fertilizer. A market which has been a disaster for many elevators and countless farmers. Against this background, we are better able to understand the forces that have brought the Farmers Elevator to the brink of bankruptcy."

"Bankruptcy!" Tom shouted. "What the hell do you mean? Why this place is as sound as…"

"Shut up, Cooper!" Jacobs barked. "Just pay attention until you're called on!"

"Gentlemen, gentlemen," Weber scolded, "let's not let our feelings run away with us!"

He then looked directly at Tom. "Yes, Mr. Cooper, bankruptcy. The Elevator has more grain obligations than it can cover with cash and commodities. In fact, it's one of the weakest organizations I've run across in all my work with co-ops."

"But…but…," Tom stammered, "I don't—but how?"

"If you'll just follow me and answer a few questions, you'll see how I came to this conclusion." Weber put down the legal pad and opened the Daily Position Book. Turning several pages, he found the entries he wanted. Running his fingers down the columns, he stopped, murmured to himself, and moved to an easel where a pad of newsprint was displayed. He uncapped a black marker and turned to Tom.

"Mr. Cooper, this Position Book shows that you have Elevator-owned corn in the amount of 50,000 bushels, wheat 85,000 bushels, and beans 50,000, in round numbers. Is that correct?"

Tom passed his hand through his hair, feeling the sweat. "Well, I don't know. Whatever the Book says is where we're at. Sounds about right."

Weber entered these numbers on the newsprint.

"Now, let's look at the Warehouse Receipt Book. This Book indicates that you have issued Warehouse Receipts in the amount of 110,000 bushels of corn, 180,000 of wheat, and 90,000 of beans, again in round numbers. Right?"

"Sure—that is, I suppose so."

Weber penned a second column on the newsprint, then added the totals.

"This adds up to 160,000 bushels of corn, 265,000 of wheat, and 140,000 of beans. Correct?"

Tom scowled, the arithmetic too much for his scattered thoughts. "Umm...yes...160—265—140...'bout right, the last time I looked."

"Then how come your stock measures 145,000 bushels of corn, 230,000 of wheat, and 120,000 of beans? Where are the missing bushels?"

Under a column marked "shortage," Weber listed the difference between "Obligations" and "Stock on Hand." He then burned these figures into Tom's mind.

"You are short 15,000 bushels of corn, 35,000 bushels of wheat ,and 20,000 of beans." Weber paused, then asked in a judgmental tone, "Is that correct?"

Tom's mind raced. *God! Tens of thousands of bushels short! Better think fast!*

"Well," he said, "there's still crop on the farm. You know...sales where we haven't received the grain."

"Cooper, you bastard!" Ryan broke in. "You marked me down for twenty-five thousand bushels of corn. Hell, I ain't even got that much on hand!"

"Are you saying, Mr. Ryan," Weber asked, "that you haven't entered into a sales contract with the Elevator?"

"You're damn right I didn't. I just can't believe Cooper would do this kind of thing. Hell, he didn't even ask me."

"But Gerry," pleaded Tom, "I tried to call you."

"That isn't all, Mr. Cooper," Weber probed. "What about the Commodity Credit Corporation oats?"

"Whaddya mean? Sure, we got CCC oats in the house."

"But your Warehouse Receipts show that you are holding 65,000 bushels of Government oats. And, the measurement shows only about 50,000 on hand. How do you explain that?"

Fuck! Bob sold into the oats again! He was always doing that to get cash for fertilizer purchases.

He tried to explain. "Those oats will be replaced this fall from new crop. Elevators are always moving oats to keep them in condition."

Alex Johnson snorted. "What the hell are you talking about? Those are Government oats. It's a crime to dip into them without payment in advance. And what do you mean, 'replace'?"

"But, Alex, you know how we move those oats."

"Not in my territory you don't. The law says they belong to the Government, and, by God, I'll do everything to make sure that nobody steals them!"

"Hey! Wait a minute! You callin' me a thief?" Tom rose from his chair.

Barney began to move forward, but Weber stepped in front of him.

"Both of you! Sit down!" Weber shoved Barney back to the wall and motioned Tom to his chair.

"Mr. Cooper, I'm afraid that's what we are talking about. Stealing grain that belongs to farmers and to the Government. A pretty serious charge, wouldn't you agree?"

"You're damn right!" Tom shouted. "It's a charge that isn't true! I was only tryin' to help the Elevator and the patrons…" He choked back a sob.

"Well, then," Weber said, "let's talk about Dakota Fertilizer. Tell us how that helps the patrons."

Tom gulped and shifted in his chair. All around the room there was nothing but hard, hostile stares. He tried to speak, but no sound would come from his parched throat.

"Can I have a drink?" he gasped.

Chris Odegaard came toward him, a can in his outstretched fist. As Tom stretched to take the drink, Odegaard stopped, his face beet red.

"I was on your side, Tom. Until this." Chris held up the can. Budweiser! "I got it from the pop machine this morning. You've made our Elevator into a party house—you and your friends." He crumpled the can in his great fist, beer spurting all around the mashed metal.

That fucking Star! He had to put beer in the pop machine! "I can explain, Chris. I didn't do it! It wasn't my fault." Pitiful cries of a guilty child where no exit was to be found.

Jacobs raged, "For Christssakes, Cooper! We all know that you're hooked on the sauce! Shit, you probably…"

Weber pushed himself away from the counter and walked up to Jacobs, stopping when his face was only a few inches from Barney's. "All right, Jacobs! That's enough! Any more from you and I'll personally throw you out of here! Now back off!"

Tom sat back, the fear reaction of a confrontation with Barney gradually subsiding. In its place was a more pervasive fear of Weber, a personality that dominated everyone in the room.

Moving to his place at the counter, Weber went on as if nothing had happened to derail his argument. "Now, Mr. Cooper, please tell us all about Dakota Fertilizer."

Tom began, his dry throat drenched in heightened emotion. "Well, this spring we had too much fertilizer…"

Weber interrupted. "No, Mr. Cooper. Let's take it from the beginning. When did you first begin to think of selling Elevator fertilizer?"

"Let me think. I guess what happened is that Bob ordered way more product than we could sell to our customers. With all this stuff coming, we had to find a way to move it out, or else we'd have a big storage problem."

"If I follow you, Mr. Cooper, you're saying that you couldn't afford to carry this amount of fertilizer in inventory. Is that right?"

"Yes. In fact, we were payin' demurrage on cars of product we couldn't even unload because we were full."

"So then you set up Dakota Fertilizer," Weber concluded.

"No. That wasn't the way. Star…"

"You are referring to Theodore Schultz?" Weber asked.

"That's right. Star put this company together so that he'd have additional work for his trucks. Then, Bob helped him find buyers for our surplus fertilizer."

"You sold what you call 'surplus' at a good profit?" Weber asked.

"That's right! We made about seven percent on most sales. And Star always paid cash!"

"I agree," said Weber. "The accounts show that the Elevator made about two hundred thousand dollars from product sold to Dakota Fertilizer."

"There it is!" Tom enthused. "That two hundred grand was clear profit and helped to offset any losses we might have had on grain trades."

"Mr. Cooper," Weber said, as if to a slow learner, "didn't you ever think that you should have sold the fertilizer directly from the Elevator to the ultimate buyer?"

"Sure, but I knew that any large amount of profit would only make us lose our federal tax status as a co-op."

"By my rough figures, I estimate that the fertilizer traded through Dakota Fertilizer made them…," Weber consulted his notes, "about $250,000."

"That much?" Tom blurted. "I had no idea!"

"Mr. Cooper, we weren't born yesterday. You are an officer of Dakota Fertilizer. You authorized these sales as manager of the Farmers Elevator. You knew the value of the products. You can't expect us to believe that you didn't know exactly what amounts were involved."

Tom sank lower in his chair. Weber was trying to make Dakota Fertilizer the scapegoat, when it really was the only hope of the Elevator. "But…the federal tax…"

Weber cut into this rambling. "Mr. Cooper, that's a red herring. As the manager of this Elevator, you knew that you were faced with heavy losses on grain trades and that any amount of income from fertilizer trades would not fully offset these losses. You could, as a matter of fact, have doubled your fertilizer profits at no risk of any so-called 'tax exemption' problems. Isn't that a fact?"

Tom used both hands to wipe his face. "When you put it that way, well—maybe the money would have…"

"Let me ask you this." Weber paused for effect. "Have you received any income from Dakota Fertilizer Company?"

This question awakened Tom to a real calamity. He began to sweat profusely. All the terrible facts were suddenly crystal clear. *The Elevator was broke. Fertilizer profits diverted. Money in his own pocket.*

He fumbled at his shirt cuffs, conscious of his vulnerability and aware that he was projecting his guilt to those in the room. "Yeah, I've been paid. As a director..."

"Mr. Cooper, what you have done is take a business opportunity of this Elevator and turn it into a windfall for you and your friends. You have betrayed the trust of these Board members and the patrons of the Elevator. What have you to say to that?"

'Bull in a Ring! Bull in a Ring!'

'Awright! You Frosh! Get on up here!'

They loped through the November half-light to where Coach was standing. The hulking thugs of the varsity line looming behind him.

'OK, here's the game. One of you Frosh backs get in the circle and try to fake out these big dummies. See if you can get through. Get it?'

'Awright! Let's go! Cooper! Get in there!' Coach tossed him the ball.

He trotted to the center of the circle. Then—quickly! Veering left! Head fake! Shift the ball! Breakthrough!

'Good work Cooper! Close up that circle! C'mon, you dummies! Eat that Frosh!'

The thugs closed in. Try again—fake! Fake again! Shift! The crack of shoulder pads and the heavy clump of cleat-busted dirt.

'Good work, dummies! C'mon Cooper! Get the lead out!'

Up again—circle tighter. Try to break out!

'Bull in a Ring!'

He was conscious that he was out of his chair—standing in the center of his accusers—trying to fake a path to safety.

'Bull in a Ring!'

"Sam," he looked into Lofthus's impassive face, "you do the books. You know that everything has always been on the up and up."

"I sure thought so, until Weber showed me what was goin' on." Lofthus thrust his head forward, like a rooster about to attack. "When I seen how you cooked the Position Book, I knew you was usin' the grain accounts to cover your losses."

Ben Waters took up the attack. "Me, too, Cooper. Why, the financial reports you gave me on your loan aren't worth the paper they're printed on!"

Tom turned away from these onslaughts, looking to break out of the ring.

"Arne, you tell them," he pleaded to Carlson. "Didn't I always give you fair prices on your crop?"

Carlson scowled. "Yep. Have to say that you did. But Weber showed me how you was givin' Board members good prices to pull the wool over our eyes. Makes me sick to think how you fooled me."

'Bull in a Ring!'

Like the blocky linebacker of twenty years ago, Weber moved in to deliver the final blow.

"That's enough! I think that you have heard all that Mr. Cooper has to say. Mr. Odegaard, you can go ahead with your meeting."

Chris cleared his throat. "Awright. You have heard Tom's explanation of what's happened here. Do I have a motion?"

Jacobs blurted, "Damn right! I move…"

Arne Carlson held up a hand. "Just a minute, Jacobs. We old timers hired him and it's up to us to clear up our mistake. I move that Tom Cooper's contract be cancelled and that he be given two weeks severance pay."

Contract cancelled! They couldn't!

"I'll second that," Sam Lofthus said.

Odegaard looked around the Ring. "Everybody agree?"

Nods. "You bet!" "Damn right!" "Sure."

The decision was unanimous.

Chris looked at Tom, his face a mixture of anger and sorrow. "Tom, I'm sorry for you. I liked you and you were once a good manager. I know this is hard on you, but it's going to be just as hard on the patrons when we go Chapter 11."

"But…but…Chris, you don't have to bankrupt the Elevator! Give me a chance! I can…"

"Jesus Christ, Cooper!" Jacobs bellowed. "We gave you a chance and you pissed away a million dollars! Get to hell out of here while you…"

"Jacobs!" Weber exploded. "Cool it!"

"Now, Mr. Cooper," Weber continued, "here's a letter that summarizes the Board's action. Please give us your keys and any other Elevator property you have in your possession. You will notice that the letter forbids you from entering these premises. You may not engage in any trading in the Elevator's name, beginning today."

Tom took the paper, hand shaking. The lines blurred.

'Bull in a Ring!'

He reached into his pocket and drew out the heavy ring of keys. Slowly he separated the single key for the Fury from the mass of Elevator metal. He dropped the ring on the counter, the loud clatter of the keys amplified by silence in the office. He moved to the door, the Ring parted to let him out.

Outside, the late morning sun hammered on the office steps. Images of the yard and cars shimmered in waves of heat. Dizzy with emotion, Tom wavered down the steps and leaned his arms on the Fury's roof.

Jesus! No job! No nothing! What am I gonna tell Janet? What'll I do?

Thoughts without focus ranged wildly through his mind. He had escaped the confines of the Ring only to be faced with a multiplying panorama of problems, all descended from his failure at the Elevator. Finally, the heat was too much for him and he slid behind the wheel of the Fury.

This activity exhausted his wasted energy and he slumped against the steering wheel until the greater heat of the car mandated movement. He went through the ritual of starting, no fat ring of keys to clutch. He sobbed.

As if to go home, he headed up the hill out of town. But again the unanswered questions were a barrier he could not cross. *What would he tell her? How could he break the horrible news to Chrissy? How would they live?*

At the crest of the hill, he drove into the parking lot of the KC Hall. Under its lone tree, he stopped the car and opened all the windows. He leaned back, his neck stretching against the tension of the past hour.

It was a setup! They had the letter ready all the time! They just didn't want to hear the truth! These observations were a preamble to rationalization.

Why, he'd been able to recover almost all the December grain losses! And didn't he have the hedging account? Say, they didn't even mention that! Bet that smartass, Weber, didn't even tumble onto that! And wasn't the number of new patrons way up? Hell, there wasn't any reason to declare Chapter 11. The Elevator was in good shape! Not great—but good.

He reviewed his conversation with Weber in detail. He'd been led from the start! Hell, Weber just wanted to add to his reputation as a fraud detective. Why, if he went back and talked straight to Chris—Chris would understand.

Tom started the car and drove rapidly back down the hill into Sheffield. But there weren't any cars at the Elevator. *They had left! He got out of the Fury and tried the office door. Locked! And he didn't have keys!* He pounded at the door in frustration—no answer.

A rattle of gravel made him swivel away from the door. Bob pulled up in his Blazer and opened his window.

"Ain't this the shits? I suppose they got you, too?"

"Yeah," Tom responded. "Put me though the wringer and gave me a 'Dear John' letter. The rotten bastards!"

"C'mon. Get in. At least we can sit in the cool."

"Let me get my car out of the lot. This letter says I can't come on the property." Tom waved the paper at Bob.

"So you got one too." Bob tapped his shirt pocket. "Leave the Fury at the VFW and I'll pick you up."

When Tom stepped into Bob's Blazer in front of the Club, the rush of cool air cleared the haze from his mind. He could see exactly what had happened—how the Board had made him and Bob the scapegoats for the whole mess. "Well, what do we do now? Seems like we got set up, don't it?"

"You damn betcha! But don't think for a minute that they'll ever admit it. Just look at it this way. We did all the work for damn little pay. It wasn't our fault that the markets went wild!"

"That's right!" Tom agreed. "Just the way it happened. Shit! Remember all those hours we worked overtime?"

Bob hesitated, "Yeah...well...sure. But the fact is we're out. Look at it this way. We are finally free of that fuckin' place and we can go make some real money."

"How the hell? Remember we just been fired."

"Lucky for us we got a good business goin'. In fact, I already called Star. We been out lookin' at that old elevator at Dover. With a little hard work we'll have the start of a real business."

A new business! That would be the answer to all his problems. Why, with the ten grand he had in the bank, he could...

"Bob, that's dynamite! Hell, if I hadn't quit, we could drink to the new number one elevator in town."

"You come to the right place, the VFW's closed but I got a jug with me. Here, take a pull to celebrate." Bob held out a nearly full bottle of Jim Beam.

Tom recoiled. The thought of whiskey made him physically ill.

"What's the matter?" Bob asked. "Need some fixins'? Watch this!" He reached into the back seat of the Blazer. In a small cooler, he found ice and vermouth. Like magic—a cool Manhattan appeared in Tom's hand.

Sure looked good! Maybe they did have a reason to celebrate! Anyway, one pull wouldn't hurt.

He drank. "Okay, Bob. Here's to Dakota Fertilizer. Let's make it the best in the west!"

"I'm with you on that! Say, you ever been out to Dover? To see the new business place?"

"Nope. Haven't been there for a couple of years. Not since Peavey sold that old elevator to some farmer."

Bob put the Blazer in gear. "Let's take a run out there. Star found the old guy who bought the elevator from Peavey. He made him a lowball offer and Dakota Fertilizer owns it! You'll see—it has a lot of potential!"

He turned out into Main Street. "Go ahead, fix yourself another. We got celebratin' to do!"

Automatically, Tom went through the motions. Two parts Beam—one Vermouth—plenty of ice. "Bob, you sure think of everything. Just what I needed. They had me by the balls."

"I know, I know. When they delivered my letter to my house this morning, I was on the ropes. 'Til I talked to Star."

They brooded on their shared injustice.

The Dover elevator was a small wooden structure with two metal bins for grain storage. Star's fleet of trucks was parked in its weedy yard. Rusty rails carried several hopper cars, atilt on the weakened roadbed.

"Sure don't look like much," Tom said, between sips of Manhattan.

"That's right. But me and Star figure we can add a couple of bins and get the old scale certified. Then we can start slow, using fertilizer to keep us goin'."

"Sounds good." Tom emptied his glass and refilled it from Bob's cooler. "You guys really think we could get a full-scale elevator goin' here? What about access roads? How far gone is that scale?" The questions piled on, heightened by the looming threat of unemployment.

"Lucky for us, Star has been workin' on all those problems. He had the Fairbanks Scale people out here. They say that the scale can be certified for about three grand. And the county is plannin' to upgrade the road from here to Sheffield this fall. That would make full semi loads legal all year 'round."

"How much you think it would cost to set up a couple of forty thousand bushel bins?" Tom asked, his mind racing like a runaway reactor, close to core meltdown.

"Slow down! Slow down!" Bob laughed. "We just got fired. Remember?"

Tom tried to return the laugh, but he choked on the shame of the morning's confrontation.

Bob rambled on. "Sure was lucky we got Dakota Fertilizer goin', though. Just think where we'd be if we had to start lookin' for jobs."

Tom gulped the last of his drink and refilled the glass with straight whiskey, not troubling with mix. "Yeah, but it sure hurts to have those creeps lay it on us. Hell, the Elevator Board is just as much at fault in this, and I'll bet Jacobs has been workin' on our case ever since he got elected."

"He's always been a real prick," Bob agreed. "Ever since he started to be a big farmer. I think he's against us 'cause we didn't shave prices for him. If we had brownnosed him more, he'd probably be singin' our praises."

Tom reflected. Barney *had* changed. But so had the whole elevator business. These were just growing pains and he and Bob had the misfortune to be caught in the meat grinder.

He drained the last of the bottle without using his glass. The flood of liquor set him coughing and his head swam. *Too much to drink—not used to the stuff—better get on home.*

"Bob, I got to get goin'. Jan's waitin' for me and I gotta…" he stopped. The next thought completely eluded him.

"Maybe you better let me drive you. You had too much to drink for a guy who ain't in trainin'." He smiled, a wavering, grinning jack-o'-lantern dancing against the hills behind the car window.

Tom bent over in response to a shaft of pain the shot through his temples. "…gotta…be OK in a minute…"

Bob put the Blazer in gear and bumped over the rough yard. Each lurch sent a spasm through Tom—the liquor pressing against his diaphragm, looking for a way out.

They drove back to Sheffield. On Main Street, Tom surfaced long enough to realize that he had to get home on his own. Otherwise Janet would disown him.

"Bob…lemme off…gotta take the car…"

"You ain't in no condition, pal. If the cops catch you they'll lift your license."

"Know it…gotta have car…Jan…plenty mad…"

"Well, you're the doctor. Give me a call on Monday and I'll get Star on the line for a meeting. Keep your pecker up!" Bob smiled at Tom's painful transfer between the cool of the Blazer and the furnace of the Fury. When Tom opened the door of his car, Bob accelerated away, tires screeching.

Tom slumped in the Fury—soaked with sweat—nausea now coming in waves, each higher than the last. He held them back and started the car.

With the extreme care of the very drunk, he slowly worked the car into the street and started up the hill out of town. The environment flowed past, wavy, distorted. The blast of a horn riveted his attention. He was on the wrong side of the road! An oncoming car scraped by, barely avoiding a collision, the driver cursing him. He jerked the Fury back to the right. The over-correction ran the wheels off the road. The right fender bumped a guard rail—throwing the car into the proper lane.

Gripping the steering wheel with both fists, Tom fought back the movement around him. Driving drunk was like swimming underwater. He concentrated on the road just ahead of the Fury's hood. With jerky darts from one side of the road to the other, he made the crest of the hill. He could go no farther. For the second time that day, he pulled into the KC Hall parking lot, heading the Fury into a patch of shade. To avoid the tree, he jammed his foot on the brake and the engine killed.

In the silence, alcohol won. He barely got his head out of the open window of the car before he threw up. Again and again. When sickness had run its course, he was spent, and chilled in his own sweat. He lay sprawled across the seat and lost consciousness.

CHAPTER SEVENTEEN
Turnings

Silver-hot needles of sun pierced the tattered pincushion of tree. Where they penetrated, they focused in laser-like beams of light that traversed Tom's body throughout the afternoon. These burning sensations were switches that turned the directions of his drunken dreams. Recall of the shame of failure was balanced by a confused anticipation of new possibilities. There were no voices, only blurred images that refused to come into focus.

The theme of these flickering forms was both confrontation and escape. Every time a person began to take shape, the scene faded and Tom experienced a deep sense of relief. Members of the Elevator Board appeared, nearly recognizable, and then lost substance as they attempted to speak. The comfort of escape was just as elusive. Visions of Bob and Star were defined by backgrounds of trucks and rivers of grain. They, too, were switched off.

Interspersed with these shifts of image was growing guilt. This became better defined over time and its principal figures began to take the appearance of Janet and Chrissy. At first they only stared at him. The force of their gaze danced over his mind—like sunbeams of emotion. Later, they attempted to speak to him, but no sound reached his consciousness.

In late afternoon, sun escaped tree. Light beamed into the open side window enveloping his head in a helmet of heat. He burned! Sweating and turning, the dreams lost their temporary focus and became nightmares of terrible reality. Undefined forms fought for control of his thoughts. Sick fear seized his mind and he tossed and murmured as he struggled to escape these horrors.

He awoke. Wet with sweat and horribly sick, he pulled himself upright using the steering wheel for support.

Where? How? God! Am I ever sick!

As he looked out the windshield, shimmering heat forced him to lie across the passenger seat. He fumbled the door open and laid on his stomach, head and shoulders outside the car. His dizziness passed and he collapsed with his forehead resting on the sill of the car door.

For a long time he lay in half-consciousness, new surges of nausea racking him, now less frequently. Out of the direct sun, his sweat chilled and he shivered. Consciousness came and left again.

Finally, the cold was too much and he raised himself painfully. As he looked around, he began the confusing process of recall.

This was the KC Hall parking lot! Jesus! What a stink! Must have been sick!

Then, the recollections sharpened. *No job! Those assholes! It wasn't fair!*

At least Bob had come to the rescue. They had an option—an elevator to run. Why they could probably make it real tough for the co-op!

He stared at the setting sun. *What day was it? Sunday! Chrissy would be waiting for him to take her to Luther League! Sonofabitch!*

He searched for his cap. He bent forward to pick it up; the movement ran a lance of fire through his brain. He nearly passed out. Clinging to the steering wheel with both fists, he gritted his teeth against the piercing shafts. Gradually, they passed. He slipped the Fury into neutral and started its engine.

I've gotta get home! But how can I tell them? How can I explain the drinking?

These impossible problems pounded on the back of his head as he turned the car west into the glare of the sunset, squinting, concentrating, wavering. Tom pointed the car down the road, eyes fixed on the twenty feet ahead of him. Luckily, there was no traffic, for he occasionally darted across the center line as he reviewed the approach he would use.

He spoke aloud. "Jan, honey. They fired me at the Elevator!" "I'm sorry I'm late. The meeting was…" "I can explain! You see, Bob and I…"

Spoken aloud, these statements were feeble excuses for the monstrous reality they attempted to define. How could the wreck of the afternoon be reduced to human terms?

From ditch to centerline to ditch—he wove his way until he was headed down his driveway. As Tom approached home, he drove more slowly, postponing the inevitable reckoning.

They were standing on the porch, both squinting west into the sun, watching his progress up the long drive.

He slowed the car. Carefully, he pulled up in front of the shed and turned off the engine. He sat for a moment, gathering his energy and confidence before leaving the sanctuary of the Fury.

Janet stepped off the porch and called over her shoulder. "Chrissy, please wait a minute. I need to talk to Dad."

He swung his legs out of the car and pulled himself to his feet. At once, his head swam and he grabbed the top of the car door to keep himself upright.

"Hi, honey. I need to talk…"

"Tom! You've been drinking? And, look at yourself! You're a mess!"

"But, honey! I…"

"You better get into the shed! Chrissy can't see you like this!" She stood between him and the girl, her eyes boring into him.

She didn't understand! She wouldn't listen! These observations summed up their meeting. Her anger was a barrier that his feeble excuses couldn't penetrate. Meekly, he felt his way around the car and stumbled into the shed where he propped himself erect with both hands against the wall.

He heard the car start and Janet called to Chrissy. "Come on, honey! We can still get you to the League on time!"

A door slammed and the Fury accelerated out the driveway. As Tom felt his way out of the shed, he caught a glimpse of sun on the car's windows when Janet turned onto the township road.

They're gone! It isn't fair! I'm the one who needs help and understanding! If they only knew what happened!

He lurched across the yard, each jarring step a threat to his equilibrium. By the time he reached the house, he was sick again and fell to his hands and knees in the dust of the drive.

When the spasms passed, he stood and climbed the porch steps. The coolness of the air conditioned kitchen brought instant relief. He was assaulted by the odor of his clothes and the stale taste of vomit. He tore off his filthy shirt and stained trousers. In the bathroom, he wedged himself in the shower and let water work its cure.

By the time he had finished his shower, dressed and put his foul clothing in the washing machine, Janet was coming up the driveway. He could see that she was alone. She parked the Fury and strode to the house, her feet a drum roll of anger. When she opened the kitchen door, he was seated at the table.

"Glad you're back. We gotta…"

"Tom! Whatever came over you? You promised you wouldn't drink! How could you do this to us?"

"I know. But it's worse than that! I got fired by the Board!"

"Fired? What do you mean?" Instantly her anger turned to concern and she sat across from him.

"Yeah. They think I screwed up the Elevator. They're goin' to declare bankruptcy and Bob and I…"

She interrupted. "That's a disaster! How could they possibly think that you…why you've given your life to that place!"

"That's just it! I tried too hard! Tried to juggle things so we could make back what we lost last winter. You see, they brought in this hotshot accountant and the federal inspectors. They just made shit out of me!"

"Oh, Tom!" She rubbed her hand across her eyes. They brimmed with tears. "How unfair! What did they say? What are you going to do?"

"Well, at first it was too much for me. I couldn't handle it. But Bob came by and he and Star…" His voice trailed off. *Hell, she doesn't know anything about Dakota Fertilizer. What should he tell her?*

"You see…Bob and Star and I have been trying to put together a fertilizer company the past couple of months. We got some business going and they think we can build it into something worthwhile for all of us."

"I don't understand," she frowned. "Won't that cost money we don't have? Where'll you get the fertilizer? I thought it was really scarce this year."

"That's just it! With Bob's connections and Star's trucks, we can really make a go of it!" He stood up and paced across the kitchen in irrational exuberance. Absentmindedly, he began to make coffee, his back to her. "What we'll do is work out of that old elevator at Dover and build up a grain business too."

"Really! Will that work? What about your drinking? Aren't those two the ones you need to stay away from?"

"Honest to God! That was a real accident! I was so stressed out by what the Board did to me that I couldn't help it!"

"Please! Be honest with me!" She stared at him. "You can't ever do this again! If Chrissy can't see you as a normal father, we'll have to find a way to keep you apart!"

The ultimatum stung him—both in tone and content. What had been a unifying force in their lives could tear them apart. Chrissy was their unity.

"God, Jan! This can't be a problem now! We've got to pull together or we won't make it!"

"Yes, we do have to be together. But we can't if you go back to drinking. You have to see that we love you, but we won't let drinking ruin our lives."

"This is a hell of a time to put pressure on me! Can't you see? I've just been fired! I don't need any more of a load!"

The argument ranged back and forth. Tom's anger and pleading couldn't sway her resolve.

The kettle on the stove boiled dry as they talked. At last Janet ended the conversation. "This is enough for now. We have to work at this. Let's go to bed, and we'll both feel better in the morning."

"But what about Chrissy? Don't we have to pick her up? I'll go…"

"She's not coming home tonight. She'll be staying in town with Carrie for the next couple of days."

Not coming home! Was this the beginning of the end? He stood and stretched, his body protesting the strains of the day.

"I guess that's okay. We've got to put this problem behind us so that she doesn't worry about us. It'd be better if she could see me working at Dover." *Better working than home—fired!* Work had helped him stay sober these past months, and it could do so again.

When in bed, the heat of night and emotion kept them apart. By dawn, the problems had gained strength—and their capacity to find solutions had weakened.

The first light of morning flashed into his eyes. The automatic reflex of Monday drove him to his feet and into his work clothes. Not until he was halfway downstairs did he realize that he had no job this Monday.

He took the last few steps slowly and entered the kitchen in a thoughtful mood. The absence of purpose was counterbalanced by the lack of demands on him. He was conscious, mainly, of relief. Now that responsibility had been taken away, he could be more careful in any new job.

Moving briskly around the kitchen, he gathered their usual breakfast with unfamiliar energy. Thoughts became words as he explored the possible futures that Sunday had created.

This is a real blessing in disguise! Why, I can afford to rest for a couple of days! With 10K in the bank, we don't have anything to worry about! Maybe we'll take a short vacation and then I can get down to work at Dover…

The water boiled, and he carefully poured it through the cone-shaped filter, washing grounds from the sides of the filter as the level of water sank. When he had finished, the grounds were all in a neat mass in the bottom of the filter. *That's the way! Just keep pushing and everything will come out okay!* He went to the stairs and called.

"Jan, coffee's ready!"

He heard her sigh and the creak of the bed. "I'm coming."

A few minutes later, she came into the kitchen. An obvious reserve remained from yesterday's argument that hadn't dissipated in the night.

"Morning. You all better this morning?" he asked with a smile.

"I guess so. But this is a very different day, isn't it?"

"You can say that again! Look at it this way. The heat's off, and we can try real hard not to let the next job take over!"

"I sure hope you're right. We found out that we couldn't get untangled from the last job. Maybe I should try to get work in town. That way, we could afford a reasonable job for you. It wasn't right that you had to carry the load for all of us."

"Now Jan, I don't think…"

"Listen a minute!" she interrupted. "We know how much money we need to live. And if I could come up with even a part of that, it would be better for us."

"But what about Chrissy? We don't want to leave her all alone after school."

"That won't be a problem. This year she'll be in junior high and have a lot of activities after school. And all her friends are in town."

"I see your point, I guess." He sipped his coffee and popped two pieces of bread into the toaster. "But it seems like your going to work is just another sign of how I failed."

"You've got to get that idea out of your head! You have done a wonderful job at the Elevator. You mustn't feel that you have failed them or us. We'll just put all of that behind us and do a better job of working together as a family."

"Sounds good! And, for a start, we've got some money in the bank, so there isn't any pressure on us for a while."

She hooked the slices from the toaster onto a plate and set them next to the butter and jam. "We do have a few dollars in savings. That won't last very long. Doesn't the mortgage come up this week?"

He chuckled. "I'm not talking about savings! Just last week I got a dividend check from Dakota Fertilizer so we're flush!"

"A dividend check! Whatever for?"

He considered. "Well, I've been on the board of the Company and I've helped Star put the business together. So I earned the money." The weakness of this explanation dragged the conversation to a halt.

She spread half a slice of toast with jam, carefully pruning the red edges. "Well, that will help. How much did they pay you?"

He munched his toast and sipped at his coffee. "Ummm…well, about ten thousand."

"Ten thousand dollars! How could they pay you that much?"

"You see, this is a really good business. Working at the board level, I'm cut in for a share of the profits."

"But that doesn't seem right. How could you possibly earn that kind of money? Your other job took all your time!"

"You don't understand. The money's for my advice, not for shoveling grain! It's where the future is, and it's the only reason why we aren't in deep shit with my losing the Elevator job!" His voice roughened with her questioning. *Didn't she get it? How could she look sideways at this windfall?*

"Sure we can use the money. I guess you have to be the judge of whether you earned it." Janet stood up and carried her plate back to the sink, her toast unfinished. "I still think I should look for work. Can I take the car this morning? The Ford's not running."

"Sure, I guess so. No place for me to go today." He sat back in his chair and watched her climb the stairs to their bedroom, knowing that he couldn't change her mind. He cleared the table, sloshed the dishes in soapy water and set them on the drainboard of the sink.

When he had finished, he took his cap and walked slowly to the barn, calling Chrissy's cats as he went. "Kitty, kitty, kitty…" Their yellow tiger faces popped out of the haymow door. Eager mewing called back to him. He pushed them out of the way with his feet as he unfastened the sack of cat food. When their heads were buried in their breakfast, he stood at the barn door looking out across the prairie.

The hoped-for rains had never come. The ground was a parched, cracked desert where occasional patches of green showed underground moisture. *Won't be much of a harvest this fall. Prices will be way the hell up. Poor damn farmers, they won't get any government payments with those high prices. And they won't have nothin' to sell 'cause of the drought.*

He walked around the barn and stared off to the west. There, the heat of the day was lost in the haze of morning–the land giving up the last of night-time dampness in the cool-warm of day. *Lucky as hell I went long in the futures.* He stopped. They weren't his futures any more. The Elevator would be cashing in on his good judgment. *Sonofabitch! Those fuckers will be rollin' in dough this fall. And they sure as hell will forget that I was the one who put them there!*

His musings were stopped by the sound of the Fury starting. By the time he turned the corner of the barn, Janet was on her way out of the farmyard. He waved and called, "Hey! Honey!" But she didn't hear him, and gradually the sound of the engine faded.

Resigned to the reality of her plan, he made his way across the yard to the house. He climbed the porch, the shade of the house an immediate relief from the already hot day. Inside, the small noises of the outdoors were a muted background for his thoughts.

Tom's parents' house had been placed well back from the road down a gravel drive. In summer, there were two well-marked tracks with a strip of grass down the center. Where the drive crossed the tiny stream, a wooden bridge carried the path. The bridge was made of loosely laid planks that sounded a distinctive clatter on each crossing, a sound that echoed throughout the valley, signaling all comings and goings.

At the entrance to that farmyard, a garden conducted an uneven battle with quack grass, the outcome depending upon the wetness of the spring and the time Tom's mother could spare during the busy summer. Some years the plot of worked earth extended from the small front lawn all the way to the creek; other years, the garden was only a small scar on the face of nature.

Like the garden, the house was very much in touch with its surroundings. It sat in a large grove of hardwoods, on the top of a small hill. Inside the grove of trees, the smell of woods was always evident. In fall, the entire hill was a carpet of crisp yellow leaves and the dry odor of autumn permeated each breeze, so walking out of the house was like taking a deep swallow of a very potent elixir. On wet days in spring or early summer, the wood smell was a mixture of growth and decay, the green of the leaves was enhanced by the freshness of rainy wind. Along with the new, there was an underlying hint of rot and a strong fragrance of wood returning to the soil. These smells were always with those who lived in the house.

The house was entered through a white door with two glass panels. The old brass doorknob was loose with many turnings. Dad had always sat just inside the door, his back to the outside while Mom worked at the kitchen range.

Now Tom paused, his hand on the modern doorknob of his own house–shiny, tight, and resistant to turnings. His throat constricted with memory and he peopled his new kitchen with figures from the past, neighbors who had time to visit and laugh about simple anecdotes.

He moved to the counter where the morning's coffee was waiting in a white thermos pot. He held his cup under the spout and pumped the still-hot fluid, turning his cup to swirl the liquid, just as he had in his mother's kitchen.

As he raised the cup to drink, the visions faded. Tom was alone in the silence of the present. Not even a stray thought came to him. He drank, then refilled the cup and carried it out to the deck on the shady side of the house. Sitting in one of the canvas chairs, he pulled another so that his legs formed a bridge between them. As he sat back, a calico cat came from nowhere to leap to his lap, purring with joy.

"Hello, Painted Cat!" The name came involuntarily—out of the past—the family cat of his youth. He was not aware of his welcoming phrase and the cat didn't care. It turned and turned, finding comfort.

As Tom sipped his coffee, he talked to the cat, and the future began to take shape on the jumble of the past.

"Let's see now. This is really a hell of a fix!" The cat stiffened, aware of tension. "Got some money in the bank. Don't have to worry right now." Her claws flexed and the note of her purr deepened in agreement. "But Jan doesn't feel too good about things. Got to show her that we can make it like it used to be. That we can forget all the past troubles." The cat looked up disturbed by the continued talk.

"The mortgage. Got a payment this month. That'll take about three thousand. No problem. Don't owe anything on the cars and no charge accounts. So the money's okay. But it takes about two grand a month. So I got to get a decent job before Christmas. Maybe this thing with the boys will work out."

The cat stretched and turned again, curling into a ball, conforming its body to the terrain of Tom's thighs. He shifted his legs cautiously to adapt to the animal. They both sighed. He stared across the prairie. The morning was growing into another incredibly hot day. The disaster of drought was clearly etched in the contrast between deep, clear blue sky and dusty brown of field. Day after day, this immense bowl of sky reduced all persons and things to insignificance.

"Should I stay with this business? Look at this drought. I'd be better off doing something that wasn't so dependent on the weather."

The cat stirred.

"Cool it, cat. Nothing to be afraid of."

The ringing of the telephone startled Tom. The cat sprang to another chair, complaining of the interruption. Tom jumped up, legs tingling with restored circulation and reached the kitchen on the seventh ring.

"Hello."

"Hey, where the hell you been? We been workin' since sunup!" Bob's voice carried an undercurrent of blame.

"Workin'? Where?"

"Down to Dakota Elevator, meathead! If we're gonna drive the Co-op out of business, we got a lot to do before fall. Hell, me and Star have already drawn up some sketches of how we could add some bins and make this old shack into a workin' elevator!"

Tom reflected on the dilapidated structure that Peavey had been only too glad to unload on the farmer–who had happily sold it to Dakota Fertilizer. "If you think you can make that clapped out place into an elevator, you got another think comin'. Hell, the scale ain't big enough…"

Bob snorted. "Being fired's turned your brain into mush. We go with the technology. Star figures we can manage most of our trade with electronic pad scales, and farmers will accept terminal weights when we settle up. That way, we can get going with no big investment."

Sure! Technology! That was what always held him back at the Co-op. Never anything new. "You got something there. That way we wouldn't have to remodel the old scale house, just use it for small trucks and…"

Bob laughed. "See, you ain't brain dead yet. Remember, we talked about this yesterday, but the fact is we got a lot to do. When you comin' down?"

"I'd come right away, but Jan's got the car and the Ford's on the blink. Soon as she's back, I'll be on the way."

"Can't wait for that! Tell you what. I got to run to the hardware store. I'll swing by for you in 'bout a half-hour."

"Okay, but…" Tom was speaking to a dead phone.

Leaning against the counter, he took a fresh cup from the kitchen cabinet. After filling it from the thermos, he sat at the table and turned Dakota Elevator plans in his mind.

The track is good up to the spur. Bet we could get Burlington to rework the spur so it could handle hopper cars. The memory of the cars he had loaded last winter drew a smile. *Wouldn't do to have one of those big mothers tip over.*

Let's see. *Which farmers might come over? Sure not Barney or Ryan.* His musing stopped at the recall of their anger. *How many of our old customers will believe that shit about the Elevator? Bet some of 'em will.* He drained the cup and rinsed it. *Maybe D. F. will change their minds! Man! I hope so.* A glance at the clock told him that Bob should arrive in the next fifteen minutes.

Tom tensed at the grate of tires in the yard. Hell, he's here already. "I'm comin', Bob!" he shouted.

As he rushed out the door, he met Janet coming in. "Hi, honey. You back already? I thought you were Bob. He's coming…"

"There's really trouble in town! Everybody's talking about the Elevator. And they say that you and Bob have cheated the farmers!" Her eyes filled with tears.

He stood rigid, hands clenched at his side.

"Now, listen! You know that just ain't so! We got caught in this drought and there ain't nobody who could have made the Elevator pay this year. Those are just rumors spread by the board to take the heat off themselves."

"I know, I know. But it's so horrible, hearing the whispers. And when they talked to me, I knew they saw me differently from the way they used to."

"That's it! These people are so damned two-faced. So long as you can make them some money, you're top dog. But let anything come in the way of profit, and you're just a turd in the road!"

"Some of them. But even the people we really believe in—some of our friends from church. That's the worst! They are showing they really care for us—just like we're sick or something!"

"Those sanctimonious bastards! We don't need no sympathy! We just need to have them look at the facts! Wait 'til we get our own elevator going! They'll see!"

"Tom, stop a minute! I don't think it's a good idea to go into business right now. Everybody will think that you and Bob had it planned all along. That'll just make things worse!"

"No! By God! We ain't gonna knuckle under to that kind of talk! Sure, we could sit tight for a couple of months, but I got to get work by Christmas!"

"I can help. I took a job at the meat-market. They needed somebody to manage the counter. I can do that and it will…"

"You took a job! What the fuck for? Don't you think I can handle the money situation?" His temper ran away with his thoughts. No sooner had he said the words and seen the hurt on her face than he knew the sacrifice she was making.

"I'm sorry." He held out his arms. "I'm just so tensed up with this problem that I can't think straight."

She came to him and leaned against his shoulder.

"Listen, let me try to make this new elevator go. Then, if you want to work, you can find something better."

She pushed back from him. "No, this is serious. I need to get out and deal with the opinions of people. I have to know that we can live in this town. If we can't, we need to know soon so we can look for another place."

"Don't talk like that! We can't run away!"

"It's deeper than that! These feelings about the Elevator are very strong! We maybe should go to another place and start over. . ."

"But that would…"

He stopped. Bob's Blazer roared up the drive.

"Look. I got to go. Bob's outside. I'll tell him that I can take the car and…"

"Then, I'll have to go with you. My job starts this noon and I need to have a way to get to town."

He paused before answering, trying to still the anger her decision drew from him. "All right, then. You take the car and I'll go with Bob. I'll call you at the market this afternoon and we can figure out how to come home."

"Please don't go away angry. Please love me. We need each other so much." She came toward him.

Reluctantly, he drew her into his arms. Over her shoulder, he could see Bob seated in the Blazer, impatiently looking into the sun.

"Sure, I love you. Now, I gotta go." He turned at the door and nodded to her, no longer a lover, just another person among the many he had to manage. As he went down the porch steps, he mouthed the words, "Hassles! Why can't things straighten out?"

CHAPTER EIGHTEEN

End of Track

When William Thoms came to the valley in the late 1870's, he chose to settle at Dover. There, the valley was narrow and a small rapid on the river could be diverted for a mill. Also, the bluffs were steeper at that point, giving better shelter from the wind. As time went along, Thoms developed the mill into a prospering mercantile center for the growing agriculture of the area.

However, when the railroad came to the valley it was channeled away from Dover by the bluffs. The Northern Pacific built down the gentler slopes east of Sheffield and crossed the river upstream from Dover. Since Thom's community was a potential user of rail transportation, a spur was run from the mainline to serve his mill and warehouse.

As the years passed, wagon roads and highways were built to cross the river at Sheffield. The result was a growing village where the bulk of trade took place. William Thoms moved his businesses to Sheffield in the early 1900s and the spur fell into disuse. In fact, there was no Dover until 1910, when a local businessman built a small elevator to take advantage of the availability of the spur.

About this time a few cottonwood seeds took root in the mesh of the spur. Since they were at the end of track, people took no notice of them and they were allowed to grow. Over time, the cottonwoods flexed their roots and began to distort the rails. They gradually enveloped the ponderous cast iron bumper, at the end of the track, their woody arms incorporating the bumper's metal.

Now the end of track was buried in a grove of giant cottonwoods. Rails were spread by a monstrous tree that dominated the environment–vital triumph of nature over alien organization.

From his first days in Dover, Tom had been in love with the tree. He took every opportunity to sit in its shade and eat his lunch leaning on the half-buried bumper. In the minute flexings of its growth, the tree gave him new energy to reform his life. He was happy.

The old elevator was, however, a mess. Too many years of neglect had made it a curiosity, not a working system for handling grain on a modern scale. Still, the basic structure was sound and some of its machinery could be used in the short run until the volume of business justified modern equipment. The task, these September days, was to make the elevator ready for this year's limited crop.

People in Sheffield watched these developments carefully. Many were impressed with the energy of the three partners and with the improvement of the old elevator. Most were puzzled by this sudden display of business activity. A few openly spoke about diverted profits and cheating of patrons of the Co-op.

These comments and feelings rarely reached the three at Dover. They worked their hours in isolation from Sheffield, as if separation could resolve all the problems of the past. When they thought of Sheffield or the Elevator it was with a combination of relief and optimism; relief at freedom from responsibility and optimism at knowing that their new business would be competitive from the start.

One Friday, about mid-month, Tom collected Jan at the meat market and Chrissy at school. Chuckling with pride, he enticed them with promises of a picnic.

"Dad, this is the first time you've taken me out of school for anything. What's up?"

"You'll see. Just wait. Have I ever got a surprise for you."

"Come on," Janet laughed. "You can tell us. Where are we going?"

"Sorry, it's a secret." He drove down Main Street and turned onto the road to Dover. "Got to stop by the new elevator for a second."

They drove out of town following the Dover spur. The avenue of cottonwoods along the track arched over the road so that they were moving through a green tunnel.

"I never noticed how beautiful it is out this way." Janet opened her window and the earthy smell of late summer permeated the car.

"Yeah, I kind of like this drive. It's 'specially nice on a hot day. These trees really keep the sun off the road."

"Hey, Dad! Watch out! There's a squirrel on the road."

He braked, and the animal darted to safety. "That one's always there. Must be a hollow tree somewhere around."

They came to the elevator, and he slowed as the new sign came into view.

"Tom! That's marvelous! Why, it looks like you're really in business."

Chrissy added her endorsement. "Geez, Dad. That's super!"

He glowed with pride. The old elevator gleamed under its new paint and the neatness of the yard was testimony to the hard work of the past weeks. They got out of the car and he unlocked the door to the elevator office.

Inside, the old counter proudly displayed a banner: WELCOME TO DAKOTA FERTILIZER.

"This is perfect." Janet turned and hugged him.

"Me, too, Dad." Chrissy stretched and kissed him on his cheek.

Holding them both, he said, "You bet! This time it'll really work. We won't ever have the kind of problems we've been fighting these past couple of years."

When they had explored the office, he led them to the end of the track where he placed their picnic basket on the tree-covered bumper.

"Geez, Dad! The tree is eating the railroad track!"

"Ain't that the truth! This old tree is showing us that there isn't anything we can build that it can't deal with."

They sat on a plank he had placed on two old railroad ties, stretching their legs in the shade.

"Here, let's see what Mom's got in the basket." He opened the lid. "Hey! Hamsammidges!" He gave them the name Chrissy had used as a little girl.

"C'mon, Dad. Don't talk baby talk," she laughed.

"There's a story behind the ham," Janet said, as she placed the sandwiches on paper plates. "My first day at work, I found a ham in the meat case with a date of May second on it. I asked Mrs. Jensen where I should throw it."

"I guess so," Tom said. "That'd be pretty ripe by now."

"You won't believe this, but she said, 'You don't throw that away. You just slice it and put it in the deli section. And add twenty cents to the price.' Isn't that awful?"

"Mom! We're eating! What a terrible story."

Tom clutched at his throat in a parody of choking. "Is this the ham?"

"No, silly. This is a fresh one I had specially sliced for us. I'd never buy deli meat again."

They laughed and joked through lunch. When they had finished, Chrissy ran off to explore, leaving Tom and Janet alone.

"T, this was perfect. You're so relaxed. You can see how this makes Chrissy feel secure."

"I know, I know. There never was time before. But here, we got control of the business from the start. And we can see to it that it never comes first."

Their hands came together and the barriers of the past month faded. They had turned another corner and could see the promise of a different sort of life, one that balanced work and family in proper perspective.

September twenty-sixth, a few days after the picnic, began on an upbeat note. Janet had risen early and made a special breakfast to show her support for the changes Tom had made in their relationship. The day, too, was cooperative. Cool and sunny as only a prairie autumn day could be. As he drove through Sheffield, he was happy that his days at the Elevator were over.

He turned into the Dover yard. Out of the car, he breathed deeply, the heady air rich with the aromas of fall. This was a time of year nobody could resist. Even Bob, a perennial latecomer, was pulling in, radio blaring.

"Hi, Boss! Ain't this one hell of a day?"

"You bet. Finally, things are beginnin' to go our way."

"You can say that again! I stopped at the Post Office, and we got three big orders for potash. When we fill these, I figure we'll be at about half the level of sales I made at the Elevator last fall."

"No kiddin'? We gonna have any problems fillin' them?"

"Nope. I telexed the orders to Leach. He said he's still in the doghouse at Farmhand, but his buddies at other suppliers will divert the cars our way. Of course, he'll have to grease their palms some."

"Hope he don't get his ass in a crack. Without Jim, we don't have much of a shot at gettin' the product we need."

They reflected on the tenuous foundation of their trade. Only with a good history of sales and payment could they expect to take their place as a regular wholesaler of fertilizer. Until that time, they would need to nibble at the edges of the flow, diverting what they could to channels they controlled.

While Bob and Tom talked, Star brought the Number One Kenworth into the yard. Two blasts on the air horns ended their conversation. Each raised his closed fist in a jerky mimic of a pull on a horn cord.

When he had stilled the rattle of the diesel, Star climbed down from his mobile throne.

"Hi, you jokers! How're things this mornin'?"

"Swell!"

"Fine! We got three big orders for you to haul." Bob waved the invoices for emphasis.

"Great! This is sure one perfect day!"

The enthusiasm generated by the fertilizer sales propelled them through the tasks of the morning. Even Andy caught the spirit and worked at twice his usual pace. When the other drivers arrived, they loaded one truck with wheat and sent it on the way to Minneapolis. Another truck was dispatched to Bismarck with a load of fertilizer and the unloading of a rail car of potash was begun.

For Tom, these activities made the Dover yard much like the Elevator. The only difference was that this counted for something. They were building a future for themselves rather than working for wages.

"To hell with the Elevator! Those bastards!"

"What's that?" Star interrupted Tom's mumblings.

"Oh, nothing. I was just thinkin' how this place is startin' to look like a real elevator."

"Damn right! In another couple of months, we'll have the world by the tail!"

They grinned at one another and walked over to join Bob and Andy under the cottonwoods for lunch. When they were seated on the pile of old railroad ties, they touched their cans of Coke in a toast.

Star summarized their thoughts. "Here's to September twenty-sixth. The day we turned the corner!"

They nodded and drank. Each opened his lunch speculating on what lay around his personal corner. The aimless turnings of the past were a pattern that would now be cut by a boulevard of opportunity.

As they were talking, Andy noticed a cloud of dust on the road leading out from town. "Wonder who the hell is gonna interrupt our lunch?"

"Don't be so damn grouchy," Bob clapped him on the shoulder. "It's probably another customer. Let's make him comfortable."

They watched the dust cloud approach the yard entrance. It wasn't a customer. It was one of the cruisers of the Thoms County Sheriff's Office.

"Hey! It's Jack Engle," Bob exclaimed. "Wonder what he wants. You been slippin' through town with an overload, Star?"

"Nope," Star said. "He's probably after you for your last bender!"

"Jack! Over here!" Tom called out to the officer as he emerged from his car.

Engle walked deliberately toward them. In the shade of the cottonwood, he removed his sunglasses.

"What's up?" Bob asked. "You sure look pretty down in the mouth."

Engle paused, looking down at them. "Boys, this is real tough on me. But I got warrants for the arrest of two of you."

"Warrants?"

"Arrest? What you talkin' about?"

Engle pulled two large envelopes from the briefcase he was carrying.

"Here's two indictments. They name Tom Cooper and Bob Clauson." He passed the documents to them. "I have to tell you that you have been accused of using the mails to divert business opportunities from the Farmers Elevator." He passed a third envelope to Star. "Schultz, you are an unindicted co-conspirator in these papers. That means you'll be a part of any civil case and a key witness in the criminal proceedings against Tom and Bob."

"Divert? What the hell's that mean?" Bob stammered as he ripped open the envelope.

"But, Jack..." Tom began.

"Cooper. Clauson." Engle stared at them, his size and uniform silencing their questions. "I got to tell you that you are under arrest and that anything you say may be taken down and used against you. You have a right to consult a lawyer before making any statement." He paused and removed his wide-brimmed hat, wiping the sweat off his forehead with his hand. "That's what I have to say formally. Now, I got to take you into Grandview for booking. If you want, you can drive up in your car and I'll follow along. I don't want to make it any tougher on you than it is already."

They looked at one another. Andy sat with his mouth open, a can of Coke slowly emptying itself on his leg. Star was the first to speak. "Co-conspirator? What's this all about, Jack? Can't you tell us what's up?"

Engle leaned on the iron track bumper, concern evident in his expression. "The charge is mail fraud. What that means is that you are accused of using the U.S. Mail to buy and sell products that were a part of the business of the Elevator."

"But, why's that a criminal case?" Bob blurted.

"It's the usual way business fraud is prosecuted," Engle said. "The District Attorney always says, 'You find the fraud, I'll find the mail.'

The problem is, when you use the mail in any kind of fraud, no matter how little it seems, you come under the mail fraud statute. That makes it a federal crime."

Tom sank to a seated position on the ties. "Jesus! Jack, a federal crime? What can we do? How…" He couldn't go on. The shock of the accusation was too much for him. There were no answers that could lessen the blow of the indictment.

Finally, Engle set these to rest with the inevitability of the legal process. "I ain't supposed to give you boys legal advice. In fact, all I can do is read you your rights and take you in. The rest is up to your attorney."

"But we don't have an attorney!" Bob exclaimed.

"You can hire one in Grandview. There's always one of them hanging around the courthouse. He can tell you what's coming and what you should do. Now, we better get going. You guys want to ride with me?"

Star responded. "No, I'll drive." He tossed his Coke can into the pile of ties. "Andy, you can close up here. Put a note on the door. Say that we'll be open again tomorrow. Then you better take the rest of the day off."

"Sure. Yeah, I'll do that." He stood up, conscious of his wet pantleg. He rubbed at his trousers—half-ashamed of his accident.

"Better not say anything about this downtown," Star cautioned.

"No. No, I won't."

Engle called out to them from his car. "Go to the Federal Courthouse in Grandview. It's on Minnesota Street. I'll meet you in the lobby."

The three got into Star's car, and he drove carefully out of the elevator yard, Engle close behind.

Tom was the first to speak. "God! It's just like school! Going to the principal's office, teacher right behind!"

"The hell of it is, this ain't gonna be so easy," Bob said. "Looks like we got our balls in a vise. Here, take a look at what they say in the indictment. 'TOM COOPER, BOB CLAUSON, JAMES LEACH AND Theodore Schultz did knowingly and willfully enter into a conspiracy to defraud the Farmers Cooperative Elevator.' How come your name ain't in capitals, Star?"

"It's a fuckin' miracle. I'm the unindicted co-conspirator, as Jack says. Remember when they were after Nixon a couple of years ago? Some of them White House guys were named in the indictment, but only Erlichman and Haldeman were prosecuted."

Tom recalled. "But those guys did time! They went to jail!"

"That's the way I read it," Bob grumbled. "Those assholes at the Elevator are gonna send us to the slammer if they can. Then they'll be off the hook."

"But jail! They can't do that!" Tom took off his cap and ran his fingers through his hair. "Hell, we didn't do nothin' wrong! We just…"

Bob reached over the seat and gripped his shoulder. "Take it easy. The way I see it is that it don't make no difference what we did. It's how it looks on paper. Listen to this. 'Defendants created a paper corporation, the Dakota Fertilizer Company, and by use of the U.S. Mails to perpetuate said fraudulent scheme, did violate U.S. Statute No…' That's how they're gonna hang us! They got the Company and our mail box! That's all they need to blow a smoke screen over the facts!"

Star glanced at Bob in the back seat. "I see what you mean. Dakota Fertilizer is a fact. Our mail box is a fact. Our business is a fact. The trick is using these facts to cover up the whole Elevator mess and lay it on us."

"That's the way it looks to me," Bob replied, "and the rest of this shit papers it over. Just listen! 'Defendants used said Corporation to divert business opportunities from the Farmers Elevator, causing the bankruptcy of said Elevator.'"

"That's all bullshit!" Tom exploded. "Why, if it wasn't for us, the Elevator would have gone under last fall."

"Hold it! They got that covered too. 'THOMAS COOPER, as manager of said Elevator, did enter into speculative commodity trades which resulted in substantial cash losses. To conceal these losses, THOMAS COOPER falsified Elevator records and reported fictitious sales of grain.' See, they got us comin' and goin'!"

"But you guys know that I only tried to cover up for that big loss when the Russians…" He stopped. The words 'cover up' sounded exactly like the phrases in the indictment. He had covered up. The only difference was the motive. He had honestly tried to help the Elevator. But they didn't know that. He hadn't told them. And now they were using his work against him!

Star glanced over at him and put his hand on Tom's knee. "You see? Bob's right! They are gonna use those things you did for the Elevator and say that you did them for Dakota Fertilizer. We are in deep shit! And we better start thinkin' how we can respond to these charges!"

They had passed through Sheffield and were on the highway leading to Grandview. Star increased speed. Engle matched the change, his cruiser following closely behind.

Bob continued to read from the indictment. "Here's another zinger! 'Defendants did divert fertilizer allocated to the Farmers Elevator to their own business and subsequently sold said fertilizer to farmers at grossly inflated prices.' Those sonsabitches. Them sales was at the goin' rates. And, get this. 'To conceal said sales, ROBERT CLAUSON developed a paper trail of invoices that showed that each sale resulted in a profit to the Farmers' Elevator.' Shit! That's just what it did do!"

Tom began to see the web of circumstance. "Damn right! We only sold to Dakota Fertilizer at a profit! There ain't nothin' wrong with that!"

Star sighed. "Yeah, there is. The way they see it, we are Dakota. And, because you two were workin' at the Elevator, you had a conflict of interest. The way they got it, every dollar we made should belong to the Elevator."

Bob snorted. "Sure! They should have the money! Hell every time I talked about expandin' trade in fertilizer, the Board said no!"

"That's right," Tom recalled. "Why, there were at least five times I can remember."

Star held up his hand. "You guys are probably right, but the Board had the final say. The way it looks is that they decided not to go into the wholesale business and you should have gone along with their decision. Setting up Dakota Fertilizer was a way around the Board. That's what I hear from Bob's reading."

"But, Star," Tom protested, "that's the basic issue. The Co-op couldn't increase its income. It would have lost its tax exempt status. You remember. We talked about that last fall."

Star considered. "Sure. But I'm afraid that'll get lost in the bankruptcy. They'll be sure to treat that as a red herring and it won't keep them off the scent."

"Dirty fuckers!" Bob pounded on the seatback.

They drove in silence for several miles. Then Bob raised the difficult question of Star's escape.

"How come you got off?"

Star had evidently been thinking about the same issue. He answered immediately. "Looks like they have a tighter case against the three of you. You were all working for either the Elevator or Farmhand. Me, I'm an outsider."

Bob consulted the indictment. "Kind of looks that way. Listen. 'Further, THOMAS COOPER, BOB CLAUSON and Theodore Shultz did enter into a conspiratorial agreement with JAMES LEACH whereby fertilizer allocated by Farmhand Co-op was diverted to Dakota Fertilizer where it was resold at prices well above market.' Nothin' in here about the two-price system! And Leach sure as hell is in it as deep as us!"

"Makes sense the way they write it," Tom agreed. *As if there were any sense in these bizarre circumstances.* He glanced out the back window. Engle was close behind.

When they reached Grandview, their problems were no longer in the abstract. Engle met them at the foot of the courthouse steps.

"Now, Schultz, you better wait in the lobby. I got to take these two in to get booked. Cooper, Clauson, you got a right to have an attorney represent you when you enter your plea. Do you want to call one?"

They looked at each other. This was a question never faced before.

Bob stammered, "But…I…guess…I don't know anybody."

"Neither do I," Tom added. "What can we do?"

"There will probably be a Public Defender on duty inside. He can advise you on your plea and you can get your own counsel later on.

Well, let's go in. And, remember, you boys are my prisoners—so don't act too friendly."

*Prisoners! Jesus! This is unreal! How can I explain this to Janet? How can I...*He was overwhelmed by the change in his position. From Elevator Manager to fired. From fired to part-owner. From part-owner to prisoner. His mind whirled.

They followed Engle up the steps and into the echoing lobby. In the Federal Court Office, they were once again read their rights and given the opportunity to consult an attorney.

Engle answered for them. "These boys have no attorney. They'll probably need a Defender."

The clerk responded. "Okay, Terry Cook's here. I'll give him a call."

Cook appeared a few minutes later—a young man in a three-piece suit. After glancing at the indictment, he raised his eyes to Tom and Bob.

"I better talk to you two. Come on, we can use the judges' library."

When they were seated in the book-lined room, Cook spoke. "First, there's no charge for my time today. I'm on call as Public Defender and will be paid by the Government. Second, this case is way beyond my experience so I won't be able to work for either of you down the road."

They mumbled agreement.

"Finally, have you read the charges? Do you understand what you are accused of doing?"

Tom answered. "It looks like a bunch of circumstantial evidence. Trumped up charges. The facts will…"

Cook interrupted. "Mr.…Cooper…is it? Okay. You can't take that attitude in your defense. When the federal government decides to use the mail fraud statute, they generally have a pretty good estimation of their chances of success. Not knowing any of the facts, I'd guess that you are likely to be convicted of at least some of these charges."

"Convicted! What the hell!" Bob sputtered.

"Yes, Mr. Clauson. You'll need a pretty good attorney with criminal experience to come out of this with a minimal penalty."

Tom took off his cap and twisted it in his hands. "But…convicted…that means prison doesn't it?"

"Maybe. Depends on how the judge and jury see the facts in the case. The way this indictment reads, I think they'll throw the book at you. Fraud against farmers' co-operatives is a particularly nasty charge, one that will get a lot of public support."

"But, we didn't…," Tom blurted. "Don't we get a trial? What about our side of the story?"

"That'll come out. What we have to do now is decide how you'll plead in the arraignment."

"What's that mean?"

"You have been arrested under a federal indictment and you will be booked and fingerprinted. Then you will be asked how you plead—guilty or not guilty. Then the judge will set bail or hold you in jail until trial."

"Jail! What the fuck! You just said we have a chance at a trial! How can they…"

"Mr. Clauson. Mr. Clauson. Please! With no previous record of a crime of this kind, the judge is likely to release you on your own recognizance. That means you'll be free to go until a trial has been arranged."

"Well, we sure as hell are gonna plead 'not guilty'. That's the facts," Tom said.

"Okay. You agree, Mr. Clauson?"

"Yeah, shit! I suppose so."

"All right. Now we'll go in for the arraignment. Please let me do all the talking unless the judge asks you specific questions."

The arraignment was an amalgamation of all the television court proceedings they had seen over the years. The accused prisoners standing, bewildered, in front of a process bobbing and weaving in theatrical precision. The indictment was read again. Cook entered the 'not guilty' pleas. Then the judge spoke.

"Cooper, Clauson. I am releasing you on your own recognizance. You will be required to report to your county sheriff weekly until a trial date can be arranged. Do not travel outside the state without my permission. I also warn you that any attempt to alter or destroy records related to this case will be dealt with very severely by this court."

There was no sympathy in these pronouncements. From the tone of the judge's voice, a decision had been reached. Tom and Bob were guilty, and at the mercy of the legal system. They were fingerprinted and returned to the lobby. Star was waiting for them.

"C'mon," he said, "let's get the hell out of here."

On the courthouse steps, he turned and asked, "How did it go?"

"Fuckin' awful," Bob said. "They got us ticketed to the slammer already. Not even a damn trial will fix that."

"Looks like Bob's right," Tom added. "The way the judge talked at the end, it's just a matter of time."

"Look, we can't talk here." Star said. "Let's go down to Whinney's. We can get a booth in the back where nobody will hear us."

They walked the five blocks to the bar where they often met when visiting Grandview. This afternoon it was nearly empty and a rear booth was completely isolated.

When they ordered, Tom asked for a double Manhattan without thinking. When it arrived, he looked at it with misgivings.

"I shouldn't have ordered this. I got so damn sick last time I fell off the wagon."

"Aww. Go ahead," Bob advised. "We got more problems than that. A little sauce will help you feel better."

That was probably true. In fact, the first sip was a welcome return to better times. Tom drank deeply with relish.

"Now. We got to figure out how we're going to defend ourselves," Star said.

"Shit! You don't have nothin' to worry about," Bob growled. "You ain't facing no federal rap."

"That's so. But while you were in there, I got to thinking. So I called Leach. He's already been arraigned and has been talking to his lawyer. Now, listen to this. His lawyer says that, even if you lose the federal case, you are likely to get a suspended sentence and a small fine."

"That's the first good news," Tom said.

"Hold it. There's more. His lawyer says that the big issue in this kind of case is the rap for the bankruptcy. If they can show that Dakota Fertilizer fucked up the Elevator, we could be liable for all their losses. And that could be a bunch."

Star stopped to drink and let the message soak in.

"Hell, Star," Tom said, "that could be a million dollars. There ain't no way…"

"Right! But if you three get convicted of fraud, all four of us will have to pay. And we can't go bankrupt. Any fraud judgment is with us for life."

"For life! All of us working full time wouldn't make no million before we die!" Bob's mouth stayed open in amazement.

"You got it!" Star concluded. "So, we got to think hard on how we're going to defend ourselves. And I'm in that problem just as deep as you." He beckoned to the bartender for refills. "So we better get our stories straight and be sure that we coordinate with Leach on everything we say."

They examined these problems from different perspectives throughout the afternoon. Although they continued to drink, no one became drunk. For Tom, the liquor provided a sense of detachment. He observed their conversation, a member of the audience as the tragedy unfolded. As time passed, they came to an unspoken agreement that nothing more could be done without the help of lawyers and others who might have had similar experiences.

It was Tom who summarized their collective feelings. "Seems to me that we can't go any further by ourselves. We just don't know enough about the law. And we need to get some help from somebody who knows all about co-ops. If we can't make the case that the Elevator couldn't sell the fertilizer, we are in deep trouble."

"You got it," Star agreed. "Let's get back to Dover and make some phone calls. Then we can decide about our next moves."

It wasn't until they were well on the way out of Grandview that Tom realized that he hadn't even called Janet. God! *I was supposed to go to the homecoming game tonight. Chrissy's going to play in the junior high band.*

"Sonafabitch!"

"What's that?" Bob asked.

"Oh…nothing…just that I didn't call Janet. Can't imagine what she'll think about all this."

"Me, too. The old lady won't like this a bit. Main thing is that we won't have the money she likes to spend. That'll put me in the doghouse."

Star offered another perspective. "You guys been thinking about what they'll be saying in town? This will be in the papers tomorrow and there'll be plenty of talk about us."

"It sure as hell will shoot any business we might have for this fall." Bob thumped the dash with his fist in frustration.

"Good thing we got some money in the bank and don't owe a bunch of people right now." Star turned to look at Tom in the back seat. "When you guys were in with the judge, I got to thinking. We got enough in the bank to pay for some legal advice. What say we get together tomorrow and hash this out?"

"Tomorrow won't work. It's Saturday and we can't get hold of any lawyers 'til Monday." Tom said.

"That's right. I forgot. But on Monday all of us better meet at Dover and plot strategy."

With this agreement, they fell silent for the balance of the trip. It was full dark by the time they reached Sheffield. The lights of the high school football field showed that the homecoming game was under way.

Tom glanced at the crowd as they passed the field, wondering what this disaster would do to Chrissy and Janet.

At Dover, they scattered to their cars. There was none of the optimistic chatter that had held them together during the past month. Instead, each fled to look for his own solutions.

Tom drove back to Sheffield and parked near the football field. Like so many other times, he sat in the Fury, his forehead resting against the steering wheel. In a way, the car was his sanctuary, a familiar place where nothing could intrude, where he could gather whatever energy remained to deal with the problems outside.

Finally, Tom raised his head and focused on the crowd leaving the game. For a moment, he was still a part of the team. *Got to get ready for next week. They'll be depending on me.*

Then Janet opened the passenger door. Chrissy was behind her, talking with friends, proud in her band uniform.

Janet began to speak, then stopped.

"Tom, where…" She stopped as the whiskey smell reached her. "You've been drinking again. Why did you have to come to the game? Here comes Chrissy, and she'll see you."

"You don't understand. I…"

Janet had already turned away and was speaking to Chrissy.

"Honey, Dad isn't feeling well. So you and I will ride home with the Swansons. Then you can stay with Carrie overnight like you planned."

"But Mom—Hi, Dad. Did you see…"

"Honey, come on now. You can tell Dad all about the band when you come home tomorrow. Hurry up! The Swansons may leave without us."

Sending Chrissy on her way with a gentle shove, she bent over and spoke to him through the open door.

"All right. I'll ride home with the Swansons. They'll drop me off at our place. Then you can try to explain why you did this to us again." She slammed the car door and stalked off after Chrissy.

Pitying thoughts turned endlessly as he waited for the traffic to move past. When there was space, he started the Fury and entered the queue of cars heading for downtown Sheffield.

As he passed the VFW, he felt the urge to share his troubles with the regulars at the bar. The thought was immediately driven from his mind by the surety that the friendships of the past would be changed by the news of the day. There was no refuge in that place.

Resigned, Tom took the road up the hill and out into the prairie. Traffic quickly thinned as cars exited the main highway at each country road. Highway 13 was clear when he turned off for their farm.

No one was at home. The stillness of dark enveloped him as he shut off the engine and got out of the car. He stretched, stiff with tension. *Was it only this morning that everything had looked so good?* There was no answer—just timeless silence. He leaned against the car with his hands in his jacket pockets.

"God, please help me. You've got to…my family," he choked with emotion. "Please protect Chrissy and Janet. Don't let this ruin their lives." The prayer went on, pitiful in its simple requests. Slowly, his hands came out of his pockets and clasped one another. He tried to remember one of the prayers his mother had used. But he couldn't make his lips form the words. He could only hold his clasped hands against his forehead. His thoughts reached out into the silence. He was not comforted.

He wept without tears. Sobs of frustration. Prayers giving way to curses.

"Those dirty motherfuckers! That god-damned Jacobs! Why the hell do I have to take the blame for their screw-ups?"

"Oh, God! Please…"

"Justice! Fuck! Guilty until proven innocent!"

"Just let me get out of this one. I'll never…"

His monologue was finally stopped by the sound of a car slowing for their driveway. Quickly, he jogged for the house. A conversation with the Swansons would be too much for him now.

By the time the car entered the yard, Tom was securely inside the porch. As Janet thanked her driver, he snapped on lights for yard and kitchen. When she came into the house, he was seated at the kitchen table.

The soft voice she had used with the Swansons was replaced by an angry, abrupt barrage of questions.

"Where were you? Who were you drinking with? Just how long do you think…"

He jumped up and grabbed her by the shoulders. Shaking her into silence, he said, "Shut up! Dammit! We got problems that are much bigger than drinking. As you can see, I ain't drunk! Now sit down and listen!" He pushed her roughly toward a chair.

Now she was crying. "Tom, you've never hurt me before!"

He wanted to go to her and hold her, but the wall of his anger was too high. He moved to the counter and hit it with both fists.

"This afternoon I was arrested! Do you hear? Arrested!"

Janet raised her head. "Arrested! What for? Were you drunk in the car?"

"Jesus Christ! Get that out of your head! Bob and I were arrested because they say that we cheated the Elevator. They're going to put us in jail! Can you understand that?"

She stood, her arms folded. "No, I don't understand. Who arrested you? Please tell me."

"Okay. Here, look at this!" He unfolded the indictment and tossed it on the table.

She picked it up and read. "United States of America vs TOM COOPER et al. Defendants did conspire…created a corporation to…falsified records in order to…"

"This is terrible! How can they say such things about you?" She slumped back on her chair. "What does this mean?"

"It means that I'm probably going to go to jail!"

"But why? When you tell your story, there won't be any way they can prove these things."

"Huh!" he snorted. "You weren't in front of the judge in Grandview! He thinks we're guilty as hell! And that isn't all of it. When the federal government gets done with us, we have to face another trial to decide how much we'll have to pay the Elevator. It's one big fucking mess!"

Janet's questions gradually built the bizarre structure of the case against him. For each option or solution she offered, he countered with the overpowering logic of the complaint.

"Oh, Tom! It looks so hopeless! What can we do?"

"That's just it. I can't see any way out. No matter how strong my story is, they'll twist the facts to show that the bankruptcy was my fault."

"But what about these crazy accusations? Like this one, 'Defendant COOPER did knowingly mark patrons' grain as sold without customers' consent.' What about that?"

"That's a good example of how it'll get twisted. See, everybody in the business marks some grain as 'sold' to cover in case they're short. I did that to be sure we kept our license. What a laugh! Now I'll go to jail for trying to help the Elevator!"

He alternately paced the kitchen and sat, dejected, at the table. She read and re-read the complaint. With each reading, the bands of law drew tighter.

It was well into September twenty-seventh before they gave up in despair.

CHAPTER NINETEEN
October Haze

Early October was a time when everyone involved in the Elevator scandal experienced much of what is good and bad about small town life. Those outside the Sheffield community were interested in this new topic of conversation. Farmers who were likely to lose money in the Elevator bankruptcy were angry and saw the arrests as a natural outgrowth of business failure. Members of the Elevator Board were confused by the legal tangle surrounding them and thankful for a convenient focus for blame.

Bob and Tom were no longer regulars at the VFW. Star was continually on the road and saw Kate at rare intervals. Consequently, Janet and Chrissy were the only ones involved in the turmoil of opinion. Sympathy and concern were their portion. Mrs. Jensen's approach to Janet at the meat market was typical.

"Oh, Janet, I just heard about Tom and Bob. It's so terrible! Is there anything I can to do help?"

"No, thank you Agnes. There really isn't anything to do but wait for a trial. Then Tom and Bob can tell their story."

"Don't you worry! It will come out all right. Those two are hard workers and have been real good to farmers. That will fix it all!"

Janet accepted these predictions, but didn't believe them.

The three conspirators had very different experiences. The first was a complete halt in their business at Dover. No customers came into the yard during the first week in October. The only business was the wholesale fertilizer trade where distance preserved the flow of orders and deliveries.

There was, however, an abrupt halt in the availability of fertilizer. Calls to Farmhand went unanswered. Finally, Tom was able to reach Leach at home.

"Jim? This is Tom Cooper. Haven't been able to reach you at work."

"Not fuckin' surprising! I got fired on Monday!"

"Yeah, I figured as much. Business is dryin' up damn fast. Can't get anybody to give me a price quote at Farmhand."

"Those bastards won't trade with you guys anymore. You better lie low when the stuff in the pipeline is cleared out."

"What do you mean? We still got orders comin' in."

"Sure, but you won't be able to give them buyers any more price breaks. You can make a few nickels by buyin' wholesale from the mines. But the days of good profits is over!"

"But that'll put us clear out of business! Hell, we can't make ends meet with the measly ten percent we can make on wholesale!"

Leach laughed bitterly. "You got it! This is the end of Dakota Fertilizer! If we somehow survive this lawsuit, you'll be just another country elevator—scratchin' along to make a go of it!"

They were silent for a moment, then Leach continued. "And that ain't the worst of it. The postal inspectors were here already this morning, tryin' to get me to turn government witness."

"What's that mean?"

"Just this. They'd cut me a deal to get off with a suspended sentence if I'd give them the lowdown on you boys."

"What lowdown? Shit! We're all in this together!" Tom sat down heavily in his office chair, another aspect of tragedy looming.

"Sure, we know that. But they were settin' me up to say that it was your idea. They'd rather get a couple of us in the pen than have everybody get off with a slap on the wrist. And, believe me, they'll be after you guys to see if they can split one of you off as a prosecution witness."

"Well, there's no fucking way that we're gonna knuckle under to that! Hell, we know the true story and we're gonna tell it!"

"I'm glad to hear you say that, Tom. I hope both you and Bob are real strong, 'cause they'll put plenty pressure on you."

"Don't worry, Jim. We'll stick together on this one! Well, I suppose I better get going on the phone and see what I can salvage from the orders we got."

When he told Star and Bob about Leach's conversation, their anger focused on the postal inspectors.

"Those assholes!" Bob shouted. "They think they know all about the fertilizer business! Shit! Bet none of 'em has ever been on a farm!"

"Yeah," Star agreed, "but think of what they've done to us. The only business we've got left is sendin' the trucks over the road hauling other people's product."

"That's so," Bob added. "You ain't seen nobody in here to trade with us, have you? We might as well close up shop and help with the truckin' however we can."

Tom returned to the legal issue. "And what about the prosecution evidence thing? We gonna stick together on this?"

"Sucking A!" Bob said. "There ain't no way these assholes are gonna drive a wedge in this company!"

"Goes without saying," Star agreed.

The phone calls to customers went about as Leach had predicted. When they quoted new prices to their buyers, they were told that the competition in the regular fertilizer market was keen. Unless Dakota could deliver unallocated material and competitive prices, they were just another supplier, and a small one at that.

Sorenson in Montana summed it all up for Tom. "This fertilizer thing's beginnin' to break. The poor crop out here has shut down demand. Hell, I'll bet you we see a fertilizer glut by early winter. Me, I'm not buyin' a pound until spring. Then I'll fill up the bins at bargain prices."

This news came as a surprise to Tom. He hadn't thought of the possible effect of the drought on farmer demand for fertilizer.

"Am I hearin' you right? You think farmers won't be buyin' as much this fall?"

"You bet! Shit, my big operators are just the same as me. They'll go with minimum fertilizer on the wheat this fall and wait to see what spring does."

"If you're right, we're sure in trouble on the fertilizer end."

"That ain't all, if what I been hearin' is true. These last couple of days, the phone's been burnin' up with calls about you guys. What's the scoop?"

Tom gave him the outline of the case against the three and how they planned to defend themselves. "When we tell our story, it'll all blow over."

"Well, I sure hope so, 'cause right now you guys ain't got a very good reputation in the trade."

"What the fuck's that mean?" Tom shouted. "We've been treatin' everybody more than fair!"

"Yeah, but they're sayin' that you used Co-op fertilizer to do it. While we all got good deals, you guys got all the gravy!"

Tom was stunned. *Sorenson was a good friend. If he felt that way…*

"But Marv, you were in on this from the beginning. Didn't you co-sign a note for Star?"

"Yep. But I talked with my lawyer after that and he said to steer clear."

"Whaddya mean! Why did he say that?"

"He said that us elevator managers would have a serious conflict of interest if we set up a competing company. Me, I don't need no such hassle."

"Marv, you know I ain't no crook! I was just tryin' to help the Elevator and…"

"Tom, I like you. But I ain't so sure about Leach and Clauson anymore. There's somethin' wrong with the situation and, until it's put right, you better go slow with the business."

Others he called weren't as open as Sorenson. Most didn't have time to talk with him. A few simply hung up when he gave his name.

The few remaining orders in process were also problems. Buyers continually called to confirm delivery and prices. Several of those calls resulted in cancelled orders—the reason being "to avoid receiving stolen product."

For Dakota Fertilizer, trade simply ceased to exist.

Star summarized the situation for them. "We ain't got enough business to keep this place goin' the way it is. We got to cut expenses, and here's what I think we should do. First, we lay off Andy and Joe, and cancel the lease on one truck. Then, me and Bob go on the road with two trucks. Tom, you stay here and see if you can drum up loads for us. How's that sound?"

Bob was the first to reply. "Okay with me. I got the license. Tom don't."

Tom added. "I'll go along with that. Sure's gonna be hard on Andy though."

"Don't worry 'bout him," Bob said. "We got enough problems of our own."

The prophecy became ever more accurate over the next weeks. Tom could barely keep the two trucks busy with loads from other elevators. The drought had created a glut of transportation, and he had to bid near cost on most contracts.

His experiences with people he counted as friends were the opposite of Janet's. Her first interactions were filled with sympathy and support. Nearly every customer at the meat market had a kind word for her. They all spoke of mistakes and predicted that everything would turn out for the best.

The difference in their interactions distanced them even further from one another. When she described the comments of others, he countered with suspicion and anger. Finally, the difference was too obvious to be overlooked.

"Dammit! I don't want to hear any more about those sanctimonious bastards! The women butter you up and the men put it to me!" He raged around the kitchen, fists clenched.

"Tom! Don't be so bitter! They really do mean what they say."

"You bet they do! And what they say is that they're gonna put me in jail!"

"Please! Look at it from their side. They have only heard the bad things about the case. They don't know what you really did and…"

"Jesus! Now you, too! Does everybody think I'm a crook?" He stalked out of the house, slamming the door behind him.

They later made up for this episode, but the sting of words couldn't be erased from their minds. He continued to wonder whether she really believed in his innocence, and she couldn't drive out the feeling that he no longer trusted in her loyalty.

These emotions caused Tom to turn inward. He increasingly kept his own counsel and said little about work or legal matters. He also began to drink steadily. Not enough to limit his behavior—but enough to be obvious to Janet and Chrissy. Whiskey again triggered a confrontation between them.

Chrissy was away from Sheffield with the junior high band when Janet turned their aimless conversation to his behavior.

"Chrissy's gone tonight."

"Ummm–yeah. So what!"

She studied him, her face without expression. "You don't seem to notice her anymore. Can't you see that she needs you to reassure her? She's as worried about things as you are."

"Probably. But you'll have to handle it. I got enough problems on my plate right now." He rummaged through papers on the kitchen table. "Where the hell's that yellow pad I was workin' on?"

"Tom! Listen to me! You are changing! You are angry all the time!"

"Christ! Don't you start preachin' to me!"

She continued as if he had not spoken. "And you're drinking again. This time it's serious! It's not just parties this time; it's every day!"

"That's my business. If I need a little support, I've got to get it from old Al. All my friends have bailed out!"

"Don't say that! It only makes it worse. Whiskey is destroying you. You have no time for us. You don't even talk to Chrissy. Can't you lean on us instead?"

"That's it! I probably would, if I could be sure you were on my side!"

She interrupted, now angry. "That's not right! We support you all the time! Both of us know you're right, and we show it in every way we can." Janet blinked back tears as she struggled for control.

"Yeah, sure! The way you two show it is to make more problems for me. Hell, I…" He stopped, but the words had already done their damage.

"If you really feel that way, Chrissy and I should go away for a while. Then you could be free of our problems, and it would be easier for you."

He raised his head and looked at her. The inner voice pressed for what he really wanted, but anger remained in charge. "If that's what you want, it'd probably be better for Chrissy to get out of town for a while!"

Janet was stunned. "Okay," she murmured. "I'll think about it this week and see what Chrissy would like to do." She got up from the table and stumbled into the living room where she cried into the night.

The tensions in their lives increased day by day. The futile hours Tom spent at Dover only heightened his anger and frustration. Despite this downward spiral, he remained at least marginally in control of himself. Alcohol was still a tool and not the master.

The next crisis came abruptly. A call from Star set it in motion.

"Tom, I got a load for Minneapolis from Grandview Co-op. Won't be back for two days. See if you can get me a back haul."

"Sure. I think there's some elevator machinery lookin' for a ride to Fargo. I'll track it down and you can call from the Cities."

"Okay. And, you better watch TV tonight. Grandview is doing a special on the big Elevator scandal. You won't want to miss it." He laughed sardonically.

"No shit? What do you suppose that means?"

"I'll bet it's our friends on the Board. Probably that fuckin' Jacobs, lookin' for more ammunition to set the public against us. Well, gotta go now, talk to you later."

Tom and Janet watched the special in their basement room.

"And now, here's Jenny Morrison, our Grand News expert with a story of corruption in Sheffield. Jenny, what's up at the Sheffield Co-op?"

The camera cut to a slim, well-dressed young woman standing in the parking lot of the Farmers Elevator.

"Jerry, what we have here is an example of growing problems in American agriculture. Farming has become big business. And it draws people looking for ways to make a fast buck. The Farmers Elevator here in Sheffield is now in bankruptcy proceedings, all because its farmer owners misplaced their trust."

"What! That goddamned bitch!" Tom growled.

"…then, three years ago, the Elevator Board decided to hire a new manager. Thomas Cooper was brought in to increase business. And he brought in his friend, Bob Clauson, to manage the fertilizer division."

"Wasn't Bob already there?" Janet asked.

"Sure! But what difference do the facts make?"

"They set up a competing company, Dakota Fertilizer, to siphon off fertilizer to be sold on the black market. They involved James Leach, a manager at the big Farmhand Co-op in St. Louis and a local trucker, Theodore Schultz. This business was so good that the four men were able to buy and equip their own elevator just down the track from Sheffield." The scene shifted to Dover and to the 'Welcome to Dakota Fertilizer' sign.

"Those rotten bastards! They've even been snoopin' around Dover!"

Now Morrison stood in front of one of Star's Kenworths.

"Dakota Fertilizer owns a fleet of these heavy trucks. In a few short months, this company has become a major hauler of farm commodities."

"Shit! Star had them trucks long before Dakota Fertilizer ever got…"

"…moving fertilizer and grain which should be a part of Farmers Elevator's business . ."

The scene shifted to Sheffield, where the reporter stood in front of the Elevator office along with Barney Jacobs.

"Mr. Jacobs here is a member of the Co-Op Board of Directors. He has consented to comment on…"

"I'll bet that asshole has…"

"Tom, please! Don't let this get to you."

"…you first get the idea that something was wrong at the Elevator, Mr. Jacobs?"

"You could smell it for the past year." Barney's round face enclosed a gleeful grin. "Cooper and Clauson were always scheming and cooking the books and…"

Morrison interrupted, probably conscious of the potential liability of this line of comment.

"Yes, Mr. Jacobs, we can see that there are problems here at Sheffield."

Again the scene shifted—this time to the Grandview Courthouse. On the steps, Morrison continued her story.

"Three of the men, Cooper, Clauson and James Leach of Farmhand Co-op, have been indicted by a federal grand jury on charges of mail fraud. The U.S. Government will try to prove that the men defrauded the Farmers Elevator. While the U.S. Attorney was unwilling to comment to us, there was a clear sense of confidence that this crime will be punished and that the Elevator will be able to serve the farmers of Thoms County as it has in the past. For Grand News, this is Jenny Morrison in Grandview."

Tom leaped up from the couch and twisted the TV control to 'off'. He whirled and blurted to Janet. "How the hell are we supposed to get a fair trial with that kind of shit being spread around?"

She agreed, sharing his anger. "It's unfair! She practically said that you three will be convicted!"

"That bitch!" He nearly spat with rage. "If only I…" He groped for words and actions, but nothing could correct the damage that this report had done.

"What will become of Chrissy? Some of her friends are sure to have heard this terrible stuff. They'll make it hard for her!"

"Chrissy!" he shouted. "What about me? Sure, they'll tease her some, but they won't put her in jail!" As soon as he said this, he acknowledged his selfishness. "Yeah, yeah, you're right. We got to think of her. What should we do?"

"Maybe this is the time for her to visit my mother. She could go to school in Minneapolis with her cousin for a while, until this mess gets sorted out." She sighed. "But that's just what the worst of them want. To break us up!"

"Guess that's right," he said. But he could see no way to hold them together. "How can we keep her from hearing about all this crap?"

She wiped her eyes. "I guess I'd better pick her up after band practice tonight. Then maybe I can drive her up to Mom's tomorrow."

"That'll work. I'll get Bob to pick me up and we'll try to figure out a way to get our story out and fix some of this bullshit!"

When Janet brought Chrissy home that night, Tom was already in bed, drawn up in a fetal position, trying to shut out the recall of the news report.

'…*the three men*…'

'…*a competing business*…'

'…*indicted*…'

He turned restlessly, until Janet's voice called from the kitchen.

"Tom, are you asleep?"

"Yeah, almost. Don't bother me now."

They didn't.

In the morning, Tom and Janet reviewed the newscast. They found no points where they might gain a purchase for their levers of argument. In retrospect, the story was a tightly-drawn net that tied up the case of U.S. vs COOPER et al. in a neat package.

Chrissy was puzzled by the planned visit to Minneapolis.

"But, Mom! I gotta be at band practice every day. Mr. Nelson says that anybody who misses will be cut!"

"Honey, Dad and I want you to visit Grandma. You know how much you like to be at her house and how much fun you have with Kirsten."

"Yeah. But Mom…"

Tom interrupted. "Chrissy, Mom and I have decided you should go. Better get ready now, so you can be in the Cities by tonight."

She stared at him. Gulping back her sobs of frustration, she clattered up to her room.

"Oh, Tom! It's already starting! She is being shoved out of our house! Let's not send her!"

"Nope." He thumped the table. "She's gotta go. I got too much on my mind to worry about her, too. In the Twin Cities she won't have to see all this shit!"

Bob's car horn cut the conversation.

"I got to run. Bob's outside. You call me at Dover when you get to your Mom's. Tell Chrissy that I'll call her." He grabbed his cap and a yellow pad and turned to the door.

She reached out to him. "Please, Tom, wait! Please say goodbye to her! She needs to know…"

"Ain't got the time now! I'll talk to her on the phone tomorrow!"

The door closed behind him. Janet held out both arms as if to draw him back, to hold them all together.

Tom swung into the Blazer and Bob sped out of the yard.

"You see that TV bitch?" Bob asked.

"Yeah. Wasn't it the biggest pile of crap you ever saw?"

"It's bullshit alright. But we're the only ones that know it. What you suppose them rubes in Sheffield think about us now?"

"That's the problem," Tom said. "They've made up their minds that we're guilty. Makes it a hell of an uphill fight for us to convince any jury."

"That's what I thought."

They drove in silence for a couple of miles.

"Looks like my old lady pulled stakes on me." Bob glanced over at him, shaking his head.

"Huh? What you mean?"

"The old bag just took all the cash in the house and caught the bus for Chicago! She's goin' home to her folks!"

"Ain't she gonna support you?"

"Nope," Bob grimaced. "She's seen the handwritin' on the wall. No more easy money and some real tough times ahead. Hell! We can't make this month's mortgage payment!"

"But, where's the ten grand you got from the Company?"

"I got that salted away. She ain't gonna get her hands on that! Hell, that's all I got for a new start when this thing blows over."

"Well, same thing's started with me. We sent Chrissy to Minneapolis today. Sent her out of town."

"Good idea! Them vultures would just pick her apart!"

On their drive through Sheffield, they imagined stares from people who recognized the Blazer.

"Jesus!" Bob said through clenched teeth. "It's started already! You see how old Jepsen scowled at us back at the stoplight?"

"Yeah. Better bug outa here! Everybody's seen that fuckin' news program."

As they entered the Dover yard, Bob slammed on the brakes. Their new sign was covered with sprayed graffiti.

CROOKS.

A dripping summary of the town's opinion.

"Those dirty fuckers!" Bob spat. He bounded out of the Blazer and rubbed at the paint. "The shit's already dry! They must have come out here right after the program!"

Tom was stunned. Rejection was one thing. To have it painted for everyone to see was another. He hung his head in shame.

"C'mon!" Bob called. "Let's see if they did any damage to the truck."

The truck was as they had left it, and there was no other evidence of vandalism. However, the painted sign had shaken both of them.

Tom summarized their feelings. "Those fucking pricks! Ain't it enough that we gotta be shown up as crooks in everybody's living room? You know, this kind of crap can get real nasty."

"That's a fact," Bob agreed. "If this keeps up, one of us will have to sleep in the truck."

"I can't believe it! Two weeks ago we were sittin' on top of the world. Now look at us!" Tom climbed the steps to the Dover office and unlocked the door.

Bob slumped against the counter. "Look, we gotta think of somethin' to do. Just sittin' here and waitin' for the axe to fall ain't the right approach. Now, I been talkin' to my brother-in-law. He's an attorney up at Fargo. He thinks we'd better try to do a deal."

Tom stopped in his aimless sorting of invoices. "Do a deal? That's just what Leach said we better not try. If we stick together…"

"Nope! That's what the Feds want us to do. Keep us all in the soup and then put it to us at the trial."

Tom considered. "Well, if your brother-in-law is right, we'd all have to go along with the deal. Or else whoever is left will sure be holdin' the bag."

"I suppose." Bob turned his back to Tom and looked out the office window. Nothing was moving in the yard. "So long as we got nothin' to do, I guess I'll run out to the house. Give me a call if Star comes in."

"Sure. Can't imagine that there'll be any business after the TV special."

After Bob left, the day dragged on. By noon, Tom had finished all his accounting chores. The only interruption was an anonymous telephone call.

"Hello, this Dakota Fertilizer?"

"Yeah, this is Tom. What can I do for you?"

"I'm an old customer of yours at the Co-op and you already done plenty enough for me."

"Huh?"

"Just callin' to say that I heard the TV last night. Sure was glad to see that you crooks are gettin' what's comin' to you."

Tom hung up in disgust. The harassment made him feel even more alone. He walked out into the yard and sat under the cottonwood tree.

Thoughts tumbled across the image of the tree and its bumper. Why couldn't they just leave us alone? He sank to his knees and tried to pray.

"Oh, God! Please give me the…Please help us to…Please keep Janet and Chrissy…"

He gave up. His whispered pleas wafted into empty air and no release came, only a sense of loss. He was a person severed from community, with no reserve of spirituality to soften his loneliness.

Star returned early in the afternoon, a fresh breeze of strength. He looked to a future where there might be a way out of their dilemma.

"Hey! Why you so down in the mouth? Suppose you saw that TV report?"

"Yeah. Did you?"

"Yep. I caught it in a bar in Monte. Most of western Minnesota stations covered it. Pretty bad!"

"Damn right! And you saw what they did to our sign. Some sonofabitch called this morning to tell us how glad he was about the TV news."

Star scowled. "Now that's real bad! But that report was so slanted that some people are askin' if we been railroaded. I heard some guys in Monte say that the Elevator Board ought to be arrested too. That comment of Jacobs probably did us some good."

"I hadn't thought of that," Tom mused. "Maybe you're right. People might think that there's other rats on the ship."

"Well, we got to look at this from every angle. Can't let it get us down. Where's Bob at?"

"Oh, he took off this morning. Had some stuff to do at home."

"How's he takin' this?"

"'Bout the same as me. Oh, yeah. He was talkin' with his brother-in-law—he's an attorney—he thinks that we should try to do a deal with the Feds."

"What?" Star grabbed Tom by the arm. "What kind of deal?"

"You know—admit to some of the stuff and see if we can get off easier."

"Boy! That's just what Leach warned us about. All we need is one of us to feed the Feds what they want to hear. Then whoever doesn't deal is gonna get screwed! Gimme that phone!" He reached over the counter to take the instrument from Tom.

Star dialed Bob's number and frowned as it rang again and again. There was no answer. He hung up.

"I don't like this at all. You suppose he's gone up to Grandview to do a deal?"

"Aw, c'mon Star. Bob wouldn't do that to us. He'd stick with us on whatever we agree to do."

Star leaned across the counter and handed the phone back. "Maybe. But he's been talkin' about a deal for the past week. This TV thing may have been too much for him. Let's call Leach."

Tom dialed Leach's number and found him at home.

"Jim? This is Tom. You hear about the TV program on us last night?"

"You bet! It was even run on one of the St. Louis stations this morning. Sure is a piece of shit!"

"The reason I'm callin' is that Bob thinks we should do a deal with the Feds."

"Fuck that!" Leach shouted. "We do a deal and the Elevator will be in fat city on a civil suit!"

"What do you mean?"

Leach explained. "If we do a deal, we'll have to admit that we pulled a fraud on the Elevator. Then they'll sue us for everything we've got, and they'll collect without even going to court!"

"You mean that even if we get off on the federal case, we gotta prove that our business didn't hurt the Elevator?" Tom glanced at Star who was following one side of the discussion.

"Damn right! My attorney says that we got a chance to lay off some of the charges in the indictment. If we can, we'll probably get some kind of suspended sentence. Then, when the Elevator files a civil suit, we'll be able to say that we were just part of a bigger problem. That way, we won't have to ante up for all the Elevator losses."

When Tom relayed this information, Star said, "Just what I thought. Ask him what his attorney says we should do."

"Jim, Star wants to know what your lawyer thinks is gonna happen next."

"He thinks the Feds are gonna try to split us up. Star's the most likely candidate, 'cause he ain't indicted."

"Star's worried that Bob may be the weak link. He's been talkin' 'deal' for a week."

Leach considered this news. "Say that's bad. We think Bob's real vulnerable. He could be a key witness for the prosecution and that would put us in deep trouble."

"That's what Star thinks. What should we do?"

"Let me talk to Bob," Leach replied.

"He ain't here now. He went home this morning."

"Gimme his number. I'll talk to him there."

"He ain't at home. We tried a few minutes ago."

"Son of a bitch!" Leach enunciated each word carefully. "I'll bet he's on his way to cook a deal with the Feds!"

"C'mon, Jim. Bob wouldn't do that!" Each time Tom assessed Bob's loyalty, he lost some confidence.

"I don't agree," Leach said. "You go track him down and call me right back when you've found him! We gotta see what's up!"

Tom slowly set the phone on its cradle and looked at Star in amazement. "He thinks we better find Bob!"

Star started out the door, beckoning to Tom. "Let's get over to his house. We can check on the VFW and Elks Club on the way."

They took Star's car and examined all the cars parked on Main Street. No Blazer.

Bob's house looked empty as they pulled up to it. Blinds were drawn in the front windows and the garage door was closed.

Star turned into the driveway. "This don't look good. Let's see if we can get into the house."

They found the front door open. A trail of clutter led from the living room into the kitchen. Both Bob and his wife had obviously left quickly, taking only things of value with them.

"What a mess! This don't look like their house." Tom shook his head and kicked his way into the kitchen.

"That's for sure." Star agreed. "One thing you could say about Bob's wife, she was compulsive about this house."

They stood in the kitchen. On the table by the phone was a pad of lined paper that was covered with notes.

Star picked it up. "Look at this! 'Turn off gas' and 'Don't forget to let the cat out'. Somebody's plannin' a long trip!"

Tom peered over Star's shoulder. "Yeah, and look at that note on the bottom. 'Call Harry about GV.' Harry's the name of his brother-in-law. That GV could mean that he's workin' on the deal at Grandview!"

"That's so." Star looked up from the paper. "Tom, I think Bob's done it. And I think he's been plannin' this for quite a while. I don't buy the notion that his wife left him either. One thing about her is that she is Bob's woman. Remember how she defends him when anybody criticizes him?"

"I guess you're right. But what do we do now?" Tom slumped into one of the kitchen chairs.

Star cleared the table and pulled up a chair across from Tom.

"We better have us a little strategy session. First, see if the phone works. We better call Leach."

Tom picked up the receiver. "Got a dial tone. Let's see, the Missouri area code is..." He dialed, and Leach answered at once.

"Jim, this is Tom again. We're at Bob's place. Looks like he's skipped out!"

"Jesus! Any idea where he went?"

"No. Only there's a note that says 'Call Harry about GV'–Harry's his brother-in-law."

"Hmmmm," Leach mused. "Sounds like he's splittin'. I was afraid of this. After your call I talked with my attorney. He says that we each need to get our own lawyer. When you boys get yours, have them give my guy a call." He gave Tom two numbers where the attorney could be reached.

"Jim," Tom asked, "do we really need all these lawyers? Can't your man work for all of us?"

"Guess not. Bob goin' over to the other side will mean that each of us better work as hard as he can to keep out of the slammer!"

"But ain't we all on the same team?"

"Still are—far as the Dakota Fertilizer goes. But each of us is named differently in the indictment, and we gotta defend ourselves against those specific charges."

Tom considered this. Holding his hand over the phone, he spoke to Star. "He says we each need an attorney."

Star reached for the phone. "Here, let me talk to him."

"Jim, this is Star. What's this about separate attorneys?"

"Umm…I see. That, too?…Well, okay. We'll call you as soon as we get them lined up."

He replaced the phone. "Well, good buddy, we got us some thinkin' to do. Way I see it, we gotta make the company go. Without that bread, we can't pay no lawyers, and no bills."

"That's probably right," Tom said. "But there ain't no business."

"Not here. But when I was in the Cities yesterday, I made a deal with Cargill to help haul out grain from their elevators in Iowa. There ain't no drought there and they need to get ready for a bumper crop."

Tom lightened. "That's good news! I heard that they were getting full."

"Yep. Now we need to get them trucks on the road. I already talked to Andy, and he can start back to work tomorrow. About the other truck—-you got an up-to-date license?"

"No. Never had one."

"Hmmm…that means we got to hire Joe back, too. Let's see, we'll need some cash to operate for the next month, until we get paid by Cargill. You still got any of that ten grand?"

"Most of it," Tom said. "Didn't need to dip into it too far, what with Jan workin'."

"Okay. Let's you and me each put up five to seven thousand for operating expenses. That'll give us about six weeks to get some cash flowin' again."

"What about Bob?" Tom asked. "He's still a part of this show. And Leach?"

"Only way is we gotta face them with the facts. We'll ask Bob for his ante. If he won't come up with it, we work a buyout on his stock. I got it all thought out."

"Sounds good to me! Let's give it a try." Tom extended his hand to Star and they grinned at each other. A small sign of hope.

CHAPTER TWENTY
Metamorphosis

The new arrangement worked. The three trucks were continually on the road throughout the rest of October. And it looked as if the company might be able to make the payments on the truck leases and meet wages for Andy and Joe with a little left over for Tom and Star.

However, these weren't good days for Tom. As long as he had plenty to do at Dover, he was fine. He could work with intensity and interest to make up loads for the drivers and could grasp the dynamics of the company in his record keeping. His problems occurred on those days when work was slow. Then he wandered around the Dover yard and started futile projects to improve their little elevator. And he drank.

There was always a bottle or two of whiskey in his desk and some ice in the office refrigerator. These he viewed as necessities, ways to recharge his energy.

At first, Janet tried to remind him of his promises, but the anger that resulted gradually wore her down, and she became resigned to his withdrawal. She lived her life in calls to Chrissy in Minneapolis and in making her job serve as the interface between the Coopers and Sheffield.

As the weeks went by, Tom found ways to avoid talking with her and Chrissy. When their phone rang at home, he got up and went outside, often to sip at one of the bottles he kept in the barn. When he reentered the house, she tried to tell him about Chrissy. These attempts always led to feelings of failure on his part and to angry exchanges.

"For Chrissakes! I know I ought to pay more attention to her! Can't you see that I can't talk to her without cryin'? If I hadn't fucked up our lives, she'd be back here with us!"

"You mustn't be so hard on yourself! We love you and support you. That's the only way we can get out of this mess!"

"Ya mean pity! 'Cause you're always givin' me sympathy. I need help, not moaning about us and Chrissy!"

"All right, then. If that's the way you want it, you'll have to tell me what to do. And, you better do it soon! We can't go on like two strangers!"

He stormed out of the house that time, roaring off in the Ford to spend the night at Dover. Alone with his bottles.

Early in November, Bob's 'deal' was confirmed. Leach's lawyer had received word from the federal prosecutor that Bob was a key witness and that he could be deposed by defense lawyers. When Tom shared this information with Cook, the Grandview Public Defender, he was told that he must find a criminal lawyer to try his case.

"I've made an appointment for you with Sam Freitag. My advice is that you go to him and see if he'll take your case. He's got the experience and could do a good job for you."

"Can't you continue?" Tom pleaded. "I'd rather stay with you."

"Mr. Cooper, this is way beyond my experience. It wouldn't be ethical for me to take your case. Now, you go see Freitag and work it out with him."

This was the problem he took to Janet.

"Okay," he said, "here's your chance. I gotta go see this Freitag at Grandview on Wednesday. You wanna go along?"

"Why, of course. I'll take the day off work."

"Don't let's hear about that damn job." He growled. "Do you wanna go or not?"

"Yes. What time do you need to be there?"

"Two o'clock."

"Shall I pick you up?" she asked.

"No. I gotta pick up some parts for the trucks. I'll run up in the Ford and meet you at Freitag's office."

On Wednesday, Tom waited in front of the lawyer's building..

Where the hell is she? Long as I gotta go through with this shit, she could at least be on time?

After a few more complaints, he saw the Fury turning onto the street ahead of him. He stepped out of the Ford and waited impatiently for her.

She came at a trot. "I'm sorry. I was talking to Chrissy and…"

"Yeah. Yeah. Let's get in and get this over with!" He turned his back on her and stalked up the steps to the lawyer's office.

The plush reception area did nothing to raise his hopes. Instead, the surroundings only added to his sense of anger and shame. They contrasted dramatically to the crude environment at Dover.

Freitag was the stereotypical successful middle-aged attorney whose three-piece suit and conservative tie were designed to inspire confidence. It had quite the opposite effect on Tom. Freitag's success was just another standard against which his failure could be measured. He was speechless with rage and frustration.

"Now, what can I do for you folks? Your call said something about a criminal case."

Janet turned to Tom, who was staring, mute, at Freitag. She answered. "We…my husband…is under indictment for mail fraud. You may have heard about the Sheffield Elevator. Tom is—was—the manager."

"Oh, yes." Freitag tilted his high-backed chair and steepled his fingers. "That seems like a pretty open and shut case. Diverting business opportunity by an employee…"

Tom interrupted. "But that's not the way it happened. I was just tryin' to help out the Elevator…"

Freitag held up his hand. "Excuse me, Mr. Cooper, but you were helping yourself. Isn't it true that you were a part of a company that profited from trades that the Elevator might have made?"

"Yes, but…"

Freitag went on relentlessly. "And didn't you conduct Elevator business out of your personal checking account?" Evidently Freitag knew a great deal about the details of the indictment and was able to go to the central issues in the case.

Tom leaned forward on the edge of his chair. "That money! I paid it all back…my check…"

"As I read it," Freitag continued, "you paid the money into a hedging account that is in your name, with a balance of something like one hundred thousand dollars."

"I can explain that account!" Tom said, his face reddening.

"I hope you can, Mr. Cooper, because it looks very much like you were building a nest egg at your employer's expense."

Janet could keep quiet no longer. "Mr. Freitag, Tom isn't that kind of person! He gave his whole life to the Elevator. He may have done some things he shouldn't have, but he was under pressure. Anyway, we didn't use one penny of the money they say he took!"

"I'm glad, Mrs. Cooper, because that's the only defense I can see. Your husband will have to show that his actions were of the sort that any reasonable person might have taken under the circumstances. But let's talk strategy for moment. This defense will take a great deal of preparation. The publicity you've received means that we must respond to each count of the indictment in terms that the average citizen can understand. And that takes time and money."

"How much would it cost, Mr. Freitag?" Janet asked, her hands working the gloves she carried.

"I'd say a minimum of forty thousand dollars for preparation and another twenty thousand for the trial itself."

Tom gasped. "But…I don't…we don't have that kind of money!"

Freitag sighed. "Criminal defense doesn't come cheap, Mr. Cooper. Don't you own property? Can you borrow against your home? Or have you friends who might lend you money?"

Freitag's glasses glinted in the afternoon sun—lenses magnifying the greed in his eyes.

Tom slumped in his chair. "There's no way we could raise that kind of money! We don't have more than twenty thousand equity in our farm. And nobody we know has enough to help us."

Freitag considered these facts, then got up and moved to the side of his desk. "I'm afraid that I can't help you, Mr. Cooper. If you can find a way to finance the defense, please call me and we can discuss an arrangement. But I will have to insist on payment in advance. It's a policy of this firm."

Janet stood up abruptly, her anger driving her. "I just don't see why Tom should have to pay for defending himself against something he didn't do!"

Freitag attempted to educate her as to the ways of legal practice. "Mrs. Cooper, you must face facts! The evidence against your husband is overwhelming. In fact, lawyers are talking about the Sheffield Elevator fraud as one of the prettiest schemes they've seen. You had better believe that the U.S. Attorney thinks he's got an airtight case. I wouldn't be honest with you if I didn't say that your husband's best defense is to admit to the charges and hope for a reduced sentence."

Tom stood too. "Dammit! I can't admit to something I didn't do. I tried to do my job in the best way I knew how."

Freitag cut in forcefully. "Mr. Cooper, I'm a busy man and I can only say that you are deluding yourself with that kind of talk. You must recognize that you did commit illegal acts and that you must defend yourself to reduce the consequences. When you realize your predicament and have the money, call me and we'll see where we go. Now, if you'll excuse me…" Freitag resumed his seat and began to leaf through papers on his desk.

Janet and Tom looked at one another in disbelief and made their way out of the office in confusion. They pressed closely together in order to pass through the office door—as if there were answers and freedom outside.

On the street, they stopped. Tom, in a rage, blurted, "Jesus Christ! Did you hear that bastard? He's sayin' that I'm a crook! That son of a bitch!"

"I know! Oh Tom! Let's go home and work this out." She pulled nervously at his sleeve, conscious that others on the street were watching.

He tore away from her grasp. "What the hell is there to work out? They've got me hogtied and ready to send up the river! Dammit! I can't even get them to listen to my side of the story!"

She opened her mouth to speak, her expression a trigger for a violent reaction. He turned on her, finding a focus for his anger.

"Just how the hell can you know? I'm the one they're after! You don't have any idea how it feels!"

"But, Tom, I love you! Together, we can come out of this! Please, let's go home!"

He looked at her, teeth clenched, almost spitting his words at her.

"Home ain't where the answers are! If I'd spent a little less time at home and more on my job, I wouldn't be in the soup now!"

As he spoke, he had an inner sense that he was crossing the last of a series of lines that encircled their marriage. He watched the hurt grow in her eyes and a small, little-heard voice attempted to stem the flow of his anger. *She's the only one you can count on. If you lose her, you'll be all alone!* In a perverse way, these semi-conscious thoughts only intensified his rage. He lashed out—wanting to give pain.

"You take the car and go home! I'm gonna try some other places around town."

"But…let me stay with you!" She rubbed the tears from her cheeks with the back of her glove. "Tom…please!"

He shook his head. "Now, you listen!" He clutched her arm, gripping fiercely and shaking her as he growled. "You get in that car! I got things to do and I don't need no weepy woman tellin' me that I got to go home!"

"Oh!" she cried. "You're hurting me!" She bit her lip to stop sobbing and looked helplessly at the few passersby who turned their heads to ignore the quarrel.

Rage was a force beyond measure that was overcoming all his basic inhibitions. Janet was now the focus for his anger.

She wrenched her arm from his grasp, standing, crying and rubbing her arm. "Tom what's happening to you? This isn't like you! Don't do this to us!"

"You heard me! Take off!" He wheeled, leaving her standing and staring after him.

Tom stomped along for several blocks, pushing past others on the sidewalk. When he turned a corner, Janet could no longer see him. At first, she began to follow. Then, remembering his violence, she crossed the street to the Fury and sat, her arms folded on the steering wheel and her head bowed. She cried, silently—then with deep sobs.

The intensity of her sorrow was a culmination of all the emotions of the past months, a final capstone on a tower of grief.

"Oh, God!" she cried. "Don't let this happen!"

After nearly a dozen blocks, Tom slowed and he became aware of his surroundings. *Where was he going?* Then, recall made him stop. *He had shouted at Janet! Hurt her! Sent her home! How could he?*

He turned back on his tracks, walking, then running the blocks toward their car, mumbling as he ran. "Honey! Please wait! I didn't mean…I'm sorry…" The intense effort made his teeth ache and he was forced to go more slowly. At last, he turned the final corner and could look down the street in front of Freitag's office.

All he could see was the wink of the Fury's brake lights as Janet entered the Sheffield road.

He stopped, dismayed at what he'd done. Now she, too, was turning her back on him. Was everybody going to let him down?

He hunched his shoulders and jammed his hands deeper into his jacket pockets—then set off in slow pursuit of the Fury.

After several blocks, his self-pity became so great that he staggered in waves of remorse. His surroundings were only a blur, a mixture of impersonal store fronts and restless flux of traffic. Then the blinking red neon of a bar directed his footsteps.

When he entered, it was like coming home. With growing relief, he slid into a booth at the end of the room and waved a tentative hand at the bartender.

"Yessir. What'll it be?"

"Uhhh…how's about a Man on the rocks?"

"Sure thing! Comin' right up!"

"Say, better make that a double."

"You bet!" The bartender moved glasses, bottles and measures with a priestly veneration, each movement a ritualized act. When the fresh, cool liquid came to rest in front of Tom, its aroma turned back the veil of despair that engulfed him.

Like an experienced lover, he caressed the glass, making little designs in the beads of moisture. As he raised the glass for the first sip, he felt a companionship with countless others like himself—outcasts from community.

He sat in the booth for hours, alternately sipping Manhattans and holding his head in his hands, sunk in a reverie of self-pity and desperation. He was unaware of his surroundings. The brown color of his jacket and cap merged with the dark background of the booth. In the half-light of the bar, he faded so that others took no notice of him. The waitress occasionally replenished his drink. Even she did not talk to him beyond essential words of one syllable. He did not exist.

The alcoholic haze was so thick that he did not perceive the conversation in the next booth until the "Elevator" theme broke through. Two truckers were talking.

"Yep. Sure has been one hell of a problem. But damn good thing they're starting to get the place shaped up."

"Ain't that the truth! Tell you what, though. Without that Pete, they wouldn't be gettin' to first base."

"That's so right! Hey, you hear what he done with that asshole, Jacobs?"

"No. And, I don't want to hear anything about that fucker. He screwed me out of two hundred dollars freight on the last load I hauled for him—and you better believe it's the last one!"

"You'll like this. Old Pete, he's sittin' in his office after work one day last week when in marches Barney, blowin' off steam like usual."

"So what's new? That bastard is always fumin' about something."

"Just listen! Pete he says, 'Hi, Barney. What can I do for you?' Barney swings his fat ass into a chair and says, 'Got to sell some corn, and I want to get the top dollar from you. Remember, I'm on the Board now and I'll be able to see that I get a fair shake.'"

"Fair shake! When did that prick ever want anything fair?"

"Dammit! Shut up and let me finish! Pete, he leans back and says, 'Barney, that's just a real good idea. Here, you fill out this contract and set the price you think you ought to have.' He pushes one of them sales contracts 'cross the desk. Jacobs, he grabs it and curls them sausage fingers 'round a pen. He says, 'Here's what I'll take. Make it twenty-five cents over Minneapolis, cash on the day I deliver.' Pete, he kind of frowns and says, 'But ain't that a little high? That'll make it hard on other patrons.'"

Tom was now fully alert. How many times had this scene been played out in the past? Barney pressuring him for special treatment. Now, poor Pete was on the hot seat.

"Barney, he don't bat an eye to this. 'Piss on them guys!' he says. 'Here's the deal!' And he writes the twenty-five cent figure on the contract and signs it, throws it on the desk in front of Pete and says, 'Okay, you sign that as Manager and I'll pick the delivery date.'"

The speaker paused to drink. A beer bottle thumped on the table. "Now, here's the good part."

Tom strained his head back against the wooden partition of the booth to hear the result of Pete's predicament.

"Pete picks up the contract, folds it and puts it in his pocket. He stands up, and you know how big and tough he can be. He says, 'Okay, Jacobs, this is the end of the shit you been pullin'. I'm takin' this contract to the Board meeting at the end of this week. What we're gonna find out is which one of us they'll fire! 'Cause I sure as hell ain't gonna stand for any special deal for you or anybody else!"

"No shit! Why, good for old Pete! What did Barney have to say to that?"

"The way I hear it, he just went white and stomped out. But the best part's still comin'."

"C'mon, give! What did the Board do about it?"

"They took about ten minutes and voted Jacobs off. Between old Odegaard and Gerry Ryan, they took the hide right off Jacobs. Even told him his trade wasn't welcome at the Elevator!"

"Sonofabitch! I can't believe it! Jesus, that Jacobs finally got what's comin' to him!"

They were quiet—apparently reflecting on this good news. Tom was dumbfounded. How could Pete have faced up to Barney like that? Somebody so mild and easygoing?

The storyteller spoke again. "Can you imagine what would have happened if Cooper was still manager?"

"Sure. Jacobs would have his deal and Cooper would probably have a piece of it himself."

"Naw. Jacobs hated his ass. Instead, Barney's got his price and Tom would be tryin' to figure out how he could cover the cost by jockeyin' the books."

"Maybe. But you got to remember, Cooper's probably a crook and he had to be pullin' the wool over the farmers' eyes for a long time."

"Could be. Anyway, let's drink to Pete. There's a guy that's gonna shape up that Elevator!" The thread of their conversation led off into other topics.

Tom sat staring at the opposite wall of his booth. A crook! But Pete! Why hadn't he taken a hard line with Barney? If he had, he probably wouldn't be out of job now. If only…

The impossibility of this line of thought quickly took control. He was in a box! He hadn't faced up to pressure. And he wasn't as good a manager as Pete was proving to be.

He shrunk down in his seat as the truckers left their booth. They walked past him, taking no notice. When they had gone, he moved as if to leave.

"You want another one?" The waitress looked over at him as she cleared the truckers' booth.

He sank back into his seat. "Oh, okay, bring me another Man."

When the drink arrived, he concentrated on it and drained the glass in one long pull while the waitress watched.

As he noticed her, he scowled. "That was a little on the short side. Better bring me a double and I'll hit the road."

But he never did. Throughout the evening, he continued to drink, more slowly now. The customers in the bar came and went. They paid no attention to him. When they looked his way, they avoided his staring eyes.

By the time the bar closed, he was thoroughly drunk. He staggered out the door to the sidewalk. There he stood, alone. Finally, the urge to urinate was too much for him and he leaned against a car while he relieved the incredible pressure.

"Not feeling so hot, mister?" A patrolman had stopped his cruiser and was standing next to him.

"Huh? Hell…fine now. Gotta get to my car."

"Sorry, Mister. You're in no condition to drive. Where you from?"

"What the fuck's it to ya?"

"C'mon. Get in the car and we'll go down to the station." The officer easily manipulated Tom's feeble resistance and bent him into the back seat of the cruiser. There he slumped across the seat and passed out.

The night in the drunk tank was mostly one of mental oblivion. Whenever Tom surfaced, there were only disconnected images of his recent experiences. Something about a car he needed to follow; an intense pull that nearly raised him from the rough bunk. But the car always disappeared along with the compulsion to follow it.

There were also images of Pete at the Elevator. These pictured Pete as a driving manager, dictating orders to faceless beings. In these scenes, there was a figure that Pete confronted. When he did so, the figure wilted and Tom lapsed into unconsciousness.

In the morning, one of the officers came into his cell.

"Mornin', Mr. Cooper. How are you feelin' today? You sure had a pretty good snootful last night!"

Tom was unable to follow the conversation; he only groaned and buried his face in his pillow.

"C'mon, now! You gotta go in front of the judge. Before you do, you have a right to consult an attorney. Not that it'll do much good!"

Attorney! Those assholes! They were out to get him!

"Mr. Cooper! Can you hear me? What's your attorney's name?" The officer shook him gently.

*Name? That jerk…Sam…*his thoughts surfaced briefly. "Freitag."

The officer stood up, amazed. "Sam Freitag? I wouldn't have believed it! Well, I'll give him a call to see what he suggests." He shook his head and left, locking the cell door behind him.

Call…that bastard…tell him… and he drifted off, now into a region where unconsciousness was gradually transformed into sleep. As the alcohol wore off, he began to rest peacefully.

"Say, Cooper! You awake?"

Tom rolled over, rubbing the grit from his eyes. "Huh? Yeah, guess so. What? Hey! Were am I?"

"You're in the Grandview drunk tank. You were arrested last night for being drunk and disorderly."

Drunk tank? Arrested? "But what for? Hell, I…"

"Hold it!" the officer held up his hand. "I talked with the officer who arrested you. Lucky he caught you in time. You were gonna drive off. If you had, you'd sure as hell have hit somebody!"

Drive off? That was it! "Jesus!" he exclaimed, "I gotta get outta here! My wife…" he lurched upright, head whirling.

The officer caught him by the shoulders and lowered him to the bunk. "You still ain't in no condition to go anywhere. Anyway, you still gotta enter your plea. That's what I came about. Sam Freitag says he ain't your attorney. That so?"

"Goddam right! That asshole!"

The policeman scowled. "Hold it! Sam Freitag's a damn good attorney, but he ain't representing you. Who is?"

Tom bowed his head. There wasn't anybody and he was in even deeper trouble now. "Nobody, I guess."

The officer rubbed his chin. "Well, then, you'll have to wait 'til tomorrow when one of the public defenders can enter a plea for you."

"Tomorrow! No! No! No! I gotta get home! My wife! I gotta see her!"

The officer paused, his hand on the cell door. "Sure, sure. When court opens tomorrow at ten, you can enter your plea. The judge'll probably let you off with a fine, since you weren't actually driving. Now, you better clean up and get some real sleep."

The door clanged shut.

Tom leaped up from the bunk and grabbed at the bars. "Hey! Come back!" But the blue uniform receded, and he was alone.

Throughout the day, he alternately paced and called out. When the evening meal came, he tried to reason his way out with the jailer.

"Please! You gotta let me out! At least lemme phone my wife! She'll be worried about me!"

This request had to be honored. The jailer led Tom to a phone at the end of the cell block.

"Be sure to reverse charges," the jailer said. "Push that call button when you're finished."

Tom drew the phone to his side. Shakily, he dialed home. The operator came on the line.

"Good evening. Thank you for calling with AT&T. How would you like this call to be billed?"

"Collect from Tom."

"Thank you, Tom."

The connections clicked their way from Grandview to Sheffield and he could hear the ringing of their phone. One. Two. Three. Four. Five. Six.

The operator broke in. "There doesn't seem to be any answer, Tom."

"Let it ring a couple more times." He listened intently.

Eight. Nine. Ten. Eleven.

The operator came back on line. "Would you like me to keep trying?"

He stared, gripping the instrument. "No, I guess not." He replaced the phone on its hook and sat numbly at the little table. *Where was she? Why wasn't she looking for him?* Then he remembered.

Oh, God! Why did I talk to her like that? Why...

The jailer interrupted. "Okay, Cooper. Let's get back to your cell."

"But I didn't get any answer. Lemme..."

"Sorry. You got your chance. You better try again in the morning. It's night-night time now." He laughed.

Tom marched ahead of the jailer to his cell. A new home, one he had better get used to.

When the dreams came, they were all variations on the theme of enclosure. He was hedged with piles of grain. As they grew, they slithered toward him and became live worms that rubbed against his legs.

He woke sweating, grasping at the blankets that had wound themselves around his body. Gratefully, he released himself and got up to drink from the little basin in his cell.

Back on his bunk, faceless crowds edged ever-closer to him. These visions were all the more horrible, since the beings had no recognizable features. As they approached, they chanted in accusatory fashion.

He responded in a delirium of words.

You gomme wrong…

I ain't guilty!

They came closer.

Please! Lemme 'lone!

The lights came on. A jailer rapped on the bars of the cell.

"Hey! Cooper! You got the DT's? Better wake up and stop yellin'. You'll disturb the beauty sleep of these other drunks."

He rolled over, awake, and desperately frightened.

"Leave the light on! Please!"

The jailer relented, and Tom spent the balance of the night in a trance between sleep and wakefulness, carefully avoiding the terror of dreams.

In the morning, he was taken to a judge. Tom's defender had persuaded him to plead guilty and offer no excuses. This proved to be a sound strategy, and he was released after paying a fifty-dollar fine and receiving a lecture on his behavior.

When this ordeal was over, he tried to reach Janet, again with no success. His anxiety heightened, he hurried out into the streets to search for the Ford.

He could not remember where he had left the car and it took nearly an hour to find it, so it was noon when he was finally on his way back to Sheffield. His fears grew during the long drive. *Something was wrong at home! Maybe she had been in an accident! It would all be his fault!* He urged the Ford to its maximum speed, wheels shaking in protest.

Through town. Testing the legal speed limit. Up the hill, tires screeching on the curves. Out on the prairie, past the KC Hall. Racing down the ruler-straight road. Quick turns. Left! Right! Then into his farmyard.

The Fury sat in the garage! It looked okay! She would be waiting...

He jumped out of the car and ran clumsily up the path to the porch.

"Jan! Honey! I'm back!" He rushed in through the kitchen door. "Jan! Anybody home?"

She was gone.

He walked softly, so as not to disturb the silence, over to the table. Next to the sugar bowl was an envelope, addressed to him. He opened it, already knowing the sadness it contained.

"Tom," he read, "I'm sorry to have to write this. But there is no hope for us as things are. I've taken the bus to Minneapolis to be with Chrissy."

He sat down, heavy with grief.

"Please don't try to get in touch with us until you have things straightened out. The way you hurt me in Grandview tells me that I'm not important to you any longer."

Not important! God in Heaven! The only one who counted for anything at all!

"The keys are in the Fury. The checkbook is in the glove compartment. I hope and pray that things will become all right with you and that we can get back together. You are the only one I have ever loved. I still want to be with you. Janet."

Tom propped his head on his hands, elbows on the table, staring at the kitchen counter, where she was always standing, laughing, talking. He looked at the chair across from him, where Chrissy carried on her animated conversations.

They were gone!

The house was suddenly hostile, communicating its rejection of him as the wrecker of its soul. Silence pressed in on him.

He walked aimlessly onto the porch and stared across the prairie.

They were gone!

There was nothing here for him—he walked to the Fury, started it and drove slowly back toward Sheffield. The brink of the hill signaled an escape of sorts, a poor but welcome refuge from the emptiness of landscape. He drove down the switchbacks. At the bottom, he took the turn for Dover and bumped over chuckholes filled with fall rain. There was a light in the office.

Inside, Star sat at the desk, pocket calculator in his hand.

"Hey! Hello! Where the hell…" Then Star saw the pasty face, the staring eyes. "What's wrong? Here, sit down."

Tom fell into the offered chair. "Jan's left me," he gulped. "I got drunk in Grandview. Hurt her. And she pulled out. Can't blame her."

"Jesus! You poor bastard! How'd that happen?"

"Guess I was too mad at lawyers and all the other stuff. Tried to take it out on her one too many times."

"But she'd never just leave!" Star protested. "She's always ready to work anything out!"

Tom spoke—almost a whisper. "This time I really fucked up. Got put in the drunk tank for a couple of days. She probably thought I was the one who run out. Here, read the letter she left." He held out the crumpled envelope.

Star read it carefully, folded it and handed it back. "I see why you're so upset. Way it looks to me, you gotta show her that you got things under control before she's gonna come back."

Tom nodded. "And just how the hell can I do that?"

Star considered. "I'm glad you caught me here. I was just doin' some damage control. Listen to this." He paused and drew on his half-glasses. "The case against us is pretty strong, but they need Bob to really make it stick. I think we can break that link by pointing to his role in all this."

"How's that?" Tom asked. "He's likely puttin' the whole thing on me."

"You remember the train ride? When I was last in Montana, Sorenson gave me a note that Bob had written to Leach. It was lyin' on the table in the bar car and he picked it up when everybody left. Here, read it."

Tom puzzled out Bob's familiar scrawl. "Jim. Looks like Tom will go along with our idea. He'll be on the train. Let's get together and see if we can get him to use the Elevator to corral some of that Farmhand fertilizer."

When he had finished reading and looked up, Star said. "Yep. I read it the same. He and Leach cooked this up and roped us in. You to get the product, me to set up the company. I think that this paper is dynamite for us, a way to put the blame where it really belongs!"

The facts! Man! Would that ever help!

"Well…looks pretty good." Tom nearly smiled, but then sadness took over. "Hell, it's probably too late."

"Nope. I disagree," Star said. "We gotta get a good lawyer and use this paper to weaken the Fed's case. Then you can cut a deal with a plea bargain, so the blame gets passed around. You bring in some of those Board minutes where they tell you to stay out of the fertilizer business and I think we've got a fighting chance. What say?"

Tom reflected. "Maybe. But how will we ever get anybody to take our case? That Freitag bastard wanted forty grand on the barrelhead just for me alone."

"That's a hell of a lot of money," Star agreed, "but I've been doin' some callin' around. I think we can get a young lawyer to take this on for experience. Maybe about ten grand total."

Tom snorted. "Great! Where we gonna get ten grand? I'm damn near broke and the Feds have blocked the money in the hedging account I opened."

"Ten grand's no problem." Star said. "With our cash flow now, we'll be…" He glanced down at the pad on his desk. "…flush about that much by the end of November."

Tom gazed steadily at him. Star was the friend he needed now, somebody who would take up his problem and help him find a way to solve it, a replacement for the strength he had always drawn from Janet.

He grimaced. "Well, if you say so, I'm willin' to give it a try. Gotta do something to put my life back together."

Star nodded. "You sure do. Now, with you at the phone, we can keep the trucks rollin'. You try to get the booze under control, and I'll help. 'Cause I'm one of them that helped make the problem."

This admission was too much for Tom. His throat constricted and he stepped to the office window to look out. Tears blurred the image of the Dover yard.

"Don't take it so hard, old buddy." Star said. "We can beat this together, and get your family back. Just wait and see!"

This time, there was no optimistic handshake. Tom and Star agreed, but without the confidence of last month. They both realized that their problems were almost unresolvable.

Tom tried. He spent most of his time at Dover. Often, he slept there at night. The few trips he made home were too emotionally draining and usually resulted in heavy drinking and ever-slower recovery.

To some extent, Star's plan worked. The trucks were on the road full time and a positive cash flow began to occur. Star himself was almost always driving. His contacts with Tom became fewer. By late November, they communicated mostly by phone.

Tom was virtually a recluse. He did not go into Sheffield except to pick up packaged food at the convenience store. There, he placed his packages on the check-out counter and looked elsewhere as the clerk added them up.

He also avoided the issue of his broken family. The letters from Chrissy and Janet went unopened. Tom simply collected them from the mailbox on his infrequent trips to the farm and dumped them on the kitchen table.

He did not call, nor did he answer the phone. Twice, when he was at the farm, he let the phone ring. Knowing it was Janet, he did not have the emotional strength to talk with her. He lived at Dover, and the wreck of Dakota Fertilizer was his life.

One day during the week before Thanksgiving, he was busy at Dover with December hauling arrangements when Star called.

"Hi, there!"

"Where you callin' from?" Tom asked.

"I'm at Minot. Be there late tonight. Got anything for me in the next couple of days?"

Tom looked at the chart of truck contracts. "Nope. Nothin' 'til after Thanksgiving. You gonna take some time off?"

"Hope so. If I can get back before the weather turns bad, I'll lay up for a few days." He roared with laughter.

Tom joined in, a participant in the growing relationship between Star and Kate. "Know what you mean." He grew silent with envy.

Star went on. "Big storm comin' up. How's things there?"

"Nothin' here. It's warm as hell. Just started rainin' a couple of hours ago. What's comin'?"

"They say rain turning to sleet this afternoon from the west. If I hit the road, I'll be in front of it. Well, gotta go. See you tomorrow."

When Star hung up, Tom went outside and looked at the sky. It was almost totally obscured by gusts of driving rain.

"Not much fun to drive in this shit," he mumbled.

The weather kept him at Dover that night. When he turned off the tiny TV after Monday Night Football, the rain was rattling heavily on the office roof. "Sounds like it's startin' to sleet. Hell of a night for a drive. Hope he stops somewhere."

Tom rolled himself in the gritty blanket he had been using and pressed his back against the side of the worn couch. Soon the clatter of the sleet settled his thoughts, and he fell into a deep sleep, protected from the icy outdoors.

Sleep was so complete that he was totally confused by the ringing of the phone. He fumbled on the floor beside the couch, looking for his alarm clock. Finally, the insistent ringing drew him to his feet and to the phone on the counter.

"Hullo. Who's this?"

"Tom? Tom? Is that you?" A hysterical female voice rang in his ear.

"Yeah. This is Tom. Is that you, Jan?" His hopes rose.

"Tom! It's me. Kate." She broke off, sobbing.

"Kate!" He was now fully awake. "What's the matter?"

"Oh, Tom! It's Ted! The police just called. He's had an accident on the KC hill!"

"An accident! What happened? What'd they say?"

"They wouldn't tell me! And, I haven't a car so I can't go out. Please, please go, Tom! Oh, God!" She wept.

"Sure. Sure. I'll get right out there. Don't worry, Kate. Star's a helluva driver. He's probably just off the road. I'll call you back soon's I find out what's what."

He hung up and went to the window. The night light in the elevator yard glistened off a sleek coating of ice. Everything was imbedded in crystal.

"Holy shit! This don't look so good!" He pulled on an extra coat and found a pair of heavy mittens under the counter. Damn good thing Star was such a careful driver. It'd take a pretty good hand to deal with this kind of weather.

Out in the yard, Tom nearly fell several times on his way to the Fury. He took long minutes to scrape the glaze of sleet from the windshield and more time to turn the car on the glassy surface of the yard.

He made good time through town. The streets were level and not too slippery. Looking up, he could see flashing red lights halfway up the hill road.

"Sonofabitch! Does look like somethin's wrong! Don't let it be..."

He drove up the first switchback. A little too much accelerator and the car swung crazily. Sweating, he got it under control. With one set of wheels off the road, he could negotiate the curves, barely.

As he reached the emergency vehicles, he saw two police cruisers. On the right shoulder of the road, a small station wagon was nosed up to the rocky embankment.

On the other side, down a deep ravine, Tom could see the white of Star's trailer, the front end lost in the sleety dark of the gully.

He stopped, got out of the Fury and staggered to the nearest cruiser. He rapped on the window and it opened an inch.

"Officer, what happened? I think that's one of our trucks down there."

"Hell of a thing! These two folks," the officer gestured to two white faces in the back of the cruiser, "they were goin' uphill and spun out. The truck was comin' down. In order to miss the car, the driver took her down the hill!"

"How is he? Where..." Tom stammered, not wanting the answer.

"Not so hot! We got to cut him out of the cab!"

Tom leaned further forward, the sleet rapping on the exposed back of his neck. "But how is he? Is he..."

"'Fraid so! Didn't have a chance. That trailer came loose and ran right over the cab!"

Tom stood up, dazzled by the revolving lights, a bizarre display of glistening beauty. Down below, two more emergency vehicles began to climb the switchbacks toward them.

One of the people in the back seat got out of the cruiser to stand by him.

"There was no way we could stop! He saved our lives! Jesus God! If only we'd stayed in town!"

"Wasn't your fault," Tom mouthed the empty words. "Star should have known better than to try to get home."

A wrecker and an ambulance arrived and Tom joined several people as they slid down to the Kenworth.

"Hey!" one called. "Give us a light down here! We gotta see where to start cuttin'."

A light beamed down on the crumpled cab. Washed over a gleaming mop of blond hair. Plastered with sleet and blood. Molded to the shell of Ted Schultz.

Now they were all gone!

CHAPTER TWENTY-ONE

This Bud's for You

"Oh God of grace and glory, we remember before You today our brother, Theodore Schultz. We thank You for giving him to us to know and to love as a companion in our pilgrimage on earth. In Your boundless compassion, console us who mourn. Give us Your aid, so we may see in death the gate…"

The measured reading of these timeless lines was an incredible conclusion to the wild frenzy that had been Star's life.

Tom sat alone in the rear pew of Our Savior's Lutheran Church. The sparse congregation was testimony to the ambiguity of community opinion concerning the Elevator case.

"We are gathered here today to pay our final respects to Theodore Schultz. Among us, he was always a source of energy and joy…" Reverend Nelson paused, as if asking mourners for some hint as to the desired message. "He will live on in our hearts and forever be a storehouse of enthusiasm on which we might all draw."

Energy. Enthusiasm. Joy. All elemental forces of life now enclosed in a gilded box.

For Tom, the eulogy was the ultimate irony. Ted—Star—was life. He could only be experienced—never diverted nor suppressed. Now that tremendous force was gone, leaving only a smoky memory, already fading.

Tom looked around the church. He knew most of the mourners. Star's brother and two sisters. His mother. And sitting alone in the middle of the church, Kate. Tom had seen her as she walked past his car, almost unrecognizable in grief, a person whose joy had been extinguished.

Kate's appearance had been more of a shock than he had expected. She seemed withered, actually smaller and more vulnerable, not the same lusty person who had partied with Tom and Star only a year ago. In her transformation, Tom saw an image of himself, a structure that looked human, but had only a flicker of life at its center.

"In his final act, Theodore Schultz made the ultimate sacrifice; his own life in trade for two others. The young family in the small car will live and experience the goodness of life because of his instinctive decision. That must be his example to all of us. Let us, in his memory, spend our lives to the good of others and to the greater glory of God!"

Kate was now crying openly, her sobs tearing at the lump in Tom's throat. He, too, had made a sacrifice—his family and future for the intangible betterment of his patrons. God! What a joke! In comparison to Star's achievement, his was a colossal failure! The beneficiaries had turned his gift into a present danger, and his torment had only begun. Unlike Star, he was upright, perpendicular in the face of the universal condemnation that isolated him at the back of the church.

Reverend Nelson came down from the pulpit. "My friends, there will be a short graveside service at Riverside Cemetery. Following internment, the Ladies Aid Society will be serving refreshments in the Assembly Hall. The Schultz family has asked me to invite you to join them for a short social hour."

He paused, his eyes sweeping over the congregation, and then he resolutely led the pallbearers down the aisle toward the hearse waiting outside.

Tom stood, his eyes linked to those of other mourners who watched Star begin his last trip over the road. As they filed out, he found himself next to Kate. She took his arm, not speaking. They moved together to the Fury where Tom bent to open the door.

"Oh, Tom! I just can't believe this! We were going to be married, and now there is nothing!" She covered her face with her hands, blotting out the sight of the passing hearse.

"Kate, I know." This was the only thought that could find voice. The others, unspoken—even unformed—churned in the void of emotion. Kate's loss was personal and monumental. His was only an element of a total disintegration, one more leaf torn from the tree of his life.

They followed the stream of cars. They passed the VFW where they had come together in the only social life they had known—activity replaced by emptiness. The single traffic light where Star had always managed a rolling stop with a single down-shift of the sparkling Kenworth. Now the procession, too, could do its rolling stop, secure in the ultimate right of way of death over life.

They approach the bridge where the three had laughed their way to River House. Star was still their leader, but only for this last trip. They swung out along the river, tires forcing their way through the slush left over from the storm. At Riverside, they drew up in a straggling line behind the hearse. Tom got out and walked around the car to open Kate's door, the wind whipping his clothing.

Kate swung her legs out of the car and stood by him, pulling her coat around her. Holding her turned-up collar with one hand, she clutched Tom's arm and they followed the other mourners to the open grave.

When they were all assembled, Reverend Nelson began. "Almighty God, by the death and burial of Jesus, Your anointed, You have destroyed death and sanctified the graves of all Your saints. Keep our brother whose body we now lay to rest, in the company of all Your saints and, at the last, raise him up to share…"

As the service went on, Tom could not see the promise of the passages. He was conscious only of the barren landscape—of the raw earth of the grave, and of the incredible fragility of all those standing around him. They were all so temporary—and he was less permanent than the others. The loss of Chrissy, Janet and now Star were open holes in the jigsaw puzzle of his life—holes that could only be filled by those exact pieces. No others would do.

Kate shivered and clung tightly to his arm. He took her hand and wrapped his arm around her shoulder. He, too, began to shake in the cold emptiness of Riverside.

Ray Jacobsen and his son cranked the coffin into the ground—a ritual these two would repeat for most of those assembled. In Sheffield, the body belonged to the Jacobsen Funeral Home and not to God.

"In sure and certain hope of the resurrection to eternal life through our Lord Jesus Christ, we commend to almighty God our brother, Theodore Schultz, and we commit his body to the ground. Earth to earth, ashes to ashes…"

But not 'joy to joy' or 'life to life'. In this commitment, there was a sense of finality for Tom. There was no hope. It had been sucked out of him by the very social life that should have given him support and comfort.

Reverend Nelson faced the mourners, his face red from the wind that blew his thinning hair. "Please join the Schultz family at the Assembly Hall. Go in peace." He led the mourners away from the grave, the shoulders of his dark coat now thick with the light snow that had begun to fall. It was coming down in a steady veil, blurring the shapes that crowded together, life seeking life, security from the death that was all around them.

Kate and Tom shuffled along at the end of the group. By the time they had walked the hundred-yard distance, they were thoroughly chilled. Tom helped Kate into the Fury and slid behind the wheel.

He started the engine. "Thank God, it's still warm." He pulled off his gloves and flexed his fingers over the warm defroster airflow. The windshield wipers scraped two arcs in the white blanket that covered the car as Tom and Kate silently watched huddled figures disappear into cars.

The cars began to leave, while the snowfall increased, erasing the temporary presence of life—filling in each tire track and footprint to create a level surface on which nothing was recorded. In this empty waste, tombstones were pitiful upthrustings of hope for resurrection, covered by time and nature.

Kate was sobbing quietly, her head bowed. She was shivering and holding her folded arms close to her body.

Tom sat back and put his arm around her. "Don't take it so hard. C'mon. Sit back and try to get warm." He drew her closer and tried to still her shaking.

Finally, all the other cars had left, and only the hearse remained. Numbly, Tom watched the Jacobsens remove their equipment. The chrome-plated winch was put in a canvas bag and slid into the hearse—where Star had taken his last ride. The canopy covering the grave was shaken free of snow, folded and bagged. Then the false-green mat that had hidden the pile of raw earth was carefully cleaned and neatly packaged.

The hearse drove off and they were alone. The Fury purred softly and raised the temperature for them. Snow brushed faint fingers against the windows, sometimes becoming audible when driven by wind gusts. Tom became relatively comfortable.

Kate's sorrow, however, seemed to increase. She turned on the seat and hugged him tightly, her face buried in his coat.

"Oh, Tom! He's gone!" she mumbled. "What will I do?"

He patted her back. "Try not to think about what's over. We've gotta look ahead and try to make the best of it."

What a joke! Look ahead! Just what was out there for him? Now that Star was gone, there was no support for the theory underlying his defense. It would be his word against that of Bob and Leach. No jury would believe that he wasn't the prime mover in the scheme.

"But..." she began, "there's nothing..."

He interrupted. "Believe me, I know. Didn't I tell you, Janet's gone? Left me and went back home."

Kate sat up and looked at him, her eyes filling. "Oh, Tom! I didn't know! Won't she come back?"

"Maybe. Depends on how things go. Gotta stop drinking. Gotta get this mess out of the way."

She pulled herself close to him again, her cheek touching his. "Oh, it's all so terrible!"

That was right! Terrible! What was the chance that he could find the paper Star had gotten from Sorenson? Had it been in the truck? Would the Schultz family let him look through Star's things? Probably not. He sighed. It sure was terrible!

The warm wetness of Kate's face against his was a trigger to his emotions. He shared her sorrow and held her closer. As the void of loneliness filled, they became aware of the physical self each held. She moved her arms under his jacket and gripped his shoulders, pulling herself tightly against him, her breasts pressed against his chest.

Tom was immediately conscious of her once-vibrant personality, of the earthy joy she portrayed. He took her shoulders and held her away from him. As he looked into her tear-streaked face, he saw a fellow traveler on a road that began in desperation, a road that lead into an unknown future.

He held that face in his hands and kissed her gently.

"Kate...I..."

"Don't talk..."

He slipped her coat off and draped it over her with his arms under the fabric. He drew her back to him and returned her desperate hugs. His hands roved down her back, finding space inside the waistband of her skirt to trace the roundness of her hips.

The rhythm of their strivings was almost mechanical in its regularity. At the same time, they both became aware that they were accompanied outside the car. They sat up.

The gravesite was enveloped in a cloud of steam. A Bobcat loader was rutting in the pile of dirt, and dumping its loads into the open grave.

Each bite of earth released a cloud of steam as the relatively warm dirt was exposed to the freezing wind.

"Oh, my God!" Kate held her hands over her face.

"Jesus!" He stared, fascinated by the diminishing pile of dirt.

The Bobcat finished its work, and with a few reverse passes over the grave, smoothed the cover over Star. Then the driver raced his machine to its trailer.

Tom could watch no longer. He put the Fury in gear and drove hastily out of the cemetery.

Kate rearranged her clothes, her face turned from Tom. He stared at the road through swirls of snow.

At the next intersection he stopped. "Where to?" he asked.

"Better take me home," she whispered.

"Yeah. Guess so." And they drove silently into town.

As he stopped the Fury in front of her apartment house, she looked directly at him.

"I understand what happened to us. But it wasn't right. We were turning away from Star and Janet. Maybe it'd be better if we didn't see each other again."

Another one! Wasn't there anybody who...?

"Suppose you're right," he said. "Sorry if I hurt your..."

"Don't say it! We are both to blame! Now we better forget it!" She got out of the car. Before she closed the door she said, "Thank you so much for helping me today. Let's try to remember the good times we had."

He watched her walk up to her door, a person walking into the past. *The memories inside that door...*

He broke off these thoughts forcefully, jamming his foot on the accelerator—sending the Fury skidding up the hill out of Sheffield.

This was the day before Thanksgiving. *Thanksgiving! What was there to be thankful for?* He gripped the steering wheel savagely, forcing the Fury around the curves, wheels sliding from side to side.

The view of prairie at the top of the hill surrounded him. In all directions, there was nothing but the white bowl of snow. No people. No traffic. The KC Hall parking lot was empty. The road was a straight channel, marked by wisps of grass showing brown against white, guiding him into emptiness.

Tom slowed the car, moving tentatively into the uncertainty of snow. The emotions of love, failure, frustration, friendship were gone. He was like the prairie—frozen and lifeless.

Star dead! Kate withdrawn! Bob a traitor! Janet and Chrissy... He gritted his teeth, willing some positive signpost to guide him into the future.

There were no tracks on the road, and the growing dusk made it difficult for him to gauge his progress. The road to his farm was barely recognizable, faint tracks crossing in the snow—just like last year. *The blizzard that had caused it all!*

"Fucking weather!" He wrenched the wheel to avoid a skid into the ditch.

At the entrance to his driveway, he stopped and rolled the window down to empty his mailbox. Its door swung free in the wind, and its contents were half-buried in snow. He shook the papers violently before bringing them into the car.

"Goddamn mailman! Could at least have shut the door!" He drove into the yard and ran the Fury into the shed.

With his hand shielding his eyes from snow, he stumbled up the path to the house, his shoes filling with snow at each step. On the porch, he stamped his feet and pushed open the kitchen door.

It was cold inside, and dirty. The overhead light shown on the debris of his life. Dishes on the counter. Tracks on the floor. Piles of unopened mail on the table.

He threw the new collection into the pile. "Jesus Christ! The fucking furnace must be out!" He clattered down the steps into the basement and peered into the furnace room. The basic test routine confirmed his suspicion.

"Sonofabitch! Out of oil! There's no way anybody will come out in this snow!"

Tom went over to the Franklin stove and peered into its firebox. "Better get this goin' before I freeze to death." He went back upstairs and scooped up the letters and papers on the table and carried the armload back down to the stove.

The papers went into the bottom of the firebox and a few sticks were placed on top of them. Shakily, he scratched a match into flame and ignited the papers. Instantly they caught fire, and the chimney began to draw.

The room brightened, and he reached his hands toward warmth. He stared into the fire, watching the papers blacken, curl, and burn.

One was a letter, addressed to him. As it began to smolder, he reached into the stove and pulled it out.

Chrissy's writing. He pinched the smoldering edges of the envelope and then drew the letter out of its scorched cover.

'Dear Daddy. We miss you. Why don't you write? Please call us on Thanksgiving. School is fine, but I'd rather be back home. How are the cats? I love you very much.' The short sentences were like chunks of ice in his chest, choking him.

He crumpled the letter and tossed it back into the fire. He had no answers to those questions. They were silenced by flame.

Tom stared at the fire for a long time, adding wood as it ate. The room grew warm—just like last Christmas. Images rose in the fire and disappeared. Not defined—vague recollections of the past—oxidized by the rushing heat of the present. He sank back on his heels, arms folded on his knees, chin resting on his arms, peering into the flames.

When this position became too uncomfortable, he stood. Legs tingling, he walked stiffly to the little bar in the corner of the basement. Most of the cabinets were empty. One bottle of Beam. He put it on the counter and opened the old refrigerator. Ice and four six packs of Bud.

"Well, better have one. Gotta celebrate. Thanksgiving is coming." He filled a glass with whiskey, snorted and downed the drink. With a refill in hand, he switched on the television set and sank onto the sofa. He used the remote control to search the channels—rejecting each offering—frustrated by the endless commercials.

This went on for the first half-bottle of Beam. Then he sat mesmerized by flickering shapes on the screen until he fell asleep. He slept without dreams. Fourteen hours later, the ringing of the upstairs telephone woke him.

Groggy with sleep, he groped his way up the stairs. "I'm coming… hang on."

There was only a dial tone by the time he reached the kitchen phone. "Shit! Why the hell can't they wait? Wonder who it was." He stared out the window over the sink. The day was very cloudy and a light snow still fell. "Must have got a couple of inches. Good thing there wasn't too much wind."

He hung up the phone and searched the disorder in the kitchen for food. All that was left was a half-eaten package of cookies and a can of tomato juice. He wolfed the food, pacing to keep warm in the chilled house. When he had finished eating, he turned on the sink faucet to clean his hands. No water came.

"Fuck! The damn thing's frozen up! What the hell next?"

He stomped down the stairs into the warmth of the basement. The laundry room faucet still worked and he splashed water over his face. As he dried his hands, he twisted the selector on the television set.

"About noon. Wonder if there's a game on?"

There was.

"Welcome to Pontiac, Michigan. Here in the Silverdome, the Detroit Lions will try to get back on track against the Buffalo Bills. The two teams have been struggling…"

Tom listened to the description of two failed seasons as the commentators tried to paint this game as a turning point well worth watching.

Each comment of the announcers drew a loud response from Tom. "Hell, them turkeys be lucky if they don't fall down comin' on the field!"

The commercial came on. "Brought to you by Anheuser Busch, makers of Budweiser Beer. Remember, this Bud's for you! And by…"

The message got through to him. He took one of the six packs from the refrigerator and nestled it close to his side on the sofa. Can in hand, he toasted the weekend athletes who celebrated their victories with Bud.

An afternoon of futility–O.J. Simpson setting an NFL record with nearly 300 yards rushing—the Lions winning 27-14. The announcer attempted to make sense of these unbelievable facts. "Would you have expected this kind of hard-fought…"

"Hard-fought…shitdem dopes…" he mumbled through the haze of Bud.

Again the upstairs phone rang. Tom frowned at the interruption. "Shaddup!…no use…" He rolled over and slept.

By Monday, the Beam and Bud were gone. He had continued the cycle of waking-sleeping-drinking. Alcohol and the lack of food were taking their toll. He was weak and no longer thought clearly.

"Wonder what day it is?" Each morning he asked this question, looking out of the kitchen window. When no answer occurred to him, he reentered the basement, where warmth and darkness prevailed, comfortable in the cocoon of his misery.

Now that all the alcohol was gone, the sanctuary of the basement began to lose its appeal. Tom had a growing feeling that he had to go somewhere. Something he had to do.

"Better get packed up." He rose slowly from the sofa and deliberately climbed the stairs into the kitchen, then, holding the railing, up the flight of stairs into their second-floor bedroom.

The wreck of his presence had washed over the remains of Jan's presence. Clothes were scattered where they had fallen. The bed was rumpled and stained with sweat.

He picked his way through the mess to the closet. There he selected the few remaining clean clothes and bundled them into a cheap suitcase. With the bag in hand, he shuffled down the hallway past Chrissy's room. The open door showed the order she had left behind. Bed crisply made. Dresser neatly arranged. Light cover of dust over everything. Tom pulled the door closed and thumped down the stairs. Shrugging into his jacket, he looked around the house. It was time to leave.

Outside, he paused and surveyed the yard. The house and its people had created an island of security in the ocean of prairie. Now the house was struggling–losing the energy needed to keep the prairie at bay.

Small drifts of snow reached their hands toward the house; shaking it in the wind as if to empty it of humanity. The barn and sheds were already partly buried in the relentless piling of white. This was Dakota winter: bare fields, constant press of wind-driven snow, with all the snowfall piled around the few obstructions men had placed between the Rockies and the Mississippi. The bare patches of dirt in the tilled fields were frozen iron-hard.

Tom stepped down from the porch and plowed his way through drifts to the shed. Snow had reached in through the open door and partly covered the Fury. He brushed snow off the windshield with his arm and tossed his suitcase into the back seat.

The car started reluctantly, as if it would rather stay in the shed. But as it warmed, it responded to his pumping of the accelerator pedal. Racing the engine, he backed the car through the drifts in the yard and up the slight hill in front of the house. The hill provided the added momentum needed to blast through the drifts of the driveway to the plowed avenue of the township road.

At the junction with Highway 13, Tom stopped. His normal pattern was to turn right to Sheffield. This morning, he hesitated. There was nothing in that direction—*no Elevator job—no Dakota Fertilizer—no Star—no friends either.*

He turned left and let the Fury accelerate—he was headed west, just as he and Janet had done years ago, looking for something new in the beginning of their lives together. Then, their car had been a magic thing that transported them to adventure and opportunity. Now the car was a refuge and means of escape.

He drove on.

After an hour's drive, he came to an intersecting highway. To the left was the freeway—Fargo–Minneapolis. To the right were familiar towns—Grandview, Winnipeg. He turned right.

In the early afternoon, he reached the outskirts of Grandview. "Cenex." "John Deere." "Hardees." His subconscious fastened on the bright orange lettering. He was hungry.

The Fury slipped smoothly into the drive-in lane and he wound down the window to peer at the posted menu. "Good afternoon. Welcome to Hardees. How can we help you?"

"Uhhh…gimmee…" He scanned the options, confused by the disembodied voice. "Gimme…let's see…a mushroom burger and a chocolate shake."

The response was immediate. "Mushroom burger and a chocolate shake. Would you like an order of fries?"

"Huh? Fries? I guess so."

"That will be $4.25. Please pull ahead."

He drove to the service window and drew his wallet from his jacket pocket. Inside was only one bill. Five dollars.

"Shit! Ain't got no more money!"

He handed the bill to the smiling girl behind the glass panel and received his change and the bright bag of food. He drove away and found a corner in the Hardees parking lot where there were no other cars. With the motor idling, he worked his way through the meal.

Tom was confused. Why was he in Grandview? The purpose he had felt as he left home no longer drove him. *There was nothing he needed to do—no place he had to go. What would happen when he finished eating?* He turned on the Fury's radio. "…are the standings in the Western Division. Tonight's game between the Vikings and the Packers will be a chance for Green Bay to halt the Viking's rush to the title. We'll be carrying the game on this station and on GVTV. Remember, turn down the sound on your television and let our Al Kane give you the real color."

"Vikings and Packers. Sure would like to see that. Could be a helluva game." He munched on the last of the French fries, thinking about the match between Fran Tarkenton and Bart Starr. "Bet they'll really knock heads!" His face brightened at the prospect. Somebody else under pressure, with Tom Cooper on the sidelines, a chance to enjoy the drama of competition without the risk and responsibility.

He decided at once. "Hell, I'll just find a motel…" He tossed the empty Hardees bag into the back seat and drove the Fury out of the parking lot.

Apparently he wasn't the only one with the urge to watch Monday Night Football. Every motel was filled on both sides of Grandview. All that was left was the old Granger's Hotel in the center of town. He stopped on Main Street and got out of the car. As he reached for his suitcase, he remembered.

"Fuck! Ain't got no money!" He slumped back into the car. "Could go back home. Don't wanna do that." His eyes roved the streets—alternatives considered and rejected. Was there no way he could stay in Grandview?

Then he noticed the strings of bare bulbs waving in the late afternoon wind. 'Nelson's Used Cars. Cash for Clean Cars.'

"That's it! Don't need this old beater no more!" He started the Fury and began to pull out into traffic. "Wait a minute!" He stopped. "Gotta clean this up a little. 'Clean Cars'—okay, we'll clean her up!"

Enthusiastically, he jumped out and began to scoop the piles of trash in the back seat into an old blanket. Hardees bag. Empty Beam bottles. Stacks of legal papers. Old gloves and caps. They all added to the bundle he made. When it was assembled, he took it down a nearby alley and forced the lump into a dumpster. Brushing the dust from his clothes, he strode back to the Fury, almost cheerful.

Nelson wasn't impressed. "Where did you get this antique? Looks like something the wind uncovered behind the barn!" He laughed and peered under the Fury's hood.

"But she's a good car." Tom protested. "Always starts—and…"

"Look mister, this one's just like my old lady. She's fine for me, but you can betcha nobody else wants her."

"Well, what's it worth?" Tom asked. "I ain't got no use for her now."

Nelson considered. "Tell you what. I think I can clean her up and maybe somebody will want an old timer for his kids. I'll give you $100."

"A hundred bucks! You gotta be kiddin'! Why, she's still a good runner!"

Nelson began to walk toward his trailer house office.

Tom ran to catch up. "Say! Wait! Can't you go a few more bucks? How about…"

Nelson turned. "Okay. Must be the Christmas spirit. I'll give you a hundred twenty five—and that's all."

Tom stared. *A hundred twenty five! Well, that would do it for a few days. Then he could…*

"Okay. I'll take it."

"Then it's a deal. Bring the title into the office and we'll settle up." Nelson went up the steps of the office, the trailer listing under his weight.

Title? Where the hell…He rummaged in the Fury's glove compartment, tossing maps and papers on the floor. There it was! He dusted it off and smoothed it into some semblance of a legal paper.

The transaction was brief. Nelson examined the title and checked Tom's name against his driver's license. "No security interests. Be a hell of a thing if anybody'd lend money on that wreck!" He laughed. "How you want your money? Cash or check?"

"Better gimme cash."

Nelson counted out the bills and Tom pocketed them. Suitcase in hand, he paced back down the street to the Granger's Hotel.

The hotel was untouched by the bed and breakfast movement. It remained very much the same as it had been for the past thirty years. Dusty. Worn out. An anachronism kept in place by the few elderly residents who had no families and nowhere else to go on their aimless journey toward death.

It smelled like a nursing home. Weak disinfectant masked the odor of stale sweat and urine. One old man sat in a worn armchair, mouth gaping wide in catatonic sleep.

The desk attendant was an old woman who eyed Tom suspiciously as he set his bag in front of the counter.

"Yeah. What you want?"

"Like a room. All the motels are full. Must be the big game."

"Game? What you talkin'bout?"

"It's the…never mind. You got a room?"

"Suppose so. That'll be twenty bucks a night. Just you sign the book. How long you wanna stay?"

He did a quick mental calculation. Twenty bucks. Three nights would be sixty dollars.

"How about four nights? That okay?"

"Makes no difference to me. You pay in advance and you can stay as long as you want."

He scrawled his signature in the stained register and handed over four twenty dollar bills.

The woman carefully smoothed each bill and placed it right side up on the counter. She drew them into a stack, tapping them as if they were a deck of cards.

"Room 26. Up the stairs at the end of the hall."

He took the key from her and carried his bag up the creaking steps. At the end of the second floor hall, he found his door set at an angle off a small landing that led to another flight of stairs marked 'Exit'.

Inside, the room had the barren landscape of an old-time hotel. A narrow iron-headed bed stood in one corner. A small dresser and mirror teetered on splayed legs, leaning against the wall for support. In one corner, a plywood cubicle had been built to enclose a tiny sink and a battered stool.

"Sure don't look like the honeymoon suite," Tom said. "If the TV works, it'll do."

The television set was rather new. It perched in another corner, faced by an armchair whose stuffing strained at the threadbare fabric.

He tossed his suitcase on the bed and opened it, stacking his small collection of clothes on the dresser. Then he closed the bag, and left the room, taking the 'Exit' stair.

In the alley behind the hotel, he detoured around garbage cans to the main street. A few blocks down the street, he found the "Off-Sale" sign he was searching for.

He entered the store and again did his mental arithmetic. About forty-five dollars left. Gotta save some for…the reason escaped him, but he transferred one of the remaining ten dollar bills to his jacket pocket.

Then, in a growing swell of anticipation, he paced the aisles, pushing a small shopping cart. Gleaming bottles reflected the bright lights of the store and his eyes shown with reflected images.

He filled the cart with bottles of whiskey, mix, five six-packs of Budweiser and several bags of ice. At the check-out counter he carefully arranged his purchases and reviewed his selections as the clerk rang up the items.

"That'll come to $35.50. Gonna have a party?"

"Sure. Sure." Tom added his reserve ten to the bills in his hand and passed them to the clerk. As they went into the till, he placed the bottles and six-packs in the suitcase.

"Here's your change, mister. Five, six, seven, eight, nine dollars and fifty cents. Thanks much, and have a good one!"

With ice bags dangling by their strings from his fingers, he marched back to the hotel. In his room, the ice was hung outside his window and the liquor arranged on the dresser. His clothes went back in the suitcase and it was stored under the bed.

With great anticipation, he made his first Manhattan. Perfect! He drank it looking out the window at the growing dusk. The second and third drinks were consumed as he watched the evening news. The advertisements for hamburgers and junk food were suggestive.

"Better get some munchies for the game," he muttered. This purchase required another trip outdoors and his last five dollar bill. Now he had only four dollars and fifty cents—plus some loose change he had collected in cleaning the Fury. He sighed at the memory of the car.

Back in the room again, he sank into the armchair, fresh drink in hand and open bag of potato chips propped on a rickety wood chair.

Frank Gifford painted the situation for him at the beginning of Monday Night Football. "…biggest game of the season for these two teams. The Packers come to Met Stadium hoping to derail the Vikings. Minnesota is in first place and wants to stay there. Don, how ready are these teams?"

Meredith grinned an earnest response. "They're at nearly one hundred percent, Frank. I look for a wide open passing game. Tark and Starr are both healthy and they've traded off on leading the league in passing this season. Yeah, I look for a real barn-burner tonight."

"My view, exactly," Gifford agreed. "We'll be ready for the opening kickoff right after these messages."

The picture shifted to a boisterous gang of laborers. Oil drillers—muscling heavy pipes–horseplaying their way to a bar. Then the message. "…on the job and working hard all day…for all you do, this Bud's for you!"

Reflexively, Tom reached over to a six pack and snapped the tab on one of his cans of Bud. He raised it in salute along with the figures on the screen. This scenario was repeated with each of the commercial breaks during the first half.

The fire-bearing caveman brought his treasure to the horned chief. Only to be told, "I said 'Bring a Lite', Ogg!"

Tom laughed, an active participant in the events he watched. "Dumb bastard! Anybody knows that a light ain't a LITE!"

At the half, the score was tied at six to six. Neither quarterback had been effective against strong defenses.

"Don't you agree, Dan, that we're likely to see some new offensive formations from both clubs in the second half?" Gifford asked.

"Gotta do it," Meredith responded. "The defenses are having a field day!"

"Hell, I can see that," Tom mumbled. "That offense looks like it's playin' flag football!" He finished another can of Bud and tossed it at the metal wastebasket. It missed.

The offenses did change, but so did the defenses. At the end of the fourth quarter, the teams were still tied and the Vikings had taken possession at their own forty-yard line after a failed Green Bay field goal attempt in the snow that was covering Met Stadium.

Tom stared at the screen, a fog of drink descending between him and the game. "Fuckin' Vikings. They ain't got a prayer!" He opened the last can of Bud and sipped at it while the announcers set the stage for the final minutes.

"With no timeouts left, Tarkenton has his work cut out for him. The clock shows one minute and thirty seconds left."

"That's it, Frank." Meredith added. "But they don't call him 'Tark the Shark' for nothing. He's done the impossible before and we've got a real exciting finish going here at Met Stadium."

The players returned to the screen and lined up on the ball. The noise level rose to a roar, and Tarkenton waved his arms to quiet the crowd.

The first two passing attempts were wide of the mark, but they used up little time.

Tom grew more animated as the drama unfolded. He clutched the beer can and tried to advise Tarkenton.

"Right…right…flanker's open! Ohh, shit!"

On third and ten, Tarkenton retreated to pass. As the Packers came on, he deftly flipped the ball to a waiting back. The Green Bay defenders tried desperately to recover. It now was a first down on the Packers forty yard line.

Tom was on his feet, swaying and waving the beer can. "C'mon… hurry it up!"

"…gives the Vikings a first down with forty seconds left. Tarkenton brings them up on the ball. Strong left. He takes the snap and throws it out of bounds. That stops the clock with thirty-five seconds to go."

Two more failed passing attempts ran the time to five seconds.

"No time for the field goal unit. They're on the ball. It's snapped. Time has run out! Tarkenton is scrambling! He fakes a pass and takes off! The Pack has him cornered at the twenty—hold on—he breaks free! Touchdown! The Vikings win it!"

The bedlam at Met Stadium went on until that moment when a commercial would have maximum impact. This time the actors were playing touch football. A long pass. Caught! More horseplay and another bar.

"For all you do, this Bud's for you!"

Tom again attempted to toast the happy players, but he fell back into his chair. Emotionally drained. Drunk.

CHAPTER TWENTY-TWO
Winter Walk

The next three days were a waking-sleeping nightmare of images and sickness. The struggle between his body and alcohol was one of the most difficult he had ever experienced. Gut-wracking nausea was followed by raging chills and, finally, exhausted sleep, but not the sleep of recovery; instead, he was in a purgatory between consciousness and oblivion as terrible visions contested for his mind.

In his nightmare life, Tom was continually pursued by images of guilt, all pointing ghostly fingers at him. Often these scenes were peopled with those he had known in Sheffield. Chris Odegaard, grey and formidable, denouncing, out of character; "Cooper, you fucking crook!" Barney Jacobs, in the robes of a judge, pronouncing his sentence in front of a jury of familiar patrons. Pete and Helen, arm in arm, shaking their heads and in unspoken looks—a greater condemnation than words.

The more bitter pictures were those of his family. Janet, in the dress she wore on their honeymoon, crying and looking off into a misty future. Chrissy, with a scar on her face, holding her hands to fend off his affection. Tears washed down his face, making the pictures blurred and, at last, washing them from his mind.

As he recovered, these images were replaced by scenes from the distant past. They became visions of his childhood; an idealized representation of a happier time. He was transported into the past, his mind finding there the protection it required to prevent immediate insanity. These visions focused on the time when his father and mother were in their early adulthood, strong, happy and full of expectation. He was young, unbounded, and free from the worries of responsibility.

The security of these dreams began to dominate his body. For yet another time, his physical self had won the contest with its chemical invader. But this time there had been a shift of mental ground. There were no more feelings of guilt, no yawning caverns of loneliness, and no demands pressing for attention.

When he was fully awake, on the fourth day, he was only dimly aware of his surroundings. The wreckage and stink of his room were facts that his mind rejected; the results of a shipwreck of another life on which he floated—a survivor.

Tom's first conscious acts were to clean his room. He picked up the empty whiskey bottles and beer cans. The rubbish of junk food was scraped into the wastebasket and the sparse furniture arranged in a pleasing order. He straightened the bed covers, turning them down as if for another night. For a moment, he was partly aware that this was something he had learned from—Janet? Who was that? His attempt to cope with this question was a failure. No amount of concentration could recall her relationship to his life.

He began then to work on himself. He stripped naked and folded his filthy clothes into a tidy package which he placed under his pillow. Awkwardly, he used the small sink and washcloth to give himself a much-needed bath. When he had finished, he took his final set of clean clothes from the old suitcase. As he stood holding the folded garments, he saw another fleeting vision of Janet, standing next to him, trying to speak. But the image receded and no sound came to him.

As he slowly dressed, he whistled quietly an old ditty his father had loved. He timed his dressing to the rhythm. *Dad couldn't wait for him. If they were going for their walk, he had better get ready.* His shoes came last. Carefully, he pulled the laces tight on each foot, lace ends exactly equal. Then he made two loops, just like Mom said, and wove them into a neat bow. To be sure, the bow was tied into a final knot; *it wouldn't do for the laces to come undone during their walk.*

When he had finished, he took his jacket and cap from the hook on the back of the hallway door. The cap was set squarely on his head and his jacket zipped halfway up. He glanced around the room. Catching himself in the mirror over the sink, he inspected his work. *Everything right! Good! Mom and Dad would praise him for his carefulness and hug him roughly—their love spilling over in their eyes.*

He moved deliberately out into the hallway and closed the cracked door on the immediate past. Walking carefully, hands in pockets, he made his way down the flights of stairs into the hotel lobby. There, he hesitated for a minute, not knowing how to proceed. The desk clerk, seeing him for the first time in four days, asked, "Going out Mr. Cooper? Better bundle up. It's going to be a nippy day."

Tom hesitated and stared at the clerk. "Huh? Yeah. Oh sure. I'm ready, I guess."

"If you're hungry, you can still catch lunch at the truck stop. It's just round the corner."

Tom smiled. *Lunch. Yes, that would hit the spot. And he still had plenty of time before he had to be on his way.*

He took up the tune he had been whistling earlier and descended the hotel steps two at a time on his way into the street. Sure enough! The diner was only a block away and the aroma of frying was sufficiently diluted by the cold to be inviting. He hurried along.

Inside, most tables were empty. It was now early afternoon and both lunch and coffee crowds were gone. The choices of seating confused Tom for a moment and he needed the nod of the counterman to find his way to a corner booth.

He slid into the seat and took off his cap, placing it precisely beside him. With folded hands, he looked toward the waitress who brought him the single, soiled menu.

"Care for coffee?"

"Okay, I guess. And maybe some orange juice."

Mom had always insisted on his orange juice for breakfast. When he was very young, it was one word—oranjoosh, later, a joke shared with her throughout her life, now a returning memory to trigger others that blurred his vision while he stared at the menu.

The waitress broke into his thoughts. "What'll it be? Care for the ham and eggs?"

"…ummm, sure. That will be fine." He returned the menu, glad to be free of her questioning presence.

He sipped coffee. Over the rim of the cup, he could see his mother again, her smile, which always grappled with the mood of the day and, invariably, won. Slowly, her questions about his plans would raise his uncertainties and fears. All these would melt away in the light of her love and support. *You bet! Mom was always on his side and he couldn't let her down. Especially not now.*

"Here you go!" The waitress placed the filled plate in front of him. As she backed off smiling, Tom felt the wave of caring that always enveloped him when his mother was around.

"Gee, thanks Mom." He mumbled.

The waitress turned away—not hearing.

He began to eat, his mind turning over recollections of the thousands of meals he had eaten as a boy. The family gathered after morning chores, before the farmwork of the day. Sometimes, when he had a disagreement with his father, these meals were uncomfortable and he built a wall of cereal boxes around his plate, a refuge from the shame he felt. But then, Mom broke into his withdrawal and patched the rift between him and Dad so that they could go out together, father and son.

These thoughts turned in his mind as Tom worked slowly through his meal. Finally, the waitress's impatience broke through his reverie and he once again became aware of the need to be on his way.

He looked at the rumpled check and carefully added the numbers. $3.65. Well, better leave four dollars. *Got to tip. That's what Mom says. He placed four bills on the check and carried it to the counter.*

"Everything okay, mister?" the waitress asked as she entered the transaction in the cash register.

"Huh? Oh sure. Keep the change."

He turned nervously and pulled his cap firmly forward as he left the restaurant. Outside, the day was bright, filled with sun and warm for December. He drew on his gloves and looked along the street in both directions. The only activity in sight was a truck driver across the way checking tires on his rig.

The truck, with its idling engine, drew him. He walked quickly across the street and waited by the cab for the driver. *He was supposed to go in this truck and it was a good thing that he had finished his lunch in time.*

The trucker returned to the front of the rig, humming. He stopped, surprised to see Tom.

"Hi. What can I do for you?"

"Well, I need to get down the road. Can I ride with you?"

"Sure, don't see why not. But I'm going south—toward Sheffield. How's that suit you?"

"That's just great! That's where I need to go!"

"Only problem," the trucker continued, "is that I'm only goin' as far as the Highway 95 turnoff. Got to go east on 95."

"No problem for me," Tom replied confidently. "I can make it the rest of the way on my own."

"Well, hop in then."

They both climbed into the cab, warm from the running engine. The driver eased the truck away from the curb and moved it through its gears, out of town. Once on the road, the momentum of the rig was transmitted to Tom. He leaned forward as if to speed them on their way.

"Say, you seem pretty anxious to get on with it," the driver remarked.

"Yep. Got a lot to do when I get home."

"Oh. You live in Sheffield?"

Tom was confused by this question. *Sheffield? Did he live in Sheffield? No, he lived on a farm with his parents. Or, maybe, just with his Mom.*

"Ummm—no. I live out of town. On a farm."

They drove on for a time, silent, each with his own thoughts, the driver wondering at Tom's simplicity and thinking that he should recognize him. But, intent on the frosty road, he put each tentative identification aside. Tom peered ahead, as if looking for some landmark. He had a growing feeling that he had an appointment to keep and that time was running short.

At last, the driver spoke. "Say, fella, I got to be turning off on 95. You want to keep on with me?"

Tom turned to face the driver, the visor of his cap just shading his eyes. "Well…no. I guess I better get off when you turn. I got to keep going ahead."

"Okay. Suit yourself. But there won't be much traffic from now on. It's already four and it'll be getting dark soon."

"That's all right. I don't have that far to go and I don't mind walking a little."

"Say! Wasn't that some game Monday night? You gotta hand it to them Vikings—they never quit!"

Game? What game? He racked his brain—the name 'Vikings' seemed vaguely familiar.

The trucker sensed Tom's confusion. "You know. The Packers-Vikings game. My God! That Tarkenton's really somthing!"

"…yeah…" Tom mumbled.

"The bar I was at went wild! Hell, I got away with a half-dozen of them foam purple footballs! Bet old Jerry wonders where they went!" He laughed and tossed a half-sized ball to Tom.

Catching the ball easily, Tom knew that this was important. *Football! Why he might even have a game to play!* He massaged the supple ball between his hands and practiced holding it as if for a pass.

"Say! You handle that thing pretty good!"

"…umm…yes, I guess that I can still do my job."

"Can't remember where I seen you before. You play college ball?"

Tom thought. *College? Yes. He had a recollection of the game.* "That's possible."

They went on. Then the truck slowed and stopped.

"Well, this is as far as I go. Good luck. Just hold up that Vikings ball and you'll get a ride pretty soon!"

"Gee, thanks. I'll see you later." Tom stepped down from the cab, swinging the door closed.

As the truck ground off up the Highway 95 grade, Tom gazed after it, tossing the little football—toss, catch, toss, catch—confused for a moment as to where he was. Then he looked in the opposite direction, to where old 95 once crossed the Thoms River. Now the bridge was closed, unsafe for modern loads, but open to hikers and hunters. He began to walk down the short approach to the bridge, pulled by an urgent need to be on the other side of the river.

In the middle of the bridge, he stopped and leaned on the railing. Open water below, where the current accelerated to pass the bridge pilings, fascinated him. He stared at the patterns in the water—hearing voices, faint at first, then clearly,

"Sure, son. The river is always moving. Even under the ice it's pulling and pushing, making a new way for itself."

He turned to look to his side, expecting to see his father. Nobody stood there, but the voice continued.

"The river's like what you got to do when you grow up. It's hemmed in by banks and covered with ice. But it can cut its own way and through the years change its whole direction. You can do that too, son; just keep at it."

He straightened and moved away from the railing. *Sure, that's what he had to do. Keep moving. Get to where he was supposed to go; that way he'd be doing what Dad said.* He continued to cross the bridge, staying on the crusted snowmobile track and walking down the far approach.

At that point, the track intersected a heavily traveled path where snowmobiles followed an abandoned railroad right-of-way leading to Sheffield. Without hesitation, Tom turned to his left, setting off toward Sheffield on the raised embankment. On each side, frost covered trees arched overhead so that he was walking in a white tunnel, faintly sparkling in the waning afternoon light.

Other voices accompanied his walk coming and going—many from his college days–his professor of economic history giving a lecture on agriculture.

"American agriculture is a joke!" the professor scoffed. "Its economic structure bears no relationship to food production. When farmers ask for cost of production, they are crying for a concept that doesn't fit on the balance sheet for modern agriculture, American-style! And the same holds in Canada."

He could still hear the puzzled murmurs of his classmates.

"What's he talkin' about? Sure, you got to make more than you spend. But, professor, why do people farm?"

"Because they're damn fools! They farm land that has an inflated value due to investor bidding. They work against a tax system that uses capital gains as an incentive for investment. Anybody with a big cash flow can get huge tax savings by buying into a losing farm operation!"

Tom strode on; the lecture continued. He listened intently, knowing that his teacher was right. His suppressed experience came through to acknowledge the truth of the analysis.

"But can't farmers still make it?" asked another student. "After all, they are really productive and the world needs to be fed!"

"Huh!" his professor exploded. "That's the biggest joke of all! Nobody, hear me, nobody cares about feeding anyone else! In fact, the more productive agriculture becomes, the more surplus we have. And that stays in the warehouses! It doesn't get to third-world countries!"

How right that was! He remembered Mom talking about Ezra Benson when he was Secretary of Agriculture and how the crops in the 'Ever Normal Granaries' should be in the bowls of the needy.

He walked on, staring past the shadows of trees, looking at his own ghostly image marching ahead of him into the dusk, accompanied by other voices, some strong, others whispers of another time.

The voices were like tracks on a worn record, jolting his mind from one scene to another, confusing in the rapidity of shifts across years, incomplete, as letters randomly scattered across the muddled desk of his mind. Clear and sharp, however, as if the speakers were striding along with him on his winter walk.

The dry cold of late afternoon triggered memories of other early winters. That afternoon in Collegeville when his team was to face the invincible Johnnies—undefeated in their march to an NAIA championship.

He could feel the fear in his stomach as they walked across the frosty field on their way to the visiting team dressing room. Glassy slivers of November sun were like pins ready to freeze these poor specimens in the St. John's scrapbook.

His coach had perceived their anxiety as an icy lump that each player had to embrace and thaw with whatever courage he could muster.

"Now, I been thinkin' about them Johnnies. I know we have no business bein' here today. They're 9 and 0 and we're only 5 and 4. But, I got a feelin' we're gonna to surprise 'em! And we're gonna beat 'em!"

All of his teammates had stared at Coach, unbelieving at the insanity of his idea. Beat the Johnnies? At home? No way!

Coach went on. "Here's how we're gonna do it! All season, we been relyin' on our runnin' game and long passes. Now, this week we been puttin' in those swing passes to our halfbacks. Well, today we're gonna swing the ball out to Cooper and Larson on sixty percent of the plays!"

Cooper! Oh, God! Those Polacks will kill me! He had fought the urge to vomit and felt the physical wash of fear through his body.

"In fact, we're gonna use 39 Swing and 28 Swing the first time we get the ball. And we're gonna score on these guys!"

These numbers burned in his mind. They were his plays!

During the warm-up, he had been unable to hold the ball. Dropping pass after pass, he eyes glued to the enormity of the Johnnie players and the perfection of their errorless drills.

Surprisingly, Concordia had held the awesome Johnnie machine on the first possession and it was time for the offensive unit to try themselves. In the huddle, he fumbled at his chin strap with the freezing wind murmuring in the ear holes of his helmet.

"Swing 38 left on 2!" The quarterback's call was as uncertain as the entire strategy.

Tom had made his initial cut, turned and thrust frozen fingers at the speeding ball. On target! On time!

In his gloves, his fingers flexed. Muscular memories of long-forgotten skills. His eyes focused on the little purple ball as it floated in front of him, coming to him over the snow, its spiral giving perfect flashes of molded lace in the dying sun. He crouched as the ball dropped into the pocket of his arms.

He planted his foot, swinging the little ball into his left arm, the right poised to fend off would-be tacklers. His right leg crossed over the left, and he began a broken field run, weaving across the snowmobile track with the high-stepping stride of a gifted runner.

Four times that afternoon, Swing 38 had led to a Concordia touchdown. When the final moments were played out in the brassy November light, they had upset St. John's 37-24. Coach and Tom were carried off the field into the steaming heat of the locker room.

Impossible joy! The game ball held in his arms as he stood naked in the shower, the team singing the improbable ballad:

Stewball was a racehorse.
I wish he was mine!
He never drinks water.
He only drinks wine!

For the fleeting moment of this vision, he was Stewball, all-conference halfback. He ran on, untiring, lowering his head to stretch for goal line yards.

But the image faded and he pulled up from his run, his breath coming in frosty clouds. One hand went to his jacket pocket for warmth—the other cradled the purple ball—*game ball!* Then the achievement of that long-ago afternoon receded as if it were an experience of another person, a page out of the *Tribune* sports section to be read and forgotten.

By now, the last light of afternoon had gone, and dusk was filling in the pools of shadow at the sides of the track. Ahead, the lights of Sheffield appeared around a curve, where the old right-of-way had bent to enter along the river front.

As Tom walked, the overhead arch of trees widened and gradually gave way to low shrubs and weeds. At the same time, the mass of the Elevator dominated his field of vision, a black shape, now dim in its enveloping steam, sharply dark against the white hills in the background.

Tom was pulled toward the Elevator as if it were the focal point of his life. Everything came together in the wood and concrete of its structure.

This Elevator was different. No longer was it a threat, a place associated with the bitter failures of his life. Fear and failure played no part in the emotion he felt as he approached downtown Sheffield. This was a sort of homecoming, not to Sheffield, but to the experiences of another life. He felt a placid sense of well-being. Anticipation pulled him along the right-of-way to the place where the remaining active tracks ended.

Tom stepped between the bumpers at the end of the line and matched his steps to the spacing of the ties, barely visible in the snow. *Careful now! Don't step in the cracks between the ties!* He moved past the business district, past the flashing sign of the VFW Club.

He bypassed the Elevator office, turning its corner to a battered door in the old building. Inside, dark, artic cold, and quiet. The pull from the past enfolded him. No words, just happiness.

And there it was: the manlift. Tom stepped on a platform, ball in one hand, the other holding onto the lift. He stood, waiting for the familiar fear, but it didn't come. He felt only the urge to go—to start—to where?

He pulled the control rope. As on countless other times, he felt the sensation of height and, along with it, the thrill of time, of knowing the completeness of events.

Tom Cooper counted for little. The prairie, grain and the organic whole of man's work in Sheffield were the purpose. His was to ride with experience, to unify in his own mind the past and the now.

Up, past empty floors toward faint winter light in the head house. Arrival. Firm tug on the rope. The lift platform halted, level with the catwalk that led out across the silos.

The pull of memory now overpowered all Tom's other senses. Pathway toward home—familiar snowbanks. Walk carefully! Slide one foot—then another—across the bridge. Then step up onto the porch.

Then—down—down. Twisting and turning through time until the last bright flash. Now resting on the concrete tunnel of silo six—waiting for a blanket of grain.

The next spring a Colorado trucker stomped into Pete's office at the Elevator. "Say, Pete, them hayshakers over to Roggen don't want no more of these Viking balls in their corn!" He laughed and tossed a dusty purple ball to Pete, who caught it.

"Where you get that?" Pete asked.

"It was in the last load you sent to the Roggen feedlot."

Pete chuckled. "Bet it was them kids playing in the tunnels under the silos. Gotta get a lock on that door before somebody gets hurt!"

The phone rang.

"Hello, Farmers Elevator, Pete speaking." He paused. "Price of No. 2 corn? We're payin' $2.50 delivered this week."

The caller responded. Then Pete said, "You'll sell 10,000? Fine, c'mon in and sign a contract. Great! So long!"

He punched a blinking button. "Hello. Who? Tom Cooper? Sorry, he's no longer with us."

"Hello, Farmers Elevator…"

PRAIRIE PERPENDICULAR

Harvest bounty, golden grain.
Time, dust and changing cultivar.
Leveling landscape, blotting stain.
Of all that's perpendicular.